D1825263

The House on Rue Obscure

Echoes of the Cathars: Book 1

Chantal's story

1999

Sarah W. Sparx

Copyright © 2015 Sarah W. Sparx

All rights reserved.

ISBN:1523943319

ISBN-13: 978-1523943319

FOR FULVIA FERLONI

as promised a long time ago in Singapore

AUTHOR'S NOTE

This is not entirely a work of fiction.

Cordes-sur-Ciel exists, as do its strangely named streets of Rue Obscure and Rue Chaude. There really is a water-collection tunnel that runs behind Rue Chaude, too. It's also a fact that the Cathar heretics found refuge in the town almost eight hundred years ago, while the legends of their well-hidden treasure have been told and re-told down the centuries.

If there is a Number 8, Rue Obscure in real life, however, it is not *my* Number 8.

I visited Cordes-sur-Ciel one sunny Sunday morning at the turn of this century and thought it the most romantic place I had ever been. When I read up on its history and discovered the many Gothic mysteries surrounding the town, it hooked me. I knew I had to set a novel in it.

If you're ever passing through the deep south-west of France, I heartily recommend you drop by Cordes-sur-Ciel for an hour or two.

CHAPTER ONE

There was something wrong with the child.

In the chilly French evening, she wore only pink leggings and a navy blue Minnie Mouse sweatshirt, but it was more than that. The way she stared straight down the shadowed alley made Chantal feel invisible, even though barely thirty feet separated them.

As the child walked, she traced a continuous line with her fingertips along the ancient buildings. She never broke contact, faithfully following into the deeply inset door-frames and on across tightly closed, wood-shuttered windows. If it was a game, she was playing it with fierce concentration.

Her pace finally faltered when her fingers met air at a passage between the stone houses. The weak light from the nearest wrought-iron streetlight, high above the ground, only deepened the gloom in this little lane. A couple of tentative steps weren't enough for the girl to bridge the gap. Her reaching fingers fluttered in the cold air like weeds in running water.

The child's unspoken need drew Chantal closer. The girl cocked her head, wary as a wild animal, at the faint scrape of Chantal's shoes on the uneven cobbles.

"Are you all right?" Chantal asked in French, pitching her voice low and soft. "I won't hurt you."

The slender shoulders relaxed a little. "I'm exploring."

Chantal looked into the girl's face. From beneath a neatly trimmed brunette fringe, clear green eyes gazed without focus. Tiny, irregular jerks of her eyes suggested a habit of trying, without success, to see. Who would let a blind girl roam the streets alone?

"Is your mother near here, or your father?"

"Papa's in the shop, checking the answer phone. I got bored."

"Shouldn't you go back to him? He'll be worried about you."

The girl's chin jutted. "He's always worried. But I'm nearly six and I know all these streets."

Chantal saw a way to serve the child's needs and her own. The narrow alleyways made a badly-lit maze, its layout almost perfectly preserved from the thirteenth century when Cordes-sur-Ciel had been founded on this remote hilltop in southwest France. Memories from her last visit, four years earlier, were too hazy to help her navigate through the dusk. The only people she'd seen to ask for help had been out-of-town tradesmen, packing up their tools for the night, and their advice had proved worthless. "You're just who I need. I'm lost and—"

"Are you? Don't you live here?" interrupted the girl.

"No, I live in London and I'm visiting for a few days," Chantal explained patiently. "Now, if we can find your—"

At that moment, a roar reached them, reverberating down the narrow street. "Louise! Louise!"

"Let me guess," said Chantal dryly. "You're Louise?"

The bellow sounded again.

Louise nodded and turned her head in the direction of the dying echoes. "Papa! *Ici!* I'm here!" she called. "Come on," she added, reaching for Chantal's hand. "We'd better go. Then I'll help you find your way."

Chantal couldn't refuse the girl's trusting gesture. She

did wonder, though, how the owner of that powerful voice would take this innocent hand-in-hand intimacy with his missing daughter.

She didn't have to wait long.

A broadly built man appeared in the dusk at the top of the lane. His streamlined silhouette suggested he, too, wore no jacket or coat. He was striding out, long legs covering the downward yards effortlessly. When he spotted the two of them, he accelerated. Chantal dropped Louise's hand and stepped back as he charged the last few feet.

Ignoring Chantal, he bent over his daughter. She disappeared into the shadow of his body, her sweatshirt merging with the dark tones of his crew-neck pullover. For an awful moment, Chantal thought he might become violent and force her to defend the child.

Then he began to talk, and she relaxed, hearing the relief behind his stern words. It sounded like she had wandered off before.

"And you know you move like a cat these days," he finished, "so I can't hear you either. You *must* tell me when you want to go. Do *not* disappear like that."

Louise muttered an apology and snaked an arm up and around her father's neck. He dropped a kiss on her head in reply and straightened up with her securely in his arms.

Chantal shifted her eyes up to his. She judged him to be in his mid-thirties. Dark, wiry hair, cut short to control its springiness, added to his height. So often she looked across at a man, or, worse, down. It wasn't easy to be a woman who stood an inch under six feet.

"…*The mighty redwood on the coast*
Enjoys a stature few can boast…"

The English poem ran through her mind just as he snapped in French, "What exactly were you doing with my daughter?"

Bilingual almost all her life, thanks to her French mother, Chantal couldn't unscramble which language she'd heard. As she drew breath to sort it out, Louise lifted her head. "She's from England, Papa. Maybe you spoke too fast."

Her father arched an eyebrow. In faultless English, but with scarcely less vehemence, he repeated the question.

She answered briskly, keeping to English. "I was trying to bring her back to you. A child like that out alone…"

"A child like what?"

Chantal cursed her lack of tact. She picked her next words with more care, aware Louise might speak enough English to follow the conversation.

"A child of five out alone so late. I was trying to encourage her back to you when you arrived."

His eyes narrowed. "You needed to learn her name and age to do that, did you?"

Chantal's patience began to unravel. "*You* shouted her name down the street. *She* told me her age." Her vowels became more clipped as the need to put this ungrateful giant in his place swelled. "Perhaps if you kept a closer eye on her, you wouldn't need to treat a well-meaning stranger like some kind of molester."

Instead of a rapid-fire retort, there came silence. His deep-set sockets shadowed his eyes and hid any clue of what he was thinking. At last he said, "You don't have children." It was a statement, not a question.

She gave a tiny shake of her head.

His lips compressed. Naturally narrow, they now vanished. His voice deepened as he said, "Maybe when you do you'll find it hard to be detached about something so precious."

His change of tone touched her. She stopped feeling she had to defend herself. "I'm sorry if I scared you. I know I must have looked like a man in this light. I'm very tall."

"Madame…or is it Mademoiselle?"

Instinct made her want to tell him her marital status was none of his business, but she knew his question simply reflected French courtesy. "Mademoiselle," she muttered.

"Well, Mademoiselle, I assure you, I never mistook you for a man." His nostrils flared slightly—whether in amusement or suspicion, she couldn't discern. He hitched Louise more closely into his arms. "We'll say goodbye." He nodded and turned towards the hill.

"Wait, please, I…" Asking for help never came easily, and this man's surliness didn't encourage her. Still, she'd have been silly to pass up the chance to ask a local for a way through the labyrinth of lanes.

He swung back to her.

"She's lost," Louise piped up in French, seemingly remembering Chantal's difficulty.

"I'm afraid I need directions," Chantal admitted. She stuck with English; if she now spoke perfect French he'd want to know why she'd not understood him before. It wasn't worth the effort.

"You're early for a tourist."

The man's aura of command nearly made Chantal justify her presence in the holiday town in late March. At the last minute she bit the explanation back. She owed him nothing. "My great-aunt lives…" She stopped and amended her words. "My great-aunt's house is in Rue Obscure. If you could point me the right way, please?"

He frowned. "I didn't know any English people had bought along that street. I've watched every property deal there for months."

Irritation flashed through Chantal. The cold had percolated through all the barriers of her clothing, shriveling her appetite for a conversation about real estate. "English people can have French relatives, you know." She hoped her tone sounded more civil than she felt. Antagonizing him now would only backfire on her.

He shrugged. "I bought a house on Rue Obscure last Friday. It's been on my mind." He shook back his sleeve, and silver glinted from the heavy steel case of his wristwatch as he glanced at it. "I wasn't planning to visit my new property till tomorrow, but we could walk there with you now. We have a few minutes."

Her forehead prickled. A personal escort from Louise's father was the last thing she needed. She opened her mouth to insist she'd manage alone, when the little girl came to her rescue by yawning enormously.

"It's been a long weekend, eh, *petite*?" Her father stroked her hair, his hand covering her head like a cap. "And school tomorrow. Better get you home and in the bath instead of checking on Number 8. It can wait."

Chantal blinked in confusion. Surely Number 8, Rue Obscure, was Aunt Jeanne's house number, the house she'd always sworn she'd never sell? If Chantal had misremembered the number, she hoped she'd still be able to recognize the house by its unique door-knocker.

"Is that clear enough, Mademoiselle?"

With an inward groan, Chantal realized she'd missed his instructions. Painting a studied look on her face, she asked him to repeat them. "If you wouldn't mind. I'd like to be sure I've got them straight."

She felt grateful when he went through the directions again with only another arched brow as comment on her inattentiveness.

She thanked him with something approaching warmth. "*Au revoir*, Louise," she added to the girl, who gave her a big smile in return. Her father nodded to Chantal and in seconds the pair had disappeared into the deepening twilight.

She stood alone.

The cold breeze strengthened and made the dark street twice as lonely. Chantal shivered. She longed to be in a hot bath with a buttery croissant and coffee in easy reach. Her stomach growled enthusiastically at the prospect. Hours had passed since she'd grabbed a stale sandwich at Heathrow Airport. It had been even longer since the taxi had driven her to the station from the North London house she shared with her mother, Helene.

Soon after the news of Aunt Jeanne's death had reached them, Helene had taken to her bed, complaining she had a migraine developing. In a crisis, especially one that demanded emotional energy, Chantal's mother could be relied on to take herself out of the picture. If practical excuses weren't at hand, she would simply become ill.

In this case, a quick mental reckoning had made it clear that Helene and Chantal were the only close family members available to make the trip to Cordes. Helene's parents were dead; Chantal's uncle, Helene's brother, was halfway through a month's business trip to Vietnam; and most of their other French relatives lived in Canada. Lastly, Chantal's sister, Lotty, the academically gifted fraternal twin with whom she had frustratingly little in common, was excavating Aboriginal sites in northern Australia. Or possibly, by now, in Papua New Guinea— Lotty wrote infrequently and never called.

With Helene retiring to her sickbed, Chantal had shouldered the responsibility of the journey to France, solo. She would have made the trip regardless, but would have gladly welcomed company and support on such a sad errand. Helene's parting words were how fortunate it was that Chantal's jewelry business hadn't succeeded, making it easy for her to leave England for a week or two.

Alone in the Cordes evening, Chantal took comfort against both the cold air and the still-raw sting of her business collapse by wriggling more snugly into her plain black scarf. Her overnight bag dug into her right shoulder and she slipped it down to her hand for some relief.

If only Cordes were an easier town to bring cars into, but even residents struggled to garage and park their vehicles anywhere close to their front doors. Knowing this, she'd left her small rental car by one of the lower town walls, and, coming up the less familiar side of the hill, she'd soon lost her way.

Muttering the directions like a mantra, Chantal trudged over the cobbles, relieved she'd opted to wear flat-soled sneakers.

On either side, the unbroken façades of medieval stone and half-timbered buildings soared two and three stories up into the darkness and turned the lane into a bone-aching wind tunnel. Around a corner, in line with the giant's directions, she found herself in the *Halle*, a small square almost filled by the covered marketplace. Twenty stone columns supported the massive wooden beams that in turn shouldered the burden of the red-tiled roof. On hot summer days, she'd seen tourists and locals alike sink into café chairs set in the shade beneath; on market days, the dignified space lent a Middle Ages grace to the chatter of late twentieth century shoppers and stallholders.

Now, Chantal hastened past the echoing emptiness and skirted the old town well. She spotted the gap in the buildings ahead that would take her down a steep alley called Les Rampes towards Rue Obscure.

At the foot of the alley, she turned right and knew at once where she was. Jeanne's house, with its promise of food and warmth, lay only a hundred and fifty yards away, but across her onward path loomed an arched, black mouth where one of the old buildings bridged the street one story up. With no flashlight, and no nearby streetlight to pierce the dark, she had no choice but to follow the blind girl's example.

Fingers trailing along the rough stone wall, belly taut against the inevitable headwind, Chantal stepped into wintry shadow, where it was forever the thirteenth century.

CHAPTER TWO

Rue Obscure was well named. All Chantal could see from inside the long archway was a grimy hoop of twilight ahead. Relying on her fingers to steer her, she extended her stride, keen to escape as fast as possible.

As she emerged, rejoining the modern world of 1999, the wind eased and her spirits rose in counterpoint. The buildings to the left dropped away sharply and though she could see nothing of the wide views across the pastoral Cerou Valley, she still caught the change of the air's scent from stone to earth.

On her right, the houses stood shoulder to shoulder, each unique in width and height, but alike in having their front doors opening straight into the street. In the last dregs of light, she couldn't make out any street numbers. At last, a stout wooden door under an unusually prominent lintel felt familiar.

Chantal drew closer to examine the knocker and saw with relief that it was the one she remembered. On her last visit, aged barely twenty-three, it had embarrassed her. The part attached to the door was in the form of a naked woman. The knocker itself was in the shape of a well-endowed, equally naked man. The two bodies, inevitably, made contact at hip level.

Typical Aunt Jeanne.

A tightening in her throat threatened the tears she'd not had time to shed. This wasn't the moment, either. She needed to get inside, get warm, and start planning how she was going to sort out her great-aunt's affairs.

And her funeral.

With her height, Chantal had no trouble reaching to the back of the weathered lintel to feel for the front door key. Most of the townsfolk of Cordes still used simple, trusting ways to store their spare keys, at least during the off-season.

The lintel held nothing.

A moment later, she recalled the other hiding place: under the geranium pot by the door. This would have suited Jeanne's five-foot-two frame better. And Madame Nazac's, too, the neighbor who cleaned for Jeanne. In their recent hurried phone call, Madame Nazac had offered to tidy the house for Chantal's arrival. But the space under the flowerpot held no key either.

Small tendrils of panic twined in her stomach. What now?

It was too early in the year for local hotels to be open. She'd have to drive the half hour back to Albi, the small cathedral city to the south, always supposing she could find her way back through Cordes' maze to her car. She leaned her head against the front door to think.

The door swung inward and the light inside, though dim, cramped her pupils. Surprise, then relief, coursed through her. Madame Nazac must be inside, finishing the cleaning.

Blinking, Chantal stepped into the narrow hall. Its flagstones bore grooves from almost eight hundred years of wear: one track went left to the dark kitchen, and another ahead to the steep oak stairs. Right, towards what Jeanne had called the parlor, the floor remained level. Food and bed had always dominated the lives of this house's inhabitants.

Chantal's eyes adjusted to the light that seeped from the landing above. She stopped. Aunt Jeanne had fallen down these stairs to her death a scant two days before.

And her broken body must have landed here, where I'm standing.

Resolutely, she climbed the first few stairs. "Madame Nazac? *C'est moi*, it's me, Chantal!"

A thump came from above. She paused, her foot hovering above the fifth stair. "Madame?"

Heavy shoes pounded along the corridor above her, coming ever closer to the head of the staircase.

A muffled figure stood above her, its face strangely distorted in a vivid shade of mulberry.

Chantal's chest tightened.

A second later she saw the man wore a thick scarf, wrapped up to his eyes.

He launched himself down the staircase. Astonished, she gripped the hand rail and stood her ground, trusting he would stop.

He reached the tread above her. Deliberately, he changed direction, throwing his weight against her. He was short and his shoulder caught her between her breasts.

The impact tore Chantal's grip from the rail. She slammed back against the wall and lost her balance. Her left hand snatched at his coat to stop her fall, but missed.

Helpless, she rolled backwards, down onto the flagstones.

Bright lights exploded behind Chantal's eyes as her skull smacked back onto the floor. Her attacker vaulted over her and raced out of the open door.

She couldn't chase him. Winded, every breath hurt. Stabbing pains in her head made her nauseous and for long minutes, she lay on the cold floor, groaning quietly. When she finally levered herself into a sitting position, she gingerly tested her joints and bones and found nothing sprained or broken.

"That would be perfect," Chantal muttered. "Two broken necks in the family in as many days." The weak joke cheered her a little.

With an effort, she lurched to her feet. The intruder probably wasn't coming back, but she wouldn't risk being unprepared. If the muffled man had had a direct role to play in Aunt Jeanne's death, then she'd been knocked to the floor by a murderer.

She needed to secure the front door, fast.

The heavy iron bolt rammed home easily, but the hasp was loose. A few hard shoves and it would give way. She needed the key.

Leaning heavily on the wall, she shuffled into the kitchen and groped for the light switch. A faint, lemony smell greeted her as she kept her eyes shut while the old fluorescent tube flickered on and off, gradually warming up to the task of staying lit full-time.

The work surfaces—all dark wood, except for a splash of cheerful orange and white from an oilcloth protecting the small breakfast table—had been cleared and wiped clean. Set into the far wall was a wide fireplace, its cavity lined with fleur-de-lis patterned tiles and its hearth occupied by a wood-fired heater. Between the heater and the door to the hall stretched an expanse of linoleum flooring in white and black squares. The checkerboard colors had long since faded to deeper gray and paler gray, but Chantal could detect the recent traces of a mop. Madame Nazac had already done her work.

The spare key for the front door hung in its old place, on a hook behind the kitchen door. Almost as long as her hand and weighing more than a pound, the cast-iron key turned smoothly when she tried it in the lock, and the satisfying clunk of the barrel turning and securing the entry loosened some of the knots in her jaw muscles.

She wasn't safe yet, though. There was a chance her attacker hadn't been alone. He might have left a partner lurking in the house. She had to know.

Should she call the police? They'd take time to come, too long for her abraded nerves to bear. She decided against carrying a kitchen knife. She doubted she could bring herself to use it, and it might get used against her.

Finally, after a swift check of the parlor, she braved the climb up to the second floor. Her legs wobbled with the aftermath of the recent shock, and her head ached in agonizing rhythm with her heartbeat. Despite the pain, she crept cautiously along the hallway to the only open door, that of the largest spare bedroom at the far end.

The light was on. Even from the corridor, Chantal could see enough mess to make a teenager feel at home. Several large plastic holdalls, overflowing with clothes, claimed the center of the room, and a tumbled stack of hardbacks covered more of the polished floorboards. She moved into the doorway for a fuller view.

A closet door hung ajar, clothing askew on the heavy wooden hangers inside. Nearer to her, several photo albums leaned against a light wickerwork chair, threatening to topple it. One small album, bound in red, lay open on the chair seat. It was hard to tell if the intruder or Aunt Jeanne had left the mess.

She spotted the large front door key beside the albums on the floor; it matched the one she had used a few minutes before, and it explained how the man had got in. With an effort that set her skull pounding again, Chantal picked it up. Now she knew she had both keys to house's main entry, her shoulders relaxed.

The two other smaller spare rooms lay undisturbed. Aunt Jeanne's bedroom also looked peaceful. Her great-aunt's handsomely enameled jewelry box, in tones of turquoise and royal blue, sat on the old walnut dresser next to her antique set of silver-backed brushes and hand mirror. Chantal flipped the box lid back to reveal Aunt Jeanne's usual clutter of rings and bangles; it looked full.

She shook her head in bewilderment and at once regretted it, as pain jagged through her eyeballs. Whatever the intruder had come for, he'd gone, and she was alone in the house.

Back downstairs, the hunt for painkillers became a pressing priority. A free-standing cabinet with ornate carvings functioned as Aunt Jeanne's pantry. A glance inside revealed that her great-aunt's taste for luxuries hadn't changed. Roasted pistachios. Tins of artichoke hearts. Packs of anchovies nestled beside tall gift boxes of Belgian chocolates. The rich aroma of coffee oozed from the unvarnished wood inside, enveloping the high-end deli assortment.

The drawers below the pantry bulged with jumble and unopened mail. At last, Chantal found a basic first aid box under the sink and, with relief, washed down a couple of aspirin.

The liquid woke her stomach, and it rumbled. After the ordeal she'd endured, she needed to progress her recent fantasy of food and a hot bath into comforting reality.

Soon, the old toaster buzzed away as it worked on a couple of English-style bread slices from the tiny freezer in the equally small refrigerator. Chantal had visited enough French kitchens to know that housewives who shopped daily didn't need much chilled storage. However, with only a bottle of champagne and a half-used jar of pickled gherkins, the fridge looked unusually empty, even by Aunt Jeanne's standards.

She walked over to the bathroom that opened off the kitchen. Aunt Jeanne had never organized to move it upstairs, closer to the bedrooms. Chantal peeped inside. The tapestry of Lady Godiva, nude on her horse, still hung on one wall, but its sepia and ocher tones had faded so much that the initial impression was of a two-headed centaur. Chantal's gaze skated past the image and settled on a nearly full container of expensive Italian bath oil that perched on the rim of the claw-footed, cast-iron tub.

She couldn't resist.

While the water ran, Chantal set her toast plate on the

bath rim. Off came her raincoat and wrinkled clothes, and on went a thick magenta-toned toweling robe from behind the door. It was ludicrously short and surely clashed with the russet tones in her hair, but no-one was watching.

She sniffed lightly at a cuff and caught a poignant trace of her great-aunt's favorite Givenchy perfume.

This time, Chantal had no defense against her grief. The recent attack on the stairs had left her composure as wobbly as her legs. Aunt Jeanne had been the much younger sister of Chantal's French grandfather, and she and Chantal had grown close, perhaps helped by an age gap that was a little more than parent-child yet rather less than grandparent-child. Chantal had visited, alone, every year or two from the age of ten. No one could make her laugh like Aunt Jeanne, and no one ever listened to her as closely as her great-aunt. Chantal's tears flowed unchecked for long minutes.

By the time the pain had ebbed and left Chantal's throat croaky, the bathroom had grown humid and fragrant with night-scented flowers. She wiped condensation from the little mirror over the medicine cabinet and a pair of red-rimmed, smoky gray eyes looked back at her, from under dark eyebrows. She grimaced at the sight of her blotchy cheeks and turned towards the cheerier prospect of the tub.

The film of bath oil glistened on the water, now just a few inches from the lip of the tub. In a nod to her great-aunt, she dropped the big wooden latch on the door to make the room more cozy and private. She knew Aunt Jeanne would have approved: in life, she had taken creature comforts very seriously.

The hot water drew Chantal close, like iron filings tugged by a magnet. She was so near to easing her bruised body, yet she held back and delayed the moment of pleasure. She knelt by the tub and held the back of her right hand just above the surface. The heat rose like a lover's breath. A fraction lower and water touched skin in a formal kiss. Chantal introduced her left hand in the same way.

It was a delightful game, gentle yet sensuous. She was at a Regency ball with beaus greeting her on every side. She immersed her arms to the elbows. The water enveloped them like black velvet gloves.

Time to dance.

She stood, pointed her right foot and dipped it in no further than her ankle. Warm at last, it felt as if encased in the softest kid leather. She placed that foot on the bottom of the tub and the left foot joined it. The heat along her calves was that of the sheerest silk stockings.

Slowly, oh, so slowly, she lowered her hips down through the steam, through the bath oil, and into the near-scalding water. Immediately, the heat began to work, soothing bruises and relaxing travel-weary muscles. She heaved a huge sigh of thankfulness.

Her sigh started small waves. Her hands joined in and stirred the water more. Now the waves lapped the underside of her breasts like a partner's hesitant first touch. More steps of the dance followed, with more caresses. They died away again, leaving her wanting more.

Who was her partner? He was taking liberties, delicious liberties. They danced to the edge of the floor, her head on his shoulder. The waves grew taller. He dipped his head and heat covered her nipples. He was good at this, very good.

Who was he?

An unsmiling face flashed up in her mind. Deep-set eyes, topped with wiry, dark hair, stared down on her.

She breathed in sharply. His expression challenged her, promising to give no quarter if she dared confront him.

How could she have summoned this forbidding man to be the dance partner of her dreams? An hour before, he'd walked away from her without a backward glance. He'd had one area of softness, though: his daughter. There'd been such intensity about him as he reclaimed Louise that it made her wonder if he'd lost someone else precious.

A metallic rattle from beyond the kitchen scattered her thoughts.

She jerked upright, heart pounding. Water slopped onto the floor. She scrambled out of the tub and snatched for the robe. If the muffled man had returned, she refused to cower away and give him free rein.

Thuds reached her. He was trying to force the front door, and didn't care how much noise he made. The rattling grew louder. Surely he'd break through any second.

The only possible weapon in the bathroom was a Venetian glass bottle. She grabbed it firmly by the neck and raised it to her shoulder, ready to shriek like a steam train's whistle to startle him.

She drew a deep breath and threw the door open, prepared to face the muffler-wearing man.

CHAPTER THREE

Five hard shoves and the hasp holding the bolt on the inside of the front door gave way. The bruise it gave Berenger's shoulder hardly compared to his irritation at having to break into his own house. His fist closed over the heavy door key, newly copied and duly received from Jeanne Lamarque's lawyer.

How on earth had the bolt slid across to secure the door? No one was in the building, and there was no back exit, except to a high-walled yard.

The mystery was explained when he stepped through into the low-ceilinged kitchen. He caught the sound of faint shuffling from behind the bathroom door at the far side. Madame Lamarque had evidently failed to vacate the house, despite the explicit arrangements he'd made with her lawyer.

The kitchen had shed much of its usual clutter. He hoped it meant she'd finished all her packing, but a glance at the open pantry told him she'd not even begun. Berenger gritted his teeth. He had a scant six weeks to get the place converted before the summer season began. It was almost impossibly tight, without the ex-owner delaying the project at the outset.

He stared at the bathroom door, irked enough to consider ordering the old lady out. Before he could, she flung the door open.

Instead of the petite seventy-something-year-old, the English tourist shot out.

Over her shoulder she wielded a green bottle as if it were a weapon. With her other hand, she was trying to hold a too-short, too-small, too-pink bathrobe as close to herself as she could.

Surprise robbed him of speech.

She looked equally shocked but beat him to the first words. "*You?* I…get out. Now!"

Her vehemence rekindled his irritation. "What the hell are you doing in my house?"

"This is not your house. How dare you barge in?" She took a step towards him, the bottle at the ready. Her wet hair hid its color, but she had to be some kind of redhead if her fiery defiance was anything to go by. Her eyes were gray, though, rather than green, breaking the stereotype of redhead coloring.

"It is my house," Berenger bit out. "I didn't break in." He chose to ignore the hasp that he'd forced and instead held up the heavy front door key. "I paid a small fortune for this on Friday. It makes me the new owner." He took a step closer but she stood her ground. "And it makes you a squatter."

"Don't be ridiculous! This is—"

"A charming squatter," he interrupted. He let his gaze track down below the robe's hem. Long, smooth inches of heat-flushed skin led to her bare feet. Even though Louise was the only woman in his life these days, he had to admit the sight had its attractions. *Concentrate.* "Charming, but unwelcome. I want you out."

"Will you listen?"

"Now." Berenger deliberately echoed her earlier order.

She banged the bottle down on the garishly covered kitchen table in frustration. "I'm Jeanne Lamarque's great-niece."

"Forgive me if I say the family resemblance is not exactly striking." She had to be nearly a foot taller than her great-aunt. Tall and lithe enough to fit comfortably in his arms. His throat clogged, and he cleared it impatiently.

She was talking again, insisting on her right to be in the house. For all her doggedness, he could see how pale she looked. Her white face contrasted sharply with her pink legs.

He cut across her. "Very well, Mademoiselle. I accept you are who you say. It certainly explains how you let yourself in. But I have plans for this house, and they don't include free bed and board for any long-lost Lamarque relatives."

"You're planning to throw me out dressed like this?" She clamped the robe more securely around herself. A hint of fragrance reached him. Its heavy, exotic notes of amber and patchouli didn't suit her. She should have chosen a lighter floral or fruit scent. Notes of orange blossom, or berries.

This isn't a wine-tasting competition. Annoyed with himself, his tone grew caustic, "So get dressed. Go and join your great-aunt, wherever she's moved to."

This English woman drove every vestige of good manners from him. Shocking her from her bath should have brought an apology to his lips, rather than a series of sharp remarks. Even if he was in the right.

She looked like he'd slapped her. "With my great-aunt? But she's…that's…"

Berenger had no idea why this comment had struck home so much harder than his previous ones, but he knew he liked her better in fighting mode. Provocatively, he drawled, "What? Her new place not grand enough for you?"

She shook her head slowly. "You've no idea, have you? Aunt Jeanne fell down those stairs two days ago." She gestured with her chin at the hallway behind him. "She's in the morgue. In Albi."

His jaw sagged.

"Yes, dead. On Friday. That's why I'm here. To sort out her affairs and the funeral."

He ran his hands through his hair, giving himself time to gauge whether she was telling the truth. He didn't want to believe it, not when he thought about how important the building renovations were to his business. To Louise's future. The shadows under the woman's eyes convinced him, though.

Damn it.

"I'm sorry for your loss, Mademoiselle." He cleared his throat. "As you say, I had no idea. I was away all weekend. You must, of course, stay here while you make your arrangements." How long could they take? Three days? Four?

She remained silent, apparently assessing his change of heart. He could hardly blame her.

"Thank you," she finally muttered, pulling the robe taut around herself again.

The fabric stretched over the curve of her breasts and his mind supplied the detail he could not see. Heat flickered within him, but he ignored it. A gone-tomorrow tourist was the last kind of companion he needed. "Is there anything I can do to help?"

She didn't reply.

Now what was wrong? "Shall I call the packers? Arrange storage?"

In response, she moved around the table, putting it between them like a shield. At least that hid her bare legs.

"There is one thing, Monsieur."

Her gray eyes lifted and drilled into his. Whatever was coming, it didn't look friendly.

"My Aunt Jeanne loved this house. It was like another family member to her. She'd never have left it willingly. I want to know exactly what you did to force her to sell."

"Force?" Berenger hissed at the unfairness of her

accusation. "Your aunt approached *me*. A month ago, out of the blue. I'd given up on her ever agreeing to sell and—"

"So you'd tried to get your hands on this house before?"

"My lawyer called her lawyer with fair offers, Mademoiselle." The ice in his voice didn't slow her down.

"And that didn't work, did it? Because she'd never sell. Not for a million francs."

"Try this number then." Berenger named a figure in Euros.

Her eyes became round coins as she did the conversion and then narrowed again. "However much, Aunt Jeanne never cared about money, except as a means of preserving this house. To her, it represented a piece of living history. She wasn't going to let it out of the family."

"Evidently, she changed her mind."

"What made her?"

His lips tightened into an angry line. "I didn't stop to ask. I simply named a figure and she accepted. I suggest you take it up with Lelou, her lawyer."

"Oh, I will, Monsieur. I'll find out everything I can. I don't know much about French law, but I doubt a sale made under duress would count."

"*Duress?*" he exploded. "It was a straightforward business deal. You're paranoid."

"A deal that went against everything I know about Aunt Jeanne. A deal you were desperate to make! I don't know why this house is so vital to you, but I bet it isn't what Jeanne valued it for. Its hundreds of years of history, the lost tunnel and the—"

"Tunnel?" This piece of information startled him.

"Exactly. You've some other reason for wanting this house so much. That's why you made repeated offers for it. It's why you're furious I'm here, in the way of your plans. When people want things badly enough…well, you can say I'm paranoid. I say it's simple logic."

"Here's a piece of logic for you then, Mademoiselle." He leaned across the table, his weight on his knuckles. "I'm wondering why you're so fierce about this. Perhaps you're upset because your great-aunt is dead. But perhaps you're angry because you've lost out. Eh? You were going to inherit and now the house is gone?" It gave him satisfaction to see her flush and step back. "Don't worry," he went on, pressing his advantage. "You'll get the money instead."

"I don't care about the money," she snapped.

"No? What a…" he stopped, hunting for the right English word. "…noble-minded family. Not one of you is interested in money."

"But you are."

"I like what money buys," he said shortly. "Security. A future."

"For your daughter."

He straightened up from the table. The argument had gone on long enough. Time to get back to the essentials.

He dug a business card out of his wallet and dropped it on the table. "As we've discussed, the sooner you finish here, the better. If you need help, ring me. Anything to speed your departure."

She stretched a hand to the card but made no effort to reach over for it. "Could you…?"

He almost smiled at her worry that the robe would gape. He handed her the card.

"Well, Monsieur Berenger Morel," she said, reading it. "You'd better tell me how many days' grace I have to stay here. The funeral details won't take long. Finding out what drove Aunt Jeanne to sell up, though, that could take more time."

"You do your detective work in your own time, Mademoiselle, or put up with workmen in here. Starting Thursday." Three full days. Then she could take her chances with dust and noise.

"And what will the workmen's job be? To destroy

23

incriminating evidence?"

He shook his head in exasperation. He turned his back on her, but at the kitchen door he paused. "Why don't you accuse me of murder, too? Maybe I stole her jewelry and threw her down the stairs when I was done?"

He hauled open the front door and strode forward, ready to slam it behind him. Having only visited the house three times, he hadn't got into the habit of ducking. He hit his forehead, hard, on the lintel. Pain seared his skin, and he clamped a hand to the cut. He left the door swinging open.

Outside, a drizzling rain had started. This was turning into a lousy evening. He swore vehemently all the way to his car, parked illegally two hundred yards away. Only when he reached it did he realize that, between the arguing and the diversion of the pink bathrobe, it hadn't occurred to him to ask the English tourist her name.

CHAPTER FOUR

It took Berenger barely two minutes to drive downhill to his home. He managed it one-handed, using the other arm to staunch the blood flow with his shirt cuff. He swerved past the trim box hedge border that encircled the fountain in the gravel forecourt, and braked viciously. A shower of stone chips spurted from beneath the SUV's tires and rained down on the chateau's yellow-plastered walls.

The sound soothed him a little.

The chateau, the largest and most elegant house in the area, had been lived in by the Morel family for over two hundred years. Built on the lower flanks of Cordes' hill shortly before the French revolution, the building had started as a modest farmhouse. Successive generations of ever more prosperous farmers, vintners and, eventually, civil servants, had added to its dimensions. Unconstrained by the city walls that hemmed in the houses higher up, and with the protection of the steep hill behind, the chateau stretched out across its well-groomed, gently sloping lawns like a cat in summer sunshine.

Currently, three generations of Morels lived in it, with Berenger's widowed father, Armand, a retired diplomat, sharing the house with his son and granddaughter.

Berenger's younger sister, Anne, had effectively moved out as soon as she had left for university, but Berenger had stayed put, bringing his bride, Mireille, to live with him when they'd married eight years before.

A security light came on and made it easy for Berenger to back into his space in the three-car garage. The outer door closed at the stab of a button, and the courtesy light stayed on long enough for him to walk through the short, stone-flagged passageway, past various utility rooms, into the main hall. Here, a long Persian runner covered the antique parquet floor, and marked the entry into the living areas of the building.

Armand came out of the family room to meet him. As always, he was crisply dressed, with a silk cravat carefully tucked into the open collar of his tailored shirt. Twice Berenger's age at seventy-two, he looked a decade younger, and his love of cycling kept his large frame lean and his skin tanned, even at the end of winter. In contrast to the smoothness of his dress, his silver hair bristled, its very short cut ideal for under a cycling helmet.

He blinked as his son passed under the glass-drop chandelier. "*Mon Dieu*, Berenger! There's blood all over your face! What happened?"

"Later, Father. I promised Louise I'd say good night when I got back from checking the new property."

"You can't go to her like that. You're covered in blood."

Berenger halted, staring ahead at the staircase. "It's not as if she can see it."

"She can smell it, though."

Berenger threw up his hands in irritation and sprinted up the thickly carpeted steps without answering. Nevertheless, upstairs, he first washed and put on a fresh shirt before gently opening the door to Louise's bedroom.

His daughter lay on her side, facing him. Her straight dark hair spilled over the white pillow behind her, reminding him of the fisherman's nets they'd seen that weekend at the end of a wide beach, spread out to dry on the pale sand.

He tucked Louise's favorite stuffed giraffe into the crook of her arm and sat down gently on the bed.

"Are you awake, *petite*?" he asked softly.

Louise's eyes stayed shut as she rocked her head slightly to say 'no'.

If she'd been half awake her eyelids would have fluttered, though the eyes beneath would have registered nothing. Two years since the accident, and there'd been no change in her blindness. No progress. Berenger closed his own eyes for a long moment, shutting out the soft light from the corridor, shutting in the harsh frustration.

When he opened them, he saw Louise's shoulders rising and falling with her steady breathing. He dropped a kiss on her cheek and stood up, careful not to rock the bed and disturb her newfound sleep.

Downstairs, a glance in the hall's gold-framed mirror showed him the cut on his forehead was clotting well, though the skin around it remained swollen and inflamed. He shrugged at his reflection. With no important customers or contacts to meet for his wine business in the near future, it didn't matter if he looked like a battered prizefighter for a few days.

At the dining table, his father had already sat down, and was talking to their housekeeper, Ah Wong, as she set out warmed plates. As usual, their conversation revolved around Armand's passion for collecting celadons, the eerily beautiful, green-glazed ceramics from China, about which the diminutive Asian woman knew an astonishing amount. A similar age to Armand, she wore her silver-gray hair scraped back in a tight bun and dressed every day in a starched white tunic over black crepe pants. Despite having lived in France with the Morels for almost fifteen years, she still favored this traditional uniform of a Taiwanese housemaid.

Ah Wong broke off her conversation with Armand as

soon as she saw Berenger. "Louise is OK? All asleep?" Ah Wong's concern for the girl never eased. He guessed it lay rooted in her past, in the loss she'd only referred to once, of loved ones killed during her family's flight from Shanghai to Taiwan in the late forties.

He reassured her that Louise had fallen asleep.

Ah Wong bustled past, her head hardly reaching his chest.

When he sat down, she spied the cut on his forehead and came closer to squint at it. "Ssss," she hissed, blowing air through her teeth in a Chinese sound of disapproval he had come to know very well. "Sss. You fight?"

"With a door frame that was too low."

"Sss. You too tall for old houses." She shook her head. "I want to serve dinner. Where is Monsieur Sanders?"

Ah Wong had set the table for three. As yet, there was no sign of their American house guest. Wilbur Sanders was a Ph.D. student, completing his research into the Cathars, the heretic sect who had found sanctuary in Cordes centuries before. Armand acted as Treasurer for the local history society, a group that had taken Wilbur under its wing in the three successive years he had visited Cordes.

This was the first time the Morels had hosted him. Berenger knew his father would have invited Wilbur sooner but for Louise's blindness and the time and effort her therapy took up. The fact that Wilbur now boarded at the chateau signaled Armand's acceptance that his granddaughter's sight would not return. Berenger had funneled his dismay at his father's lack of faith into impatience with their guest. Right now he blamed Wilbur for keeping him from his meal.

"Wilbur called while he was packing up at the library in Toulouse. He should be here any minute," Armand offered.

Ah Wong sniffed and returned to the kitchen. Berenger's stomach rumbled in accord. The cooking smells from the kitchen suggested a *daube,* a rich beef stew, and he was ready to attack a double portion. He reached for the wine bottle.

"I hope Wilbur finds what he needs," added Armand. "He's only got another ten days of his study break left."

Berenger made a vague noise. Their guest's research didn't interest him much on a good day, and today was far from rating that highly. Instead, he read the wine label. Not one of his wines, or even a local Gaillac vintage, this ten-year-old bottle came from Cahors, an hour's drive to the north. The area produced reds in a powerful and robust style that, suitably matured like this one, would make an excellent foil for the stew.

"Did you hit your head at Number 8?" his father asked.

Berenger nodded.

"I've some news about your new property that will interest you." Armand was on the town council and very little happened in Cordes that he didn't soon hear about. "I ran into Laurent, your young cellar man. His mother cleans at Number 8."

"I know. And I know Madame Lamarque's dead." He explained how he had heard. A frown weighed down his features as he described his new house's unwanted visitor.

"How are you going to cope with the delay?"

"Get my hands dirty for a couple of weeks, I suppose, to speed up the work," he answered. A grim smile slowly erased the scowl. "Could be worse. The builders won't slack off or pad the bill."

He was on the verge of telling his father about the English tourist's wild accusations when Wilbur walked in.

As always, Berenger found their guest's body shape perplexing. About forty, Wilbur was of average height but wide across the shoulders and reed-thin, with arms that hung about six inches too long for his build. For all his leanness, there was a suggestion of wiry strength about him. He wore his stringy, dark blond hair tied back in a ponytail.

The conversation switched to English. Wilbur's

modern French lagged behind his competent command of medieval French and his even stronger grasp of the older Occitan language, once spoken by the Cathars and many others through medieval southern France.

Wilbur sat down beside Berenger. "Haven't seen you for a few days. How was the trip with Louise this weekend?"

Berenger and Louise had driven to the Côte d'Azur. This late March weekend had become a tradition for them, to spend private time away together. Two years had passed since Mireille had died in the car crash, and since Louise had lost her sight the same day.

"Good." Berenger managed a slight nod. Even now, he found it hard to talk about.

His father glanced at him and promptly led Wilbur into a debate on Cordes' many strange stone carvings. Scholars could argue for hours over the symbolism of monkeys and leering faces. Quietly grateful, Berenger watched his father, knowing Armand had deliberately guided the conversation, but also aware that his father delighted in hosting a scholar who appreciated his town's history.

The discussion on carvings lasted most of the meal. Left to his own thoughts, Berenger inevitably pondered Number 8. It backed onto his wine-tasting store on Grand' Rue, the main street through Cordes. The shop, and the customer relationships it helped foster with tourists each year, sold the output from his vineyards. His land was all in the local Gaillac region, and most on the Cordes plateau nearby.

Despite its excellent location, the store struggled. He'd known why for some time: it was too small. There was no room for anything but tasting tables and wine, and tourists wanted to try food matches and browse for local food specialties to go with their purchases. The problem had been finding space to expand. The neighboring stores on Grand' Rue were too expensive, and Number 8, the property almost directly behind, hadn't been for sale. He could remember his relief when Madame Lamarque had suddenly offered to sell.

Other vintners in the region traveled regularly, signing up distributors, and promoting their wines in person. Berenger refused to leave Louise or his cherished vineyards, and that left the shop as his key selling tool. The tourist had put her finger on it when she guessed he was building for Louise's future. The shop *had* to succeed.

Over cheese and fruit, Wilbur dropped the subject of mysterious carvings and turned to him. "Hey! I should be congratulating you, Berenger. You're the proud owner of a new property, right?"

Berenger frowned at the reminder of his immediate problems. "A new property, yes, but with a squatter. The old owner's great-niece."

Wilbur dropped a peach but deftly retrieved it before it could knock over his wineglass. His head swiveled between his hosts, making his ponytail swing, as he waited for an explanation.

Armand gave Wilbur the key facts.

The American turned back to Berenger. "She's staying in the house? How long for?"

Berenger didn't usually find much common ground with the scholar, but he welcomed this genuine concern. "Tonight and who knows how many more nights."

"Won't this throw your schedule for fitting out the shop? Send her to a hotel."

Wilbur's words made sense but they brought back an image of the woman's face. Tired and pale, but defiant. Short of picking her up and flinging her into the street, he couldn't have got rid of her. He changed the subject. "Lamarque's niece mentioned a lost tunnel somewhere under Number 8. Do you know about it?"

Wilbur's stare made Berenger think of an owl about to swoop on a mouse. Armand laughed at his guest's eagerness and with a wave handed the floor to him. "Though I do wonder how my son can know the pedigree of every local vine but not the basics of the town's history."

"Vines are alive, Father. Stones aren't." It was a well-worn topic between them. He turned to Wilbur. "Tell me, if this tunnel exists, could I get into it somehow and use it for extra storage?"

Wilbur leaned on the table and made a steeple of his fingers, tapping the tips together in a staccato rhythm. "It probably exists, but no one knows how to access it. Old documents I've accessed with your father's help—" he nodded at Armand who smiled in return, "—refer to two tunnels running through the limestone. They drain seeping rain via cisterns into the town's wells. The lower tunnel we even have a map for, and it drains into the little fountain in the rock face on Rue Chaude."

The rhythm of his tapping fingertips slowed and stopped. "The other tunnel is said to run under Rue Obscure but no one knows exactly where, or for how far. There's an outlet into the main town well in the *Halle*, about thirty yards down the well shaft. Some people thought it must belong to that lost tunnel."

"Why don't they take a look?"

"They did, about twenty years ago, when we were in Mexico, unfortunately," chimed in Armand, setting down his delicate coffee cup. "They abseiled down and shone lights into the outlet, and all they could see was a foot-wide channel cut back into the bedrock. It turned a corner a short distance in, cutting off all view."

"The History Society has a photo of Rue Chaude's tunnel," Armand added. "Its floor was dry but it was barely six feet wide. Number 8 has enough storage room, surely?"

Berenger shrugged. "Free space could have been handy, that's all."

Soon after, Wilbur excused himself. Despite being a mature student, he kept distinctly young-student hours. From what Berenger had seen, their guest preferred to do the bulk of his work at night and rarely surfaced before lunch. Dinner was his version of brunch.

"I've got some correspondence to finish," Armand said. "Sending out feelers to New York for a large celadon bowl with a peony design. Of course my able adviser in the kitchen will probably suggest trying for something less common, like twin fish."

"Take her advice. You say she's usually proved right," answered Berenger absently.

"I'd rather get it right myself."

The petulant note in Armand's voice hooked Berenger's attention. He gave the older man a considering look. "And if your father had spoon-fed you the subtleties of Chinese ceramics from birth, your strike rate would probably be as good as hers. I'd pick her brains and be grateful if I were you."

"If you were me, *mon fils*," sniffed his father in retaliation, "your civil service career would be well-established by now and you wouldn't have farm dirt engrained in your palms." He stalked to the door.

"And I'd be unhappy."

"Would we notice the difference?" Armand paused with his hand on the door handle but didn't look around to see how his barb had landed. "You'll lock up, won't you?"

Berenger grunted.

After his father had gone, he went to stand by the French doors that opened out onto the rear terrace. He had more pressing things to think about than his father's griping.

He pushed back the heavy velvet drapes. The light in the room turned everything outside black, but his gaze traveled up Cordes' southern flank, that rose sharply above the terrace. Up there, and a hundred yards to the right, sat the English tourist, in his house. He didn't know her name, yet she had barely left his thoughts.

That had to stop, and soon. A pretty face and long legs

weren't enough. Since Mireille had gone, women had been very low on his priority list. He had, however, identified precisely what he needed in a future wife: someone local, who shared his love of the land, understood the demands of his business, and didn't treat Louise's blindness like a handicap. If potential wives were wine, the tourist would barely rate as *vin ordinaire*, let alone *premier grand cru*.

She'd set herself up as an adversary, not a lifelong ally. He'd bet that right now she was scheming to sabotage the house sale. His fist clenched around the edge of the drapes.

He knew too well his tendency to handle conflict in a fire-ready-aim style, but this was too important to get wrong. What was that saying about catching more flies with honey than vinegar? A plan for handling the tourist at Number 8 began to distill, drop by honeyed drop, in his mind.

CHAPTER FIVE

At nearly nine the next morning, Chantal plodded downstairs, wearing jeans and a sweater, her one change of clothes from her overnight bag. She gripped the hand rail, unsure of her feet in the gloom. The only light came from beams knifing through cracks in the ancient shutters and front door.

The sight of the high-backed, wicker-seated chair she'd jammed under the front door handle reminded her of Berenger Morel's abrupt departure the previous evening. His string of swear words had added a couple of new and juicy expressions to her already competent colloquial French. On the downside, he'd cost her hours of sleep as she'd lain in Aunt Jeanne's old-fashioned spare bed, playing their argument over and over and fretting at the problem of what—who—had driven Aunt Jeanne from her beloved home.

At one point in the night, she'd nearly got up to fetch the little pouch of macramé yarn from her purse. She knew that puzzling over new knots and patterns for her jewelry would distract her and eventually send her off to sleep. The problem needed solving, though, not avoiding, and she'd shrugged the idea away. Her tossing and turning had gone on.

Jeanne had been born in Number 8 and she'd repeatedly vowed to die there, too.

At least she got that wish, whatever else was going wrong in her life.

Unlike her older brother and sister, Aunt Jeanne's imagination had fired at a young age with the tales of their home. One of Cordes' oldest buildings, Number 8 was tucked snugly inside the innermost ring of the town walls. Its first occupant had been the infamous Roland Fleurie, the man who allegedly led his neighbors in a deadly attack on three Dominican inquisitors in 1233. Chantal knew Aunt Jeanne had bought out her siblings' share of the house—she'd joked often enough that the purchase had crimped her financially and put a stop to her old ways of carefree travel.

To many, an ancient house would have been a dismaying burden, but Chantal knew what delight it had brought her great-aunt. Aunt Jeanne had for years invested a generous share of her love and funds into the ancient stones and timber beams, preserving the fabric of the building as a priority ahead of the interior fittings. Scarcely a letter or phone call emerged from Number 8 without a report on its state of health and future plans for its longevity.

At times, Chantal felt her great-aunt had married the house. Certainly she had remained unmarried, despite gleefully claiming a succession of local suitors. The idea that she would willingly sell Number 8, without so much as a mention to her family, was unfathomable.

Just as out-of-character was the idea that Aunt Jeanne could have been bullied or threatened in some way. Even by an unsmiling man with cold blue eyes who would have towered over her. Aunt Jeanne had always been feisty. If an intruder had come calling, she'd have struck back. A half smile crept to Chantal's lips. Most likely, her relative would have dashed for the antique cutlass she'd acquired in a souk in Tangiers, and threatened to cut off his ears. Or something a couple of feet lower.

Lying in bed, Chantal fretted at her lower lip. In the shuttered darkness, she admitted she'd overreacted with her suspicions about Berenger, too. She must have sounded half-crazed. He might have the best motive to bully Aunt Jeanne out that Chantal knew of, but that hardly explained her cold fury when she'd faced him across the table, and her heartfelt vow to wreck his purchase of the house.

She punched the mattress in frustration. Why had she been so bitter?

Then it hit her.

Steven.

Steven, her one-time lover. Her one-time angel investor. The metallic tang of last year's loss soured her mouth. She refused to let it get as far as her stomach. He wasn't going to wreak havoc with her life again. She'd worked like a demon and cleared most of her debts. She'd learned some hard lessons, too. Whatever lay ahead, Steven had no part in it.

But it did explain everything about the way she'd acted in the kitchen. Steven had made a fool of her. And then he'd conned her so that she'd lost her business too, her precious jewelry business that she'd worked so hard to build. And someone, by trickery or bullying, had made Aunt Jeanne lose what was deeply precious to her. Her subconscious had made the link long before she had. She hadn't been able to extract revenge against Steven, but she'd been hunting it for Aunt Jeanne. Berenger had been right in her sights.

Now, with a bright morning on the other side of the front door, Chantal still intended to dig into Aunt Jeanne's bizarre decision to sell, but she cautioned herself, too: she should check whether revenge was called for before she took any irrevocable action. She twisted the chair out from its defensive position under the front door handle and carried it to the kitchen. With the shutters pushed back, sunshine streamed in and lifted her spirits.

It was too lovely a day to be vindictive, or afraid.

She found some scented loose-leaf tea and hummed while it brewed. Sitting in the chair that had recently been on sentry duty, she wished Berenger could have left with a better opinion of her. Lord knew why, when he was such a challenging man to be around. It had taken all her will to stand her ground against him. The blue of his eyes added pounds of pressure to his direct gaze.

The hot drink cleared her wits enough for her to change focus and make a list of jobs for Jeanne's funeral. Sleuthing would have to wait. She jotted down several items and added a final one about finding her way back to the rental car to bring it closer to Number 8 so she could unload her small suitcase.

Berenger's parting remark about murder came back to her. *Had* someone pushed Aunt Jeanne to her death? Chantal walked into the hall and gazed up at the stairs. They were steep and their centuries-old rises a little uneven. The question was, how had Jeanne, a fit seventy-year-old, fallen down them after decades without a tumble?

So much for delaying the detective act.

She grimaced and shook the railing that rose beside the stairs. It held firm despite the wrenching it had received in her tumble the night before. She probed the back of her skull lightly and found nothing worse than a slight bump and some tenderness.

Tread by tread, she climbed up. The polished wood wasn't slick, not even under her socks. When she reached the top, she turned around and descended slowly. There was nothing that could have tripped Aunt Jeanne.

A fatal fall, an unexpected house sale, and an intruder. Two events might be coincidence, but three?

Cold needles prickled the back of Chantal's neck. A sharp rap at the front door made her yelp. She spun around.

Intruders don't knock.

More likely this was a friend of her aunt's, someone who hadn't heard of her death. Chantal's shoulders sagged at the prospect of breaking bad news to a stranger.

She opened the door.

Madame Nazac stood outside, wearing the typical garb of French country housewives in the midst of morning chores: a buttoned-up pastel-colored polyester housecoat over a printed dress. In her mid-fifties, she barely came up to Chantal's chin. Chantal couldn't keep her eyes from the older woman's head. Since they'd last met, Madame Nazac had taken to dyeing her hair. Gone was the gray-streaked, dull brown hair, now replaced with an unnaturally fiery red that clashed with her flushed cheeks. She carried a small wicker basket covered with a tea towel.

Her visitor's rapid patois drowned out Chantal's greeting. Slowly, she began to adjust to the dialect. She could tell Madame Nazac was apologizing, repeatedly, for not coming by the evening before.

"*Calmez-vous, Madame!* Please, calm down." Chantal drew Madame Nazac through into the kitchen.

"I would have called earlier, you know, but your shutters were closed."

"I slept late after my journey. Please, sit down. There's fresh tea in the pot. Or I could make coffee." Tea was not, after all, a normal French morning drink.

"Tea, for a change, thank you." Madame Nazac settled herself on one of the kitchen chairs and pulled back the cloth on her basket. "And you must have some *beignets.*" Inside were deep-fried golden choux pastry shapes, dusted with icing sugar. They were just the kind of comfort food Chantal craved after her broken night.

Madam Nazac talked on, her French growing more intelligible. "Our car is getting so unreliable, but Paul, my husband, says he can fix it. And he does, but then it develops another problem. Can you believe it, four hours stranded on the other side of Albi! It was nearly eleven before we got a ride back. I just hoped you'd find the door key under the pot."

"Actually — a man had taken it. He was in the house, looking for something." She related the attack in a few, terse details.

"But you must tell the police! See a doctor, too."

Chantal made a sound she hoped would pass for assent. She'd not decided what to do about the police. "Have you seen anyone like this intruder before? Short and stocky and with a mulberry-colored scarf?"

"I'm sure not. But I'll arrange for a new hasp to be put on your door as soon as possible. A strong one. And a new, modern lock too. I encouraged Jeanne a few times. There are so many tourists here in summer. But Jeanne…" Madame Nazac shook her head.

"Not good at taking advice."

"She always knew her own mind." Madame Nazac reached out and squeezed Chantal's hand. "Paul and I will miss her. She was a good neighbor. She didn't poke her nose into your business, but she'd help if you needed it. That's what counts. Some people couldn't see past her clothes."

Chantal smiled at an old memory. "The orange caftan." The outrageous garment summed up her relative. It was a short step from Aunt Jeanne's unique wardrobe to Chantal's concern about her great-aunt's out-of-character decision to sell.

"Three weeks ago she told me she was selling up," said Madame Nazac. "Such surprising news."

"Did she say why?"

"The house was getting too much for her. She'd had a spate of repairs this year. Did she not tell you?"

"She did mention a fuse box fire, but nothing since." Chantal paused, as dates tumbled through her mind. "That was the last time we talked, well over two months ago." She had still been working frantically back then, fixing the Steven debacle, and more time had slipped by without hearing from Aunt Jeanne than she'd realized.

"The fuse box fire was the worst." Madame Nazac shook her bright red head. "I know she kept losing things, too, then finding she'd put them in odd places. But there, we all get older."

Chantal's eyebrows shot up. "Could she have been ill?"

Her companion heaved a sigh. "She looked very tired in the weeks before she decided to sell. I offered to help with more cleaning, whatever she needed. She refused, rather brusquely. Not like her usual self at all."

"So you did think something was wrong with her health?"

"I wondered, but I only saw her once after that, very briefly. It was last Thursday, and I was rushing. She looked much brighter. Said she'd found a little apartment in Albi to rent while she looked for a place to buy. The packers were due on Saturday to put things into storage. They came, too," she added, "but of course no one was here after she… I put their card on the sideboard in the parlor." Madame Nazac paused. "The odd thing is that the last couple of times I cleaned, the house was spotless, as if Jeanne had stopped living here. But if so, I don't know where she'd gone."

They sat in silence, sipping tea. Madame Nazac spoke first. "It's a comfort Monsieur Morel is the buyer. He employs a lot of people on his vineyards and the estate. This house backs onto his wine store. Now he can expand."

Chantal's senses went on full alert. "And this expansion is vital to his business?"

"Laurent says so. You remember my son, Laurent?"

Chantal nodded. Laurent would be about twenty now. She recalled he'd been a young lout, who'd worried his parents endlessly. "And he works for Monsieur Morel?" Given a choice, she'd have chosen military school over Berenger.

Her tone must have conveyed her opinion because

Madame Nazac raised her chin. "Monsieur Morel has been very good to Laurent. Given him a chance at the winery. Since he started work, there's been no more…" She sighed. "Well, we're very obliged to Monsieur Morel."

Chantal remembered Aunt Jeanne mentioning Laurent in a phone call. He'd taken one joyride too many, one that ended in a crash and the other car's driver in intensive care. Laurent's future had looked bleak at that point.

How obliged had his parents been? Enough to help force a sale?

Chantal stamped on the thought. If she suspected the Nazacs, she'd have to suspect all the Morel employees. Year-round jobs weren't exactly abundant in the countryside.

Madame Nazac drew in a breath sharply. "But I'm forgetting. This house must belong to Monsieur Morel now! And here we are, me letting you in to stay, and both of us with keys…"

Chantal watched the woman's cheeks again compete with her hair, as she grew more flustered. She couldn't resist asking, "Does this put Laurent's job in danger?"

"No, no, but I must inform Monsieur Morel. He'll know what to do."

"He already does," said Chantal dryly. "He came here last night. We have a…temporary arrangement."

Madame Nazac's shoulders sagged with relief. "Ah, that's good. He'll be such a help to you. You couldn't find a better man. Such a shame about his family."

Chantal's curiosity overcame her urge to make a curt remark about her experience of his goodness. "Do you mean his daughter? I met her, too, last night. He didn't say anything, but I guessed she was blind."

"She is. His wife died in a car crash near here, two years ago. Little Louise was in the car, too. Something must have hit her head in the crash. They've tried everything. It's such a shame. She's only five."

"Poor wee thing," muttered Chantal. "How does he manage the business and care for her? It must be hard."

"He lives at the chateau with his father and they have a housekeeper to help. As the crow flies, their house is quite close." She twisted around to point diagonally up the street. "It's over there, and straight down."

"And he's not found a new partner yet? Or even a wife?" Chantal's tongue had taken on a life of its own.

Madame Nazac shook her head. "Never even looked at another woman. Laurent says he goes to business dinners on his own, even if they expect him to bring someone. His wife, Mireille, was very beautiful, you know. Long black hair and huge green eyes."

"He's still mourning her, then."

"I'm sure. Anyway, what woman would be good enough to be a mother to Louise? He adores her." Madame Nazac finished the last of her tea. "I'll have to go soon. But can I ask about the arrangements for Jeanne?"

Chantal nodded soberly. "I've got a list. There's a lot to do."

"Did your mother give you names of people who might want to attend the service? There are several people here in town who Jeanne saw often. I could give you a list and phone numbers."

Chantal wasn't about to reveal the very limited practical help her mother had offered, but Helene had at least put ticks beside names in her address book. "That would be very helpful, thanks. I'll check them against what Mum's given me."

"And will she be coming to the funeral?"

"We'll see." Chantal cast about for a reason that would sound legitimate, rather than the truth that Helene had well-honed tactics for avoiding emotionally charged events. "Her health hasn't been too good recently."

A question occurred to Chantal as they crossed to the front door. "Madame. You found Aunt Jeanne on Friday." She hesitated.

"It was the afternoon about three o'clock. Don't distress yourself, Chantal. I don't think she was lying here alone long."

Chantal nodded slowly. "That's a comfort…"

"And I'm sure it was very quick. There was no blood, nothing."

"But her face. How did she look?"

There was a pause. "Shocked, Chantal. She looked shocked."

CHAPTER SIX

An hour later, Chantal headed out on her errands. Having managed to park both legally and much closer to Number 8, she had retrieved her suitcase, and now wore smarter clothes and make-up. She strolled west, her face turned to the view of the Cerou Valley spread out to the horizon in a patchwork of pastoral greens and arable browns. In daylight, even under a weak spring sun, Cordes always turned on its charm.

At the end of Rue Obscure, she turned right and passed under the Porte des Ormeaux, the massive defensive gateway that pierced the innermost of the town's five rings of ramparts. Unlike the night before, she barely noticed the cooler air in the shadow of the thirteenth-century stonework. The cobbled road forked and Chantal took the right-hand option. Even this early in the year, she had to dodge around a knot of tourists photographing the multi-storied Gothic splendor of the famous Grand Ecuyer restaurant.

She puffed up the steep hill, ignoring the medieval glories, and concentrating on her first mission: to charm an appointment with Aunt Jeanne's lawyer, Lelou, before the end of business hours. She hoped the priest and the undertaker would be more flexible about seeing her, under the circumstances.

The Saint Michel church clock chimed eleven and the sound made her hurry. Like most French towns, Cordes would close for a two-hour lunch at twelve.

Lelou's office, Madame Nazac had told her, sat almost on the brow of the hill, near to the town hall. A few moments later, the sight of the French *tricolor,* hanging solemnly from a short flagstaff angled out over a doorway, indicated she was very close.

She looked around and spied a discreet brass plaque beside a tall, narrow door, denoting the premises of Aristide Lelou, *Notaire.* Chantal entered, her arrival announced by the faint tinkling of a small brass bell. Brown floor tiles and darker wood on the reception desk absorbed what little light made it through the venetian blinds on the window to the street.

An older woman sat at reception. Her up-swept coiffure and twin set and pearls suggested she'd walked off the set of a 1950s movie and never updated her look. To Chantal's relief, the woman proved responsive to her plea of urgent business.

In two minutes, Chantal found herself upstairs in Lelou's office, sitting deep in a well-padded leather armchair. Her great-aunt's lawyer was a slight man of about sixty-five, with a sharp nose and sleek, pale silver hair brushed back off his low forehead. He made her think of a white rat.

"*Alors,* Mademoiselle. You say you have come to discuss the affairs of Mademoiselle Lamarque, your great-aunt. I assume you have her permission for this? Or must I telephone her?"

Chantal frowned. "Surely you know the situation, Monsieur Lelou? As her legal representative. Has no one told you?"

Lelou raised a shoulder and an eyebrow in synch. "The situation?"

She took a deep breath. The words, she knew, would very soon become familiar and flow smoothly, but for now they lurched over her tongue like a drunk crossing a plowed field. Telling Berenger the night before had been her one practice so far. "Aunt Jeanne…she is…on Friday. She fell down the stairs, you see."

Lelou's eyebrow descended and joined its partner in an expression of evident concern. "She is injured, incapacitated? This is the issue?"

Chantal tried again. "Aunt Jeanne is dead. I've come to Cordes to arrange things. Her funeral."

Lelou's chin shot out, making him more turtle than rodent. "*C'est impossible!* I was talking with her only last week. Are you sure?"

She bit back the obvious retort and stuck to the facts about how Jeanne had been found, where her body lay, and how the police had informed her family in England.

Lelou rubbed a hand across his face. "This is such a shock. I should have been informed sooner. There will be much to do. Her financial affairs…"

"But first, her funeral. That's why I'm here. Aunt Jeanne never discussed it with me, but I expect you have her will and can tell me her wishes."

Lelou dragged his hand down off his face. "I do have it, of course." His eyes flicked to a small stack of manila folders on the corner of his desk.

Chantal's followed but the angle prevented her making out any of the names labeled in bold sticky letters.

"Before we discuss anything confidential, however, I regret that I must ask Marie," Lelou nodded to the door, "to make inquiries to confirm matters. Normally, I would have expected to hear directly by now of such alarming news."

Chantal shrugged. Lelou seemed as bothered by the failure of his bush telegraph as he was with protecting Jeanne's privacy. She decided to play it his way because she had the perfect topic to fill the time while they waited.

He walked to the door and called to Marie to come up. Seconds later, her shoes clacked up the short flight of steps and he explained the task to her. Chantal had enough time to drop her purse and use the retrieval as a way to read the file names. Sure enough, she saw Jeanne's name on the top document, which made sense given the recent property transaction.

When Lelou returned, Chantal opened the topic uppermost on her mind. "On Friday you conducted the sale of my great-aunt's beloved house to Berenger Morel." She had meant it to be a straightforward opening statement, but it came out as an accusation.

Lelou looked at her sharply. "At her explicit request," he snapped.

Chantal smiled inwardly. The lawyer had given away confidential information without meaning to. "Tell me why she wanted to sell, Monsieur. It goes against everything I know about her."

He shook his head. "She had every right to sell."

"And I'm asking if you can tell me *why* she would sell something she loved so much, without first discussing it or seeking help from family and friends."

"There's no mystery, Mademoiselle. Your great-aunt believed the house was becoming too difficult for her as she grew older. The repairs. Some minor accidents. It happens."

His words confirmed what she had heard from Madame Nazac.

"You don't think she was harassed into selling?"

"Harassed?" His tone suggested she'd lapsed into Mongolian.

"Threatened. Bullied. Coerced."

Lelou waved the notion away like an early summer fly. "Ridiculous! Your great-aunt willingly offered her house for sale. She knew she would have a keen buyer in Monsieur Morel who had approached her on the matter in the past. And so it proved. I may add she got a good price."

"But not even a quarter of a million euros could replace a unique home she'd devoted herself to for a lifetime."

Lelou's eyes bulged and flicked across to the stack of folders again.

"I didn't peek in the files. Monsieur Morel informed me of the price when we were discussing my right to stay in Number 8 while I make arrangements for Aunt Jeanne."

"It is his house now, without question. If he permits you…"

"For a scant three days."

"That's more than he needs to offer for a property he purchased fairly. In this very room. At twelve on Friday."

Outside Saint Michel chimed the quarter hour. Its short peal reverberated in Chantal's head and a revolutionary idea began to form. She stretched forward. "At twelve o'clock? You had power of attorney to sign on my great-aunt's behalf at that time?"

Lelou pulled himself up straight in his chair. "*Précisement*," he answered with dignity. "As soon as Monsieur Morel and I had finished signing the deeds, the bells began tolling noon."

"And Madame Nazac told me she found Jeanne dead about three in the afternoon."

"*Voilà*. An eventful and most regrettable day for your great-aunt, but all within the law."

"You don't see it, do you?" She strained even further forward.

A silver eyebrow rose.

"What if my aunt had died before you signed on her behalf?"

Lelou froze, staring at her. "*Impossible*," he whispered for the second time in their meeting.

She couldn't blame him. It would mean an appalling legal tangle. "It isn't impossible. We don't know when she died, only when she was found."

A quiet knock at the door heralded Marie's arrival. Her

eyes at once fixed on her employer's rigid features. "Monsieur Lelou? Is something wrong? I can assure you that matters are as Mam'selle here has explained. I spoke to the police in Albi. Mademoiselle Lamarque died at her home on Friday, from a fall down the stairs." She glanced at Chantal and murmured towards Lelou, "Her neck."

Lelou kept his gaze on Chantal as he asked, "And did they mention the time of death? It is a question of the gravest importance."

"Yes. They were quite specific." Marie referred carefully to a note in her hand. "Mademoiselle Jeanne Lamarque died between eleven and one."

Lelou slumped back in his chair and squeezed his eyes shut. "*Catastrophe,*" he muttered.

"Monsieur Lelou?" Marie's concern dragged her a few steps into the office.

Chantal's mind whirred. Uncertainty over whether the house sale was legal would give her time, surely, to investigate what had happened to Jeanne. Berenger would no longer be able to dictate terms to her.

Lelou drew a deep breath and gathered himself. "Marie, please call Albi again and put them through to me. We need a tighter time frame. This two hours is no good. No good at all."

*　*　*

Chantal collapsed into a café chair in a sunny spot at the edge of the covered marketplace. Her old friend Saint Michel chimed for 11:45, but she had no appetite for an early lunch. What she needed was a strong coffee before she tackled the next item on her list. After the revelations with Lelou, her priorities had undergone a reshuffle. Berenger had leapfrogged the priest and undertaker to take pole position.

She'd left Lelou flummoxed and barking contradictory instructions at Marie. Any minute now, he'd be calling

Berenger's lawyer to inform him of the knotty problem they'd uncovered. When he'd announced that step, Chantal knew at once she'd have to tell Berenger the news to his face. Not to gloat, but because she'd hate him to think she was hiding behind the lawyers, afraid to face him.

The waiter took her order for a *noisette*. She looked forward to the dash of cream smoothing the espresso's bitterness, while the caffeine revved her mind. Till it arrived, she let her attention float and simply watched the passersby, enjoying the counterpoint of their modern clothes and cameras against the three-story stonework and arched windows of the Maison du Grand Fauconnier across the way. The medieval masons had surely been the technological giants of their age.

Here in Cordes, built as a refuge for the persecuted Cathar sect by Raymond VII, a sympathetic local nobleman, the buildings rose to far less awe-inspiring heights than in the Catholic centers. Cordes contained no crenellated spires or majestic stained glass windows casting jeweled shadows onto the huddled congregation below.

Cathars, she had learned from Aunt Jeanne, lived frugally, disdaining the ostentation of the Catholics, and were happy to worship in one another's homes or out in the oak woods and fields.

The *noisette* materialized and brought her back to the twentieth century. She sniffed at the coffee, its sharp aroma helping her focus on what she'd say to Berenger. Not a chance he'd take the news quietly and let her think on her feet. She hunted for the clearest way to express the new problem and its impact on their respective rights.

She dropped coins on the table, and from her seat, scanned up and down Grand' Rue for Berenger's wine store. Once she remembered to look in the rough direction of Number 8, she spotted the sign "Cave" down to the right, announcing its wine wares. The store's street frontage did look narrow; she could see why expansion might be a good thing.

She stood, threw back her shoulders and marched towards it.

CHAPTER SEVEN

Two wooden barrels, cut in half vertically, stood guard either side of the wine store's doorway. One supported an open display box with three red-sealed bottles nestled in wood shavings. From the top of the other barrel spilled a green fountain of ivy, its natural form softening the hard angles of the stone wall behind it, and evoking an echo of vine leaves.

Insert chapter seven text here. Insert chapter seven text here. Insert chapter seven text here. Insert chapter seven text here. Insert chapter seven text here. Insert chapter seven text here. Insert chapter seven text here. Insert chapter seven text here. Insert chapter seven text here. Insert chapter seven text here. Insert chapter seven text here. Insert chapter seven text here She stepped over the threshold and a muffled gong sounded. Display racks lined the left-hand wall, full of bottles standing in ranks like soldiers on parade. The bottles' predominantly white labels glowed against the dark timber of the shelving. Ahead, through the body of the shop, Chantal saw several chest-high tables designed for tasting activities, each a small planet orbited by two or three bar-stool moons. Down the right-hand side ran a long, glass-topped serving counter, backed by rows of wine glasses, tumblers and water jugs.

The shop held one person. Wearing a navy pullover over a crisp blue-and-white-striped collared shirt, he stood behind the counter, staring at several large sheets of paper spread out before him. The casual glance and quarter-smile Berenger lifted towards his new customer froze when he recognized who had entered.

The low ceiling accentuated his height. She watched his look of welcome ebb away and decided to stay close to the door. No point wandering too far into the wild beast's den.

"Mademoiselle. These plans delayed me." He jerked his head at the papers in front of him, his tone formal. "I had intended to call on you today."

"What about?" Not for a social chat, she was sure.

"To renew my offer of help in several ways. Not out of a sense of neighborliness. This leopard hasn't changed his spots." Another man might have smiled as he said it, but Berenger remained deadpan.

His reference to a wild animal slightly unnerved her, so soon after her mental image of his shop as a lair.

"Every day counts," he continued. "The sooner you leave, the better."

"I understand your urgency, but I don't need your help. Thanks all the same."

His mouth tightened at the corner. "So why are you here? You've come to buy wine?"

She drew a deep breath.

Here goes.

"I've come to tell you that Number 8 may not be yours. Our lawyers are looking into it. It all depends on the timing."

He straightened up to his full height, his head nearly brushing the beam above him. "Explain." They both knew he meant it as an order, not a request.

"You signed the papers with Lelou moments before twelve. He had power of attorney to sign for Aunt Jeanne."

"I know all this. I was there," he snapped.

Chantal cut to the crucial uncertainty. "He didn't have the power to sign for a dead woman. And Aunt Jeanne might have been dead at noon. No one knows."

His eyes narrowed. "The police must."

"Lelou called them. They say she died over lunchtime but they can't say exactly when." She recalled the look on Lelou's face when his repeated urging for a clear-cut answer from the police had made no headway.

A line of white now rimmed Berenger's nostrils. "Congratulations, Mademoiselle. You must have had a busy morning, finding a reason my sale shouldn't go through." He tore a hand back through his springy curls. "Then you ran rings around old Lelou, even with your basic French. He must have been distracted by a foreign siren invading his office."

She let his continuing mistake about her French language ability pass. But *siren*? She gave herself a mental shake. This was Berenger Morel, a man who didn't give an inch. He hadn't paid her a compliment. He was simply impatient of anyone who'd allow female charms to sidetrack them.

His voice cut through her thoughts, demanding to know exactly what the police had said.

She struggled to answer. "You'll hear it all from your own lawyer soon enough, I expect. But I believe the window for the time of death is between eleven and one."

Feature by feature, his face locked into rigidity. "But I signed at twelve!"

"That, Monsieur, is the problem."

He gripped the edge of the counter as if to restrain himself from vaulting over it. "No, the problem, Mademoiselle, is that a gold-digging relative from England is determined to keep hold of a house she thought she'd inherit, no doubt to turn it into a quaint holiday home to rent to a bunch of Johnny-come-latelys, who wouldn't know a decent glass of Cordes Blanc if it climbed out of the bottle and threw itself down their ignorant palates!"

Having the expected storm raging at last brought Chantal a kind of relief. She'd enjoy holding onto her temper while he lost his. She replied evenly, "I told you last night. What I care about, very much, is my great-aunt, and what happened to make her sell. I don't care about the money."

"And who owns the house if it isn't mine?"

Damn, damn, damn the man.

Lelou had been in such a state that he'd let slip the house would come entirely to Chantal if the sale proved invalid. Her sister, Lotty, had gone unmentioned, and it hadn't been the moment for Chantal to probe the will's details. In Lelou's office, she'd been touched that her great-aunt's age-old promise of leaving her the house had been genuine. Now, in Berenger's wine store, the legacy had become an accusing finger, pointing straight at her. She retreated a step and muttered, "I do."

"I knew it." His eyes were black disks in shadowed sockets. "And do you want it?"

She'd not had time to think. Events kept blindsiding her, like spooks leaping out along a ghost train.

As she cast around for an answer, a memory from her very first visit to Cordes surfaced. She and Aunt Jeanne had stood side by side in the hall on two kitchen chairs— for that visit, only, they were the same height—and peered at a master mason's mark on the lintel over the front door. With her fingertip, Chantal had traced along the chiseled lines of the stylized capital 'A' with an arrow balanced across its apex. She'd shivered in the knowledge that another human, a skilled craftsman, dead for centuries, had carved them. Raised in a London house that dated back no further than Queen Victoria, and whose construction truths lay hidden behind wallboards and dropped ceilings, Number 8 had been a place of wonder.

Did she want the house? Did she want it for Aunt Jeanne's sake more than her own? And did she really want the house more than the money?

She could only shrug.

"Well, *I* want it." Berenger added to the emphasis of his words by straining forwards, his shoulders bunching under his weight. "So take my quarter of a million euros, and go back to England and spend it. I'll get on with what I have to do here."

"It's not my decision. It's up to the lawyers."

"I'm not waiting for them." He pulled back and scooped the plans into a pile. "Lawyers take forever."

"I can't solve that problem."

"You create them." Swiftly, he rolled the plans up.

Chantal persisted. "Believe me, I'm trying to solve the one about Aunt Jeanne selling the home she loved."

"I'll believe you when I've double-checked every word you've said. You'd better leave. We're not all sightseers with time on our hands." He looked pointedly at the door.

She opened her mouth to retort that she had plenty to do, too: arrange a funeral, empty a house. Track down a short intruder with a mulberry scarf.

Let's not forget him.

Instead, she shook her head. Why waste effort on this rude man?

She had one foot in the street when Berenger called out. "Wait! You'd better tell me your name before you go. I can't keep thinking of you as 'the English tourist'."

She threw him her sweetest smile—and walked off without saying a word.

*   *   *

It took every shred of Chantal's willpower not to look around to see the look on his face. She concentrated so fiercely that she missed the side alley back down to Rue Obscure, and ended up well along the eastern stretch of Grand' Rue.

Cordes had enjoyed a renaissance in the 1940s with the

57

arrival of all kinds of craftsmen and artists, and these days the main street's stores offered everything from gemstones and handicrafts to small art galleries and even working artists' studios.

All had closed for lunch. Nevertheless, the professional in her insisted she stop to assess what was on offer. The priest and undertaker would be busy with their main meal of the day, and she had time to browse. As she enjoyed window displays of fine leatherwork, pottery, silver bracelets and crystal pendants, the problems of the morning faded.

When she'd last visited the town, she'd taken a course in stained glass-making, and that experience had helped her truly admire craftsmanship. Now, she saw the same stores with the eyes of businesswoman, albeit a failed one. *A wiser one*, she told herself.

Chantal's jewelry specialty had been to fashion antique beads into new earrings and bracelets. She'd been planning to branch out into knot jewelry, when her business failed. Her jewelry looked a good fit with the ranges selling along Grand' Rue. The prices of some of the items were remarkable and Cordes attracted hordes of international tourists during the warmer months. There'd be worse places to relaunch her business.

She could move out of her mother's London house and base herself at Aunt Jeanne's. At twenty-seven, wasn't it high time she struck out to live on her own, without her mother, and without any man, either? Her trade contacts in London all knew about the debacle of her jewelry deal with the big fashion store chain, whereas here she had no reputation, good or bad. Rue Obscure was not a main street, but she could try turning the little parlor into a showroom to supplement sales from other outlets along the main street.

If you get Number 8.

She'd have sworn she heard Berenger's voice in her head, challenging her again. She paused to think. Losing the house with all its good memories and intriguing legends would be a wrench, but for her business it might be a boost. She'd have thousands of euros instead of a house that needed constant care. There'd be more than enough money to clear the last debts, rent a place to live near to the town, create exciting new jewelry pieces and slowly rebuild.

Chantal mulled over her options until she reached the fortified eastern gate. It bore the name *Portail Peint*, the Painted Portal. She peered closely at the huge stone blocks, willing a trace of medieval color to reveal itself. What had the gate looked like in its days of finery? And, if it had never been painted, where had its name come from? More old puzzles hovered in the air all around her: what had happened to the Cathars' long-lost treasure? Had Roland Fleurie really thrown those inquisitors into the well? And did a long-lost tunnel run somewhere beneath Number 8?

She banged a fist lightly against the stonework. The olden-day puzzles paled beside the modern ones. The reason Aunt Jeanne had sold her beloved house, and Berenger's role in it. A last question made her roll her eyes: would his face crack if he smiled?

The trailing savory scent of food caught her attention and her stomach rumbled slightly. Her watch told her Saint Michel would soon chime one. If she ate a good meal now, she could make do with a snack from Aunt Jeanne's pantry later, and the time spent eating lunch would give her a chance to read over her aunt's funeral wishes that Marie had hurriedly copied for her.

She'd only glimpsed the words at Lelou's and needed more time to absorb them. Her great-aunt had specified burial in a cardboard coffin, and Marie said the papers contained a list of suppliers of such ecologically friendly caskets. Pure Jeanne, but probably not the undertaker's preference. She consoled herself with the thought that a disappointed undertaker would be a breeze after her encounter with Berenger Morel.

In fact, restored by a good lunch, she had no difficulty with either of her afternoon meetings. The funeral preparations were well in hand by the time she said goodbye to the priest and crossed the little square outside the church. Grand' Rue had emptied out as closing time drew near, and in moments she had descended Les Rampes and turned hard right towards Number 8. The long, shadowed passageway lay ahead, but the late afternoon light from the west pierced almost to its heart and kept the ghosts at bay. Chantal sauntered through it and paused on the far side to enjoy the view once more.

The sharp scent of wood smoke spiked the air. Despite the rapidly cooling day, she leaned against the ramparts and gazed south. Down in the valley, the low sun cast long shadows from the occasional elm trees in the hedgerows. A breeze ruffled her hair. This would be a perfect moment to feel a lover's strong arm around her shoulder, his jacket a warm haven to burrow into. How long had it been?

Chantal sighed. If Prince Charming ever showed up, she wouldn't trust him. Not after Steven and his golden grins. She was alone. That was how it had to be.

.

CHAPTER EIGHT

That evening, the ceramic wood-heater on the kitchen hearth substituted for a lover's warmth. The heater should have drawn well, but Chantal struggled to coax it to stay alight. When it finally began to emit cheerful crackles, she decided it had been worth the oily smell of firelighters that now pervaded the room.

She pulled a chair as close to the heater's warmth as the flex on Aunt Jeanne's old phone would allow. Taking a deep breath, she made a call to her mother. She felt obliged to report in, like a soldier out on patrol, but didn't expect much support in return.

After receiving a catalog of Helene's numerous little struggles to manage without anyone else in the house, Chantal described her progress with the funeral arrangements. She left out all mention of the intruder and also tried to gloss quickly over the mystery of Number 8's current ownership. Helene, however, seized on the issue. The energizing prospect of so much money flowing into the family, and for an asset she had never liked, dissipated her sickbed languor like the sun on morning sea mist. Chantal found herself receiving armchair detective advice on how she could find proof of when Aunt Jeanne had died.

"Even if the house is ours," concluded her mother, "we can still offer it to that local wine merchant. Think of what we could do with the money!"

Chantal hugged to herself the knowledge that any decision on the house would be *hers* not *ours*. That revelation could wait for another call.

She tilted her head back, following the heater's flue up to the beamed ceiling. Aunt Jeanne had often repeated the secret to wood beams strong enough to carry a heavy load for hundreds of years: oak, soaked in lime-water for up to twenty-five years. Her aunt had given her ceiling the hidden support of two well-disguised modern steel girders, but after seven centuries the oak beams could be excused a little sagging.

Chantal's attention drifted back to her mother's voice. She was still talking about ways to spend the proceeds of the house sale, and the topic grated on Chantal's nerves. Helene's own father had been born at Number 8, but that family connection carried no weight with her. And the reminder of the unsolved puzzle of why Aunt Jeanne would ever sell her cherished home added to Chantal's irritation.

She switched to the offensive, knowing it would bring the tiring conversation to an end. "Madame Nazac asked if you would be coming to the funeral. What shall I tell her?"

Helene's fatigue rolled back in as quickly as a fog bank in the English Channel. "I couldn't, darling. My health." She sighed deeply. "Explain to people. It's not what I'd hope for."

A minute later, Chantal placed the handset back on its cradle above the rotary dial. Duty done, she heaved a deep sigh of her own. Her last question to her mother had been to check on Harry's welfare, and she'd been pleased to hear his appetite hadn't waned in her absence. She yearned to have the cat for company at Number 8, something warm and alive and friendly.

Without him, she decided to fill the two or three hours before bed with other sources of comfort. She made a light snack from tins, and, after she'd eaten, fetched her latest jewelry project from her purse.

Almost without looking, she secured macramé yarns onto a small clipboard she used as support when traveling. Her fingers deftly teased apart the bright scarlet and pure white strands below the main knot and placed them in the right sequence. She was trying to weave a heart-shaped knot to stand proud of the surrounding weave. Using a bead of the right shape would have been easier, but it wasn't the effect she wanted.

As she tacked the strings to and fro, her thoughts did the same. She had to probe the possibility that Aunt Jeanne had, in fact, been ill. Her doctor might have found a sudden and serious illness. Wouldn't it be like Jeanne to keep it a secret as long as possible? With her flamboyant nature, she might have wanted to go out in a blaze of glory. Chantal thought of the hints her great-aunt had dropped about her wild early years. Travel, parties. She'd have needed money to recapture those times, money that for years had been lavished on Number 8.

If Aunt Jeanne had been ill, her death could easily have been an accident. Then Berenger Morel would be in the clear.

After an hour, she dropped the macramé. The square knots refused to taper and her neck felt as twisted as the strings in her lap. She stood to stretch and found her legs had also seized up after her busy day on foot. To limber up, she crossed the worn hall flagstones into the parlor.

So far she had only glimpsed inside this room, as part of her mission the night before to reassure herself there'd been no hidden second intruder. The parlor had changed little from her previous visit four years earlier. A tall dresser still displayed four rows of a blue and white dinner service, the plates' color breaking up the starkness of the whitewashed wall. Opposite stood an oak sideboard, its surface cluttered with antique pottery and glass ornaments. A ruby-toned Persian rug over the dull brown floor tiles added some warmth, as did the two chintz-covered easy chairs and a long ottoman that had lived under the street-front window as long as Chantal could remember.

Aunt Jeanne had added something new to the room since Chantal's last visit, though: a long thin rug now hung on the wall that faced the street window. The runner reached right to the floor and its poor placement niggled at Chantal's sense of proportion. It should have been mounted higher up. She flicked back a corner, looking for a reason for its odd position.

Sheltered behind it lay the door to Aunt Jeanne's study, a room she had often jokingly referred to as her *scriptorium,* and a part of the house Chantal had forgotten till this moment. During her great-niece's visits, Jeanne had largely put on hold the three activities she conducted in this office, meaning Chantal rarely had cause to enter.

One activity concerned paperwork and phone calls for whatever cause *du jour* her aunt was busy championing. Chantal couldn't recall a single visit in which her aunt hadn't had a battle to lend her prodigious energy to.

Another activity revolved around her never-ending research into the history of Number 8, Cordes and the Cathars. The third activity, presumably less relevant since Aunt Jeanne had reached retirement age, related to her work translating books and business documents between Italian and French. The Lamarque women tended to have a knack for languages; Chantal's mother also dabbled in translation, mostly between English and French.

If any room might hold a clue about Aunt Jeanne's state of mind near the end of her life, or hint at a new enemy, surely her office offered the best opportunity.

Chantal twisted the door handle, half expecting it to be locked. Instead, it opened easily.

The smell of old paper that greeted her made her think of rats in damp corners, but she knew her sister Lotty would have breathed it in to the depths of her lungs and dreamed of libraries. And Lotty would have been nearer the mark: books lined almost every square foot of wall, mixed in with ring-binders and document boxes in bureaucratic shades of mottled gray and dark green.

Two filing cabinets hunkered under the shelves, and a massive antique roll-top desk, filling a quarter of the small room, stood under the shuttered window. Beyond the window lay another part of the house she'd not yet re-visited—a small paved yard, enclosed with high walls, and boasting a disused medieval water cistern.

Chantal doubted the intruder had made it into this haven of research, though Jeanne's trademark mess of haphazard piles of paper made it hard to tell. She wondered if the hanging rug outside the door might have been for extra privacy as much as the more likely explanation of keeping drafts at bay.

She sat down at the swivel chair, another vintage piece, and immediately discarded the plump cushion that had lifted Aunt Jeanne to a comfortable working height. At this new, lower angle to the desk, Chantal could see the side of a document box, half-hidden under loose papers. She pulled it out. Its contents label bore the words *Eye of the Needle*, written in Aunt Jeanne's round hand. Chantal knew the phrase from the Bible story, but it meant nothing else to her.

The box contained sheaves of paper and a scroll tucked in at one side. On the outside of the scroll, Aunt Jeanne had printed the words *Discovered behind the fireplace, 1997*. Chantal cocked her head, remembering the repair job two years back, triggered by crumbling bricks in the fireplace. Jeanne had had them patched but also put in the wood-heater for greater convenience.

Intrigued, Chantal carefully unrolled the coiled paper. At first glance, it looked like an electrical diagram, with a solid black line running down the center of a large triangle, while two dotted red lines ran across. Then she deciphered the words *town well* beside the vertical line and realized she held a map of Cordes, with the triangle representing the hilltop and the plunging black line its four-hundred-foot-deep well. She guessed the horizontal red lines to be the encircling town ramparts.

Several tiny symbols, all meaningless to Chantal, speckled the map. One symbol, close to the upper dotted line, looked like an Egyptian hieroglyph for an eye, but rotated ninety degrees to stand on its end. Another eye shape had been drawn well down the pyramid. Next to the upper eye sat a little flower. Nothing remotely resembled a needle. Without a legend or scale, it wasn't much of a map.

Near the top of the box, she found a photocopy of the scroll, and this time Aunt Jeanne had covered it with comments in faint pencil. Chantal leaned closer to try to read it and her neck spasmed in protest. She kneaded the tense muscles and then rubbed her eyes.

Torn between curiosity and fatigue, she pulled out papers held together with a brass split pin, determined it would be the last thing she checked before bed. With relief, she found the bundle to be a series of letters, legibly typewritten in passable modern French and dated three years earlier. The writer, W. Sanders, used letterhead from Columbia University in New York.

As Chantal read the letter's presumptuous tone, she visualized Sanders as a man. He was apparently a student of the medieval era in southern France, and summarily requested the essence of Jeanne's research into Cordes in general and Number 8 in particular, without showing willingness to share any insights in return. He wanted to know what the 'Eye of the Needle' meant to Aunt Jeanne. He asked if she had seen it referenced in documents about Cordes—if so, specifically which—and if she believed it represented a physical place or feature in the town—again, if so, which and why. That Aunt Jeanne had obviously responded to this arrogant approach surely reflected her great-aunt's true passion for the town's history.

The second letter made clear that Sanders disagreed with Aunt Jeanne's opinions about the Eye. Chantal could infer from his reply that her aunt believed it to be a metaphor referring to Cordes itself, reflecting how hard the town's defenses made it for any who were not welcome to gain entry. Sanders pushed her to consider if it could not be a structure or structures, such as the town's massive gates whose entrances stood tall and narrow. This time he offered a quatrain in Occitan to support his theory.

Chantal's eyes glazed over at the unfamiliar language. She bundled everything back into the box. Any further clues in Aunt Jeanne's study would have to wait. Bedtime beckoned.

As she reached for the study's door handle to leave, she saw its key—small and malnourished compared to the front door's monster—in the lock. On a whim, she locked the door behind her, before slipping the key into a narrow-necked Victorian glass vase on the sideboard.

In the bathroom, Chantal rummaged in the medicine cabinet above the sink for pharmaceuticals that would suggest a recent illness. Mostly, she found quack remedies for digestive disorders in dark brown bottles. She consoled herself with the option of talking to Aunt Jeanne's doctor directly.

A final annoyance was finding she'd forgotten to buy new toothpaste. The tortured tube in her toilet bag refused to yield any more. Wrinkling her nose, she used a little of Aunt Jeanne's old-fashioned tooth powder. Its gritty texture and corn flour-bland flavor made her screw up her face.

"Use lists more," she scolded herself as she flung her empty toothpaste into the trash. "If Prince Charming ever did ride by, you'd forget his name and number before the second date."

CHAPTER NINE

"I want this dream to stop," whispered Chantal. Her hands twisted in the thick bedspread, seeking comfort. On the wall opposite, an ugly stain swirled in a poisonous shade of mustard. At its outer edges writhed a mass of tiny fingers that clawed their way downward. The stain reached the wooden floorboards and the fingers began to inch towards the bed.

Something else moved at the corner of her vision. She twisted to the right and saw the wall rippling in lazy waves. Chantal knew for certain it was solid stone, two feet thick, and hadn't moved in hundreds of years. She knew with equal certainty that it was undulating towards her.

"Make it stop," she urged herself. The mustard vortex now swirled a mere hand span from one of the stout oak bed legs. Flecks of scarlet had bloomed in it. Drops of blood.

"No!" she shouted. Her voice sounded loud and strong. In her nightmares, she could never speak.

What if I'm awake?

"But I can see," she reasoned rapidly, trying to use logic to calm her pounding heart. "The house is pitch dark at night. I must be dreaming."

She held her hands in front of her face but couldn't see them. They did nothing, however, to block out the creeping stain. It remained plainly visible, though its colors had begun to fade. The fingers still scrabbled towards her.

She bit her lip. The sharp tang of blood filled her mouth. Could you taste in dreams?

She knew the door out to the hall lay to her left. Dream or not, she'd risk bolting to it through the dark if she could only reach the light switch. But which side of the door was it? The haze of fear fogged her brain.

From under the bed, a thin voice giggled.

Panic hit.

She shot out of the bed covers and raced to her best guess of where the door opened into the corridor.

Her left temple slammed into the door jamb. Adrenalin numbed the pain. It also cushioned the shock that she was obviously awake. Her breath came in short sobs as she swept the walls either side of the door for the switch.

Again and again, her hands scraped up and down. At last, she felt the smooth plastic. On the third, agonized try, her fingers hooked onto the switch.

Weak yellow light filled the bedroom. Relief and air flowed into Chantal in equal measures. She peered around the bedroom, ready to confront her recent terrors.

Her insides turned to ice. The red-flecked puddle swirled over the carpet. The wall had retreated, but it continued to ripple.

In all the miserable months of bad sleep that Steven had caused, she'd never suffered crazy visions like this. She clenched her jaw. Tiny pieces of Jeanne's tooth powder grated between her teeth.

From near the head of the stairs came a mechanical whirring. Her head snapped around to stare down the hallway and confront the next horror. A gong in the grandfather clock struck a mournful note, then another. Silently she counted each stroke.

Twelve for midnight.

"Perfect. The witching hour." Her flicker of courage soon burned out. In the long shadows cast by the bedroom light, the clock face morphed slowly into a gargoyle whose gaping mouth grew larger and larger. Folds of cloth, medieval style, draped its head. Its mouth stretched to fill the clock face. She couldn't bear to wait to see how big it would grow. Or what would spew from its mouth.

The steep stairs to the hall looked normal. Would they stay that way if she stepped onto them? They led to the kitchen with its bright light. She balled her hands into fists. Mad visions or not, she had to descend.

At her first step onto the ancient tread, Chantal remembered what had brought her to Aunt Jeanne's house. The thought of that fatal fall almost made her stay with the gargoyle. She'd lose her mind if Aunt Jeanne's ghost rose before her, head lolling at a crazy angle on its broken neck. She rubbed her eyes to erase the sickening vision and grasped the handrail resolutely.

The kitchen offered sanctuary. For once, the fluorescent light came on smoothly. The white surfaces of the little fridge and the old cooker wore a halo of blue, but the effect was more odd than scary. All the same, Chantal didn't feel brave enough to open cupboards or the bathroom door.

She settled on the draining board by the sink and rested her head back on the wall. At least this one behaved like a wall should.

As her shoulders relaxed, a clanging began. At first, it rang like metal on stone, a master stonemason chiseling letters into a tombstone. But then the volume swelled, and the kitchen filled with it as if transformed into a belfry with crazed bell-ringers striving to outdo one another.

Rather than the sound descending from bells above, though, it rose from the depths of the house. First rhythmic, then staccato, the noise had no pattern. It disoriented her, echoing through her, spreading and filling her head. The noise became a spear, aimed at her eardrums, angled to pierce through to her brain.

She couldn't fight the madness. Curled into a ball of wretchedness, with her hands over her ears, she screamed to drown out the terrible noise.

CHAPTER TEN

The jolt of her head as it rolled forwards snapped Chantal awake on her perch on the draining board. From neck to knees, she had chilled to the stiffness of a marble effigy. Memories of the night's horrors returned but, slowly, her senses reassured her. The bizarre clanging had ceased. The appliances had returned to their regular plain white once more. Her watch read seven-thirty in the morning.

She coaxed herself to open the bathroom door. Everything looked as it should. Even after a long, hot bath, however, she had to steel herself to climb the stairs and move past the grandfather clock. It looked benign, its brass fittings gleaming. In the bedroom, she threw open the shutters. The walls had reverted to their job of holding up the ceiling again.

Chantal dressed in her favorite tight jeans and deep red sweater. Bright colors she reserved for jewelry, never clothes. She headed down to make breakfast.

A knock startled her still-raw nerves. She put down the toast she'd coated with apricot jam and fetched the front door key from its kitchen hook. Opening the door carefully, she met an extravagant spray of flowers danced a foot from her face. Shafts of sunlight turned the daffodils and jonquils from yellow to gold. A thrilling scent of spring hovered in the air.

A man's hand held the flower stems firmly. Tendons ran like fine steel ropes beneath his tanned skin. His hand looked capable enough to drive off a dozen demons. The last dregs of her night-time fears drained away.

She lifted her gaze directly to Berenger's eyes. The blue ice of the day before had dissolved to deep summer seas. More formal than at their first meeting, he wore a coat and tie with a black pullover and gray dress pants.

"Good morning, Mademoiselle."

"Monsieur." Despite a cup of soothing breakfast tea, Chantal's throat still rasped slightly from her screams in the night, and she tried to clear it.

An awkward pause followed.

"These are..?" After their recent fights, she doubted they could be intended for her, but he did seem to be offering them.

"For you. I'm trying a new approach," he said, his gaze roaming across her face as if trying to gauge her reaction.

"And in return?" She reached for the bouquet.

He moved it out of reach. "Your name, please."

"Flowers first."

With a small shrug, and a rare gesture of acquiescence, he handed them across. Their hands touched lightly, a scant square inch of skin. Her nerve endings lit up like fairy lights on a Christmas tree.

Where did that come from?

"Chantal Harrison." She put out her hand to shake. It looked like politeness. With luck, he'd never guess it was an experiment to see if the sensation would return. His hand engulfed hers in a firm shake. This time, the contact with his warm, dry palm shot searing heat to the pit of her stomach.

Two out of two.

"Berenger Morel, at your service," he replied formally.

Yes, please, said the treacherous little voice. She tried to

73

ignore it. "The flowers are lovely, thank you. My name seems a small price for them, though." She shot him a sharp glance. "Was there anything else?"

"Yes. But time is short. If I may explain?"

He'd piqued her curiosity. "Then you'd better come into the kitchen while I put these in water. Watch your head on the lintel," she said over her shoulder as she led the way.

"One hard blow usually drives things into my skull." The dryness of his tone made her smile.

"There's tea in the pot, if you'd like some." The polite exchange stood in stark contrast to their previous meetings.

"I drink coffee, but don't bother."

Not a total contrast, perhaps.

She opened the cupboard under the sink where she thought she'd seen a tall vase.

"You look tired," Berenger commented, testing the weight of Aunt Jeanne's breakfast table before leaning against it. "Uncomfy old bed, or have I bought a ghost along with the house?"

Chantal had her back to him, reaching across the scratched steel sink for the faucet, so he never saw her eyes widen at his uncannily accurate guess. Not that hallucinations were ghosts, but both were desperately unwelcome nighttime visitors. And the word 'ghost' reminded her of Aunt Jeanne's tale of Roland Fleurie. He'd died young, supposedly haunted to an early grave by the shades of the dead Dominican inquisitors.

Maybe Fleurie had been haunted, but Chantal hadn't. No vengeful black-robed figures for her, just gargoyles and clanging church bells. And she was sure that Aunt Jeanne, despite her healthy respect for the afterlife, had never seen a ghost.

She wasn't about to share any of her thoughts with Berenger, though. He must already think her unbalanced with her insistence on understanding Aunt Jeanne's motives for selling. "Old bed," she managed as she looked around for the best place for the vase.

He nodded.

She opted for the center of the table and walked a little further around it than necessary, to keep her distance. The sight of the bright yellow flowers against the orange and white spotted oilcloth cheered her, reminding her of fruit displays on a market stall.

"Well, to business," her visitor said, the brusque tone re-entering his voice and commanding her attention. "I have an appointment to see Grenier this morning. He's been our family lawyer all my life. I want you to come with me."

That explained the smart clothes but not much else. "Me? Why?" She gripped the back of one of the kitchen chairs.

"Because I want you to hear from the best legal mind in this area that your aunt's death changes nothing about the sale. Lelou is a solid lawyer, I think, but—"

"Don't knock him," she interrupted, relieved to hear that there were, apparently, no fresh complications to deal with. "He confirmed what you said about your past attempts to buy this place."

"I said he was solid. But Grenier practiced for years in a top partnership in Paris. He's semi-retired now."

"You already know his opinion on the matter, do you?"

"No." His hand swept back though his hair in a gesture of impatience she was beginning to recognize. "We've only managed to exchange phone messages. He's been out of town."

"Maybe he won't say what you want to hear."

Berenger's brows lowered and he folded his arms. "At least he'll say it to a native speaker. Lelou was probably oversimplifying for your French."

"My French?" she said mildly, resisting the temptation to fold her arms in reply.

"Being able to talk to a five-year-old isn't the same as

following a discussion on French law."

"Granted." She tightened her grip on the chair, knowing the time had come to deal with his misapprehension. "Here's the thing, though, I do—"

He cut her off. "So, if we both go and hear what Grenier thinks of this situation, I can translate for you. If, as I hope, this is all a fuss over nothing, you can get back to your arrangements here. Like the packing." He threw a meaningful glance at the half-open pantry and its well-stocked shelves.

She rolled her eyes. "I haven't forgotten the packing. But this translation offer. It isn't necessary. I—"

Again, he overrode her, standing up from the table to make his point. "Yes, it is necessary. I want access to this house. By yesterday, frankly." He jabbed a strong finger hard on the tablecloth. "That means I need you working to clear up Jeanne Lamarque's affairs. You won't, as long as you think this house might be yours, or that there's something in your idea about your aunt being scared off."

She slapped the chair's back with her right hand. So be it. He listened about as well as he smiled. She'd let him translate, and she'd test his honesty. "OK, we'll do it your way. But I'll need a few minutes to change."

Berenger inspected her clothes. "That fluffy top's fine. It's almost the color of one of my favorite Rhône wines, one that's blended from Syrah and Sincault varietals."

"I'll choose my own clothes, thanks. But for your future reference, this pullover is one of my favorites, and it's blended from a mix of lambswool and angora."

Berenger inclined his head in acknowledgment. She almost thought a smile tugged at his lips, but dismissed the idea. Not this man. He didn't do smiles.

Upstairs, she debated whether to change the sweater or not. She didn't want Berenger thinking she'd followed his suggestions. On the other hand, she knew she looked good in it. In fact, she looked terrific. It clung softly to her breasts without being tight. The deep shade of red set off her auburn highlights.

She kept it on and teamed it with slim-fitting black wool pants and low-heeled pumps that would cope well with the cobbled streets. Back downstairs, Berenger ignored her choice of clothes and merely checked his watch.

They set off, turning left to take the shortest way to the town center. Clouds chased across the sun. In the shifting light, the ancient stones along Rue Obscure turned from gray to maize and back to gray. Despite her terrible night, Chantal found a new sharpness and clarity in everything she saw. Somehow, she'd woken with better than 20/20 vision.

A strange feeling rose in her chest. It was bubbly, yet made her feel tense at the same time. At first, she blamed it on their brisk pace. When it didn't ease as they reached the brow of the hill, she paid it more attention.

It's happiness.

It had been so long since she'd felt it that she'd not recognized it. Covertly, she glanced up at Berenger's profile. Could she be enjoying his company?

As they passed his wine store, a short, stocky young man emerged through its door, his neck warmly wrapped in a dark scarf. He threw Berenger a respectful greeting. Something about him was definitely familiar. "Is that Laurent Nazac?" she asked.

Berenger nodded.

She hadn't seen Laurent since her last visit but one, about seven years back, yet something told her she'd seen him much more recently.

Then she made the connection: a short, stocky man hiding in a scarf. Her intruder. He could have been Laurent. He'd have known where to find his mother's key for cleaning Number 8. An employee might help his boss cover the tracks of a crime. Motive. Opportunity. It was a good start.

"Here." Berenger broke in on her uncomfortable

thoughts. They stood outside a stout door set into a medieval façade. The stone bulk of Saint Michel soared to their right. Glancing up at it, Chantal saw two gargoyles arching out from under the church's roof line. One resembled a leaping stag and the other a hooded monk. She shivered, remembering the grandfather clock's transformation. Her subconscious must have projected an image she'd seen on her walks. She had absolutely *not* seen the face of a long-dead Inquisitor.

They climbed the narrow stairs to Grenier's office.

Forget ghosts and bells, listen for how honestly he translates. And say as little as possible, or they'll pick up on your French.

Grenier's plump, florid face turned puce at having what he termed 'the other party' present. Berenger insisted. It didn't surprise Chantal that he got his own way. Grenier hitched up his exquisitely cut suit pants and sat heavily in his wing-backed office chair. It creaked under his weight.

The discussion began. Chantal couldn't fault Berenger's translation. He passed the lawyer's words on faithfully, whether the information ran in his favor or not.

In truth, the visit added little to what Chantal had learned from Lelou. The legal mess could be untangled only by determining the time of death. Like Lelou, Grenier had quizzed the police and received the same answer. The police were treating it as an accident.

"You may tell your…companion…that probate on her great-aunt's estate will be subject to the same delay. If she is her aunt's legatee, neither of you will be able to access the money or claim the property till this is sorted out."

"I lose my money *and* the house, for months and months?" Berenger roared.

Chantal felt a rush of sympathy for him, and even a little for Grenier who recoiled into the safety of his chair. It took a mental image of Aunt Jeanne looking scared and haggard for her to regain a proper perspective.

Berenger pushed Grenier repeatedly to find ways to break the deadlock. The lawyer tapped his fingertips on his nose as he considered different angles. "Perhaps if your estate and the legatee's were fully commingled…" he offered at last.

"Which means?"

"It means you'd need to marry this young lady."

Berenger stopped translating. He rolled his eyes to the wood-paneled ceiling and stayed that way, staring upwards.

Grenier cleared his throat. "I will continue to search for more palatable and practical options, of course."

Chantal bade Grenier a simple goodbye and went to the head of the stairs. Behind her, she heard him say to Berenger, "I'm sorry you're in this situation, but I can tell you the Council's not sorry the old dame has departed. Without her energy, the petition will lose steam. Good for traders like you and me, eh? *Bon.* I'll be in touch."

Berenger came down the stairs, hammering his heels into the ancient timbers. The explosion couldn't be far away. He averaged one a day at present, and Chantal had been in the firing line for all of them. Not that she would leave before he gave her an explanation for Grenier's final comment. She pointed to the café she'd visited the day before. "Let's get that coffee."

"Great," snarled Berenger. "I haven't got my property. My money's out of reach in the lawyers' accounts. And you want to chit-chat over fancy cakes."

Chantal rounded on him. "No, I want explanations. And information. Too many odd things happened in Aunt Jeanne's last couple of months. You are still, by far, my top suspect. I don't care if you think I'm paranoid. I don't care if you think I'm desperate to hang onto a pile of old stones for sentimental or commercial reasons. But I do care about what happened to my great-aunt. She gave up on something she valued deeply, and I know what—" She broke off. "I know what that would have been like for her," she ended, awkwardly.

Blue eyes regarded her intently. Finally, he nodded. "We'll go up to Place de la Bride. Grenier owns a share in one of the cafés there. If we boost its business maybe his legal fees will drop," he added grimly.

He chose a table by the window. "Before you start arguing again, this is my territory, my tab," said Berenger. He signaled to a thickset man in his late twenties whose cheerful smile shone all the brighter for the contrast with his close-cropped full black beard. The smile widened when Berenger, using simple French and a little English, introduced him as Martin, Grenier's stepson. Chantal had forgotten how interwoven the ties in a small town could be.

"Martin helps out here between his shifts at the lab in Toulouse."

"University pharmacology lab," added Martin, as he ran a swift appraising glance over her pullover. "I'm the mad chemist, *moi*, here to serve whatever poison you like."

Chantal let his teasing wash over her before heading to the restroom.

When she returned a few minutes later, she could hear Berenger and Martin speaking in the local patois. After two days in Cordes, Chantal could follow their conversation easily.

"Tell me where this English lovely is staying. You don't bother with women these days. But I do," coaxed Martin.

"You're an old goat. This one's too good for you. And too tall."

"Who are you saving her for then? Not yourself, I know."

There was a pause. "I might be."

Chantal heard Martin snort. She could have echoed it. It helped her ignore the flush rising on her neck. She reminded herself that Berenger had never stopped loving his dead wife. If he was keeping Martin at bay, it wasn't to have her to himself. Most likely he wanted her gone as soon as possible, without entanglements to make her linger. Regardless, she was no bone to be argued over by two dogs. High time to teach the pair of them a lesson.

As she reached the table, Martin smirked and said, in thickest patois, "Well, then, here's your plump little chicken, back for the plucking."

Chantal fixed her eye on him. In her clearest, most precise, Parisian French, she said, "I'm glad you like my fine feathers. However, they're not coming off for anyone."

Four eyes bulged. Chantal allowed herself a few heartbeats of pure enjoyment before turning to Berenger. She reverted to English. "I tried to tell you this morning, but you wouldn't listen. You don't know me. So, please, stop making assumptions about me."

Berenger inhaled a breath that went on forever. "I'll certainly try, Miss Harrison. Shall we order?"

.

CHAPTER ELEVEN

Berenger sat back. His legs stretched out far beyond the table. Despite his relaxed posture, his brows had settled in a hard line. "Come on," he said, "Put me straight about Chantal Harrison."

She wanted to parry and demand he explain Grenier's comments about the petition, but she had to concede he was only doing as she'd asked. Time to make the most of his co-operation. "You'll listen?"

"I told you before. One hard blow to my head usually gets the message through. Count this as a hard blow."

"What do you want to know?"

"Who you are, what you do, where you learned French. And anything else I'm likely to have guessed wrongly about you," he said gruffly.

Chantal silently ruled out sharing most of that. She'd need to know — and trust — him a lot more than she did now. "OK. My French side. Mum's dad was Aunt Jeanne's older brother. Much older, he's been dead a while now. Mum grew up in France. For years, she's done bits of translation work. I'm always hearing the language."

"And your father's side is English?"

"Yes. Dad's a property developer, though he started out as a builder. They met when Mum had a job as an au pair in London. His workmen made such a racket that she came out to complain."

"And hey presto."

"For a while. They've been divorced fifteen years, separated longer." Her mother had escaped her London loneliness by marrying the young builder who'd made her laugh. He'd been convenient. They'd all paid the price of that convenience. She hurried on before Berenger could ask questions. "I live at Mum's in north London. Dad lives further out, near Watford."

"You're a big city girl."

She pondered the description. The city had been where she'd spent most of her time, but she made little use of what it offered. She'd always loved the countryside, especially in France, and told him so.

His eyes softened a fraction. "But you'll be returning soon. Work must be waiting."

She thought of her newly cleared debts, the few remaining ones, and her first notions about how and where to start again. In England, the ideas hadn't come. Here in Cordes, she could hardly keep up with them. "It can cope without me for a bit."

"And the people in your life, can they cope without you, too?"

Chantal picked up the unused paper straw of sugar from her saucer and tapped it on the table. "My twin can. She's—"

"Twin?" Berenger sat up slightly. "There's another Chantal Harrison out there?"

She sighed inwardly. After a lifetime of uninvited comparison and comments, Chantal had stock phrases to hand and she rolled them out now. "We're fraternal twins, so we're as different as any two siblings. She's blonde, I'm not. I'm very tall, she's not. She's academic, I'm not. Our names are about the most similar thing we have—Chantal and Charlotte—but for years she's been called Lotty."

Berenger opened his mouth to ask another question but Chantal pressed on, ticking more items off her mental list. "I'm the elder by ten minutes. We don't have a 'twin' thing, no ESP about accidents, no telepathy. Dad liked the idea of similar names and clothes but Mum refused to raise clones. She succeeded, I'll give her that." The paper straw flicked out of her fingers and skittered off the table.

"Meaning?" Berenger asked as her head disappeared under the table to retrieve the little packet.

"Meaning we went to different schools, took different holidays, everything."

"Separate *holidays*?"

Chantal shrugged, unwilling to elaborate. "Not all, but often."

Their holidays apart had started the summer she and her twin turned ten; the year their parents split up. Helene, exhausted by the marriage drama she could not avoid, had sent the girls away to relatives. Chantal still remembered how she and Lotty had clung to each other in shared bewilderment at Heathrow Airport, when the time had come for Lotty to fly to Quebec to Helene's sister there, and she to Bordeaux to be picked up by a garrulous friend of Aunt Jeanne's for the two-and-a-half-hour drive eastwards. Lotty had never returned to Quebec, but every couple of years Chantal had spent a holiday in the sanctuary of Cordes, as much at her request as at Aunt Jeanne's.

"I haven't seen Lotty since…" She paused. When had it been? Two Christmases ago?

"It's been a while, I take it," Berenger finished for her. She nodded.

"OK. So you have a sister who's not in your life much. Parents in London. What about your friends? Of either gender." He muttered the last words.

"A few friends, of course. And there's Harry."

Berenger's eyes narrowed. "Harry?"

His query set the little happiness bubbles fizzing again. "Fat Harry, to give him his full designation. Species: Felis. Color: ginger. Size: industrial."

His gaze traveled to the window and focused on something outside, as if he had suddenly grown bored with her story.

Chantal was about to insist he share some details about himself when, still looking out the window, he asked, "And was it your sister, your parents, or maybe those few friends, who took from you something that you valued very deeply? The way you think I took from your great-aunt?" Blue eyes swung back and drilled into her. "Or was it someone else?"

Under the onslaught, she dropped her eyes and stared into her coffee cup, seeing memories as dark as her espresso. "No comment."

"No comment?" he echoed softly.

Without looking up or replying, she launched into a ramble, snatching at subjects at random, anything that didn't involve Steven. She talked about her repeated holidays in Cordes over the years and how Aunt Jeanne had rewarded Chantal's growing interest in Number 8 with a promise to leave it to her. Her schooling during those teenage years came tumbling out, too.

The arrival of an enormous toasted sandwich for Berenger and her own more modest croissant finally slowed her to a standstill.

As she paused to cut into the snack, Berenger commented, "So you were the daughter of a self-made man in a school full of lords' and ladies' brats. Uncomfortable combination." He took a bite of his sandwich.

"An effective way to identify your real friends," she replied.

"It is, isn't it?" he agreed. When she threw him a questioning glance, he went on, "My father was a diplomat and where he went, we followed. He was posted all over, from Southeast Asia to Mexico. I went to four international schools in nine years. Always the new kid, trying to figure out how things worked, usually getting it wrong. I got into plenty of fights."

She could well believe it. "Did your siblings have the

same problem?"

"One sister, Anna, two years younger than me. She's more like my father, could always talk her way out of trouble."

His words fascinated Chantal; she had a front-row seat at the unveiling of a long-kept secret. With every sentence, the velvet curtain obscuring Berenger's true nature rose a little higher.

She picked up her croissant. "My turn to eat. You talk," she urged.

"What about?"

"The important stuff," she said, trying to emulate his gruff tone.

He twisted on the hard café chair and, as Chantal had done a few minutes earlier, began to fiddle with his sugar straw. After a pause in which his eyes locked on his saucer, he muttered, "Simple. Three things. First and foremost, Louise. Next, living and working here, in Cordes. Then wine. That's it."

"Cordes?"

His eyes flashed up to hers.

"What's special about Cordes?"

"What's special? Everything. I never want to live anywhere else." He bent forwards. "This is where my ancestors have lived and died. It's where I belong. Farming our land to support my family, just as they did, that's what gives my work here real meaning." He stared at his boots, thrust out beyond the table, but Chantal guessed his inner gaze saw only familiar, precious pieces of land strung out across the plateau and along the valleys.

"I hated leaving Cordes to follow my father to his next posting. I even begged him once to leave me behind, but of course neither he nor my mother would consider it. Said they couldn't bear to be apart from me."

Chantal listened, captivated. The velvet curtain had risen all the way, and in the spotlight stood a different man than the grumpy giant, a man lit from within.

"My dream," he continued, his glance flicking up to her face for a moment, "was to find a way to stay in Cordes, close to the land, and never have to leave it again."

"And how did you manage it?" she prompted, wanting him to reveal more of himself.

"A degree in land management and viticulture." He now ran the family estate, he explained, growing a mixture of sunflowers, canola and vines. The sunflowers and canola went into animal feed and oils to pay the basic bills. He intended the vines and wine to be the jewel in the estate's crown. As he described their potential, his hands waved about, adding emphasis to his enthusiasm.

"We have fantastic variety of wines in the Gaillac area, thanks to the geology. Our different styles can take you through every dinner course from soup to nuts. And we have single types, like the *perlés*, the slightly sparkling whites, that can carry an entire meal on their own, from aperitif to post-prandial. Imagine! There's nowhere like it." He took a modest bite of his sandwich and swallowed it hurriedly.

"I've been part of a group that's working to bring back a couple of the old grape varieties, too. Really old ones, like Ondenc, that grew up here on the plateau before the 1870s and the phylloxera disaster. We've had to go to Australia to the Barossa Valley." He jabbed a finger downward, towards the opposite side of the Earth. "To get the root stock, you see. From vines that nineteenth-century emigrants took with them, ones that never suffered from the disease. I've got a hectare growing up at La Picarie. It loves the free-draining limestone there and—"

"La Picarie?" Chantal interrupted, seeing an extra gleam in his eye at the name.

"A separate piece of land that came to me when my mother died. The best I've got, in fact. It's in the *Premières Côtes* area, a special designation within the Gaillac wine region for top quality white output. It's been…" He paused. "Let's say it's been a special project of mine in recent times. I've even converted the old barn there into a sleep-out to save me the drive home during pruning and harvest." He heaved a deep sigh and came to a stop. "Enough," he said shortly. "This wasn't the sort of information you wanted."

"Know thine enemy," she quipped, and wondered why it earned her a stony look.

He took a huge bite of his sandwich and chewed it with deliberate slowness as if to signal the end of the truce. Chantal was sorry to see the old Berenger return, but she had learned a huge amount about what made the man tick. With a mental shrug, she changed gears. "OK, let me ask you: what did Grenier mean about the Council and Aunt Jeanne's petition?"

He quickly wiped his mouth with his serviette and said, "Of course, your fluent French. How was my translation?"

"Very fair, actually."

He acknowledged her compliment with a brief nod. "The Town Council matter is straightforward. They want to stop a bypass planned by the regional authorities. They're worried Cordes will lose visitors who spend money. Some locals, like your great-aunt, supported it. They want to keep the twentieth century at bay, never mind the twenty-first one starting next year."

Murder had been committed for far weaker motives than protecting lucrative businesses. "As a local merchant, you're worried by this bypass?" she probed.

"Not enough to kill," Berenger said curtly. "Nor, I should think, are any of the tradesmen. As for the Town Council, your great-aunt had been a thorn in their civic side for years. This was just another skirmish in a long battle."

"You seem to know a lot about the Council," Chantal challenged again.

His chin came up an inch. "I do. My father chairs it."

Unquestionably, Berenger was well-connected. Big

landowner, big employer, hooked into local politics. This new information kept him firmly nailed to the top of her suspect list. She pressed on. "New line of inquiry. Where were you on Friday morning before you went to sign the papers?"

"Packing for a special weekend away with Louise. Witnesses include my father and housekeeper." He stuck his neck forward, coming closer to her.

She could see faint crows' feet at the edge of his eyes. They must have developed from years of squinting down lines of vines in the southern French sun. They certainly weren't from laughter.

"If I'd seen your aunt," he went on, "I'd tell the police. To narrow the time of death."

"Not if you were the one who threw her down the stairs."

"With the bypass as my motive?"

"Not necessarily. It could have been an accident, an argument that got out of control."

He rolled his eyes for the second time that morning. "And what were Mademoiselle Lamarque and I arguing about?"

"I don't know," she said. "Your bullying. Blackmail." Now, that *was* an idea. "You found out something about her. The house sale was the price of your silence. She fought back, called your bluff. You argued, struggled. She fell."

"You should write thrillers, Mademoiselle."

"Oh, for heaven's sake," she snapped, irritated without quite knowing why. "Can't you drop the formality? You know my name's Chantal."

"You should write thrillers, Chantal," he obliged.

She tore into the croissant as if it were his head. After she fought the mouthful down, she added, crossly, "You don't understand. Too many weird things have happened. Aunt Jeanne selling when she swore she never would. Aunt Jeanne falling down a staircase she'd never had trouble with." She weighed up telling him about her intruder and decided she had nothing to gain from keeping it secret. "And a man in the house the night I arrived."

"Me, you mean?"

"No. There was a man in the house when I arrived. An intruder."

Berenger sat up. "What happened? Did he hurt you?"

"He came from upstairs, running. He pushed me over on the stairs and, yes, I lay half knocked out on the flagstones for a while. And no, I didn't tell the police. I made sure he hadn't left a friend hiding anywhere, and then I locked the front door and took my bruises off to soak in a bath."

She watched Berenger assemble the sequence of events in his mind and then shake his head.

"What?" she prompted. Surely he wasn't going to criticize her choices that evening?

"Call it another hard blow on my thick skull. I was your second intruder in the space of two hours, wasn't I? Most women would have cowered and no blame to them. But not you, you came out swinging and—"

Chantal would have sworn his lips twitched in a tiny smile.

"—wearing that shockingly short bathrobe. With panache, I have to say."

She had to grin, but his face grew somber again as he sought, and held, her gaze. "I really have to stop underestimating you, Chantal. You've a lot more guts and resilience than I've given you credit for. I'm sorry that I added to your troubles that night."

Astonishment at his gracious words stole her voice. She nodded in mute acknowledgment.

"I'm sorry about something else, too," he added, his blue gaze still locked onto her. "I'm sorry I'm your key suspect. I'd rather be helping you catch that intruder and making sure he doesn't attack you again. But you don't trust me to help."

Chantal cleared her throat and found her vocal cords had freed up. "No, I don't. But maybe you can help even so, by answering a question about him."

"Go on, then."

"I couldn't see his face because it was wrapped in a scarf. But I do know he was the same shape and size as one of your employees."

He frowned. "Who?"

She parried with a question of her own. "Have you seen any of them acting suspiciously?"

Berenger threw his hands in the air. "Even at this slack time of year I employ twenty people. During harvest, it can rise to a hundred. I don't keep an hourly dossier on them all."

Chantal shrugged. "OK. I'm talking about Laurent Nazac."

"Nazac? He's had his issues. That doesn't mean he's responsible for all Cordes' troubles."

"Laurent could get a key more easily than most."

"I'll have a word with him, I promise you."

"Do any of your other employees look like Laurent? Stocky, short, straight dark hair?"

Berenger considered for a moment. "No. Will you take my word for it, or do I need to organize an identity parade?"

Before Chantal could reply, she saw a figure at the edge of the square that made her leap up. Her chair skidded back on the tiles. She barely heard Berenger's shouted question as she dashed out towards Grand' Rue.

A short, dark-haired man in a purplish scarf scuttled along ahead of her, keeping close to the buildings. At the sound of her pounding feet, he sprinted off, never looking round.

"Stop!" she shouted. "You! Stop!"

Was he Laurent? She couldn't tell.

For a small man, he moved fast. Too fast to be anything but a fit young man of twenty? Her quarry ducked down an alley. As Chantal reached it, Berenger overtook her and plunged on in pursuit.

Chantal slumped against a wall, out of breath. She felt guilty letting Berenger take over, and then alarmed.

If the man turned out to be Laurent, what would Berenger do? Haul him back? Or warn his employee accomplice to be a damn sight more careful? She started jogging to the corner.

Berenger appeared, empty-handed, chest heaving.

"He got away, one turn too far ahead of me," he panted. "Sorry."

"That," she said with emphasis, "was my intruder, as I'm sure you've realized. Did you recognize him?"

Berenger shook his head.

"Not Laurent Nazac?"

Another head shake. "Let's clear young Nazac right now." He pulled a clam shell mobile out of his shirt pocket. "I'm calling the store. Delgarde?" He shifted to French. "Put Nazac on. Well, where is he? How long's he been gone? OK, transfer me." While he waited, his lips thinned into an expression she had now seen several times. Berenger's next conversation, seemingly with a worker in the estate's winery store, yielded the same result. He snapped his mobile shut. "It wasn't Laurent," he insisted. "Why would he be skulking around the streets with his face hidden in a scarf when he's meant to be at work?"

"You tell me."

"I've promised I will when I find out."

They retraced their steps to the café and picked up their belongings. Martin shot Chantal several appreciative glances as Berenger paid.

Outside, Berenger said, "I can tell you this, Mademoi—Chantal—I want to catch this intruder. If he was in the house on Sunday, maybe he was there on Friday. He could help pin down the time of death." She saw him clench a fist. "Something has to break this deadlock."

Chantal recalled Grenier's marriage solution. Berenger

hadn't translated that bit, and he hadn't mentioned it since. Of course not, she chided herself. Such a crazy idea. "I want to find him, too," she said. "Get in line."

"And who else will you be after?"

"Aunt Jeanne's doctor," she remembered.

"You'll find it's Simon Mezaute. He's the only medic in town. I'll leave him to you."

"You don't want to push him for evidence to establish your innocence?"

"I know I'm innocent," Berenger said sharply. "You're the only person around here who doubts it."

She sniffed. "I'm going to the police, too, to see if I can change their minds, stop them dismissing this as an accident."

"Same here. Though I won't be offering myself as a key suspect. If they believe it's a case of foul play, they'll work a lot harder on when your great-aunt died."

"Sounds like there'll be a small queue for the medical examiner's door as well," she noted wryly. "First in, best answered. They won't want to talk twice."

"If it's a race, I'll back myself, Chantal. You're duty-bound to attend a funeral and play hostess soon."

"You couldn't get an appointment with the police that fast anyhow." Could he? She couldn't, but then she didn't have his connections. Nor did she share his urgency. She was after revenge and that was rumored to be best served cold.

"A challenge, eh?" Berenger reached for his phone again. While he made his call, Chantal rested against Place de la Bride's northern wall. Its parapet formed part of the same city wall that ran along Rue Obscure. Thirty feet down she could see rooftops and gardens that stretched out to the second defensive ring. The stones felt slightly warm beneath her fingers, and the Cordes plateau stretched before her, speckled with the green of spring. The breeze tantalized her with the scent of lilac from a tree hidden from view below.

"I should have taken a bet with you." Berenger's voice broke in on her reverie. "I'm seeing Bastien, the medical examiner, at four, then the Inspector. He's an old friend of mine, Olivier Riberon."

She pulled herself up straight. Damn those contacts of his. Her frustration had to show. Now he'd gloat. Instead, his words amazed her for the third time that morning.

"You could come along."

"*Me?* What exactly are you proposing?"

"We'll do the interviews together. You try to prove I'm the villain. I'll build a case for the defense."

"You'd be squandering your head start."

"I don't need one," Berenger said calmly. He stood alongside her and stared out at the view. "I'm not guilty."

"But why would you want me along? You know I can't trust you."

"If we're enemies, to quote you, I want to stop you creating more obstacles." He glanced sideways at her. "And that means keeping you very close."

Yes, please, said the treacherous little voice.

"In any case, I want to be there when you eat your words." He turned to her, but his deep-set eyes lay in shadow. A day ago, she'd have felt she was talking to a mask but, already, she had learned to read tiny movements in his face and to listen for nuances in his tone. Right now, she sensed he found the situation as amusing as she found it confusing.

She'd enjoyed his company far too much this morning. How could she maintain a healthy skepticism with the little voice popping up to distract her? And it would, if she spent more time with him.

"Afraid your pet theory will prove wrong, as soon as the investigation introduces a few basic facts?" Berenger prodded.

She might be learning to read his face, but she had to admit he had begun to learn how to push her buttons. On balance, she judged she had more to gain than lose from the offer. Probably. She gave in. "When shall I expect you?"

They fixed the time.

"*Bon.* It's a date," announced Berenger.

The word reverberated in her head. She suppressed it firmly. "No. What we have is an appointment."

"An appointment, then, to kick off our new partnership." Berenger halved the distance between them. "As a part-Frenchwoman, you'll know men and women in this country often seal deals with a kiss."

Chantal's stomach flip-flopped. He stood so close that she could pick up his scent, nutmeg-warm. Her mouth parted. His face was inches away.

Insanity.

She'd agreed to an alliance, but not this sort. Not with a man she'd be mad to trust. Ducking her head, she thrust out her hand. "And as a part-Englishwoman, I'll shake instead."

He took her hand, enclosing it in his. Instead of shaking it, he lifted it to his lips. They brushed her knuckles in a soft caress.

The breeze intensified, the rustling of the first spring leaves in the gardens growing more agitated.

Could Berenger sense the parallel sensation he'd roused in her? She lifted her eyes to search his face. And his expression hit her, full frontal.

He smiled.

Oh, Heaven help her.

It crinkled his eyes and put twinkles in their blue depths. It opened his mouth so she could see his strong, even teeth. But much more than that, it opened the man: she glimpsed his loneliness, his toughness, and his capacity for fierce loyalty. And for a moment, she let herself imagine being his partner.

She sagged back against the wall.

"Till later, Chantal." He strode off across the Place.

She watched him go with her hand pressed to her

pullover. Her heart rattled around inside her, as loose as a coin in a washing machine. Another smile like that one, and it'd bounce out of her chest. She'd lose it forever.

CHAPTER TWELVE

Their meetings with the police in Albi finished as the afternoon light began to fade. Chantal fastened her seat belt in Berenger's dark green SUV and settled back, drawing brief comfort from the light embrace of the black leather upholstery. What she could see of the police building's functional, contemporary architecture held zero charm compared to the glories of Albi's vast medieval brick cathedral. She'd enjoyed views of it on their journey into the city. With Pont Vieux, the aptly named old bridge, and its low stone spans in the foreground, the scene showed scarcely any sign of the modern age.

She closed her eyes, letting her thoughts drift back. Before her police appointments with Berenger, she'd had a busy time finalizing Jeanne's funeral service with the priest and, with Madame Nazac's help, letting various friends and contacts of her great-aunt know about the ceremony.

Delicate probing of what Madame Nazac knew about her son's whereabouts that morning and the previous Friday had led nowhere. Laurent's doting parent claimed he worked conscientiously, without even a love interest to divert him.

As Berenger turned the ignition, Chantal opened her

eyes. The lengthening shadows across the soulless car park stirred the embers of her fears. Soon she'd be back at Number 8, alone. Would the madness strike again?

She stole a glance at Berenger as he reversed out of the parking space. The tendons on his neck stood out like steel hawsers as he craned around. Hands, bones, muscle -– strength coiled in all of him. The gargoyle faces would be almost bearable if he were there to reach out to.

He hadn't transfixed her with another smile. This morning had clearly been a -– wonderful -– aberration. For a moment, she'd seemed to mean something special to him. Had he detected her response to his kissing her hand? If so, she'd bet he'd liked the sense of control it gave him.

It would suit her fine if his smiles stayed as rare as pig's wings. A respite before the next one would give her time to grow a hide thick enough to withstand it. Maybe. Where this man was concerned, her outer layers had thinned to mere wafers in the space of—what?—a handful of meetings. She could cope with the fire of his anger, but his smile had scorched her in a very different way.

"Well, what's your verdict on our meetings?" His voice broke in on her brooding.

Chantal managed a small smile. "I wish I had a photo of Riberon's face when you prompted me to tell him my suspicions about you. I bet that doesn't happen too often. Accuser and accused in the same room."

He gave a short, humorless laugh. "Didn't shake his pig-headed conviction that there was nothing to investigate, though."

"And I thought you Morels had the police in your pocket," she added mischievously.

"If we did, Bastien would set the time of death after noon last Friday, and no questions asked."

Berenger had pushed the medical examiner repeatedly on the issue. He'd asked about further tests, bigger and better laboratories, and had finished by doubting, out loud, Bastien's capabilities. It had taken all Chantal's tact to calm things down.

The medical examiner said he'd contacted Aunt Jeanne's physician, Doctor Mezaute. Jeanne's health complaints had been ever stiffer joints and a delicate stomach that struggled with her rich diet. Mezaute had lately prescribed nothing stronger than sleeping tablets, and Bastien had found no trace of suspicious substances.

The sleeping tablets tallied with Madame Nazac's description of Aunt Jeanne looking tired. Insomnia afflicted many older people. Overall, a solid medical excuse for Jeanne's out-of-character behavior over the house sale looked unlikely. The evidence pointed to scare tactics again. So far, one man fitted that frame particularly well. And he sat the width of the gearbox away, the formal dark wool of his dress pants not quite obscuring the power of the long limbs beneath.

She stared at the road ahead. They had left the plane tree-lined boulevards of Albi behind, and now the horizon shifted in height and color as they ran past fields of young, green wheat and others plowed and waiting, their chalky earth empty.

"It was a blessing to hear poor Aunt Jeanne died instantly," Chantal mused after a couple of silent miles. "But did you hear how Bastien put it? He said there was nothing to show it wasn't an accident. My intruder could have knocked her over, like he did me. That would look totally accidental."

"So you're not giving up?"

"Not at all. But Riberon has pretty well closed the case. Accidental fall. Possible harassment, but no clear link to death. Intruder seen in house after death –– probably opportunistic. End of file, end of case. We're on our own."

We? If Berenger had noticed her Freudian slip, he showed no sign as he concentrated on a series of sharp bends.

Chantal kept talking to cover her gaffe. "I thought Riberon was very casual about Mulberry." They'd coined the intruder's nickname on the way to the police station. "More worried about lecturing me on secure locks than what Mulberry was up to."

"He never did have much imagination. Ninety-nine per cent of break-ins are simple thefts, so that's what he sees."

"If Mulberry was a thief, I don't think he found what he was hunting for in the back bedroom, you know. I'm sure he left empty-handed." She sighed. Where to next?

Berenger supplied the answer. "Come and talk to my father. He'll give you the Council angle and let you check my alibis. Maybe he can find more suspects for you, too."

"Would he accept being grilled by a stranger?"

"He worked as a diplomat. If he doesn't want to answer, he'll refuse charmingly and leave you feeling grateful."

"Perhaps I can meet him soon."

"Come for dinner tonight."

"Thank you." She accepted at once, not caring if he thought it odd. A few more hours away from the house and its demons would be very welcome.

A few more hours to get to know Berenger, too.

"Good." He made a brief call to warn of the extra setting at dinner. "Louise will be pleased to meet you again. She'll be up a little while yet."

At Louise's name, the mood in the car grew awkward. Chantal tried to broach the subject of how to handle Louise's blindness.

At last, Berenger took pity on her. "Come on, ask."

"I'd hate to say anything to upset Louise — or any of you. I know a bit about her from Madame Nazac. My main concern is how to act around her."

"Like yourself," said Berenger gruffly. "Remember she's in her own house. Don't try to do things for her, and don't move anything."

She thanked him and they drove on in silence. The fields were fading in the half light. Their smudged outlines reminded her of Berenger's love affair with Cordes and wine. Reminded her of him, as if she needed it.

"I wondered," she ventured, "about your first name. I've never heard it before. What does it mean?"

"Sorry, there's a fee for names around here."

There was no mistaking the teasing in his words. She glanced across. No, no new smile. But what was this fee? A kiss? She drew a breath as she remembered the scent of him up close and the warmth of his lips on her hand.

The topic hung, unresolved, between them. They reached the houses at the foot of Cordes and Berenger swung the car uphill.

"I thought you lived that way." She pointed along the lower road.

"All women like to fuss over their looks before an evening out, even a casual one. Will ten minutes do? I'll wait by the car, since I can't park up here."

He meant well, but two minutes alone would be enough for her in Number 8. She fished the door key out of her bag, but, even in the twilight, could see something had changed. A small, modern lock, sized for a regular key, replaced the gaping hole that had accommodated its cast-iron cousin. Madame Nazac had kept her promise and relied on Chantal's common sense to find the new key under the geraniums.

Inside, the bright brass of the new hasp, secured by four large screws, glinted in the hallway light, and, next to the vase of Berenger's flowers, a spare key weighed down a note from Madame Nazac. Chantal debated offering Berenger the second key, then decided against it. Not until she could be certain of his innocence.

She quickly checked all the rooms, upstairs and down. Having Berenger in calling distance gave her courage. Nothing had been disturbed. Rapidly, she brushed her shoulder-length hair to make the russet tones gleam, avoiding the sore patch where her skull had collided with the flagstones. Eyeliner diverted attention from the shadows under her lashes and enhanced her gray irises. A black pullover highlighted her necklace of graduated white and scarlet cloisonné beads. A matching bracelet completed her outfit.

Throughout the short stay, the house behaved itself. No madly clanging bells, no undulating walls. She went back to the kitchen for her coat, and the sight of Berenger's flowers gave her an idea. It took only a minute to put into action.

Berenger leaned against the car, his hawkish profile lit by a street lamp. She approached with one hand behind her back.

He gave her a quizzical look.

Looking him in the eye, she brought out her hand. It held a small spray of golden jonquils culled from his large bouquet in the kitchen. "The fee. Let's have it. Your name and its meaning."

Amusement twitched at his lips. The faint echo of his one true smile sent warmth coursing to her fingertips. She knew she'd read him right.

"Berenger. Bear-like. I was born grizzling and with a shock of black hair."

"Shame you grew into a mild-mannered blond," she joked as they climbed back in the SUV.

"Isn't it?"

The vehicle rolled past a zigzagging alley that led upwards towards the main square. The Nazacs lived somewhere along it. "You promised to tell me how Laurent explained his absence."

"True. I cornered him at lunchtime. He'd said he'd run his father to the garage at Les Cabannes on his moped. The family car broke down Sunday night and was due to be picked up today. The little fool," he added.

"Why's he a fool?"

"For sneaking off work in the morning when he could have used a few minutes of his lunch break for a private errand. That's for a start. Plus, he should have asked one of us to drive Nazac senior there in a proper vehicle. He has a bad leg and the last thing he needs is to fall off a scooter."

"He's a fool for lying about it, too." Chantal explained what Madame Nazac had said. "His mother would have known if the car had been waiting to be picked up and if they needed Laurent's help with it, but she was sure he was at work. So I reckon he was somewhere else. Running through Cordes, maybe, with you at his heels."

Berenger's fingers tightened on the wheel. "I'm sorry."

"What for?"

"For not cross-checking his story. That was sloppy. I'll do it tomorrow and get to the truth of his movements." He hesitated. "And I'm sorry I remain your number one suspect. Clearing Nazac won't acquit me in your eyes, but it'd be a damn fine start if one of my employees wasn't in the frame with me."

"It wouldn't solve whether the house is yours."

"You might think better of me, though."

Her mouth went dry. Berenger Morel cared what she thought? Perhaps there had been something fueling that wonderful smile, after all.

CHAPTER THIRTEEN

Berenger swung the SUV through two widely set stone gateposts topped with carved acorns. Chantal read the property's name on a neat plaque as the SUV's tires crunched over the gravel driveway. In the headlight's beam, she saw a small fountain and the wings of a two-storied house that stretched away into the dark. Her father Terry's house in Watford sprawled generously, but she thought the one in front of her looked even larger.

"Lagrotte?" she asked, repeating the house's name. *Not remotely grotty or down-market.*

"The story goes there was a cave or grotto around here that local shepherds used for shelter. Maybe my ancestors built the house over it, because I've never found it." He pulled up between the fountain and the house and cut the headlights. A brass lantern hanging from the entrance porch replaced the car's piercing beams with a warm glow. "No one calls this place by its name anyhow," he added, as he climbed out.

"So I've heard."

Louise tugged open one side of the chateau's double front door for them, her wide grin welcoming them in. Ready for bed in Roadrunner pajamas and a purple dressing gown, she gave her father a hug and then bestowed another on Chantal.

"Did you get lost again? Did Papa find you?"

Not waiting to hear the answer, Louise raced back up the wood-paneled hallway, calling to her grandfather. Chantal found it hard to believe she was blind. The girl's evident confidence helped her relax.

"I'll take your coat," Berenger said.

As she turned to let him help her, she caught sight of a family photo near the hall phone. In the portrait, Berenger, in an open-necked shirt, sat a little behind a dark-haired woman in her late twenties. She appeared to be leaning back into the protective crook of his arm. On her lap perched a plump, almost bald, baby in a pale pink romper suit. The woman gazed serenely at the camera, scarcely smiling. Chantal stared back at the image that must surely be of Mireille.

The jeweled turquoise tone of the roll-neck top Mireille wore intensified the green of her huge eyes, and Chantal took in the classic lines of her high forehead and sharp cheekbones, and an aquiline nose. The lips lacked a little fullness and disappeared into the corners of her mouth, but that minor flaw accentuated the perfection of her other features.

If Berenger noticed what had captured her attention, he said nothing and gestured her ahead of him up the hallway. Louise appeared again through a doorway, eagerly tugging a man in his early seventies by the hand. Another man might have looked ungainly in such a situation, but Armand Morel's upright posture and the refined cut of his clothes, from the neatly folded cravat to the knife-sharp creases of his trousers, conveyed elegance and control. Chantal felt grateful to Berenger for giving her the chance to smarten up.

Her warm feelings cooled considerably at Berenger's introduction.

"Father, this is Mademoiselle Chantal Harrison. She's

come to mine you for information and to check up on me. On top of which, we're giving her dinner."

"My dear young lady, what a pleasure." Armand extended his free hand over Louise's head to shake hers, and his smile etched deep lines in the corner of his eyes. Perhaps years of diplomatic training had given the Armand the knack of instant charm, but Chantal felt genuinely welcome. The creases on his face had to be laughter lines, incised by years of enjoying the company of all kinds of people.

"It's a rare pleasure to have some feminine company at dinner," her host continued. "Louise, alas, can't stay up too late in the evening yet."

"When I'm six I'm going to stay up till eight o'clock every night," Louise announced.

"We'll see about that," replied her father, restraining his daughter by her shoulders.

Armand took advantage of his temporary freedom to usher Chantal into a large reception room. To the left lay the dining area with an eight-seater table set for four. Family seating filled the opposite end of the room, the furniture angled towards the TV and an adjacent fireplace. A large potted plant with drooping branches helped separate the two areas.

"You'll forgive the informality, Mademoiselle, but this room is more convenient to the kitchen for our housekeeper, Ah Wong, and the fire's warmed it nicely."

"It's lovely," she answered with sincerity, drawn to the dancing flames, and relieved to see a fireguard in front of it to protect Louise. She debated inviting Armand to call her Chantal, but sensed he would prefer a level of formality.

"And, here, a little aperitif." Armand held out a glass of lightly sparkling white wine. "One of my son's vintages. If you can believe something as fine as a *perlé* could spring from a winery run by this bad-tempered giant."

The diplomat's combined bouquet and brickbat made her want to smile, but instead she raised her glass.

"Berenger, is this the one you said could take a drinker from aperitif to post-prandial?"

"It is." He inclined his head in a small salute to her accurate recollection.

The wine tasted lightly fruity to her untrained palate. Guided by Armand once more, she sat down on a sofa covered with a tartan throw, and placed her glass on a side-table. She was just in time before Louise bounced onto the cushion next to her.

"Be careful, Louise!" Berenger warned.

"I am being." Her answer came automatically, all her attention on Chantal. "How did you learn French so quickly? You didn't speak much before."

While Chantal explained, Louise's fingers reached for Chantal's jumper, exploring its softness. Their discussion soon moved to Chantal's jewelry and make-up. Chantal found the girl's rapid eye movements less disconcerting than their green color that kept reminding her of the photo in the hall. The photo of the woman Berenger had never stopped loving.

"I'm afraid our little one is starved of female things," observed Armand. "It's a shame. She's never been a tomboy."

"Your housekeeper doesn't…?"

"Ah Wong's no good at that stuff," declared Louise. "But her cooking is yummy! She made me fried rice tonight. And she tells me stories from China."

"Then she has two skills I don't have," laughed Chantal.

"What can you do?"

"I can make jewelry."

Louise's mouth formed an admiring "O".

In simple terms, Chantal described her work and techniques before unfastening the cloisonné bracelet from her wrist and passing it to Louise. The little girl traced along the chain of beads, exploring the different shapes. "Will you make me one? I'd love one of yours. Please!"

Before Berenger or Armand could step in, Chantal promised. "I think I have something at the house I could use for you. Let me measure your wrist with my fingers."

With that promise, Louise allowed herself to be carried off to bed by her father. Armand smoothly filled the next few minutes with polite condolences on Chantal's recent loss and inquiries about the funeral arrangements.

"Do you really have time to make that bracelet for her?" Berenger probed when he returned from tucking Louise in. "I know you're going to be busy with your aunt's affairs and…other things."

Chantal ignored his reference to her sleuthing. She suspected he was testing if she might let his daughter down and reassured him it would be a quick job. Jeanne's jewelry box held a number of broken odds and ends. Of little worth in their current state, their variety of shapes could still entrance a five-year-old, including one who couldn't see color.

"Well, thanks," he murmured.

Armand asked about her jewelry making. She didn't hide that her business had failed. Inevitably, Berenger asked why. Her discomfort must have shown, because Armand tactfully steered the conversation away. She shot him a grateful glance. She wasn't ready to discuss Steven with near-strangers.

The Morels' house guest joined them a couple of minutes before dinner. He came over to introduce himself before Armand could step in. "Wilbur, ma'am, from the Big Apple. Delighted to make your acquaintance." Chantal read the frank appreciation on his face but couldn't reciprocate. His soft brown eyes sat at odds with the sharp planes and hollow cheeks of his thin face, and the contrast unsettled her.

She offered her name in polite reply, and Armand rounded out the introduction with brief details of Wilbur's studies on the one hand, and Chantal's loss of her aunt who had lived on Rue Obscure, on the other.

Wilbur's smile faded. In a moment it became evident he'd heard about the legal muddle over Number 8. Had the lawyers resolved the problem, he asked? Was she still in the house?

His interest took Chantal aback and she told him so.

He spread his hands in an expansive gesture. "Don't mind me, ma'am, I'm partisan. My young host here has been dealt some lousy luck. I said to him last night, it'd be fairer if you moved into a hotel while this gets sorted."

"The matter," said Berenger firmly, "is between me and Chantal."

She felt an absurd rush of pleasure at his defense.

Armand defused the tension by drawing them all to the table, seating her next to Berenger. Not having to look straight into his forceful blue gaze came at the price of facing Wilbur instead.

The American hadn't smiled at her since discovering where she was staying. He caught Chantal's eye. "I wouldn't want to sleep in that old place, though. Nothing like a change of owner to wake sleeping ghosts."

"There hasn't been a change of owner yet," snapped Berenger. He reached for the wine bottle as if looking for more sensible things to pay attention to.

The second mention of ghosts that day grated on Chantal's nerves and spurred her next words. "Roland Fleurie's ghost, I suppose? The man alleged to be the ringleader behind the murder of that kindly trio of Dominican inquisitors? I can tell you that if my great-aunt had ever met his ghost, she'd have wanted to shake his hand. She admired him for defending his neighbors and taking action."

"Maybe, but you do know your aunt's house has had vague but persistent stories of night-time disturbances for centuries?" Wilbur retaliated. "Not the ghosts-in-white-sheet variety, of course."

"That's right, agreed Armand. "According to items in our Historical Society library, the reports are more of odd sounds and household items mysteriously moving to new places."

"Old timbers, forgetful servants and a lack of cable TV," answered Berenger. He began to pour the wine, skipping Chantal's glass that remained half full of the *perlé*.

His impatience with the astral plane encouraged Chantal. Maybe lead pipes and a high wind from the Cerou valley had conjured up the clanging and roaring sounds that had terrified her the night before. "At any rate," she stated with more confidence than she felt, "Aunt Jeanne never had any trouble sleeping." *Until a few weeks ago.* Her mouth snapped shut.

"Good luck to you, then." Wilbur's tone suggested that by not taking his warning seriously, she deserved whatever might be coming.

"She doesn't need luck," cut in Berenger. "The house is fundamentally sound. Not everyone believes superstitions scratched on scraps of vellum."

The housekeeper's arrival with a basket of baguette slices and a large plate of paté, pickles, salamis and radishes brought a welcome distraction. Armand, ever polite, introduced Ah Wong and Chantal to each other.

After the housekeeper returned to the kitchen, he tried a more neutral topic. "Not too long before you finish up here, Wilbur. You know my Historical Society colleagues are all looking forward to your lecture to us before you leave for Columbia. Any hints yet about your topic?"

Chantal choked on a lump of bread, but held up a hand to protect herself from Berenger, his hand ready to strike her between the shoulder blades.

"Wilbur!" She croaked.

"What?" The American held up his palms in the universal gesture of innocence and ignorance.

"You're W. Sanders, from Columbia! You wrote to my great-aunt about something called—" She took a gulp of water to clear the last crumbs from her throat. "—the Eye of the Needle."

"Did you, Wilbur?" Armand asked with indignant surprise.

Wilbur turned his placating hands towards his host. "I wrote to all kinds of people at the start of my Ph.D. I had to find a unique angle for my research. It was three years ago, before I knew the situation here with her. Before I knew you guys."

"What situation?" Chantal asked.

Wilbur looked at Armand, who pinched the bridge of his nose and took a moment before replying.

"Your great-aunt, Mademoiselle Lamarque, applied, unsuccessfully, to join our Historical Society. You see—"

"Our?" Chantal couldn't help herself interrupting. "It's a private club, then?"

Before Armand could answer, Berenger explained, "It's the local boys' club for male professionals and well-off tradesmen, Chantal. They let Madame Castaigne in but only to take the minutes and make them coffee."

"Berenger, that's neither true nor helpful. Mademoiselle Harrison, the Society is, of course, open to anyone who has a genuine interest in the town's history. It seems, thus far, that it only appeals to a certain group of educated men."

"And my great-aunt and her unsuccessful application?" Chantal forced herself to keep her tone mild. No one could have been more passionate about Cordes' history than Aunt Jeanne.

Armand shrugged slightly. "It was judged there was not, after careful reflection, the kind of…fit that would make for a productive Society. Enthusiasm for a subject must be tempered…channeled…"

"She was in it for the mystery and romance." Wilbur found the confidence to contribute to the topic. "I could tell when I corresponded with her. No rigor, no method. These guys in the Society…" He leaned towards Chantal while jerking his thumb sideways at his host. "These guys are scholars. Takes one to know."

Armand's chest swelled a little, while Chantal's lips compressed.

"If only we knew more about the Eye of the Needle, eh?" said Armand wistfully. "More than scattered, tantalizing references to it being the path to true treasure."

"You know my current view, Armand," stated Wilbur. "Any Cathar treasure references are most likely to be about spiritual treasures. How to pass from entrapment in the evil, material world into the divine domain of souls and light."

"But if it weren't, eh? If it were the treasure they smuggled out of Montségur before it fell?"

"Then scholarly research will reveal it. Piece by piece, reference by reference. One day."

Armand clapped Wilbur lightly on the back. "I admire your patience and your confidence, *mon cher*. You're right, one day the Society will be part of that fantastic discovery. One day, and I hope I'm here to see it."

Chantal bit back a sarcastic comment about romantic mysteries apparently appealing to scholars and professionals as much as old ladies. She had yet to ask Armand questions about his son's alibi and the politics of the town bypass. Antagonizing him would not help her cause.

The conversation halted as Ah Wong wheeled in tureens of vegetables, a platter of freshly grilled flounder and a jug of garlic and white wine sauce. It gave Chantal time to consider how best to show her support for the "old lady" and ruin Wilbur's appetite into the bargain.

"You may have done my great-aunt a favor, actually." Chantal smiled sweetly at Wilbur as she handed him the sauce. "I think you piqued her curiosity. A year after your correspondence, she found an ancient map of Cordes, speckled with strange symbols, including eye-shaped ones. She filed it next to your letters."

The porcelain sauce boat rang loudly against Wilbur's plate as he lost his grip on it.

"Found it where?"

"A map written on what?"

"What symbols?"

Wilbur and Armand's questions tumbled over each other. She glimpsed Wilbur's look of mingled amazement and jealousy before dropping her eyes to her food. No need to let him read the triumph and satisfaction on her face.

Carefully flaking her fish, Chantal continued as if she hadn't heard their insistent queries. "And Aunt Jeanne filled a whole document box with further items she'd gathered on the topic."

Armand craned forward into her peripheral vision. "But Mademoiselle, this sounds like a marvelous discovery. You must let us look at it all, see that is appropriately curated and cataloged and—ahem—correctly attributed to Mademoiselle Lamarque."

Wilbur leaned in too. "It could reveal a whole new chapter of Cordes' history. She'd have loved that, you got to admit."

Chantal looked across the table at their eager faces, glad of the whim that had made her lock the study. "Gentlemen, I'll take a proper look at it all first. I wouldn't dream of wasting the time of scholars with what might be no more than a haphazard collection by an old lady." She couldn't resist a light emphasis on the final two words.

A volley of laughter in her left ear made her jump. Berenger's hand slapped the table as he rocked back in his chair. His three dinner companions stared at him, none more genuinely startled than Armand, who watched his son's convulsing shoulders as if they had sprouted wings.

"Go on, go on!" urged the laughing winemaker. "Don't stop. Best dinnertime repartee in weeks." He raised his glass to Chantal. "You win on points."

His father shook his head. "Enough. Do something useful and pour the wine."

Chuckling, his son obliged.

They ate the fish in near silence. It gave Chantal a chance to appreciate Ah Wong's cooking, and to wonder how the Asian woman had come to be so far from home. To break the increasingly uncomfortable quiet, she voiced the question.

Armand answered at once. "She was our amah in Taiwan, on my last overseas posting. Celestine, my wife, and I, we'd had plenty of servants over the years, you know, but none like Ah Wong. Remarkably efficient and intelligent."

"She keeps us all organized," added Berenger. "And her Taiwanese French mesmerizes the local tradesmen."

"Indeed it does. So when Celestine became ill shortly before we were due to return to France, it made sense to ask Ah Wong if she would come back with us to help with the housekeeping."

"But her own family in Taiwan?" asked Chantal.

"Nearest relatives all passed on, and she'd been a widow with no children for many years. Anyway, she came, and did more and more as my poor Celestine could manage less and less." He cleared his throat. "It's been seven years since we lost her."

"I'm sorry," murmured Chantal, the clawing ache of her loss of Aunt Jeanne returning.

Ah Wong came in to clear the plates.

"We were saying how we couldn't manage without you," said Armand with a smile.

Ah Wong made a noise that could have been agreement or its opposite.

"The meal was delicious, thank you," offered Chantal. She rose to pick up the large platter that wouldn't fit on the trolley with the tureens and dirty plates.

Ah Wong waved a hand at her. "Is OK, I come back."

"I'm up now, it's the least I can do." She walked ahead to the kitchen door and held it open for the older woman. Once they were alone, Chantal asked for directions to the restroom. Ah Wong nodded and pointed the way out into the main corridor and around a corner.

Coming back a few minutes later, Chantal found herself unsure which door led back to the dining room. She guessed and reached out a hand.

A hiss from behind startled her.

"No, Missy, you not go there! Master's private room."

Chantal pulled her hand back as if the handle had been red-hot. The woman's indignation at her honest mistake made her flush with guilt. She hurried towards the door Ah Wong indicated.

Which Master's room, she wondered as she re-entered the family room.

To her relief, Wilbur had gone, and Armand sat in one of the armchairs with a coffee. Berenger was pouring another. He took her order and then said, "I'm going to check on Louise. This is your chance to suck the information you wanted out of my father."

"Come, Mademoiselle," invited Armand with an expansive gesture as Berenger left. "After our earlier revelations, whatever you need will be simple, I'm sure. And you made my son laugh, for which I sincerely owe you."

So I'm not the only one he scowls at.

She settled into the armchair next to Armand's. He quickly confirmed Berenger's movements on Friday. His son had gone straight from the chateau to Lelou's office, almost running late. There hadn't been time for him to detour to Number 8.

Chantal thanked him. "And now my great-aunt, if I may. I know Aunt Jeanne was a great one for causes and petitions of all kinds. Some would have affected the Council and its business. Could she have stepped on a hornet's nest of some kind?"

Armand swirled the coffee in his cup. "You want to know if anyone would have reason to scare your aunt away, or do something worse? No one on the Council felt that strongly, I'm sure. She had been battling with us, and others, as you say, for years. Why would anyone get murderously angry now?"

"The bypass petition."

His eyes, a lighter blue than Berenger's, narrowed slightly. For the first time she could see a strong likeness between father and son. "You are well-informed, my dear, and so soon. I should have expected it. Berenger has no time for unintelligent women."

She said nothing, but kept an expectant expression on her face.

"The bypass has been an issue for months. Likewise the petition so vigorously pursued by your aunt."

"Perhaps it had reached a critical point?"

"I couldn't say. Mademoiselle Lamarque didn't provide us with progress reports on her campaign."

"But you'd know."

"I'd be happy to furnish you with the Council minutes if you'd like. They're a matter of public record."

Chantal suppressed the urge to roll her eyes, as she experienced the downside of his years in the civil service. Before she could work up real irritation, he offered her a small peace token.

"I was driving through Souel early a couple of weeks ago," he said, naming a neighboring hamlet. "I saw your aunt walking down the street. Rather early for visiting, but not if she were staying there and out for a morning walk. Perhaps she stayed with friends there? If so, ask them why she had left Rue Obscure."

Two weeks ago. Right in the period when Madame Nazac thought Aunt Jeanne had ceased sleeping at Number 8. Chantal found herself smiling at him in thanks.

Berenger appeared at her shoulder and indicated the time. "I know you have a busy day tomorrow with the funeral. Can I drop you home?"

All notions of detective work left her. Her heart began to thud. In the hallway, Armand, once again charm personified, helped her slip on her coat. She made her goodbyes almost mechanically, while in her head, she tried pretending that her apprehension stemmed from the prospect of another night of hallucinations. Only when she stood alone with Berenger in the chilly night air did she admit the real issue. She was afraid of herself, with him. She'd come so close to letting him kiss her that morning. Wanted him to.

"A new moon." Berenger gazed up at the crescent. "Let's walk, shall we?"

"Mmm." She could summon up no more than that tiny sound. When his arm came around her shoulder to guide her over the gravel towards the chateau's stone gates, her remaining powers of speech ebbed away.

He dropped his arm, but before she could mourn its loss, he tucked her arm around his in the old-fashioned style. It made her feel safe and excited at the same time. They headed along the moonlit road in silence, their long-legged strides fitting perfectly, even as the road grew steeper.

She reveled in how Berenger's wrist and hand felt beneath her fingertips. There was a scattering of hair below his shirt cuff and broad, solid bone under that.

She wanted this in-between time to go on forever, just walking in the moonlight, saying nothing. Too soon they turned into Rue Obscure, with Aunt Jeanne's house only a minute away. There was no doubt he wanted to kiss her. There was no doubt she was going to let him.

They reached Number 8 and their pace slowed to a halt. She heard Berenger heave a deep sigh and risked a look at this face. There was tension in the muscles around his jaw. Thank God he felt it, too.

Uncoiling his wrist from hers, he turned to her and drew her into his arms. He pitched his voice very low, but she caught every word. "This time, Chantal, I'm not going to shake your hand."

CHAPTER FOURTEEN

She had slipped into his arms like a key into a well-oiled lock. Berenger had expected hesitation, second thoughts. Her willingness nearly made him lose control and crush her to him. With an effort, he clamped down on the urge. This one he wanted to get right.

They fitted perfectly. He'd known they would. He dropped a gentle peck on her left cheek. He did the same on the other cheek, a little closer to the full curve of her mouth. Her breath fanned him in a soft caress as he moved across her face. She returned his kisses. The scent of apples floated around her.

Everyone double kissed in France. He had no plans to stop at two. A third kiss landed on the corner of her mouth. She moved against him and her breath drifted across his lips again. His veins felt too small for the blood in his body.

At last their mouths met, lips parted. He lifted a hand from her waist to run his fingers up through the heavy screen of her hair. He reached deeper into her, exploring gently with his tongue. In reply, she traced the sensitive area inside his lips.

The pressure in his blood made him dizzy. It was

making him hard, too. He was powerless to stop it. She increased the pressure of her hips against his, her breathing growing heavier. His own breath rasped in and out.

A door banged up the street and Chantal jumped. He drew back a couple of inches. She moved back a foot and loosened her arms from his neck. Galaxies formed, bloomed and died while she stared at him in silence.

"Chantal?" His voice came out husky. He yearned to pull her close again. His body felt naked without her against it.

She wiped her hands down her face. "Sorry." She turned and fumbled with the front door. Once it was open, she half turned to him again. "I'm sorry."

The door closed behind her, leaving him bereft.

*   *   *

A scant seven hours later, and he was back at Rue Obscure. Invisible strings had pulled him from his bed, but he'd paused to look in on Louise before he left. Fast asleep, her dark, straight hair now fell across her cheek, drawing attention to her long eyelashes. So much of Louise reminded him of Mireille, but Mireille had gone forever. And he was messing around with a woman who'd be heading back to London in a few days.

Berenger shivered. The dawn chill trickled down the collar of his heavy jacket. What was he thinking to be back here so soon?

The front door at Number 8 drew him across the street. He stopped on the very spot he'd kissed Chantal the night before. The memories drove the cold from his bones.

Celibacy must be the problem. A man in his mid-thirties wasn't designed to be alone so long. It had to happen sometime. Chantal had all the curves a man could wish for, topped by russet waves made to run his fingers through. Physical attraction, nothing more. He could handle it.

Only he couldn't.

Every time he thought he had this woman correctly categorized, she taught him he'd made another round of wrong assumptions. It had been a long time since a woman had aroused and intrigued him. Of course, her persistence and quick wits had stirred up nothing but trouble for him so far, but the challenge of proving his innocence and solving the mystery of her aunt's time of death kept Chantal permanently in his thoughts.

Her vulnerability attracted him too; he could sense it in her, coming from a deeper place than her grief for her dead great-aunt. He wanted to learn what—who—had hurt her, and he felt the glimmerings of a desire to shield her from any more pain.

Berenger crossed the road and leaned on the parapet overlooking the mist-wreathed valley below. The haze in the air blurred the edges of everything at the foot of Cordes' hill. It reminded him of the change in Chantal's eyes the day before, up in Place de la Bride.

So often he met gray steel in her gaze. But yesterday they'd softened from unflinching metal to vulnerable smoke. It had happened when he'd taken her hand to kiss it. He knew he'd grinned at her like a wine buff faced with a free lifetime's supply of 1945 Château Mouton-Rothschild. And Mademoiselle Chantal Harrison, who had dealt him more surprises in two days than most people in a year, had been thrown off balance herself. He smiled again at the memory.

A cry from somewhere nearby dragged him back to the present. He crossed to Number 8's door in four long strides and strained to listen. Could he hear sobs? Adrenalin fired through him and his heart rate jacked up by forty beats a minute.

"Chantal!" The roar was out of his throat and his bundle of keys out of his jacket pocket without conscious thought. Twice as heavy and awkward now with Number

8's huge key attached by a loop of fine wire, the jangling metal slipped through his fingers. Bending down to snatch it up, he saw the gleaming brass disk of a new lock-plate. No way in. He swore and shoved the keys back into his pocket so hard the lining ripped.

"Chantal!" He slapped his palms hard on the door. "Chantal!" The rending sobs continued as though she couldn't hear him. He stepped back, thrusting his hand through his hair to coax some inspiration.

It came.

He sprinted right, into the blinding morning sun and on into the pitch-black arch. Left up the steep alley, legs pumping and burning with the effort, and left again into Grand' Rue to his store. Breathing hard, he scrabbled through the keys for the one he needed and stabbed it in the lock. He slammed the front door shut behind him and charged on, a high stool crashing to the floor in his wake. Through the French doors at the rear, and he finally reached the tiny back yard.

The ivy-clad, seven-foot stone wall separating his shop's yard from Number 8's proved no barrier. A small stack of metal café-style chairs at the left offered an easy route over, but at the price of a few seconds of delay he could not endure.

Instead, he ran hard at the wall, jamming his foot into the stone almost at hip height. The momentum lifted him, and with his hands' tight grip on the capping stones and ivy stems, he boosted his chest over. A push-up and a twist of his hips brought his legs over the wall and down onto the heavy wooden lid of the old well.

The back door succumbed to his right boot with a splintering of old timbers. A half second later, his head nearly followed suit on the lintel. Every damn door in the house was midget-height. How did Chantal cope?

Ignoring the pain, he pushed through the door into the little scullery. Water splashed around his feet.

He ignored the closed door ahead that led down to the

basement and turned into the kitchen. The only light came from a couple of cracks in the shutters and what little daylight penetrated from the back door behind him. In the gloom, Chantal huddled on the kitchen table, her shoulders shuddering with each breath. Her nightshirt had ridden up to reveal a sweep of pale flesh that ended in white panties. He jerked his gaze up to her face.

At the sound of his boots sloshing through the water, she looked up. Her eyes were hazy smoke again, but this time her vulnerability was physical. Under her eyes, sleeplessness had printed black bruises. Lengths of tangled auburn hair draggled over her forehead. Her misery made him want to hit someone. He'd start with whoever had turned his woman of last night into this wreck.

On a ragged gasp, she said, "Are — are you real?"

The words made no sense. He gathered her hunched form into his arms, the iciness of her skin burning into his wrists and fingers. He strode into the parlor, managing to flip a light switch as he went. The floor in the front room sat an inch or two higher than the flagstones outside and the carpet had escaped a soaking.

Gently, he put her down on the divan under the window. He smoothed some of the hair from her face and kissed her forehead. "I'm going to fetch a blanket. I'll be ten seconds."

It took him only nine to return with a quilt. He wrapped her up, his mind racing. "Chantal, I've got to find the mains tap before everything down here floods." She nodded dumbly. His presence seemed to have calmed her. Already the sobs had changed to small, intermittent gasps.

Back a few minutes later, he pulled as much of her as he could into his arms. For a while, she simply buried her face into his neck, drawing strength from his comfort. Eventually, she sat up and sniffed.

"Better?" he asked quietly.

She answered with a wobbly smile.

He wriggled to pull his handkerchief out of his pants

pocket.

She blew her nose.

"Now," he said. "What happened?"

She leaned into him so he couldn't see her face. "The water was all over the floor."

"The Chantal I'm getting to know would have called a plumber and fetched a mop while she waited."

She shook her head against his chest. "Not last night. Remember what Wilbur and your father said about…disturbances?"

"I do."

I could throttle them.

He tightened his arms around her. "The tins from the pantry went marching through the house?" He hoped for a little laugh, but none came.

"It'll sound crazy. It *is* crazy. But the house tried to drown me." She spoke in a whisper. "Like those Inquisitors drowned in the well."

Struggling to keep his voice low, he asked her what on earth she meant.

"The bedroom wall last night. It turned to swirling mist. I forced myself down to the kitchen. To find brighter lights. The floor seethed like boiling water, but it roared, too. I climbed up on the table." A hiccup betrayed her effort to keep going.

This was much more than a regular nightmare. He felt uneasy. He gave her the gentlest shake he could manage. "Come on, Chantal. Tell me."

"A man appeared. A man with a donkey's head. He turned to me and brayed. I wrapped my head in my arms. When I looked again, he'd gone. I know he wasn't real, but I was so scared."

He was starting to get the picture. Too clearly. He'd shared a room at university with a student who experimented with drugs. One day, Berenger had returned to find his roommate cowering under the bed, with furniture overturned and ripped books scattered across the floor. To crown it all, the young man's terrors had made him nauseous and the ripe stench had filled the air. The memory still revolted him. He only half heard her next words.

"When I woke up on the table, I saw water on the floor. I figured I was still seeing things. I forced myself down and my feet got wet. It had turned real. I thought I was going mad. I think I screamed just before you came…" She peered up at the tenseness in his body.

He stared over the top of her head at a rug hung on the wall opposite. "Your dealer should have warned you."

She jerked in his arms.

"It's not ghosts, for God's sake," Berenger snapped, looking down at her. "You've taken drugs and had a bad trip. Recycling those old stories into a personal horror movie."

Her lashes flew wide and fire kindled in her eyes. Despite everything, his heart lifted to see it.

"Don't be ridiculous!" she snapped back. "I never, never, touch drugs. I hardly drink except a glass of wine with meals. Last night, OK, the liqueur, but I was so jumpy after our…"

"What liqueur?"

"The one at the front of the cabinet." She waved a hand at the sideboard. "Absinthe, I think. It was bright green. I only had a little, it tasted so bitter."

He barked a short laugh in his relief. "That's it! It's neat alcohol, mixed with wormwood. It's been illegal in France for eighty years because it rots people's brains."

"Strong enough to cause hallucinations?"

"What else would have done it? The one time you drink it is the one time you see donkey men."

A shadow chased across her face. He kicked himself for reminding her of one of the worst moments.

"You need a bath and a proper lie down. You won't get them here. I'll get someone to bring my car up, and I'll run you to my house. Then find a plumber, if I can.

Wednesday's half-day closing, around here."

"But I'm inviting people back here after the funeral! They can't come in to this."

"Bring them to the chateau instead."

"And the caterer will be here at ten."

"Ah Wong will call them and ensure they deliver to the chateau."

"I couldn't possibly. I would be imposing."

They tussled. Berenger won, narrowly. Even after no sleep and crazy visions, her force of will remained phenomenal.

He considered the state of the floor in the hall and kitchen. "It'll take a while to dry out. You should move down to my place till it does."

She opened her mouth to debate that one, too. Did she have to turn every common-sense offer into an assault on her independence?

He ignored her objections. "Let's just see what the plumber has to say first."

While Chantal packed clothes for the funeral, he hunted for the cause of the leak. He soon tracked it to the exit pipe from the hot water boiler. The welding had given way. Once the boiler had emptied its contents, mains pressure had kept it pumping out over the floor. He shrugged. The house *was* fundamentally sound, but its plumbing dated back decades. It didn't take spooks to explain the failure.

*   *   *

At two o'clock, Berenger watched Chantal descend the chateau's stairs and check her hair and outfit in the gilt-framed hallway mirror. Her black dress skimmed her knees. Another of her necklaces, this one with shiny black and crystal beads, added a subtle sparkle. She'd drawn her hair back in a chignon. He preferred it loose.

"Feeling better?" he asked.

She started as he spoke from the shadows, but he could see that sleep had helped erase the defenseless woman who'd clung to him at dawn. The usual, determined Chantal had reappeared.

"Yes, thanks. Much." She reset a hairpin and, eyes on her reflection, asked, "Why were you up at Number 8 this morning? Not that you weren't a godsend."

He thought fast, not ready to reveal his need for her. "I went early to check phone messages upstairs at the shop. Luckily, I passed the back door and heard you scream."

She nodded at the mirror. "And have you been able to find a plumber? And what about the back door you crashed through? Can it be patched up?"

Typical Chantal. Straight to the practicalities.

"The plumber says the problem's fixed, though things will be drying out for a while. The back door lock I haven't solved yet. We could prop a chair under the handle if you like, but I can't see any of my employees hopping over that back wall."

Creaks from the floorboards above told him Wilbur had emerged from his room at last.

"Then I shall stay at Aunt Jeanne's tonight," Chantal said. "I'm truly grateful for your help this morning and for letting my guests use your house this afternoon. But after the funeral, I won't be in any shape to socialize."

His face stiffened. "You can go to your bedroom here. Don't come down till you're ready."

"Please, Berenger."

"Is this because of last night? You and me?" An unfair question ahead of the coming funeral ordeal, he knew, but her reserve dismayed him. She had boarded a train, and it was headed away from him.

He thought she would deny it, but her shoulders slumped. "It is. You've been very kind, but," she coughed, "kindness to me doesn't make you innocent of cruelty to Aunt Jeanne."

He sucked in a harsh breath. "What do I have to do?

Catch more villains? Translate better?"

Her gaze fell. "I'm not pretending it's fair. Having to keep my guard up against you is exhausting." She darted a look through her lashes. "But it's better than being disappointed."

There it was again, the shadow of someone in her past. "But you wanted it last night, too. We both did."

"Yes."

"Listen to your heart instead of your head."

"My heart doesn't trust you either. It just…forgot last night. I'm sorry."

Forget her.

Like all tourists, she'd soon be gone. He should let her go. With an inward shrug, he confined himself to a warning. "Don't touch the absinthe."

A glance at his watch told him it was time they left. Earlier, he'd offered to drop her at the church and pick up some of her guests afterward. Fortunately, spring was the quietest time in the wine-making business, and still too early for much of the estate plowing. He tried not to think about the time he could be spending on converting Number 8.

They drove in silence. He considered telling her about his cross-checking of the Nazacs at lunchtime, but it hadn't yielded much. The parents had closed ranks behind their errant son. Both now confirmed his story about dropping his father at the garage. Berenger's effort to confirm that with the garage owner had failed: the mechanic hadn't seen Nazac senior arrive.

Berenger had gone straight on to the winery, and hauled Laurent into a quiet corner. Bolder than Berenger had expected, the youth had stuck to his story, but Berenger was sure he'd held back the truth.

Instead, he told Chantal that all the Nazacs would be coming to the funeral. "Laurent, too. A show of respectability his parents will have insisted on. You can keep an eye on him," he added.

She nodded and thanked him as she quickly climbed out of the car at the corner of Place St. Michel. A mixture of curious onlookers and guests filled the square, the latter identifiable by their dark clothing. A few had filed up the church's six shallow steps to where the priest stood to welcome them. Berenger recognized the plump form of Grenier and one of his father's fellow councilors waiting to shake the priest's hand. Come to make sure the old lady had really died, he reckoned.

Louise needed picking up from kindergarten, but he lingered to watch Chantal's slim black figure cross to the church. The chignon made her look more self-contained and remote than ever. He imagined slowly pulling out the bobby pins, loosening her hair, his fingers—

A polite toot from a car behind stopped the daydream. He spun the SUV's steering wheel and swiftly moved the vehicle on.

Beyond the town walls, in the newest part of Cordes, Louise stood waiting outside the little school, hand-in-hand with Mam'selle Rouge, her teacher. He parked and called a greeting as he got out. Louise waved madly until he reached her.

He nodded his thanks at Mam'selle, grateful as always for her willingness to include a blind child in her classroom. The young teacher smiled briefly at him and said goodbye. Louise transferred her hand to her father's.

"Do anything good today, *petite*?"

Louise swung on his arm as they returned to the car. "We learned about rubber. Did you know it comes out of trees, all sticky?"

Berenger admitted to having heard that before.

"It's got a funny smell, hasn't it?" Louise's sense of smell had grown more acute since she'd lost her sight. She often commented on scents her father could barely discern. "Mam'selle Rouge brought in a piece of rubber sheet. We played games with it, pouring water on it. All the water ran off."

They climbed in the car. "Monsieur Sanders," Louise continued, "smells of rubber, sometimes."

Berenger snorted in surprise. "Chérie, I don't think so!"

"He does. And Chantal smells of apples. And Grand-Papa smells of cologne and hair cream."

Berenger made a non-committal sound. Two out of three wasn't bad for a five-year-old.

"I like Chantal, Papa. Is she going to stay in Cordes now?"

His daughter's words twisted through his chest. "No. She has her home and family in England. She's here for…" He broke off, thinking. Chantal had never answered his question in the café. The intruder had interrupted things. He shrugged. "A few days at the most."

"But she has to make my bracelet first!"

"She promised she would." He hoped it was true. "But today is a sad day for her, so she won't do it right away." The rest of the brief journey he spent explaining what he'd said.

CHAPTER FIFTEEN

After the funeral service, the congregation emerged into the cool afternoon sunshine. While the undertakers solemnly loaded the unconventional coffin into their hearse, a few mourners who were not attending the burial came up to Chantal to offer their condolences in hushed voices. Two commented how they had seen Jeanne Lamarque as their own latter-day Joan of Arc, the inspiration and the energy behind their causes. A third warmly remembered Jeanne working on children's charities with her. Laurent Nazac and the town's doctor, Mezaute, also made their brief but respectful farewells just before the priest signaled they were ready to move on

Walking behind the priest and the slowly-rolling hearse, Chantal fell into step with an older woman. She soon learned the woman was called Odile and had been a distant cousin of Jeanne's.

"Pop music in church and a cardboard coffin!" Odile's blue-gray rinsed hairdo quivered with disapproval at the ceremony she had just endured.

"It's what Aunt Jeanne wanted," countered Chantal. The service had been pure Jeanne and every minute had hurt her great-niece as much as it had delighted her. Chantal dabbed at her red eyes yet again.

Odile stole a swift sideways glance and handed her a fresh tissue. "And you were the only family representative today. Surely others wanted to pay their respects?"

"Of course. But most of our family is overseas, it's bad timing. And my mother's health's not been good," Chantal added loyally, heading off further probing. She blew her nose.

"Who was the woman with the bright red hair who moved to sit with you?" pursued Odile.

"Madame Nazac." Chantal had been profoundly grateful for the cleaner's comfort and support. Seated prominently in the front pew, reserved for family, Chantal had been struggling alone with her tears till the cleaner came to clasp her hand.

The blue-rinsed coiffure shook again as if Odile did not deem paid help to be suitable for the front pew. Chantal began to feel tired by their exchange.

They walked to the Porte des Ormeaux in silence. Odile tugged her heavy stole closer as they moved through the chilly air under the gateway. The odor of mothballs swam up Chantal's nose.

"At least Jeanne slept in decent comfort in her last days," said Odile at length. "With me, in Souel."

The name of the hamlet Armand had mentioned roused Chantal. Despite the occasion, part of her slid into detective mode. "She wasn't living at her own house anymore?"

"Jeanne was with me," stated Odile. "She turned up at seven o'clock one morning, oh, about four weeks ago. I wasn't even out of bed."

"Did she often drop in so early?"

"Never. No need, was there? We lived just a short drive apart." Odile gestured vaguely along the road ahead. "But this time she walked, and it's a good three miles. Such a strange thing. She hadn't anything with her, just what she stood up in."

"Did she say why she arrived like that? On foot, no bag?"

Her companion remained silent, trudging steadily downhill, as if wrestling with something.

"Please, I'm trying to understand those last few days."

Odile sighed. "I was happy to have her company, of course. Life's been too quiet since my René…God rest him."

Frustration formed a hard ball in Chantal's stomach. The modern cemetery's plain sheet-metal gate lay only yards away. She tried again. "But why did Aunt Jeanne leave home?"

Odile's shoulders sagged. When she finally spoke, Chantal had to stoop to catch the quiet words. The stole moved again, but this time in a shrug. "She said she couldn't stand it anymore. Things kept breaking. But you don't walk out because the fuse box catches fire, do you? We all know old houses take lot of looking after."

They walked through the gate and down the narrow concrete path that wound between modest twentieth-century tombs, none more than hip high. The old cemetery across the road housed the rows of mausoleums, each like a miniature house. Over there, almost all the tombs sprouted tall crosses like antennae picking up messages from the afterlife. Chantal was glad Aunt Jeanne had organized her final resting place to be in this less spooky half of the graveyard.

By now, Odile was talking more to herself than Chantal. "I must have asked a hundred questions. It was as if the house itself…" Her voice died away.

The weak spring sunshine lost what little warmth it had offered. Chantal shivered. "You don't think Aunt Jeanne was ill? Couldn't climb stairs so well?" Anything to avoid the idea that Roland Fleurie's house had sprung to life with the goal of sending its occupants crazy.

Odile dismissed the idea of illness with a wave of her

hand. "You're forgetting. She'd walked over that morning. Stronger legs than me and I'm twenty years younger."

That was a bold claim, but Chantal refused to let herself be distracted. "Did she have bad dreams?" Chantal's voice croaked slightly.

Odile's eyes met Chantal's, and narrowed. "Maybe. There was this look in her eyes. It faded after a few days at my place. I remember she said she was sleeping well again." Odile paused. "She never went back to Rue Obscure except in daylight."

Chantal could guess only too well at the horrors that had finally driven Jeanne away. And what lay behind it all? Surely something more than absinthe. Chantal had suffered horribly the night before she'd delved into the little drinks cabinet. Could guilty spirits make the living see things that weren't there? Had someone woken the otherworld that lurked in the ancient timbers of Number 8 so as to scare Aunt Jeanne out?

Get a grip, girl.

They reached the grave where the priest waited. Dutifully, Chantal bent her head and made the necessary responses. She threw the first handful of earth onto the flimsy coffin inside the small vault. The heavy marble lid rested alongside. Other friends stepped up to throw their own handfuls. One older man, who Chantal didn't recognize, threw a rose. She sighed at the romantic gesture and imagined him as one of Aunt Jeanne's spurned suitors.

As the queue of mourners took their turn, Chantal moved back to Odile. "You knew she was selling her house?"

"Of course. She called her lawyer the day she arrived in Souel."

"Where was she planning to live?"

"In a rented place in Albi, while she looked around to buy. I know she only inspected brand new houses."

Somewhere without ghosts in the old stones. Who could blame her?

Chantal fretted at the problem on the journey to the chateau, opting to walk while Berenger kindly ferried a carload of less mobile guests. She'd much rather blame it all on poisons and narcotics laid by a flesh-and-blood hand than some ghostly agency. But exactly how could she tell the difference? And who on earth could she ask about it?

By four o'clock, the funeral party had assembled at the chateau, in the drawing room overlooking the sweeping lawns. About thirty people crowded the room, some sitting cautiously on the delicate Louis Quinze furniture, and others admiring Armand's celadons in the floor-to-ceiling glass-fronted display cabinet. Chantal couldn't help thinking how wryly amused her great-aunt would have been to see so many sworn opponents of the Council happily enjoying hospitality provided by its Chair and his son.

She looked for an opportunity to repeat carefully edited highlights of the conversation with Odile to Berenger. He stood over by an enormous houseplant, but she couldn't reach him. Strangers came up to her, one by one, to say kind things about Aunt Jeanne. One, dropping his voice as Armand came near to top up glasses, said he would miss Jeanne as a key ally in the struggle for the bypass.

In a brief lull, Chantal moved on, heading for Berenger, but before she had gone two steps she caught unexpected words from behind.

"Burst boiler, maybe, but look who's ridden to her rescue. Do you think…?"

Three days in Cordes and the rumor mill had begun to grind her name between its mighty stones. No surprise— the gossips would keep a close eye on all Berenger Morel's doings, waiting for the town's most eligible widower to signal a romantic move. Had someone seen them kissing in the street last night? She kicked herself for not being more discreet, even as the idea of the two of them being an official couple thrummed excitement deep within her.

Movement from the hallway distracted her. Louise

sidled around the door, head cocked to assess the position and number of people in the room. She made progress along the wall, for once trailing a finger to guide her in a room the family used less often. In her path lay a side-table where three dainty china plates held finger food.

Worried that Louise might bump into the little table, Chantal searched out Berenger. She caught his gaze with a questioning look and a glance towards Louise.

He shot her a swift thumbs-up.

Sure enough, Louise reached the table safely. At once, her fingers lightly traveled around and over the plates. Deftly, she plucked up a small vol-au-vent and bit into the puff-pastry tower. With a second pastry in hand, she turned to the room, pausing to re-assess people's location. Then she moved steadily to a nearby sofa occupied by two older men. Leaning on the sofa's arm, she began to talk to them.

The child's confidence charmed from Chantal the closest thing to a smile she'd managed all day. She looked across at Berenger and saw her feelings multiplied in his face. His eyes were locked on Louise, and his features, lit by a luminous smile, telegraphed his pride and love. She wished she could snap a photo.

Another mourner touched her arm and she turned reluctantly, tuning into the man's words. Once she'd observed the necessary ritual exchanges, she'd cross to Berenger. She smiled at the guest and made a polite reply.

A minute later, a fierce bellow startled everyone.

Berenger grasped a middle-aged woman's wrist. Her fleshy face was frozen in shock. "Can't resist passing on vile gossip, can you, any of you?" His voice filled the room.

Had he overheard the whispers about his possible romantic involvement with Chantal? Dismay washed though her at this dramatic overreaction. Why would he be so appalled to be linked with her?

"She can't see, dammit! Of course she knows her way

around this house, but she's lost anywhere new." He threw the arm back at its owner.

Chantal relaxed, despite the violence. Berenger's fury made complete sense if Louise and her protection were at stake.

The woman's alarm swiftly turned to self-defense. Her mouth pursed. "I do not pass on gossip, Monsieur. I know what I was told, and now I have the evidence of my own eyes."

"And who have you been talking to?" Berenger roared.

"To someone who knows the truth! That child's not blind. She's…" The woman's finger tapped at her forehead.

Berenger took a step closer, towering over her. Chantal almost felt sorry for her.

"I can't see," Louise's voice piped into the hushed room. "I really can't. Why does she keep saying I can, Papa?"

The woman stepped aside from her furious host and quickly pulled a twenty-euro note from her purse. She dangled it at the child. "What's this Louise? Do you want it?"

"She's not a performing seal," Berenger snapped. He tried to snatch the note, but the guest spun away. Little gasps erupted around the room.

"Papa, it's OK. It's paper money, isn't it? I heard the purse snap."

"Ah, but how much money, Louise?" The woman, pleased with herself, shook the note enticingly.

"I don't know, do I? I can't see. And I don't know my money numbers yet." Her lower lip pouted. "I'm only five."

"Well said, Louise." Chantal's words triggered a ripple of agreement.

Others clearly shared Chantal's growing sense of embarrassment. It was her fault this dreadful woman had entered Berenger's house and insulted his family. Armand scooped up Louise and swiftly moved between Berenger and his prey, while Chantal took charge of the rest of the room, making pointed suggestions about the time, and encouraging a small knot of guests towards the door.

There were more noises of assent. Within minutes, the room was clear. Madame Nazac offered to stay and help clear up, but Armand graciously refused while Chantal brought the cleaner's coat.

Berenger closed the front door behind the last guest, and set the deadlock with a vicious twist.

"I'm so sorry, Berenger. That ghastly woman," said Chantal. She leaned against the bottom of the banister for a moment's support.

"Not your fault," he said tersely.

"She said she was one of Aunt Jeanne's comrades-in-arms. I can't imagine my aunt being friends with such a viper."

"That woman was Madame Prunet," offered Armand from up the hall. "Her daughter's the receptionist at Mezaute's surgery. Perhaps your aunt found her a source of useful information for her various campaigns, nothing more."

Chantal nodded at him, grateful for the kind thought. "I hope so."

Armand moved into the kitchen.

"Thank you for getting them out so fast." Berenger folded his arms, his hands gripping hard onto the sleeves. "I suppose I overreacted. But Louise is braver and happier than any of us. Despite what she's lost. She deserves a damn sight better than ignorant accusations." He paused. "I'd better check on her again."

They returned to the front room and found Louise on the empty sofa, happily munching a canapé. Berenger reached down to stroke his daughter's head while Chantal sat next to her. "I'll make your bracelet tonight, Louise. But for now," she surveyed the room, "I'd better tidy up."

"No need," said Berenger at once.

"I'll help," offered Louise. She giggled. "Not by carrying plates. By eating up the snacks!" Chantal laughed with her and even Berenger snorted.

He excused himself to make a phone call. Chantal quietly carried a stack of dirty plates to a corner of the kitchen. She could hear Ah Wong talking to the caterer at the back door. As she returned for more crockery, she checked to make no mistake about which door led back to the lounge. The thought of entering "Master's private room" on top of the recent fiasco made her cringe.

Back in the kitchen, Louise in tow, she met Ah Wong. The housekeeper shook her head at the dirty plates Chantal had gathered.

"It was the least I could do after all the extra trouble you've been put to," said Chantal in self-defense. She took the risk of placing her hand on Ah Wong's arm. "I'm really very grateful for all you've done for me today. You've been very kind. And I promise I won't clear up anything else."

Her words seemed to mollify the housekeeper.

"You stay for dinner?" Ah Wong jerked her head to the oven. Rich smells of lamb ragout seeped out.

"Stay! Stay! Stay!" Louise danced in the center of the kitchen as she chanted.

The friendly offers tugged at Chantal.

"Yes, stay," chimed in a deep voice. She spun around. Berenger leaned on the door frame. Shreds of recent anger lingered in his eyes.

Chantal guessed the phone call had put them there.

"If you'd care to."

Unable to withstand the intensity in eyes, she dropped her gaze to his chest. Through the fine black wool of his pullover, she read the lines of his body and remembered how those heavy bones and muscles had felt, close against her. A flush crept up her neck.

"For dinner, nothing more."

Had he read her thoughts? The flush rose into her cheeks even as her gaze tracked lower. His silver belt buckle drew her attention like a magnet.

"Perhaps you'd prefer to rest upstairs for a while?"

Yes, please.

Louise tilted her head, puzzled by the one-sided conversation.

"No. Thanks." Chantal spoke quickly to drown out the little voice in her head. "This is Aunt Jeanne's day. I need to be back in her place, with her things around me." It sounded lame, an excuse to escape his unsettling presence. He must know it.

Louise began to protest until Chantal reminded her she would need time at Number 8 to find the best beads for the bracelet. That settled the matter for one Morel, at least.

Chantal declined Berenger's offer of a ride up to Rue Obscure and kept her eyes away from his. It made it easier. Every extra hour she spent with him made it harder not to give in and trust him. In the closeness of the car, if he touched her, she might surrender altogether. How could she keep her head clear to solve the mystery around Aunt Jeanne then?

Berenger shrugged at her double refusal of dinner and the ride. Chantal couldn't guess what he was thinking.

As she collected her toiletries upstairs, she realized how much she wanted to remain. The chateau meant time with Berenger, true, but it also offered normality, conviviality and a good night's sleep. She hated to swap it for the emptiness at Rue Obscure.

Downstairs, Berenger waited in silence at the front door. She looked up at him. She wanted to accept one, either, both, of his offers, but all she managed was, "Thank you again."

"You're welcome. I'll be in touch," he replied in a detached manner.

She ought to have been relieved. Instead, it hurt.

She stepped out into the porch.

CHAPTER SIXTEEN

The sun had almost dipped behind Cordes' western flank as Chantal walked out past the chateau's gateposts, and a damp chill had crept into the air. She'd intended taking the straightest route to Number 8, but the fading sunbeams reminded her of her loss and drew her further west to the cemetery.

By the time she reached the graveyard for the second time that day, the sun had sunk further to paint rosy gold on the tops of the laurels that edged one wall. A municipal worker in blue overalls still moved through the tombs, sweeping the paths. They exchanged nods.

Chantal walked to Aunt Jeanne's vault where the flowers softened, but couldn't hide, the reality of what lay beneath the marble slab. Chantal called up her three favorite memories of Aunt Jeanne and shared them with the peaceful surroundings.

She looked up at length. Movement at the southern cemetery boundary caught her eye. Two hundred yards off, a man in an oversize beret walked along outside the wall. Chantal's long sight failed her, blurred by the smear of tears. It probably wasn't Mulberry. Short, dark men in berets could be found on every street in France.

But just in case…

She went over to the caretaker. It wasn't hard to arouse his indignation at the thought of someone interfering with the dead. He took the scrap of paper with Number 8's phone number and promised to be in touch if he saw anyone hanging around Aunt Jeanne's tomb. Chantal managed to slip away before he could launch fully into a story about graffiti in another graveyard he tended.

On the way up the hill, she passed a grocer who was closing up and bought a few items for supper. She'd had an idea about analyzing the source of the hallucinations. Not only would she avoid eating anything from the house, she'd get the absinthe checked out. An evil person had to be behind the visions, not some malevolent spirit.

She reached the massive gateway of Porte des Ormeaux as a couple came through its narrow arch, wrapped up in coats and each other. She stopped to let them pass. Standing still, she got a good look at the boy. A load lifted from her. Now she reckoned she knew exactly where Berenger's wayward employee had been while they'd chased Mulberry down Grand' Rue. Or rather, she knew who he'd been with and why.

There was no mistaking Laurent Nazac, even with a curly-haired girl attached to his face. Lust was a much better reason than skullduggery for his sneaking off. With this piece of information, it would be easy to double-check his whereabouts at the crucial time around Aunt Jeanne's fall.

It would be easier to let her guard down with Berenger, too. She smiled in the darkness. Perhaps it was time she learned to trust him more. Let him closer.

*　*　*

Chantal's fingers moved the four strands of yarn in the old familiar rhythm as she knotted Louise's bracelet. After the fiasco in the drawing room, she wanted to meet her promise to the child as soon as possible. Blue, blue, green, green. Over and under, under and over. Select a bead. Push the central cords through. Tie the outer ones off in square knots beneath. The pattern was simple, with two round enamel beads followed by two ovals, and one larger heart-shaped bead dead center.

The occasional hiss and snap from the burning branches in the wood-heater kept her company, and its warmth was helping dry out the damp that lingered from the burst boiler. Chantal had dragged a small armchair from the parlor for a more comfortable place to sit for a couple of hours. The sense of peace went precisely wallpaper-deep, but she welcomed it after the stress of the previous twenty-four hours.

Dinner had been the grocer's soup and crackers, washed down with tea from a new box. With luck, she'd avoided eating anything tainted. As for the other possibility… Until these last two nights, she'd have denied the existence of ghosts as roundly as Berenger. She needed to rebuild her conviction, fast.

Chantal grimaced. Talk about a lousy set of options. On the one hand, she faced the terror of warped reality in the dead of night, the time the house always chose to attack her. On the other, she had the confusion of being attracted to a man she couldn't allow herself to trust.

Making jewelry always soothed her, though. Select a bead. Thread a bead. Knot it off. She measured the length of the bracelet. Another two beads and she would have it finished. She created a fat knot to act as a toggle and then pushed it through the loop she'd woven at the beginning of the bracelet. She snipped off the ends and added dabs of glue. Satisfied, she leaned back.

It had been one heck of an afternoon, but Chantal tried to maintain her calm mood by picking up another set of cords. These ones were for trying to develop her heart knot. Nothing like a knotty problem to ease the mind. She smiled at the awful and well-worn pun.

The grandfather clock chimed nine-thirty. Chantal stretched beyond the armchair's embrace and dropped the macramé board with its misshapen heart knot onto the kitchen table.

It was too early for sleep, too late for another cup of tea. She thought of finding something to read, and perhaps taking it to bed. Aunt Jeanne had favored the local library for her fiction needs, but Chantal hoped she'd find something tucked away in the study.

It took a few seconds to remember in which vase she'd hidden the study key. The metal tinkled against the vintage glass as she shook the key down the vase's narrow neck.

Inside the study, nothing had been disturbed that Chantal could see. Her gaze traveled around the shelves, and on a whim she pulled down a green document binder and opened the lid. The spring-loaded clip inside held down a fat wad of letters, the top one in Aunt Jeanne's hand. The upper lines had been folded over, hiding the addressee, and when Chantal focused on the words, she saw they were in Italian, a language she hardly knew. More letters lower down the stack appeared similar. Why did Aunt Jeanne have letters she herself had written? Had a lover returned them to her?

It felt too personal to probe. Chantal returned the file to its shelf and looked around.

The gray document box containing the map scroll and the *Eye of the Needle* papers lay on the desk, exactly as she remembered leaving them. She pictured Wilbur and Armand standing beside her, reaching greedily for the contents. She sniffed, and scooped the box up into her arms. Legends of treasures and mysterious symbols would make good bedtime reading, she reckoned, and help her feel close to Aunt Jeanne, without invading her privacy.

She left the box by the stairs and went to close the air inlet on the wood burner to a mere slit. With luck, she'd be able to coax the embers back to life in the morning.

A shout from somewhere outside made her jump and

curiosity propelled her to the back door. The damaged bolt clanked softly as she opened the door to the little yard and immediately shivered in the cold air.

Light streamed from an upstairs window in the wine-tasting store. It stood ajar, and the angry words grew louder. Berenger's shape appeared, his shoulders filling the window frame.

"We had an agreement!" Berenger bellowed.

"We still do," protested a man's voice.

"Someone's taken matters into their own hands. Why? It was all going fine. No one suspected a thing. Least of all…" He jerked his head out of the window. Chantal felt he'd gestured straight at her.

"It wasn't through me, I assure you."

Berenger spun away from the window, muttering in anger.

The man he had accused came to lean on the windowsill. He looked about fifty, short and lean, his head clean-shaven to hide the extent of his hair loss. She recognized him as Mezaute, the town doctor, still dressed in the dark suit he'd worn at the funeral. His black tie made an exclamation mark on his white shirt.

He turned to half-face Berenger. His profile showed a straight nose and thin mouth. "If it's been done by someone on my side…"

"It didn't come from us, did it? There's only my father and me in on it. We have every reason to keep things looking as straightforward as possible. Look what's happened now."

"What's happened that really changes anything?"

"I'll tell you. She's asking questions, that's what's changed. And believe me, she's persistent. I'm afraid she'll ferret out the truth. That could jeopardize everything." There was a pause. "I couldn't stand it."

"I'm sure you can distract her. You spend plenty of time with her. She trusts you."

"Which is more than I can say about how I feel about

you," snapped Berenger.

"Our agreement stands, Morel. I'll take steps to ensure there are no more… breaches. But as you say, it's in your interest to get things back on track, isn't it?"

She heard a sound of something slamming.

"Oh yes," came the growl, "I'll sort it out. What choice do I have?"

Chantal stood motionless in the back yard. The cool of the spring night was nothing compared to the creep of icy bile up her throat. So much for lowering her guard with Berenger and resolving to trust him more. He'd proved himself to be no better than Steven.

Inside, she jammed a kitchen chair under the handle of the door into the scullery, determinedly ignoring who had advised her on this security measure, and went to chafe her hands by the wood burner. Its residual heat eventually eased the chill on her skin but did nothing to stop the sour trickle inside her.

Berenger had taken part in a secret deal to do with Aunt Jeanne and something had gone wrong. Now he feared Chantal's questions would lead her to the truth.

She had no idea what that truth could be. The only thing she knew for sure was that her first thoughts had been right. Berenger Morel was a schemer and a bully. And with his foul temper, he could probably be a murderer as well.

Alone again, she'd have to rely on herself.

She could handle it.

CHAPTER SEVENTEEN

Chantal's brave words fled overnight. She woke in the spare bedroom before dawn, feeling more tired than when she'd gone to bed. It had taken a long time for her to drop off to sleep and, waking at six in the morning, her mind sprang into agitated life. Disjointed images of Aunt Jeanne's last weeks ran through her head. The fuse box fire, the escape to nearby Souel. The word *escape* fired adrenalin into Chantal's blood and its prickling aftermath signaled the end of sleep.

She reached out from under the warm covers and switched on the bedside light. Its mellow glow chased the dark from the bed, though shadows lingered in the room's corners. The document box she'd brought up from Aunt Jeanne's study waited on the bedside rug.

The night before, she'd been too perturbed by the revelation of Berenger's plotting to do more than stare down, unseeing, at its contents. The memory of what she'd overheard in the back yard threatened to make her miserable again, and she heaved the carton onto her lap with determination.

The typeset pages looked the easiest place to start, but they soon made her sigh. Most were photocopies of poems written in Occitan. They'd meant something to Aunt Jeanne because various lines bore fluoro-yellow highlights. Enough similarities lingered between the medieval words and modern French for Chantal to recognize *tresaur* for treasure and *peira* for the modern *pierre* or stone, but the phrases in between defeated her. She reached for fresh material.

Aunt Jeanne's hand-annotated copy of the scroll map emerged. Chantal rubbed the heels of her hands into her eye sockets, rousing the muscles to the task of deciphering the tightly written words.

Most comments clustered around the upper dotted red line and the two puzzling symbols that sat close together about halfway along it. The symbol that vaguely resembled an Egyptian hieroglyphic eye lay slightly below the shape that looked like a flower. From each symbol sprang a pencil line, leading to a word. Chantal tilted the paper towards the bedside light.

The eye symbol connected to the word *EON*. Not a word, she realized after a moment's thought, but an acronym: *Eye of the Needle*. A thrill of excitement followed. Had Aunt Jeanne succeeded in decoding the map, and with it the Cathars' true meaning for the Eye? A delightful image of Aunt Jeanne presenting her breakthrough to the local gentleman "scholars" came to her, before she reluctantly put it aside. Armand and Wilbur's words at dinner had made it clear they'd not heard of any such coup.

Chantal next followed the pencil line from the flower. It ended in a name she knew well.

Fleurie.

Fleurie—the French for flowering or blooming.

She frowned. Presumably the flower symbol didn't mean the man, Roland Fleurie. More likely it referred to his house, to Number 8. The dotted line with its flower lay high up the triangle, just as Rue Obscure lay high up Cordes' hill. She returned to her aunt's cramped writing, impatient to learn more.

Jeanne had jotted down three ideas for what the upper dotted line might represent.

Ramparts along Rue Obscure
Water collection passage (cf. Rue Chaude)
Tunnel—Lost!

Most of the other markings related to measurements. Aunt Jeanne had tried to relate the real-life elevation gap between Rue Obscure and Rue Chaude to the distance between the dotted lines as a way to test her first theory. A series of question and exclamation marks suggested the map had held onto its secrets.

Chantal set the map aside and lifted out all the other papers, scanning each, before returning them to the box. Back in went Wilbur's annoying letters about the Eye, half a ream of photocopies from journals and old poems, and, of most interest, pages with Jeanne's jottings. Yet none threw any more light on the Eye or the map.

She threw herself back onto her pillows and tapped her head against the bed head, trying to coax ideas. If—*if*—the Eye lay near Number 8, then its position on the map showed it to be a little below the house. That could mean outside the house, perhaps, and partway down the massive ramparts that plunged from Rue Obscure to the back of the houses on Rue Chaude. Or closer. Something connected to the cistern in the back yard? Yet that was only two or three yards deep, if she remembered correctly. The house's basement would surely go down twice as far as that.

Her face twisted in distaste. The basement had to be her least favorite, least-visited part of Number 8. She and Aunt Jeanne had ventured down its steps one summer, hunting for old deck chairs to use in the little back yard. Chantal recalled how she had stopped on the last wooden step above the dusty chalk floor, unwilling to leave the escape route back to sunshine. Even her aunt's cheerful conversation had not encouraged her, that long-ago day, to follow and explore among the hulking, shrouded shapes.

But the basement had to be a possibility worth checking out. The idea of sleuthing in her great-aunt's footsteps—because surely Jeanne would have gone through the same logic—warmed her. It would be a little bit like having her aunt back again. And her aunt in spirit would be a more trustworthy companion than anyone alive in Cordes. Till last night, she would have been tempted to ask Berenger along for company, but that option closed for good.

The Eye of the Needle had taken a powerful hold of her imagination, she reflected. Here she was, seriously contemplating a solo trip underground at six-thirty a.m. on a cold spring morning. If she turned on every light in the kitchen and scullery, cranked up the volume on a pop music channel on the radio, and put fresh batteries in the flashlight she'd seen under the sink, she reckoned she could handle it.

"Don't want to be like a horror movie victim," she muttered. "The idiot who checks out strange sounds in the attic, totally unprepared."

Thick socks inside her sheepskin slippers, a sweatshirt on top of her nightdress and her own winter-weight coat over the top made her the equal of the cool air in the hallway.

At the head of the stairs, the document box tucked under her arm, it dawned on her that normality reigned. In the last eight hours she'd suffered no hallucinations, nor ghostly visits. The clock ticked steadily. Down in the kitchen, where she deposited the document file on the breakfast table, the appliances sparkled in stark white. The mundane scene buoyed her spirits, and in a couple of minutes she stood in the well-lit scullery, flashlight in hand, ready.

The basement door swung open to reveal a small landing. Galoshes and rubber boots in Aunt Jeanne's petite shoe size took up half the space. Raincoats and jackets lined the wall to her left. One yard ahead, the steep wooden stairs descended into the gloom. The smell of autumn rose to greet her: damp earth, with a hint of rotting wood. At once, the scent transported her to Aunt Jeanne's open grave. She shook her head fiercely to get rid of the mournful image.

"Come on," Chantal said out loud to the shadows below. "Adventure time."

Determinedly, she swiped at the light switch to her right. A low-wattage bulb, partway down the stairs, scattered a few dusty rays.

She turned on the flashlight, threw back her shoulders and marched to the bottom. This time, she stepped firmly onto the gray floor, hewn from the chalk bedrock. She breathed in the winter-night cold and shivered.

Another weak light bulb threw shadows from where it dangled, some way back in the room. The chances of picking up the trail Aunt Jeanne might have followed dwindled as Chantal took in the scene. Much as she'd remembered, stacks of boxes nestled in the foothills of high, shrouded shapes. If anything, the jumble had multiplied since her last visit.

She strode resolutely to the nearest sheet and pulled it aside to reveal a rickety stack of cane-backed chairs. Dust flew up and made her sneeze. The cardboard boxes at her feet bulged with old magazines.

Which way? Chantal chose a narrow gap to the left of the stacked chairs. Here, the piles of junk obscured most of the light from the two ceiling bulbs. Without the flashlight, she'd have been working blind, and even with it she had no clear idea of the basement's size. A few feet ahead, a covered table barred her path till the flashlight confirmed she had room to shuffle by sideways. Dirty cobwebs hanging from the table left a gray smear across her coat.

At last, she could see the basement wall, though a further tower of wooden crates stood in her way. Through the slats, she could make out glass containers. She shook the topmost crate and the jars rattled hollowly. Moving carefully around the boxes, she finally touched the clammy chalk of the basement's far wall.

A faint draft from the left stirred the fine hair at her temple. It faded to little more than a tremor in the air between the wall and the crates. She swung the flashlight towards it.

And gasped.

Splintered brick and shards of plaster littered the floor, some of it crushed as if by passing feet. Beyond lay a pile of loose bricks and larger sheets of plaster that had broken free. The brick glowed in earthy reds with streaks of orange, untainted by basement dust. A rough, dark hole about five feet high opened out of the basement wall. The heavy sledgehammer propped alongside had probably done the damage.

Chantal crept forward and tried to heft the tool with one hand. It barely budged. Diminutive Aunt Jeanne had never swung this hammer.

She traced the edges of the opening with the flashlight's beam. Some long-dead craftsman had skimmed plaster over a single skin of bricks with such skillful texturing and tinting that it blended into the solid chalk wall. No one using Number 8's basement would have suspected anything.

And Aunt Jeanne couldn't have opened the hole. The position of the rubble pile and the litter on the floor made it clear the demolisher had come *from the far side*.

Sweat prickled Chantal's brow, almost stinging her skin as it cooled. She hugged herself, one-armed, for warmth and comfort.

Slowly, she raised the flashlight and pointed it inside the hole. Bright chalk, about ten feet away, dazzled back at her. A solid wall. Was this a dead end?

The draft reached her again and told her there had to be an exit. Angling the light, she made out a narrow strip of darkness at the left rear of the secret room. She saw nothing else of interest in the empty space.

The ceiling on the antechamber, if that's what it was, stood about five and a half feet high. Enough for thirteenth-century Cathars, perhaps, but a cramped stoop for a six-foot woman born into the twentieth century.

If she went in.

Would she?

Aunt Jeanne would have, without hesitation. A mental image of her great-aunt, gray eyes bright with anticipation, hitching up her orange kaftan to hop over the lip of the hole into the chamber, gave Chantal enough courage to think it through.

She stood stock still, eyes closed, and focused all her attention on what she could hear and smell. Any hint of danger, and she would hightail it back to the sanctuary of the kitchen.

Silence.

Silence and a scent of water. Perhaps this led to nothing more sinister than a simple drainage channel.

You wish.

Chantal took a deep breath of the basement's damp and frigid air. She would be brave and go as far as the back wall to see where it led. And then, honor satisfied, she would beat a speedy retreat to the kitchen and brew a very hot cup of tea in a very big mug.

Wrapping her grimy coat tightly around her, she ducked into the chamber. She hunched low as she hobbled towards the exit at the rear, fearing collecting cobwebs in her hair as much as scraping her skull on the chamber's ceiling.

When she reached the little exit, she saw it stood barely two feet wide. Gingerly, Chantal pointed the light at it. This time, the chalk reflected the light more softly, with the beam probing deeply along the way ahead. The passage ran gently downhill for about twenty feet, its roof line dropping slower than its floor, so that its height steadily increased. An eight-foot-high, pointed arch of crisply chiseled stone blocks marked its end, with blackness beyond.

The blocks formed an elegant ellipse.

Just like the eye of a needle.

CHAPTER EIGHTEEN

Chantal's feet rat-a-tatted back up the wooden basement stairs. A heady mix of elated thrill and bone-deep chill surged through her, and her teeth chattered in harmony with her footfalls. Slamming the basement door shut and reaching the safety of the bright kitchen only intensified her amazement at her discovery.

She had so much to think about, so much to process. But first, she had to get warm again. A quick jiggle of the electric kettle told her it held enough water. She flipped the black plastic switch. Then, with stiff fingers, she pulled a tea bag from the box she'd bought the previous evening and dropped it into the largest mug from Aunt Jeanne's cupboard.

The kettle sat stubbornly silent. Had she turned it on? Checking for a hint of growing warmth, she tapped the brushed-metal casing with her palm.

A strong shock coursed up her arm from the kettle. Her head snapped back. The force smashed her lower jaw into her upper teeth, ending the chattering. She staggered and fell heavily on her left hand, the impact jarring up to her shoulder.

Another booby-trap.

She wouldn't cry. She *wouldn't.*

Getting back on her feet posed the first battle. Breathing evenly again presented a second.

Her right palm burned from touching the electrified metal. Chantal longed to put ice on it, but that would mean opening the fridge-freezer. Every electrical appliance could be rigged to give her more vicious shocks. The fridge's metal handles gleamed as wickedly as knife blades.

She remembered little of her school physics, but she knew she needed insulation. Jeanne's rubber galoshes from the basement landing offered a solution. Jamming her toes into them as far as she could, and with her heels hanging over the backs, but not touching the floor, Chantal felt safer.

Shuffling back across the gray and black linoleum, she fetched ice for her hand and then collapsed onto a chair at the breakfast table. The pain ebbed, but the physical shock compounded her earlier excitement and cold and she shook for long minutes. Her need for the comfort of hot, sweet tea grew urgent, but she couldn't bear to touch the kettle again, and didn't trust the gas stove not to blow up either.

Water pipes, fuse boxes, electric kettles. Unless men who'd been dead for well over seven hundred years had enrolled as trade apprentices, these household accidents had a modern origin. As modern as the hand that had wielded the sledgehammer in the basement.

How good were Berenger's mechanical skills? He'd known how to turn off the mains tap. Her lips thinned in an unintended echo of her top suspect. Heck, *she* knew about mains taps. Most people did. It wasn't as if she needed any more reasons to distrust him. The comments he'd hurled at Mezaute had been enough. She tried to forget how good it had felt, for the few hours between the wake at the chateau and the words she'd heard in the back yard, to believe she could trust him.

If he walked in right now, she'd be putty in his hands.

The physical shock had weakened her defenses and the urge to share her discovery of the Eye with someone who cared about Number 8 only sapped them further. She wished she had something stronger than the chair under the back door handle to safeguard the house.

Not from Berenger, she silently admitted, but from her reaction to him.

She managed to coax the embers in the wood-heater back to life. Achingly slowly, a small pan of water on the wood-burner's hotplate crept to the boil and at last she could make tea. She scooped three heaped spoonfuls of sugar into the mug and, with her elbows propped on the table, inhaled the fumes. By the time she had sipped her way through half of the mug's contents, she felt better. Tea and sugar were this girl's preferred drugs.

Sugar.

She stared at the half-empty mug in horror.

The amber liquid now looked more like poison than nectar. How could she have made such a basic mistake? The electric shock had fried half her brain cells along with her palm.

Chantal prepared for the madness that might well be coming by opening every shutter to let in light. She didn't dare venture outside. What if she decided she could fly off the ramparts? She jammed a broom handle across the basement door to make it harder for her hallucinating self to wander back down into the darkness. Grimly, she also forced a knife handle into the slot under the door's old-fashioned thumb latch. It might delay someone coming through the passage below, uninvited, long enough for her to come up with a better plan to keep them out.

Time for happy thoughts. No basements, no intruders. Daffodils and kittens instead.

Corny, but worth a try.

Minutes later, the symptoms began, and her effort to think positively paid dividends. Beautiful starbursts of color appeared on the wood burner's enameled sides. The phone rang at one point. The ringing tones drifted as feathery gray snowflakes from the ceiling. Her rubber-shod feet grew into enormous blueberries. When she tapped them together they emitted a scent of roses.

The benign parade of colors and smells utterly engrossed her. Maybe the daylight helped. Maybe the previous trips had given her resistance, or the sugar dose had been smaller. She lost track of time. When at last she looked at her watch, it read nearly ten o'clock.

The world gradually shrank back to its humdrum self. By noon, unsteadiness in her legs remained the only trace of her experience. The sort of wobbliness, she noted, that might send an older woman tumbling down stairs for the first—and last—time.

After the excitement and stress of her morning, Chantal craved simple, quiet activities to find a sense of balance again. She began by returning the document box to Aunt Jeanne's study. As she re-entered the parlor, a passing cloud darkened the room and she hastily rearranged her priorities. Her first task had to be making the power supply safe before nightfall. The idea of a long evening by candlelight, reliant on the wood-heater for her supper, made her shudder. She noted wryly that repairs at Number 8 were becoming almost *normal*.

In the new fuse box in the scullery, she found the business card for the electrician who had done the last repairs. To her relief, Monsieur Bellec answered promptly and promised to drop round before dark. He sounded agitated by the news of more problems, and defensive. Chantal guessed his responsiveness was to demonstrate his earlier repairs could not be blamed for the new problems. As long as he came, she didn't care why.

She washed her face and dressed. Bellec might be hours yet and, after roaming around the house for inspiration, she opted for a session of sorting. Whoever Number 8 finally proved to belong to, Jeanne's clutter had to be brought under control. The job had been on her to-do list even before Berenger had pestered her with his deadlines. The bedroom-cum-storage room at the end of the second story looked the most manageable place to start. She loved the daylight that poured in too, making the murky basement seem far away.

The tumbled books, all good-quality hardbacks, took little time to stack neatly. The photo albums she turned to next proved a very different challenge.

Chantal intended only to page casually through the uppermost album, but she soon become absorbed and sank onto the wicker chair. The glimpses the photos offered of Aunt Jeanne's younger life made her wonder if at least some of her great-aunt's wild stories weren't true. On one of the pages she found pictures of camel races. One of the jockeys looked tantalizingly like a very youthful Aunt Jeanne. Curly hair escaped from under a lightweight racing helmet, and the jockey's smile revealed small, even upper teeth, just like Jeanne's. In another, her aunt stood in a desert, with the pyramids clearly visible in the distance.

In each image, Aunt Jeanne stood alone or with a group of people, never as a couple with a man. Why had she never married? The subject had come up during Chantal's visits over the years, but her aunt's knack for light-hearted comments that quickly led to other topics never gave much away.

Chantal leaned back in the chair, ignoring the creaking protest from the wickerwork, and stared into space. What had Aunt Jeanne said once, long ago? One man had slipped away while she slept, or perhaps she'd said he'd not come back as he'd promised. She'd sensed her aunt had not been sure if this man had deserted her or been prevented from finding her.

Usually, on the topic of husbands, Aunt Jeanne would joke that suitors suited her but a spouse could be a louse. And then she'd neatly turn the tables on her niece and quiz her about boyfriends, a tactic that typically led to bored shrugs, given the uneventful state of Chantal's love life through most of her teens.

Now, Chantal looked at the spine of the album in her hands and read "1946". That made Jeanne just seventeen. She must have left France for her travels almost as soon as the dreary war years ended. The other albums bore dates from 1948 through to 1953. She put them in order.

1947 was missing.

When she'd come into the study that first night, minutes after Mulberry had knocked her over, a red album had been lying on the chair. Now it had disappeared. She had not imagined it. The albums in her neat pile all had blue and green bindings. She ferreted between the bags of clothes that covered half the floor and checked the closet. No red album.

Puzzled, she checked the last pages of the 1946 album. The shots suggested Jeanne had left North Africa. The scenery resembled southern Spain or Italy. Olive groves peppered rocky slopes and the brilliance of bougainvillea blazed forth, even in black and white.

In the background of one snapshot leaned a signpost. Chantal squinted at the lettering.

"Calvi." she muttered at last. Wasn't that in Corsica? She dimly remembered Aunt Jeanne mentioning that her mother, Chantal's great-grandmother, had been born in Corsica. Jeanne might have traveled there to meet relatives.

Hurriedly, she turned to the 1948 album. There were a few village scenes, dark-clothed figures in a café, two women at a well. She did not get a sense that any of the faces held significance. One last snap showed a small fishing boat moored at a jetty. The pale letters on her prow spelled out "Jeanne".

After that, the photos changed. It looked as if Jeanne had gone on a mad whirl of sightseeing. Chantal recognized monuments and landmarks from all over northern Europe. The faces kept changing. It was as if Jeanne had picked up traveling companions, then dropped them at will. A series of photos on a freighter led to scenes from Asia. By 1953 it appeared she'd returned to Cordes.

What had happened in the late forties? Once again, Chantal scoured the room for the missing album. She extended the search to the other bedrooms and into the linen cupboard. The red book had vanished.

Someone had taken it.

One of the Nazacs? They might have kept a copy of the key for the new front door lock they'd had installed, but since Chantal had seen Laurent with his girlfriend the day before, she was sure he wasn't Mulberry.

Berenger had had opportunity yesterday, in the flood. He'd come upstairs to fetch the quilt. Her sense of time had probably been as badly distorted then as it had been after the sugar that morning. He could have been gone ten minutes or ten seconds. Maybe the album showed some secret he'd blackmailed Jeanne over. He could have sent Mulberry to fetch it over the weekend, back when the old lock opened the front door and Berenger had a key. Mulberry had failed, interrupted by her arrival. Berenger had had to find an opportunity to do it himself.

Chantal shook her head at her thoughts. They amounted to nothing more than conjecture on assumption on guess. Berenger's angry exchange with Mezaute and her suspicions over the tainted foods represented her best evidence for foul play where he was concerned. But did she have enough to interest Inspector Riberon yet?

A brisk knock at the front door broke into her musings. Monsieur Bellec waited outside, a large toolbox in each hand. He wore bright blue overalls and gave the immediate impression of being constructed of circles, from his button eyes set in plump apple cheeks, to his pot belly.

"Mam'selle." He nodded his head in brief greeting, his gaze shifting at once towards the kitchen.

"Thank you for coming so soon." She waved him in and he strode to the scullery. The fuse box's plastic catch squeaked a few seconds later.

Chantal reached the scullery door and heard Bellec

muttering to himself.

"Do you need anything?" she asked.

He glanced over and held up his hand. "Don't touch anything. I have to keep the power on while I run my tests."

Chantal had no intention of touching anything until Bellec gave her the all-clear. She retreated to the kitchen table and watched through the open scullery door as the tradesman fussed in his toolbox. He took readings, first on the kettle, then back in the fuse box. She caught the sound of a sharp intake of breath.

"*Ah, non. Non, non, non,*" came Bellec's murmur of dismay. "*C'est pas possible.*"

"What's not possible?"

He looked across at her, his button eyes wide and dark. "Someone's tampered with this."

She goggled at him.

Her emotions churned: she wanted to fist-pump at this incontrovertible proof of modern human mischief; she wanted to run away and leave the house to the person who wanted it so badly. Berenger, Mulberry, whoever. An idea occurred to her.

"Monsieur, the deliberate damage you've seen, would you tell the police?"

"Police?" he looked up, even more dismayed than before.

"You're an expert, Monsieur, they'd listen to you," she said to soothe him. "That fuse box is new, you installed it, and you can see someone has interfered with it. I've told the police my suspicions, that something is wrong in this house, but they don't believe me. Now you can give them proof."

Bellec rubbed his chin.

"As the expert," Chantal reiterated.

The electrician looked more relaxed.

"What tampering can you see?"

He shook his head. "With a little bad luck, this could

have been murder, Mam'selle."

"But what did he do?" she probed again, even as his words chilled her.

"The kettle's quite new, yet it's live. Inside, there's a wire touching the metal case. *Un moment.*" He ducked back into the scullery and Chantal heard the clunk of a large switch.

"*Bien.* The power is off." He unplugged the kettle and placed it on the kitchen table. "This is proof for the police. You must not use it again, eh?"

Chantal shook her head vehemently. She'd heat a pan on the stove till she could buy a new kettle.

"But that is not all. This man, this…criminal, he has sabotaged the circuit breaker. It should have snapped inside when you were shocked, to cut off the circuit. But it is still running. If you had touched the kettle again, you would have been shocked again."

Chantal gingerly rubbed the burned area on her palm. Its throbbing had eased, but it could have been so much worse.

"Now, I make everything safe. And yes, I'll talk to the police if you wish."

* * *

That evening, Chantal scraped together dinner from tinned items from the pantry, having inspected each minutely for any sign of tampering. In the scullery, she knew the knife handle still jammed the thumb latch on the basement door. She was getting the hang of this house— and the person who laid its traps. Without doubt, someone had spiked the contents of the pantry and drinks cupboard. Roland Fleurie and his guilt over the murdered inquisitors had nothing to do with her twentieth-century torment. Number 8 was *not* haunted.

She'd find someone to analyze both the absinthe and an armful of rations from the pantry. If the tests came back positive, then, along with Bellec's testimony, she'd have two lots of rock-solid proof to take to Riberon in Albi. Evidence he couldn't ignore.

She remembered Grenier's freckle-faced stepson, Martin, from the café on Place de la Bride. He'd said he worked in a lab in Toulouse when he wasn't helping serve coffees. He might know someone who could run tests. In the morning, she'd buy breakfast up at the Place and ask him for advice. The plan of action buoyed her spirits.

Chantal sighed contentedly into her cup of chamomile tea, and at once wished she hadn't. The warm fumes reminded her of Berenger's breath on her cheek as he'd kissed her two nights ago. It seemed more like two months since that intense experience; so much had gone wrong since. Poisonings, passageways, photo albums. Broken trust.

She couldn't think of a single person in Cordes she could safely and sensibly talk to about what had been happening, yet she needed external perspective to sift through all the swirling possibilities. Her father used to say the simplest explanation tended to be the right one, but, in the midst of overlapping events, Chantal couldn't discern the overall pattern.

One thing she did see: her father, Terry, would be the perfect person to call. She checked her watch: early evening in England. With her chair close to the wood-heater, she placed the call, eager to hear him. He picked up after four rings and the sound of his familiar voice relaxed her. She should have called him much sooner.

"We're good, thanks," he said warmly in answer to her greeting. "Tricia's just taken the dogs for a walk round the village, but I know she'd love to say hello if we're still on the call when she gets back." Tricia had been Terry's partner for several years now. Chantal liked the petite blonde for her openness and for the obvious love she had for Terry. "You keeping safe in the big, bad capital?"

He didn't know she was in France instead of home in

London, Chantal realized. No surprise, really. Terry and Helene rarely spoke and her father had never been close to Helene's family—mostly because Helene herself wasn't. As far as Chantal could remember, Terry had only once met Aunt Jeanne, soon after he and Helene married.

"Not quite, Dad. I'm fighting off criminals in sleepy Cordes-sur-Ciel."

"What? You and your great-aunt are as thick as thieves again, you mean?" he joked.

She explained briefly about Aunt Jeanne's deadly fall and the need to tidy up her affairs. The words came more fluently now than they had in Lelou's office.

"Ah, I'm sorry, love, I know you were very fond of her. But to be there on your own…" He stopped. She could hear her father's disapproval coming down the phone line in silent waves.

She knew why. "It's fine, Dad, really. Situation normal."

"You could have asked me. I'd have come with you. Moral support at least."

"I know, but it was all a shock, and then a mad rush."

"She always asks for too much help. You don't ask for enough. I wish you'd let me get you into a place of your own again, instead of playing handmaiden to Helene on top of all your business worries."

"I know you do." She took a sip of her cooling tea. "And, look, here I am, ringing for your help now."

"Good," he said gruffly.

"If you've time?" Terry had lost a few of his workaholic tendencies under Tricia's insistent influence, but Chantal had learned not to assume she could hold his attention. "This is a bit of a knotty problem."

"Better let me call you then. Don't want Jeanne's estate to rack up a huge phone bill and you to get blamed."

When they had successfully reconnected, Chantal asked, "Got a whisky in reach?"

"Will I need it?"

"Afraid so. I wasn't joking about the criminals, and I need you relaxed enough to think, not all worked up."

"Crikey, Chantal. I thought Lotty living in Papua New Guinea with pygmies would be the death of me. Wait."

Chantal grinned as she heard liquid gurgling into a glass. She raised her mug of tea in silent salute.

When Terry announced his return, she began. "Aunt Jeanne's death may not have been an accident, Dad. Someone tried very hard to scare her out of this house. In fact, they succeeded. She ran off to a friend's place nearby and she agreed to sell Number 8. And, Dad, she loved this house. She wanted to die in it. She would never have willingly sold it."

She heard her father gulp a mouthful of whisky and heave a huge sigh. "Has someone bought it?"

"Yes." She decided to leave out the ownership complication for now and quickly sketched in the key details about Berenger Morel. "If he was acting his surprise when I told him Aunt Jeanne had died, he should get an Oscar. I really don't think he knew, and yet…"

"And yet?" Terry urged.

"No one else wants the house. He has the motive. But then I had the intruder knock me over, and Berenger is far too tall to be him."

"*Intruder*?"

"A short man in a mulberry scarf." Again, she filled in quick details.

In reply, she heard the whisky glass being refilled. "They could be partners, Chantal. Or your Mulberry is in this Morel's pay. Simplest explanations, remember. There can't be different motives going on here. But, since Jeanne had already agreed to sell, what would be the point in Morel & Co killing her? Or even in scaring her any more?" He paused and Chantal could picture his brows furrowing under his thatch of gray-blond hair. "And are you certain about the scare tactics? It might have been old age creeping up on her. Failing memory, weaker judgment."

"Dad, it wasn't. I know, because I've suffered the scare tactics too." She stared up at the ancient ceiling timbers as she counted events off in her head. "In the three days I've been here, I've had three hallucinations that went on for hours, two of them seriously scary. Someone has spiked food and drink in here somehow. And two big dramas in the house; the electrician said the one this morning was definite sabotage and could have been fatal. It—"

"Then for God's sake, get out of there and come home!"

"Not till I know who's behind all this, Dad." She put her mug down and rubbed at the tension in her forehead. "I owe Aunt Jeanne that much. I hate to think of her being too scared to stay in the home she'd dedicated her life to, only daring to return in daylight."

Her father made a noise of strangled frustration.

"I'm gathering evidence to take back to the police," she went on hurriedly. "To make them accept there was foul play and that Aunt Jeanne's death needs proper investigation as more than an accident. Once I've got them working on the case, I can come home."

"How the hell can people get in and out of that house at will to set up these so-called accidents? Even in rural France they must have keys and the common sense to use them?"

"Don't worry, I've got new locks on the front door, and a stout chair under the back door. But Aunt Jeanne was more casual with security. And there's more." She hesitated, and looked around the bright kitchen, and its tightly fastened shutters. No one could be listening, could they?

"Come on, out with it," Terry said impatiently.

Her voice dropped to a whisper. "I found one more way into the house today. A way I don't think Aunt Jeanne knew about, though I'm sure she'd tried to find it. It's a long-lost passage leading underground from behind a false wall in the basement. It goes to a very narrow archway. I didn't find out what lay the other side of the arch, but someone had recently come through it, from the other side…"

A glass slammed onto a wooden table at the other end of the phone. "That's it! I'm coming down there. And till I get there, I want you in a hotel. A big one, with good security. I'll pay, just get yourself somewhere safe."

"It's OK, Dad." She tried to placate him, even as she enjoyed being the target of his strong protective instinct. She'd had too little of it growing up in her mother's house. "I've got the basement barred off too. And I really feel I'm getting the measure of this villain."

"Oh sure, right until he turns up from yet another secret passage and stands over your bed with an ax. I mean it, Chantal, this sounds serious. Get out. And while you're at it book two rooms. I'm going to clear my diary and come down there."

Chantal shrugged. "I'd welcome the support, Dad, but you always have a lot on. And I feel better just for thinking this through with you. But I'm not moving tonight." In truth, she was bone-tired after her eventful day. "I'm going to bed in a minute."

"Check the locks."

"I have. But I'll check them all again, just for you."

"I'll call you in the morning to make sure you're alive."

She chuckled. "I'd like that."

*   *   *

In the middle of the night, her palm woke her with its throbbing. An uneventful trip down to the kitchen's first aid box built her confidence. As she rummaged for painkillers, the faint sound of metal tapping on stone reached her. It came from everywhere and nowhere.

"Flashback," she muttered, firmly ignoring it. She trudged back up to bed. As she turned off the light, a final thought came to her.

Berenger would never fit through the Eye of the Needle. Whoever smashed the wall down, it hadn't been him.

CHAPTER NINETEEN

Chantal's palm bothered her as she dressed the next morning. She'd wanted to see Mezaute, the doctor, and this painful little injury gave her an excellent reason. When she rang, the receptionist offered her a cancellation. The doctor could see her in an hour, if she could get there?

She could. Expecting to be out for a while, she called her father first, reassuring him she'd slept well, and that her skull remained free of ax blades.

"I'm working on clearing my diary," he warned her, ignoring her attempt at humor. "I want to come and keep an eye on you. And next time we talk, I want to hear you've moved into a big, safe hotel."

She ducked making an actual promise and distracted her father with questions about Tricia and the dogs.

After she hung up, she checked her watch. She had enough time to walk up to Place de la Bride for breakfast. She kept her fingers crossed she'd find Martin on duty. On the way, she also kept a sharp lookout for a head of wiry, dark hair on a tall, broad body. Her luck held; she didn't see him.

At the café, her luck promptly ran out. Martin wasn't due on shift till eleven. In a dark corner of the café, she ate an enormous breakfast and pondered how best to approach Doctor Mezaute. Linking her injury to questions about Aunt Jeanne's health seemed the best route.

The doctor worked from a solid stone house in the newest part of Cordes, near the outermost town wall. The building looked a mere hundred years old. Mezaute stood waiting in his consulting room as Chantal entered. His clean-shaven head gleamed as if he'd polished it. He wore a short-sleeved white smock that reached to his hips and, below that, smart navy slacks. His dapper dress reminded her of a younger version of Armand. The first five minutes of the appointment passed in small talk about the funeral and the suddenness of Aunt Jeanne's death.

"And what can I do for you?" he finally asked.

She showed him her palm and explained how she'd come by the injury.

He shook his head. "That house needs renovating from top to bottom. Your great-aunt had a series of problems this winter."

"So I've heard. She also kept mislaying things."

"Don't we all, as we grow older," he said smoothly, probing her burn gently.

"Why did you prescribe her sleeping tablets, Doctor?"

"Sleeping tablets?"

"Doctor Bastien in Albi mentioned it. So did the friend she went to stay with when the house got to be too much." She hoped he'd pick up her emphasis on the last two words.

"It sounds as if you have been busy, Mademoiselle," he said mildly. "Now, this burn of yours."

"My palm is the least of my health problems."

His eyebrows flicked up. "You're ill?"

"I believe I have the same symptoms that drove my aunt from her house. Surely she told you about them?"

He dropped her hand. "I may be old-fashioned, but I believe your aunt's health is her private affair."

"Aunt Jeanne is dead," Chantal said pointedly. "She has

no privacy you need to protect. So please tell me, did she complain of any experiences like these?" She listed the scariest visions and sounds she'd experienced, starting with the donkey-headed man.

He tilted his head, staring at a framed print of Munch's *The Scream* that hung above his desk. "I will discuss your case, and your case alone, Mademoiselle. If you keep asking questions about your great-aunt, I shall ask you to leave. I have a duty to open files to the police…" His eyes moved to a gray cabinet at his side. It had four deep drawers with alphabet labels on each. "But not to you."

She refused to let him fob her off. "Would you say my symptoms sound like the kind of hallucinations that could be caused by recreational drugs?"

He continued to stare at the tortured face in the print. "Personally, I can think of another cause."

"Well?"

"Number 8 is haunted."

She gaped.

He cleared his throat. "A man of science must be allowed his beliefs."

"Not if they blind him to an obvious explanation under his very nose!"

He spun around to face her. "This appointment is over. Get some anti-burn cream for your hand. And move out of your aunt's house if you can't stand the ghostly company. I'm sure you have a life elsewhere to return to."

A deafening crash and telltale tinkle of broken glass from the reception area shocked them both. Shouts rose in volume. The loudest called for the doctor to hurry.

Mezaute leapt up, a curse on his lips. He jerked his head at Chantal. The message was clear: *leave my office.* Chantal led the way to the waiting room. Mezaute pushed past her to the mess of glass and a spreading pool of blood. Chantal watched for a moment. All eyes had fastened on the injured man and the chaos of the upturned instrument tray.

She slipped back into the consulting room. She'd never stolen anything in her life, but she intended to steal Aunt Jeanne's file. The mention of haunting had raised her hackles and her suspicions.

She tugged at the cabinet drawer labeled 'F-L' and scrabbled at the furthest files. Leblanc. Too far. Labarre. Not far enough. Her breath came in short gasps. Lamartine, Jean. Nearly there. Lamarque, Jeanne. She hauled the file out and thrust it under her coat.

The hubbub from the accident had started to die down. Chantal couldn't bear to be caught red-handed by Mezaute. She headed to the patio doors that led outside. She craned her neck to see if the outdoor area led anywhere but couldn't see.

The patio door handle wouldn't open. Panic blossomed before she saw the key in the lock. It turned easily.

She slipped out and into the narrow garden. Ducking under each window, she crept to the far end. An alley between the doctor's and the next house led out to the main street. She ran towards it. At every step, she expected Mezaute's arm to grab her from behind.

Joining the shoppers and early tourists, Chantal headed off into the warren of medieval lanes as fast as she could. As usual, she got lost, but she knew safety lay upwards.

She strode past an office supplies and services store, its sleek window display at odds with the heavy timber framing. An idea occurred to her and she backtracked into the store. It didn't take long for the bored teenage assistant to run off a copy of the file's contents. When Chantal emerged, she headed down the hill once more and, after a couple of tries, found her way to the doctor's surgery. She fell into step behind a large lady who was entering the building. To the left of the front desk, an archway led to the administration area behind reception. It took a moment to slip the file into a pile of papers.

For the second time in half an hour, Chantal left the doctor's. No longer rushed, she found Rue Obscure easily.

"Sorry, Aunt Jeanne," she said aloud to the kitchen as she pulled the photocopied file out of the envelope. Her intrusion had good motives, but she couldn't throw off a sense of guilt. She looked for the most recent entries. Mezaute wrote surprisingly legibly, in a large, looped hand with occasional flourishes.

Near the bottom of the last page, she saw an entry for February of the current year. Aunt Jeanne had complained of stomach upsets. Chantal remembered all the brown bottles in the bathroom. Most of those had been for indigestion, but they were hardly modern medicine.

Chantal turned to the previous page. Mezaute's writing filled it. She read the entries, hardly breathing. "Presented with burn from electric shock. Dressed wound and instructed to change dressing in two days. Complains of broken sleep. Prescribed mild sedative. Complains of weakness in leg muscles and occasional numbness. Prescribed relaxant. Presented with insomnia. Prescribed new sedative. Complains of visual disturbances. Recommended ophthalmologist. Complains of sounds in ear — tinnitus? Prescribed decongestant."

It went on and on. Jeanne had visited Mezaute no fewer than six times through mid-January and early March. Reading between the doctor's carefully constructed lines, Aunt Jeanne had suffered the same problems as Chantal. More, it looked as if the severity of her symptoms had worsened gradually. That might explain something that had been bothering Chantal: why would her normally astute aunt not reach the same suspicions that she had? The slow onset must have helped confuse her.

Chantal leaned back on the kitchen chair. What did it all mean? Mezaute had something to hide or he wouldn't have been so economical with the truth.

She remembered the angry words between Berenger and Mezaute. Berenger wanted Aunt Jeanne to sell. Maybe their agreement was for the doctor to scare Jeanne out of the house. That fitted what she'd overheard. And it fitted with the best motive she'd found so far. She had to face facts where Berenger was concerned.

If only it weren't so hard.

With a paper and pencil, she marshaled her thoughts. Next, she rummaged in her purse for a business card. When the duty sergeant in Albi answered, she asked for Inspector Riberon.

After a long wait, he came on the line, his voice dog-tired. Despite his evident fatigue, he listened without interrupting. When she finished, he asked a couple of clarifying questions about the electrician, Bellec, and the kettle before adding, "Will you be bringing in these samples you believe are laced with some drug for testing?"

She hesitated. Did this policeman have the power to change police lab results if his influential friends needed assistance?

"Because if you do," said the weary voice, "don't bother bringing in the absinthe or any other liquid."

"Why not?" She bristled. The absinthe was one of her best exhibits.

"The common hallucinogens are water soluble. A child could contaminate a liquid. It'd never stand up in court. Bring crystals, dried foods. It takes more than a basic understanding of chemistry to spike those."

"Like the sugar?"

"Like the sugar, Mademoiselle." He hung up.

She stared at the phone, weighing her options. Should she take samples to the police, or someone else, or both? She shrugged. It wouldn't hurt to see what test facilities Martin knew of.

Her watch told her a morning coffee would be in order, and she knew where she'd be buying it. Locking the front door carefully again, she sauntered along Rue Obscure, through the shadowed tunnel and up Les Rampes. The covered marketplace hummed with activity as locals sought their caffeine fix and the latest gossip. Chantal moved on to where she'd had breakfast.

Martin appeared at her side almost before she was through the café door. "Mademoiselle. *Enchanté.* I'm sorry I missed you before, but I can't handle early mornings."

Chantal gave him her brightest smile. A little honey couldn't do any harm. She ordered a coffee and then added, "And can I have a quiet word with you, too? I need your advice." She'd have sworn his chest puffed up.

When he returned with her drink, she nodded at the seat opposite. He sat down.

"I've had food poisoning." It was hardly a lie. "I rang the manufacturer to complain and they won't take it seriously. I want the rest of the food tested."

If he was disappointed she didn't want something more personal from him, he hid it well. "I could take it to my pharmacology lab. The guys there could take a look if you want."

She wanted someone completely independent of Berenger and his friends. "No offense, Martin, I'm sure you'd do a great job, but what I need is a specialist food lab." She nudged him for more ideas.

"You could try chemists," he offered. "They'd only send it off to the kind of independent testing lab you're after, though. If you're in a hurry, go straight to one of them." He didn't know any but brought her the café's Yellow Pages and suggested a couple of headings to look under. She'd started to leaf through it before she noticed he hadn't moved off to serve other customers.

"There's a simpler solution." His tone was reluctant. "You could ask Berenger."

"Berenger?"

"Bio-chem was part of his viticulture degree. Wine making's just a sexy form of chemistry, after all. He's got a nice little lab on the estate. I'm sure he could help."

Her heart thumped. Could Berenger have the skills to adulterate sugar crystals? Had she just added means to his obvious motive?

CHAPTER TWENTY

"That's all for now." Riberon flipped his notebook shut. "Sorry I had to get you down here like this, Morel, but it's procedure when we receive a credible report from the public."

"You will be sorry if you breathe a word of this," Berenger snapped back. If Louise suffered because the truth got out... His anger had been on a low simmer all through the interview. This last thought shot an incandescent dragon's breath on the cauldron of his fury.

He stood up. The hard metal chair bounced off his calves and clattered on the tiled floor of the interview room. He looked down at Riberon. "You're still refusing to tell me who told you all this?"

"I am. Standard policy." Berenger's bulk and prickliness clearly didn't bother the Inspector.

"I'll figure it out for myself."

"As you like. Just stay within the law."

Berenger strode out of the Albi police station into the flat light of an overcast late afternoon. He gunned the SUV's engine for the satisfaction of hearing it protest at the high revs. The end-of-work traffic slowed his progress through the city, but, once he was on the open road back to Cordes, he stamped on the accelerator.

Row after row of vines flew by on either side, their bare stems like black charcoal tracings across the chalky soil. Normally, the sight would have cheered him. He loved vineyards in all seasons. In the dark days after Mireille's death, when Louise lay in the hospital, it had been the estate, and particularly the vines, that had given him a few precious hours' relief. Kept him strong for his daughter.

He pushed a hand through his hair. He could hardly believe the accident had happened only two years before. It felt like another man who'd been married to Mireille, another man who'd paced the hospital, waiting for the experts to mend his little girl. They hadn't been able to.

The hurt cramped in his chest, an old, familiar pain. He'd never reconciled himself to Louise's disability. Somewhere, he knew, lay a cure.

For a full minute, he cursed whoever had found out about the arrangement with Mezaute and got the police involved. Had it been Mezaute's receptionist, whose mother had challenged Louise after the funeral? But she'd no reason to tell the police.

Then it hit him. He'd complained to the doctor at the wine store. In his mind's eye, he saw the view from the office upstairs at the rear of the building. The light had illuminated part of Jeanne Lamarque's tiny backyard.

He hit the steering wheel.

Who else but Chantal?

In her quest for answers about her elderly aunt, she was ready to seize on any clue. And to think he'd been worried about her this last couple of days when she'd not answered the phone or the door. So much for their truce to solve the mysteries around Jeanne. She'd distorted what she'd overheard in the back yard to fit her suspicions. Then she'd run to the police.

What did it take to reassure her? He'd played chauffeur, host, handyman and rescuer, and still she doubted him.

When she'd taken enough advantage, she called the police down on him. She must be laughing. Not only did she have possession of the house, she had him leaping about like a trained monkey, too.

A junction on the outskirts of Cordes lay ahead. Left would take him home. He swung the wheel hard right. He'd had enough of being used. It was time Chantal repaid her debts.

The shutters at Number 8 were folded back and a kitchen window hung ajar. She had to be in. As usual, the door knocker distracted him. The couple's eternal lovemaking tugged at him. How long since he'd been that close to a woman?

Longer than anyone would believe.

Since meeting Chantal, he'd become painfully aware of his monkish life. The descending path of her gaze on him in the kitchen the other day had been like a trickle of molten metal. He'd have sworn her rush to get away was because she felt the same tension. Pity she hadn't exploited him for *that* particular need. He'd have got some benefit, at least.

He hammered his frustration on the old timbers of the door. They shivered under his assault.

"Who's there?" Chantal's voice sounded apprehensive.

"Your errand boy!" He slapped a palm on the door.

Three seconds' silence stretched like minutes. At last, Chantal replied, "Go away. I've nothing to say to you."

This doorstep belonged to him as much as her. Two strides away, the open kitchen window beckoned, its sill level with his hips. He unhooked the window catch and pulled it wide open. A moment later, he stood on the old linoleum floor.

At the door to the hall, he collided with Chantal, who clutched a thermos. His arms encircled her of their own accord. She gasped. Half of him wanted to squeeze the living breath from her. Every gasp would soothe his disillusionment. The other half wanted to do very gentle things to her mouth. It was there for the taking, just inches below his own.

Within his arms, he found she'd changed shape. He couldn't feel the graceful lines of her lean back. He loosened his arms and scowled at the problem. She wore a thick jacket with a scarf and heavy shoes. The sight of the warm, sensible clothing slowed him down. "You're not going out for your picnic till I've said a few things to you."

Chantal used her free hand to shove him hard in the chest. "Let me go! How dare you break in here again?"

He propelled her into the parlor, ignoring her protests. He kicked the door shut and nudged her onto the ottoman.

"Thanks to you, I've spent the afternoon at the police station. You eavesdropped on Mezaute and me, didn't you? No, you sit and listen. I've had to explain that conversation to Riberon, though it's no one else's confounded business. And I finally satisfied him."

Chantal tried to say something, but he shut his ears. "Nothing convinces you, does it? I'm still the prime suspect. Next time you want help, go and find some other gullible idiot." He had to stop for breath.

She cut in, her gray eyes chilly as rain. "Yes, you are my prime suspect. You might have bought off your policeman friend with a clever story, but I know what I heard. You, your father and that doctor are in on some deal to do with Aunt Jeanne."

"The deal has nothing to do with Jeanne. It's private." Although today it seemed like half of France knew of it.

"Of course it's *private*."

"Dammit, it's true! There's a medical problem in our family."

Silently, she raised a skeptical eyebrow.

"If I had a better excuse, I'd use it," he snapped. The edges of his anger curled away from him. He flung open the drinks cabinet. It looked emptier than he remembered it. The absinthe bottle had gone. Tossed out, he hoped.

Better than thinking she'd been too inebriated to answer his calls. He slowly drew out a brandy bottle.

"Are you really going to drink that?" She sounded genuinely interested.

"Afraid I'll get drunk and tell you a few home truths?"

A spasm of irritation passed over Chantal's face. "You sure as heck don't seem to be holding back right now." She nodded at the bottle. "Go on then."

He hesitated. He didn't want the drink. It had simply been a way to show her his frustration.

"No? I thought not."

What was she talking about?

"Meanwhile, I've something to do," Chantal said. "Don't worry, I've no intention of asking for your help. And, for the record, I've never asked for your help. You've forced it on me when I've been too tired to fight you." She picked up the thermos and swept into the kitchen to latch the window. "I'm leaving. Take the brandy if you want it." She opened the front door and threw him a pointed look over her shoulder.

She might be finished with him but he'd hardly begun with her. "Where are you going?"

"I'm not accountable to you."

"Yes, you are. I'm calling in the debts you owe me. We'll start by pooling what we've found out about Jeanne's death these last couple of days."

"I'm not working with a man I can't trust." She stepped outside.

Short of shouting after her from the doorstep, he had to follow. The force field of her will dragged him into the street, trailing in her wake like a scolded dog.

He fought for control. "Perhaps you've forgotten, but a couple of days ago you were happy to use my contacts and police appointments. You didn't trust me then, either."

"But now I'm doing fine with leads of my own." She strode off west along Rue Obscure.

He pulled the front door shut behind him and heard

the lock click. By using every inch of his long legs he caught her up without seeming to rush. "Very well. I'll start," he said. "I've spoken to the neighbors here, those I could find. Number 6 is empty, it's a vacation rental at the moment. And the people in Number 10 are out of town. The neighbors further along each side saw nothing Friday lunchtime."

"And I'll tell you this much, if you think I owe you. Except for Laurent, all my leads point to you as guilty."

It was the perfect moment to pull his rabbit out the hat. "Talking of young Nazac, I've figured out what was behind his absences."

"A plump, curly-haired young lady. Congratulations."

It was like being six and hearing the biggest present under the Christmas tree was for someone else. He gritted his teeth and focused on the key point. "So Mulberry isn't one of my employees. And that means I'm much less likely to be your ogre."

"You're still the ogre. You've got private little deals you won't come clean about."

His jaw tensed. "And you haven't anything private in your life, Chantal? Hmm? How about the person who hurt you so much you can't bear to trust anyone?" When he heard her sharp intake of breath, he knew he'd hit home. He'd bet every acre at La Picarie it had been a man who'd wounded her.

She swung around to look at him. In the half-light, her eyes had taken on a new hue. Not steel, nor smoke, but bleak, like a featureless horizon on a dull day.

"*Touché*," she muttered.

Berenger pushed his hand through his hair. "You see, we both have skeletons to hide."

"At least my skeleton only affects me."

"Lucky you," he said bitterly and looked away from her.

They'd reached the cobbles below the massive arch of Porte des Ormeaux. In silence, Chantal turned left to where the street widened into Place Fontournies. Beyond, the street narrowed sharply as it twisted west, and steepened towards the valley below.

She finally paused where the road surface changed to modern tarmac. "Do you plan to follow me all the way or can I get on with my own business?"

"I plan to follow you."

"Why?" she huffed.

"Because I'm betting this is somehow to do with Jeanne Lamarque. You're obsessed. And so far, when you work on that subject on your own you turn up problems for me." He'd spoken the truth. She created trouble. But she also attracted it. He wasn't sure he could stand to see her in pain again.

Chantal eyed him appraisingly. "Then take note. I'm not asking for your help. Tag along if you must, but don't get in my way."

CHAPTER TWENTY-ONE

Chantal set off again. When she turned into the steep alley called La Peyrade, Berenger began to guess her destination.

"You're going to pay your respects to your great-aunt?" Already, he could glimpse the wall of the town's new cemetery.

She answered by turning onto a gravel track just short of the graveyard. Here, a short grass bank formed the eastern wall of the cemetery. Fifty yards along, she slithered down it to where a clump of elder trees shielded them from the graves.

"What are we doing?" Berenger asked.

Chantal put her finger to his lips for silence. At her touch, he drew in a sharp breath. She removed her finger with a soft downward stroke. Against all odds, she had given him a light caress. His heart rate kicked up a notch, but she appeared unmoved.

She stared through the tree trunks and, in a low voice, said, "Council caretaker rang me this afternoon. Saw someone around Aunt Jeanne's grave yesterday evening. Chased him off. Sounded like it could be Mulberry."

Why was he not surprised she'd organized spies around the town? "And?"

"I've come to see if he'll return now it's getting dark again. To catch him. Make him talk."

"On your *own?*" He found it hard to keep his voice quiet. The danger of her plan turned his guts to water.

"Shh!" She pulled him into a crouch.

"He threw you down the stairs!" He hoped his whisper sounded ferocious. "He could smash your brains out on a tombstone!"

"What do you care?" Her answering whisper was truculent.

"Let's just say the burning question of who owns your aunt's house will get solved faster with two of us on the job."

"Then keep up. Unless you're scared of ghosts." After another brief check, she crept forward beyond the trees. He followed.

They settled in the shadow of one of the few high-sided concrete vaults. It gave them a good view of Jeanne's grave. The still-fresh bouquets of white lilies lying on the granite slab shone through the gloom.

Berenger worried that they'd not chosen a hiding spot between Jeanne's resting place and the cemetery gate. Their position gave any grave robber a good chance of escape. Torn, he kept his thoughts to himself. He wanted the pleasure of catching Mulberry and twisting that damned scarf around his neck till he spat his secrets out like pips from a grape. At the same time, an easy getaway would keep Chantal safer. The best answer was for Berenger to get to the man before Chantal did.

The buried dead didn't bother Berenger at all, but the seeping cold did. Daylight had faded and the moon had yet to rise. One star pricked the blue-black canopy. It would only grow colder. Unlike Chantal, he hadn't come dressed for the night.

Minutes ticked by. To keep his mind off the chill, he began a mental list of better places to spend time with a woman. The Grand Ecuyer Hotel right here in town would be a good start. The food was outstanding and the restaurant had private corners ideal for an intimate dinner for two.

A drive through the vineyards to a picnic spot he knew came to mind, too. In another fortnight, the spring leaves would be out in vibrant shades of lime-green.

Would this woman even be here then? Her fluent French made it too easy to forget she was a tourist. Hello, goodbye. He owed it to Louise to aim for relationships that had at least a chance of long-term success.

Chantal's hand on his sleeve jerked him back to the present. A shadow slipped between two vaults near the gate. It halted, then moved forward. He got a sense of broad shoulders on a short body. It had to be a man. Mulberry.

Finally, the man reached Jeanne's tomb.

Berenger hoped Chantal would wait till Mulberry got busy before leaping out. In the dim starlight, he caught a gleam of metal in the man's hand. Whatever he held looked over six inches long. He leaned towards Chantal and whispered, "He's armed."

A small nod showed she'd heard.

Mulberry crouched at the head of Jeanne's vault. The faint scrape of metal on stone told them he planned to lever the lid to one side.

Chantal shot out.

Berenger snatched at her jacket, but she moved too fast for his cold fingers.

"*Arrête!* Stop!" she shrieked, running straight towards the danger.

In answer, the metal implement clattered as it bounced on the concrete slab of a nearby tomb. Mulberry whirled around and, as Berenger had foreseen, headed for the exit.

Berenger sprang to his feet and cursed at the pain from his chilled leg muscles. They headed in a three-way sprint for the gate. Mulberry paused to wrench it open. Chantal was almost upon him. Berenger darted forward to shield her from any violence.

His left foot hooked under Chantal's as he ran past her.

They both sprawled headlong on the path.

Berenger leapt up, winded, but too charged with adrenalin to feel pain. He tried to kick into top gear, but his lungs refused point-blank. Mulberry vanished ahead of him into the dark alleys.

By the time he'd wheezed his way back to the graveyard, Chantal had found a perch on a tomb next to her aunt's. Her left hand rubbed her right knee vigorously. "I *told* you not to get in my way!"

Her words shortened his temper. "I was trying to protect you. He had a weapon."

"A garden trowel." She pointed at the round-nosed tool on her aunt's grave cover. "Which he dropped. And forgive me if I can't help noticing that each time you chase Mulberry he gets away."

"He runs like a rocket! You haven't done any better."

"That's because Sir Galahad sent the damsel flying." She shivered. "Oh, do something useful. Take your shining armor and fetch the thermos."

He bit his tongue and did as she asked. The short walk helped calm him a little. He couldn't argue with her. If he hadn't pushed forward, they'd have the villain in a chokehold, coughing up some answers. Answers that might have budged the log jam over the time of death. Then the house sale might be on again.

On his way back he paused to wrap the trowel in a handkerchief. He hoped Mulberry might have left prints—and that the police would have a record of them.

As he drew closer to Chantal he saw her flexing her knee. He watched, debating what to say. In his experience, women in pain took offense very easily.

She responded to his silence with a sharp look. "This would be a good point for you to express sympathy."

He kept it short. "I'm sorry your knee's sore. Can I help you back up the hill?"

It must have hurt because she accepted his offer without the usual fight. Her weight on his arm heightened his other senses. He noted wood smoke, the exhaust of a passing car, the sweet waft from a tub of nodding freesias. His eyes stayed alert to any shifting shadow that might threaten her. Why did it have to be a troublesome tourist who made him feel twice as alive?

*   *   *

At Number 8, Berenger kicked his dew-drenched shoes off in the hall. "Put the kettle on. I'll get the wood stove fired up."

That earned him another sharp look. "Other way round."

He threw up his hands. "Please. Feel free to demonstrate your Girl Scout skills."

While Chantal shed her outdoor clothes, Berenger looked around the kitchen for the kettle. He spotted it beside the trash can. Chantal came through, and he gestured with it. "What was this doing on the floor?"

She stared at him.

He filled the kettle, and plugged it in, resting his fingers on the cold cylinder as his thumb reached for the switch.

A sharp, hot tingling made him recoil and a punch from nowhere thudded into his shoulder. His yell mingled with Chantal's shout of alarm.

She dragged over a chair and he sat heavily.

"That was either the best double bluff I've ever seen -— or it was for real."

He didn't understand her words. The shock had confused him.

"The way you went for the kettle, no flinching…I know what it's like. The kettle zapped me yesterday." She flashed him her palm, a white dressing almost filling its width. "Worse than yours, because the circuit breaker had been tampered with, too. But that's been fixed."

"It was for real, I promise," he said, his hand shaking. "Could you bring that brandy? I need it."

She came back with the bottle and a glass. "Don't you think this is going a bit far?"

"Eh?"

She poured a solid inch into the glass and held it to his lips as if he were an invalid.

"I can manage." He took hold of the glass and tried to tilt it.

She resisted. "Got the antidote handy? Cooked up a cure in your lab?"

"Hmm? It's brandy. Not your absinthe."

They struggled over the glass again. Chantal pulled it from his shaky hold and poured it down the sink. "Maybe the brandy isn't pure brandy."

"What?"

"You didn't know about the kettle. You were prepared to drink the brandy. I wonder…"

She squatted beside the wood-heater. As she prepped it, she talked. Her words painted a grim picture of the house he longed to take ownership of. She'd suffered more than he'd realized. Someone had set a series of traps for Jeanne Lamarque, and her great-niece had walked into the leftovers.

Chantal led him through her call to Riberon that morning, when she'd told the inspector both about Bellec's discovery of tampering with the electrics, and the conversation she'd overheard between Berenger and Mezaute the night before. She'd promised Riberon he could expect to hear from a testing lab in Toulouse. She'd then driven to Toulouse with samples, a trip that had taken most of the afternoon.

Berenger could see she was doing her damnedest to triumph over the hidden assailant. But plenty of questions remained.

"Why didn't you tell me the absinthe episode was your second hallucination attack?"

"Because you'd have taken it as confirmation I was a junkie. And for a while I half thought it might be old Fleurie's influence. You think even less of ghosts than drugs."

She cared what he thought. Warmth prickled through his still-chilled limbs.

"So, you see, now I know how Aunt Jeanne grew so scared she left her beloved home. Hallucinogens in the starring role and a supporting cast of household booby-traps. And you, Berenger Morel, you not only have the best motive, you have the means."

The flickering heat inside him sputtered out.

Chantal stood up. "You've got a lab to prepare the chemicals. I'm told spiking sugar takes some skill."

"I dare say," he said grimly. "But a chemist could do it. Or a medic. I bet even Martin up in the café could manage it."

"And you handled the flood well."

"The estate uses a lot of piping. But I'm no electrician."

"And you had opportunity," she drove on relentlessly. "You could have got in here by climbing over the back wall. I bet Aunt Jeanne took as little care locking that door as she did the front one."

"So you still don't trust me, Chantal? The kettle, the brandy, don't count?"

Her lashes drooped.

"I didn't do it," he said wearily. "I didn't spike her sugar or wreck her pipes. I didn't scare Jeanne Lamarque from this house."

"Do you realize," said Chantal in surprise, "that you've never denied it before? You've talked a lot, but you've never simply denied it. Why not?"

"I guess I thought I'd said it a hundred ways. I thought it was obvious. Does this mean you suddenly trust me?"

She shook her head. "I can't tell if I can trust you till I know what the Mezaute deal is all about. Prove it wasn't about Jeanne, or me. You were worried about me asking questions. You said I was persistent." The steel had spread from her eyes to her voice.

He let out a sigh. Could he afford the price of winning her trust? Could he stand to see her walk away? In her presence he felt as if he'd woken from a two-year sleep.

On impulse, he stretched forward and planted a gentle kiss on her lips. She didn't move.

"How about a bargain, Chantal? I'll tell you my secret. If it makes you trust me at last…" He paused. "…then you tell me a secret. Maybe the one about that man."

Her eyes widened. "That's a high price."

"You'll only pay if you believe me."

"I'd like to trust you," she said, reaching out to touch his hand. "I need someone to trust. I'd like it to be you."

He grasped her hand between his palms and searched her face for an answer.

After a long pause, she nodded slowly. "If I believe yours," she murmured, "then I'll tell you mine."

He took a deep breath. "OK. What you heard. It wasn't about Jeanne. It wasn't about you. It was about Louise."

"Louise?"

"Yes, my poor, blind daughter. That's what we're trying to hide. Louise isn't blind at all."

CHAPTER TWENTY-TWO

Chantal stared at Berenger in disbelief. The electric jolt had obviously fried his brain. "Of course Louise is blind. On the night I arrived, I watched her use the wall and the sound of my voice as guides."

"She's not blind. She just can't see."

Chantal pulled a face and rocked back on her kitchen chair.

"Blind people have something physically wrong," Berenger explained. "But a hundred tests say Louise's eyes, nerves and brain all work. She isn't blind…"

"But she can't see?"

"Exactly. Another part of her brain, away from the part that decodes the messages from the eye, is blocking the pictures of what she sees."

"It happened in the accident?"

Berenger nodded. "Mireille and Louise got trapped in the car wreck. When the emergency services reached them, Mireille had slipped into a coma from blood loss. Louise was fully conscious but couldn't see." His eyes focused somewhere beyond the kitchen. "Our best guess is that she watched Mireille bleed to death. The seat had pinned her in. She couldn't move to help her mother. It was so harrowing that her brain closed her sight down."

Chantal bit her lip. "That's awful," she whispered.

"And she hasn't seen anything since. They call it hysterical blindness."

"Is…" The words caught in Chantal's throat. "Is there a cure?"

"Every case is different. We've tried psychotherapy. We've tried giving it time. Nothing's worked."

"Louise's situation is difficult for all of you. But why does it have to be a secret?"

"Two reasons." He shifted on the hard chair. "You saw the first one after the funeral. People hear a whisper of the truth and they immediately think she's mentally ill. This is a small country town. Madness is something to fear, not pity or help. We want to shield Louise from that." He sighed. "The other reason came from her therapist. If Louise knows there's no physical reason she can't see, she'll end up doubting her own senses. That will only add to the confusion and guilt she's suffering."

"She must know it wasn't her fault her mother died?"

"We've told her that, of course. She may know it in her head, but she doesn't feel it inside."

"What do you tell her about why she can't see?"

"We've said something bad happened in the car crash. It hurt part of her brain and that's affected her eyes. We've also said that nobody knows if it will ever heal. It's almost the truth." The lines at the edge of his mouth deepened.

Chantal replayed what she'd overheard between Mezaute and Berenger. "So when you said to Mezaute that 'she' was asking questions and 'she' was being persistent, you meant Louise. Not me."

"You come a close second."

She aimed a playful kick towards his shin. "And the secret deal was that Mezaute and his nurses would keep quiet about her blindness being emotional rather than physical. One of them must have blabbed."

"Not me or my father. Even Ah Wong doesn't know,

and I only told Riberon today because I had to. So that leaves someone on Mezaute's side." He squeezed the bridge of his nose. "Whoever it was, I hope the damage won't be too great. Louise has been through enough."

There was a lull in the conversation. Berenger stared at his knees. Chantal wondered if his thoughts had drifted to his dead wife. The man must have gone through hell two years ago. Every day must bring a fresh reminder.

Chantal rose to fetch a small box from a kitchen drawer. "For Louise. I finished it after the funeral."

He opened the lid and looked at the alternating sequence of round and oval beads. "Thank you," he said rolling the heart-shaped one in the center gently between his fingers. "She'll love it."

"It's nothing. I wish I could do more."

"You can do something. For me." His eyes, black with emotion, locked on hers. "Tell me if you trust me now. Tell me if you believe it wasn't me that hurt Jeanne."

She couldn't doubt what it had cost him to share the truth about his daughter for the second time that day -— and still not know if he'd won her confidence.

She wanted to let go of her doubts. She wanted to trust him.

But only if it's right. Not because he would be a convenient shoulder to lean on.

Her head began to marshal arguments and weigh probabilities. But that wasn't the way. Logic would still find reasonable doubt against Berenger.

She needed to listen with her heart.

He'd given her the gift of his own faith. He trusted her to protect his child's secret. What more could she ask?

Nothing.

"I can. I do." Her voice was barely a whisper.

He smiled, and it jolted her heart loose from its moorings again. At that moment, she'd have walked barefoot to Paris for him. Instead, all she had to do was talk about Steven.

Before she could find the words, he pulled her onto his lap. This close, his eyes became a blue blur. Their mouths melded in hungry need. For once, she needed him to be dominant, to crush her so close there'd be no room for doubts. He sensed it and responded. The world shrank to the square inches of flesh where they touched.

He broke away at last and rested his forehead on hers. "Much more of that," he said, "and I'm going to carry you upstairs to the first bed I find. And if Roland Fleurie dares watch, it'll give him a guilt trip to last another eight hundred years."

"Much more of that," she replied, her own breathing shaky, "and I'll let you."

He answered with a series of feather kisses in her hair. "You're a sweet mystery, Chantal. All sober colors and self-composure. Yet under the surface," he slid a hand up her ribcage, "you're ablaze."

She leaned towards his roaming hand. "You're a dark horse yourself."

"Me? With my mother's temper and none of the Morels' moderation?"

"You with your one smile a month. Oh, the volcano erupts regularly, but in between it's hard to know what you're thinking."

A rumble from Berenger's belly proved her point about volcanic forces. They both laughed.

"If we're not going to satisfy our carnal appetites," he said, slowly withdrawing his hand, "I vote we satisfy some other ones. I'm famished."

Chantal frowned. She had barely enough safe food in the pantry to feed herself, let alone a man the size of Berenger.

"Not here, obviously," he said, chiming in on her thoughts. "I don't fancy electrocution or psychedelic poisoning." He glanced at his watch. "It's getting late for a restaurant at this time of year. We'll have to throw ourselves on Ah Wong's mercy."

Chantal slid reluctantly off his lap, instantly aware of the loss of his body heat.

"Surely you don't want to sleep here, either?" he added, looking up at her. "You may have solved why Jeanne left, but not how the culprit breaks in. Whatever game he's playing, it's not safe for you to stay here while he's on the prowl."

She thought about the mysterious underground passage she'd discovered that morning. Should she tell him?

Berenger's belly rumbled again. "Hurry up and pack. Before I starve."

The passage could wait, Chantal decided. It wasn't going anywhere, and its cold, damp air held no appeal. By contrast, the prospect of escaping the house, and into Berenger's company, beckoned like morning sun after a week's rain. The two busy days since the funeral had worn her down. Even the ninety minutes' drive back from Toulouse on the smooth main road that afternoon had strained her concentration.

She couldn't go yet, though. She had a promise to keep. She cleared her throat. "I've not kept my side of our bargain yet."

He waved a hand dismissively. "Let's wait till we're fed and rested. There's no rush. I trust you."

Did she detect a sting of reproach in his words? She looked hard into his eyes and he returned her gaze steadily.

"Do you know which hotels are open at this time of year? I should call and book a room."

His brows gathered. "You're staying at the chateau. With me."

"With you?" she echoed.

"Yes," he said firmly. "Two doors down the corridor, where I know you're safe and where you can get some proper sleep."

Fighting him took too much effort, especially when she didn't want to. No more hallucinations, lonely evenings or booby-traps. She smiled as she climbed the stairs.

It didn't take long to pile her belongings into the little suitcase. She had more than clothes to think of, though. Jeanne's medical file needed to come with her.

Back downstairs, she walked into the scullery where she'd left the envelope with the copy of Jeanne's file. Before she'd set off for Toulouse, she'd tucked it out of sight on a shelf over the ancient washing machine.

The envelope had gone.

She stepped back to peer beside the washing machine, and her heel came down on something thin and springy. The knife that had jammed the basement door latch now lay on the floor. She picked it up. Coincidence?

Berenger poked his head around the door. "What are you looking for?" he asked impatiently.

She gave him a few quick details, sketching the size of the A4 envelope with her hands, and not mentioning the dislodged knife.

"I'll look in the parlor," he offered in a grim tone. "Maybe Mulberry's been in again and moved it. Probably topped up his poisons while he was here, too."

Had Mulberry come in through the passage? Chantal hated to think of him grubbing through the sensitive information in Aunt Jeanne's file. She climbed the stairs to check the upper rooms, certain she would find nothing. She entered the spare bedroom with the photo albums.

And gasped.

CHAPTER TWENTY-THREE

On top of the wickerwork chair lay the red-bound photo album. Chantal picked it up in wonder and read the label on its spine.

1947.

Something slid from its pages and whispered to the floor.

The envelope with Aunt Jeanne's medical file.

She stared at it for a long moment and then opened the album. It opened at a photo of a young, dark-haired man squatting by a boat. He'd turned to smile over his shoulder. The snap had caught him as he painted a name on the boat's prow. Chantal could read the letters 'J' and 'E'.

She snapped the album shut.

"I've found it," she called out and scooped up the envelope with her free hand.

Berenger met her at the foot of the stairs.

"He's been here. Mulberry. For sure," Chantal said. She thrust the album at him and shook the loose papers out of the envelope. A quick count confirmed the pages were all there.

She became aware of Berenger's questioning gaze. "I

saw this red album upstairs, the night I arrived. Yesterday afternoon—gone. Now it's back." She shrugged helplessly. "Seems Mulberry can come and go as he likes, despite the new front door lock. And I checked the back door before I set off with the samples at lunchtime."

Berenger swung away, leading the way back to the scullery. There, the back door bolt still hung loose, but the door itself was locked, as she'd left it.

"We'll get this lock changed, too," Berenger said. "If he came in through the front door, even once, he might have found a spare key to this back one. And since I crashed through the bolt…"

She stared through the back window. It was impossible to see his shop against the kitchen light, but she could imagine it. "Do you really think he comes in via your place?"

"It's possible, during opening hours. I look after my keys better than your aunt did, so I doubt he can access the shop at night."

She picked up the knife from where she'd left it on top of the washing machine. Telling him about the passage would be a first mark of her new-found trust in him, a warm-up for talking about Steven. "See this? I found it on the floor five minutes ago, while I was searching for the envelope. But when I left for Toulouse, it was still jamming this latch." She pointed with the knife handle at the slot under the thumb rest.

"You think Mulberry camps out in the basement, waiting for his chance to roam around the house?"

"I think Mulberry is small enough, just, to get in through a hidden passage I found down there this morning. I suspect it links to the lost tunnel for anyone who can squeeze through the Eye of the Needle."

Berenger looked concerned.

"Chantal, I think you must be confused. Dreams, the hallucinogens in your food, you know…"

"Do you want to see?" It seemed the quickest way. She

reached for the latch.

Berenger's stomach gave another thunderous rumble. He reached out to stop her opening the door. "Feed me first. Then I'll do anything you want. Tunnels, stakeouts, whatever."

Chantal shrugged. The Eye of the Needle had been real, she was sure, and it wouldn't run away while they ate.

Five minutes later they sat in Berenger's SUV, winding down through the dimly lit streets to the chateau. Chantal nursed the red album and envelope. Her thoughts traveled back to the graveyard and Number 8. "Let's call Riberon tonight," she suggested. "Tell him we've got the trowel for prints, and that Mulberry's trying to desecrate Aunt Jeanne's grave. And that he seems able to enter Number 8 whenever he wants. By whatever door," she added in a mutter.

"And you'll mention you're calling from the chateau and no longer suspect me?" It was hard to tell in the gloom of the car, but she sensed a smile tugging at his lips.

"Absolutely." She owed him that much, at least.

Berenger glanced across. "Louise is just starting her Easter vacation. If it's not raining tomorrow, how about we take a break from all this, and go for a picnic?"

"I'd love to," said Chantal warmly, "It'd be my first quiet day since I arrived."

* * *

The chateau felt peaceful as Chantal and Berenger walked down the utility passage from the garage. Berenger carried Chantal's suitcase.

"Is Louise in bed?" Chantal asked quietly.

"Yes, she'll have gone an hour or more ago." Berenger sighed. "I'll go and kiss her goodnight in a minute."

"Will she still be awake?"

"No. But she'll check at breakfast on whether I kissed her. Ah, watch out." He spoke in a more urgent tone as they arrived in the hallway. Up the corridor, Ah Wong, who must have had sharp hearing, stuck her head out of the kitchen door.

A hiss of disapproval greeted them as they took off their coats. "You very late. You not ring."

"I know, and I'm afraid there's two of us needing a late meal. You remember Mademoiselle Chantal Harrison, I'm sure. She's also going to be our guest for a little while."

"Nice to meet you again, Ah Wong," said Chantal politely.

The hissing subsided. "I remember. She help when I say not help."

Stricken with illogical guilt, Chantal looked down the corridor at her accuser. Something flickered across Ah Wong's face. A wink? Or simply a twitch?

"Chantal doesn't know how we do things here." Berenger's large hand felt warm on Chantal's shoulder as he guided her up the corridor. "Now, Ah Wong, I apologize for not letting you know I couldn't make it to dinner, but what can you feed us? I need to eat before I faint."

"You very lucky. Is chicken chasseur tonight. Easy to make hot again, and I make plenty."

"That sounds lovely, Ah Wong." Chantal hoped her enthusiasm would make up for her apparent faux pas in carrying dirty plates on her last visit, but the housekeeper withdrew into the kitchen without replying.

"Why don't you call Riberon first, as you'd planned," prompted Berenger, "and I'll go up to Louise? Do you have his number?"

"His card's in my purse somewhere," Chantal said. "You go on up. Hopefully he'll answer and this will be quick. And Berenger—"

He looked round expectantly from the foot of the stairs.

"Would you mind if I placed an international call, too? To my father? I want him to know I'm safe here, and that he doesn't need to come. And I'd like to give him this phone number."

"Of course!" Berenger ran up the stairs as if her suitcase weighed nothing.

Riberon answered her call, sounding even more tired than before. As succinctly as she could, Chantal outlined the latest developments. Was it her imagination or did the inspector's energy level rise as she reported her location? To be fair, Riberon had interviewed Berenger promptly based on her report of the backyard conversation, but now she listened to him promising a level of help and responsiveness well above what she'd dared hope for.

She hung up and then dialed her father's home. Tricia answered, sounding pleased to hear from her, and asking at once about her health and safety. Chantal poured all the reassurance she could into her answer, and then had to repeat the effort when her father picked up the extension phone. It proved worth it: she convinced him the chateau offered as much safety as a hotel, with the bonus of a family's companionship and home comforts.

"So you're sure you don't want me to come?" probed her father. "My diary's looking good from the end of this week."

She reassured him once more, warmed by his willingness to come, but silently certain she could handle things now she had Berenger back on her team. She gave her father the Morels' phone number and promised to keep in touch.

Berenger came to the head of the stairs as she hung up. She watched as he descended, his broad shoulders blocking out most of the light from the landing above.

"Riberon says, starting tomorrow evening, he'll place one man on lookout in the graveyard for a couple of nights. We'll have to risk that Mulberry won't try again before then. And he says a policeman will come by tomorrow and pick up the trowel."

"And your father?"

"I've convinced him I'm as safe here, and in better company, than in a hotel."

"You are." He put an arm around her shoulder and drew her into the family room.

There they found Armand lingering over his coffee with a glossy catalog open at a page of images of green pottery. He rose at once to greet Chantal and when Berenger told his father about the latest booby-trap, Armand fully endorsed Chantal's moving into the chateau. His welcome seemed genuine, but Chantal couldn't shake off lingering wariness, remembering how he he'd dodged her questions about Aunt Jeanne's bypass petition.

Berenger poured two glasses of red wine and handed Chantal one on his way across the room to soak up the heat of the open fire. He toasted her and said, "Another of mine, mostly from a variety we call Braucol. Good structure, good depth of color. Its style is similar to a Cabernet Sauvignon."

Chantal made a non-committal noise to hide her near-total ignorance about what he'd said and sipped the wine.

"A couple of days under this roof, Mademoiselle Harrison, and I guarantee you'll come away knowing all the main grape varieties in Gaillac, the most popular blends and styles, and Berenger's views on their optimum cellaring times," warned Armand.

"She will, as long as you don't stuff her head full of information on your celadons," retorted Berenger.

"Are those celadons?" asked Chantal pointing at the catalog in front of Armand. After the drama of the day the father-son banter relaxed her, and she felt able to stir in a little mischief of her own.

Berenger groaned.

"Indeed they are," asserted Armand. "My hobby, though Berenger would say my expensive obsession. You might have noticed the display case in the sitting room where your guests came after the funeral? That's my Korean collection."

"And there's his other room you haven't seen, Chantal," added Berenger. "Down the corridor, worth three times as much. Full, floor to ceiling, with his Chinese collection."

Master's private room. Now Chantal understood Ah Wong's protectiveness when she had headed towards the wrong door. The pieces in that private room sounded as if they could be worth a small fortune.

"The Korean techniques reached their peak in the same era that Raymond of Toulouse founded Cordes, you know," said Armand. "First half of the thirteenth century. But the Chinese output from the Longquan kilns is probably better known because—"

Ah Wong interrupted his flow by wheeling in the serving trolley with two steaming bowls of casserole and a basket of bread slices.

"Because Longquan exported everywhere," Ah Wong said, readily picking up the thread of Armand's mini-lecture. "But later pottery made in Chinese Ming period, that not so good. We focus on pieces from Southern Song dynasty."

She unloaded the bowls as she spoke. Berenger strode to the table.

"You're an expert too, Ah Wong?" asked Chantal, taken aback.

"Ah Wong was born to it," Armand said, recapturing control of the conversation. "Her father held the post of museum curator in Shanghai before the family escaped to Taiwan. When we lived in Taipei, Ah Wong took the greatest care with my collection. Of course, I had far fewer pieces back then."

"But had too much Ming." Ah Wong gave her now familiar hiss.

"And very soon, Mademoiselle Harrison, as you may have deduced, I found I had hired not only an amah, but a very knowledgeable—and forceful—adviser."

"Come on, Chantal," grumbled Berenger. "Sit down so

I can eat. And you need food, too, or you'll be seeing hallucinations again, but from low blood sugar this time."

Chantal sat. The aroma from the chicken casserole promised an excellent meal.

"Hallucinations? Have you been ill?" Armand turned towards her.

She shook her head. "I've been the victim of chemical booby-traps, Monsieur, as well as the physical ones Berenger told you about before. Someone spiked food and drink at my aunt's house. It made me see crazy, scary things. Stone walls rippling. Clock faces turning into hooded monks."

"Good heavens. But there's no danger of that here with Ah Wong in command of the household and catering," her host assured her.

"Chantal even saw your Eye of the Needle," Berenger added, dabbing at his mouth with his serviette.

The concern on Armand's face rapidly morphed into excitement. "The Eye? The *Eye*? What did it look like?"

"A vision, Father, not reality."

"Why shouldn't it be real?" Chantal asked, irritated. "I had a map to follow, remember. Well, a diagram without a scale or legend."

"But what did you see, Mademoiselle? Did you see something physical?" Armand leaned closer, claiming her attention.

Chantal put down her fork and turned to meet his eager gaze head-on. "Monsieur, what I saw was a very tall, very narrow archway at the end of a passage that sloped downhill."

"That's exactly what your imagination would conjure up for something by that name," declared Berenger.

Chantal and Armand ignored his comment.

"And where was this passage? Mademoiselle, did it connect to your aunt's house?"

She nodded.

"And what lay beyond the archway?" Armand's pale

blue eyes were diamond-tipped drills, boring into her as his interest grew more intense.

"I don't know. I'd had enough of the cold and dark by then." She shrugged and picked up her fork again.

"But you could find it again? You could show me?"

"Yes, if it isn't all in my head, like Berenger thinks."

Armand slapped the table. "This is marvelous! I must tell Wilbur. He's stuck upstairs. Said he had to hunt through all his papers for some Cathar reference he's mislaid. He'll be fascinated."

"Really, Monsieur, I don't think he will. Last time, he was adamant the Eye was a purely spiritual reference."

"But this could be new evidence, and Wilbur's a scholar. You'll see!" Armand jumped up from his chair, sending his celadon brochure skating off the table, but deftly catching it in an outstretched hand. Chantal doubted her father, Terry, could have moved so athletically. On a whim, she began sizing up the men she knew in Cordes for those slender enough to squeeze through the Eye.

Berenger and Grenier, the well-fed lawyer, never. Armand was leaner and shorter, but still broad. Mulberry perhaps, but he'd have to strain. Mezaute, with his lean build—definitely. Wilbur she struggled to gauge. He had wide shoulders but his face was long and thin.

The door to the corridor closed behind Armand. The only sounds came from the hiss and snap of the logs in the fireplace.

Berenger sat back from his empty bowl with a satisfied sigh and reached for his wine glass.

"Now I can function again. What's it to be? Exploring, chasing, spying?"

"I'd like to tell you about something from this morning, actually, so I only need your brain and ears."

"Yours, for what they're worth. Would you like a coffee when you've finished? We could sit over there, nearer the fire."

"Thanks. Black coffee would be great." Chantal wanted

to sit beside Berenger on the sofa. With Wilbur and Armand due any second, there'd be no chance for a repeat of their closeness in Aunt Jeanne's kitchen. Frustration burned, but she fought it down.

Long-engrained habit made her stack their dirty plates.

Berenger turned at the clatter of crockery. "Leave those. That's Ah Wong's job."

"I'm creating work for her by staying here. I need to do something to contribute."

"Please, don't." Iron in his tone made her glance up, alarmed. "You mean well, but you're treading on ghosts. My mother's, to be specific."

Chantal's hand sank down and the bowls chinked softly onto the tablecloth.

"Oh, don't look so penitent," he said impatiently. "You didn't know, and I'm explaining. When Maman became too ill even to do little chores, Ah Wong took them over as if they'd always fallen to her, and we pretended that was true. And now we can't stop."

Chantal unstacked her bowl from Berenger's spotlessly clean one, and set both back in their places.

"I know you don't like accepting my help, Chantal, and you want to pay me back by paying it forwards, but this isn't the way. Anyway, you've already paid. Louise's bracelet." He tapped his shirt pocket.

"That was fun to make." She smiled tentatively.

"I'm glad." He didn't smile, but the lines around his eyes softened. The sight lifted her spirits and drew her towards him.

Before she could cross the room, Armand returned.

"Oddest thing," he announced. "Wilbur's not in his room. I can't find him anywhere. I might check in the basement in case he's after a bottle to cheer himself through his paperwork."

"Hope he knows which bottles are for daily consumption," growled Berenger. "I don't want him near my good stuff."

"*Our* good stuff," Armand corrected. "And I told him when he first arrived." He thrust his hand through his silver bristles in a gesture Chantal knew very well. "I'm bursting to share your news, Mademoiselle. If I can't find Wilbur soon, I'll have to call one of the Musketeers." He disappeared into the corridor again.

Chantal covered the distance to the sofa and sat down. She left enough room, hoping Berenger would join her. "Musketeers?"

Berenger set her coffee down within easy reach, and sat down beside her.

Yes.

"The Musketeers are the inner circle of the local History Society. You already know about that. The trio's made up of our lawyer Grenier, my father, and Doctor Mezaute."

Chantal sat up straight.

"They've been friends for years," he went on. "They're amateur treasure hunters, living in hope that one day they'll find the Cathars' long-lost treasures. You heard Father getting excited about it with Wilbur the other night."

"The Eye of the Needle being the path to true treasure. And Wilbur saying it wasn't likely to be the gold and silver kind."

Berenger nodded and leaned back, a shift that brought his leg within an inch of her knee. "Let's forget mythical treasures. You were going to tell me something about this morning."

Chantal dragged her gaze away from his knee and told him about her morning at Mezaute's.

Berenger shook his head in near disbelief as she told him about taking Aunt Jeanne's file. "You never cease to amaze me, Chantal Harrison. Never."

"I don't make a habit of being a burglar," she protested, "but Mezaute stonewalled me over Jeanne's complaints. And as for feeding me rubbish about hauntings!"

"He's always been straight as a die with us," reflected Berenger. "Do you think he was offended by you probing into things he believes should stay private?"

"It felt like he used the moral high ground to hide that he knew Jeanne's symptoms were drug-related."

"So why would he write anything down?"

"I suppose the appointment book and pharmacy scripts would show she'd visited him, wouldn't they? He had to write something, but he downplayed it on purpose. Hang on."

Chantal retrieved her purse from the dining chair. This time, she sat down closer so their knees touched.

Berenger replied with gentle pressure from his leg.

Inwardly, she grinned, then riffled through to the last pages in the envelope. "See?" She handed him the final sheet. "If I hadn't lived through the hallucinations, I'd never have recognized her symptoms."

He read the page rapidly. "Go on."

"I think Mezaute let Aunt Jeanne think she was losing her mind. Maybe even spun her the haunting line. The ratbag. He'd know Jeanne was susceptible to the idea."

"Mezaute and Mulberry?" Berenger's forehead creased. "Why? I can't see it. Mulberry keeps breaking in, so he must be looking for something. But Mezaute?"

Chantal shrugged. "We already know about the lost tunnel. Maybe something else got hidden there over the last seven centuries, something Mezaute found out about through the Society. Something he's chasing alone, with Mulberry as his henchman."

Two men who could fit through the Eye.

"It's possible, but I really think Father and Grenier would know if Mezaute had a lead. They're always theorizing over coffee at the Society. I can't see one Musketeer being able to keep a secret from the rest." Berenger frowned over the rim of his coffee cup. "And don't go thinking the three of them must be in it together.

That's going too far."

She put her hands up in mock defense.

"Did you find anything else of interest in your aunt's file? I'm not trying to pry, but we're low on practical clues again."

Chantal shrugged. "It felt wrong to read more than I needed to. I checked the last couple of pages and put it away." She considered the matter for a moment. "I'll take a proper look. While I do, you could go through the photo album." She pulled it out of her purse. "It must be significant if Mulberry bothered to take it."

"Perhaps it wasn't. He brought it back."

"Then why didn't he just throw it away?"

Since neither of them could answer the questions, they set to work.

A few Latin references in Aunt Jeanne's file baffled Chantal. Most appeared at the beginning, in a general description of Jeanne's health, recorded in the mid-1950s.

"What does this mean? *Gravida 1, para 1?*"

"No idea. I'll fetch a dictionary."

She felt the cool air as his knee left hers.

Berenger returned with the heavy tome a minute later, and this time sat shoulder to shoulder with her. "Easier to share discoveries this way."

"I agree," she murmured happily, before turning her attention to the dictionary and leafing through to the 'G's.

Grave.

Gravel.

Gravestone.

Graveyard.

The dictionary seemed to be telling its own story of their evening adventures.

Gravid.

The definition made her gulp. Never in all of Aunt Jeanne's tales of her wild youth had she ever let out a hint of *this*.

"What? A clue?"

"Oh, yes." She sat forward and stared at a hyacinth planted in a white-glazed bowl on a small side table. The swelling blue-purple buds looked about to burst into life, a strangely appropriate parallel. "It means Aunt Jeanne was pregnant and delivered a child."

CHAPTER TWENTY-FOUR

Berenger snapped upright. "A child? Boy or girl?"

Chantal tucked a stray russet wisp behind her ear and re-skimmed the first two pages before handing them to him. "Doesn't say, but the child was born in 1948." She pointed at the album on his knees. "Therefore conceived in 1947, maybe near Calvi in Corsica."

"By the man painting Jeanne's name on his boat," finished Berenger. "Could be she offered me the house in order to raise hush money to pay off a blackmailer."

"If so, the blackmailer can't be Mezaute, however much I'd like it to be him. As Jeanne's doctor, he's known about the baby for decades," Chantal pointed out. "And why would anyone care after all these years, anyway?"

"What if Mezaute found out the identity of the child, or the father, and they were high-profile people who couldn't afford the past to become public? Your aunt tried to protect one or both by paying up." Berenger flicked through the album pages, as if hunting for inspiration, and sighed. "Blackmail's one thing, Chantal, but why would a blackmailer need to scare your aunt out of her house?"

Chantal thought it through. How would Aunt Jeanne react to threats? "She'd be fighting back, trying to find other ways to raise money than sell her beloved home. The scare tactics were to hurry her up."

Berenger looked sideways at her. "It's not compelling, is it?"

"No." She threw in another tough question. "Why does Mulberry need to disturb Jeanne's tomb?"

They puzzled over that problem, tossing ever crazier ideas to and fro.

At last, Chantal threw up her hands. "I thought this secret baby would be the missing piece in the puzzle, but it just makes things murkier. We've found a love child, but it doesn't mean he—or she—has anything to do with the drugs or Aunt Jeanne's death."

"It's a three-bottle problem, and no mistake." Berenger stretched his shoulders so far back that the fibers of his pullover thinned under the strain. If the strands broke, she'd find the answer to a private mystery. What did that powerful torso look like naked?

"But instead of drinking our way to the solution, we'd do better to sleep on it." His face remained impassive, but his next words betrayed him. "Alone, in separate rooms. Or else, I'm afraid, you'd get no sleep at all."

Her answering flush betrayed her in return.

*   *   *

Chantal came downstairs later than she'd intended the next morning, thoroughly refreshed after a deep sleep. She found the family and Wilbur enjoying a continental breakfast at the dining table. Berenger gave her a rapid wink that drew her into a secret partnership and set the happiness bubbles popping again. This morning, he wore a crisp cotton shirt folded back at the cuffs. The sight only made the bubbles fizz faster.

"Hello, everyone," she managed in what she hoped was a steady voice.

"Mademoiselle, good morning," said Armand and

waved a genial hand toward the table.

Louise had swiveled around at the sound of Chantal's approach. She dropped her croissant and cannoned off her chair to wrap a welcoming hug around Chantal's waist. A red ribbon around Louise's ponytail glowed against her dark hair. "Sit next to me, Chantal," she urged.

Chantal sat down beside the girl and accepted a cup of tea from Ah Wong, who had appeared at her elbow.

"Your news of the Eye of the Needle gave me a disturbed night, you know," Armand said in mock-admonishment. "All broken dreams and wild imaginings. I told Wilbur this morning, and he was so amazed he walked into the sideboard."

Wilbur's mouth twisted. "Going to have a bruised knee."

"Not so bad, I hope, that you won't be able to come along when we persuade Mademoiselle Harrison to retrace her steps."

Wilbur gave Chantal an angry look that made her recoil.

"What?" she demanded. "I'm not going to force you into dark passages, if you don't want to go. And I'm in no hurry to go back there again, either."

Wilbur rubbed his face before answering. "My apologies, ma'am. I'm—I guess I'm a little tense with my study break finishing soon. This structure you say you saw, if it exists, it could eat all the time I have left." He turned to Armand. "I've got to stay focused on my research, Armand. You know my Ph.D. supervisors aren't giving me grades for hunting old legends. They want rigor and references—like that lost citation that had me hunting through the garbage last night. When you couldn't find me," he added.

"Always the scholar, Wilbur!" said his host, shaking his head admiringly. "Well, you know the Musketeers can be trusted to perform the preliminary research, eh?"

Wilbur raised his coffee cup in a small salute and

looked about to say something further when Berenger interrupted.

"Don't count on any 'preliminary research' today, Father. Chantal, Louise and I have plans for a picnic, and we hope you'll join us. The forecast is good for later this morning." His glanced out the window.

Chantal's gaze followed his. Outside, the light on the terrace appeared bright, yet oddly flat, and the more distant shrubs were faintly blurred. She hoped the weather forecast would prove correct. A spring picnic really needed a little sunshine to encourage lingering, and she looked forward to more time with Berenger, and watching him with his daughter.

"Where are we going to go, Papa?" Louise asked, pushing jam onto her croissant with a finger. Chantal understood that, for Louise, there had to be a trade-off between good manners and independence.

"You could try the trout lake near Loubers, if you want somewhere new," suggested Armand. "I couldn't join you there till early afternoon, though."

"Or, if you've got all day, how about Montségur?" Wilbur asked, over the lip of his coffee cup. "It's a long drive over the Black Mountains, but a truly dramatic scene when you arrive."

The American seemed to be trying to make amends for his earlier grouchiness.

"I've not visited there since the last Musketeers' trip. Majestic, but eerie, too," commented Armand.

"What's Montségur?" asked Louise.

"It's a ruined fortress on a rocky pinnacle," explained her grandfather. "The last major stronghold of the Cathars. And you've heard me talk about them often enough."

"They were the hairy kids," Louise stated and then bit into her jam-topped croissant.

Chantal blinked.

Armand took on the role of interpreter, after a quick,

wry smile at Louise.

"Almost, Louise. The Cathars were heretics. You'll remember that means they rejected many of the teachings of the Catholic Church, even though they were Christians. And the Catholic Church tried to stop them."

"Succeeded, too," commented Wilbur. "Pretty thoroughly wiped them out. That's why the resources in the library here that show how they lived their daily lives have been so important to me."

"Does anyone still live there?" asked Louise.

"In the village below, sure," the American answered her. "But not in the castle ruins. Someone betrayed the Cathars in 1245. More than two hundred of them were burned alive in a field nearby."

Chantal had forgotten the sheer scale of the butchery. Pity soured the yogurt in her mouth.

Louise, however, remained spellbound. "Didn't anyone escape?"

Wilbur turned his soft brown gaze on her. "The soldiers who had helped defend Montségur were allowed to live. And legend has it that four Cathars escaped the night before Montségur fell. They scaled the cliff at its steepest point and took their treasure, the one your granddad and his friends would love to find."

"Maybe that day is coming closer with what Mademoiselle Harrison has found." Armand clapped his guest lightly on the shoulder and looked over at Chantal, a wide smile crinkling the lines around his pale blue eyes.

She turned the topic back to Montségur. "Can you walk through the castle?"

"The walls and part of the keep remain," said Armand.

Wilbur leaned forward, a finger aloft. "But what's there now is a later structure than the Cathars', remember. People ignore that, and I guess the romance of the story and the spectacular views explain that."

Ah Wong came in to tell Armand he had a phone call, and he left the table with a look of regret.

"Why are you so skeptical about the Cathars and their treasure, then?" Chantal asked Wilbur.

Wilbur pushed flakes of croissant to the edge of his plate with his long index finger before replying. "The Cathars who came here looking for sanctuary had lost nearly everything they had, everyone they knew. Simon de Montfort's crusade against them had been protracted and pitiless, and the Dominicans conducted a vicious Inquisition for years after that, one that reached into the walls of Cordes. I believe they invented the legend as a source of comfort. A promise for the future."

Wilbur's empathy touched Chantal, and she found herself warming to him at last.

"Plus," he went on, "Everything I've learned about the Cathars shows they were strongly spiritual, and as dismissive of riches as the Catholic leaders of the day were enthralled by them."

An image of a plump prelate trying to squeeze through the Eye rose before her. The archway *had* to mark Cathar territory, a place the enemy couldn't penetrate. Beyond the stone-rimmed slit she'd glimpsed lay something of value, surely. Perhaps a safe place to worship? That would have been worth more than gold to the persecuted community.

Wilbur's short laugh cut in on her thoughts. "And if I'm wrong, then I'll bet the treasure's lost for good near Montségur itself."

Louise burst out, "Can we go to Montségur? Can we? Please, Papa! To hunt for the treasure!" Louise obviously didn't think her lack of sight would be a handicap.

Her father spoke over her entreaties. "Isn't it a rough walk up to the castle?"

"Took me about thirty minutes when I went," said Wilbur.

"Thank you. Then Montségur is out. Today, we want a relaxing picnic, not an endurance test. Now, Louise," he spoke more loudly to drown out the protest they could all see coming. "Let's take Chantal somewhere that you know, but she doesn't. If we go to the stream, you can show her where to fish for minnows, and she can tell you how many you've caught."

Louise's face was a study in conflicting desires. Her blindness did not detract from the expressiveness of her eyebrows and eyelids.

"You know, Louise," said Chantal swiftly, "at this time of year I'm not so keen on hiking. But if there were a sunny place to go fishing, that would be perfect."

"I s'pose," mumbled Louise, her lower lip protruding a little.

Her father nodded his head briefly in appreciation of Chantal's comment.

Wilbur excused himself from the table and met Armand returning. He caught his host by the elbow and drew him back into the corridor, asking him for help with something.

Ah Wong came back in to clear away the dirty plates. Chantal sat on her hands to stop herself helping.

"I hear you go on picnic today," the housekeeper said. "You must buy bread, but other food is all OK."

Louise tilted her head. "Have we got fruit tarts, Ah Wong? We always take fruit tarts. And I get the one with strawberries."

"No tart, and only a few *croquants*."

The light and crispy almond cookies were a local specialty that went wonderfully with coffee. Chantal turned to Berenger. "If you drive me up the hill, I can pick up the bread and pastries and then come back in my rental car. I'd rather have it here with me, if that's OK."

Louise bounced off her chair. "Can I come?" she asked. "Please? I can show Chantal where our favorite bakery is."

Berenger's face signaled his doubt. Chantal guessed he allowed very few people to have sole custody of his beloved daughter.

"Maybe you should stay and pack up the other picnic

food with Ah Wong," suggested Chantal, unwilling to encourage Louise if her father felt uncomfortable. She caught his eye and made a gesture she hoped conveyed 'it's up to you'.

"I want to come with you," pouted Louise. "Ah Wong won't let me help. Papa, please?"

Her father frowned at his daughter. At length he sighed. "Very well. I'll drop you as close to the bakery as I can. And, Louise, you need to sit in the back of Chantal's car."

He had made her another gift of trust. If their positions had been reversed, Chantal doubted she could have matched Berenger's good faith.

"Papa, I know that," answered Louise. "And I know to listen to make sure Chantal doesn't eat all the tarts."

Chantal laugh out loud. "And I'm going to keep a sharp eye on you, too, young lady," she retorted in fun. "No strawberry tarts are allowed to go missing before the picnic."

Louise giggled, and Chantal saw a ghost of a smile slide past the edge of Berenger's mouth.

He sent Louise off to find her coat and shoes and then said earnestly to Chantal, "Please keep hold of her hand, even in the bakery. She hears things we don't notice, and she'll be off to investigate them. She can disappear in a couple of seconds. It's curiosity, not disobedience." He pushed his hand back through his hair. "But it's absolute hell till you find her again."

Chantal held his bright blue gaze. "I promise I will take great care of Louise." And then, to recover a little of the light mood, she added, "Of course, I can't promise the same for the strawberry tarts…"

* * *

The moment Chantal and Louise arrived back at the chateau, each carrying a bag of goodies from the bakery,

Berenger opened the front door. He must have been hovering in the hall, awaiting their return. His face showed little emotion, but Chantal saw his shoulders drop as tension ebbed from them.

"Thank you," she said quietly to him. "We enjoyed that." She handed her bag to Louise and asked her to take their shopping to Ah Wong.

After Louise had skipped away, she went on, "The baker will be gossiping that a female guest from the chateau came in with *la petite Morel.* Louise cheerfully shared her news about me before I could get a word in." She slipped off her coat. Tiny beads of moisture from the morning mist clung in the folds of the cloth. "I'm sure that's what earned her a free *croquant* to eat on the way back."

"Welcome to life in a small town." Berenger shook out her coat and hung it up. When Chantal moved to follow Louise, he put a hand on her arm. "Two things. While you were out, one of Riberon's men came by and took the trowel. We're to ring Riberon for a progress report on Monday."

"Good. And the other thing?"

In reply, he slipped the bracelet box into her hand. "I haven't given Louise this yet. You should give it to her when we get to the picnic spot."

They pulled out of the driveway half an hour later, with the SUV loaded with a rug, collapsible camping chairs, a generously sized picnic hamper, and a small fishing net.

"Will Grand-Papa come?" asked Louise from the back seat.

"He says he'll drive out to meet us if he gets finished in time," Berenger replied. "So we'd better save him a fruit tart."

"He likes *croquants* better."

Chantal let their conversation flow past her. The mist hid most of the scenery from view, but it didn't obscure a road sign to the nearby hamlet of Souel. She needed a break from the mystery around Aunt Jeanne and her last weeks with Odile, and felt glad of the distraction when Berenger drove past the turning to the main Albi road. He took them due east, on a small road she'd not traveled before.

"Papa, this isn't the way to the stream."

Chantal marveled that the girl could tell their route when she had nothing to go on but the twists in the road and the engine speed.

"It will be, Chérie, but we've a stop to make first."

"Where?"

"I think you'll work it out in a minute. Help me keep it a surprise for Chantal, OK?"

The sound of a drawn out "oh" indicated Louise had figured out her father's plan.

The road climbed up from the valley, and at first Chantal could see no more than the verge beside the road, its grass pocked with white scars from the chalk that lay below the thin soil. As they climbed, however, the mist thinned rapidly, and golden sunlight suddenly bathed the road ahead.

At one sharp bend, Berenger threw a glance in the rear-view mirror and pulled over in a lay-by. "We're here. Louise, we won't be a minute."

"OK, but I'm counting it. One-a-thousand. Two-a-thousand. Three—"

"This is where we get out, Chantal."

Intrigued, Chantal obeyed. They met at the back of the SUV, and her gaze followed his finger, due west.

The breath caught in her throat as she took in the view.

The sun had burned off the top of the cloud perched on Cordes. She could see the buildings on the upper shoulders of the hill, floating on the thick mist that still circled the lower slopes.

Berenger's voice was in her ear. "That's why we call it Cordes-sur-Ciel. Cordes-above-the-sky."

"I've never seen this view before," she breathed. "It's

like a fairy tale."

Berenger's hands tightened on her shoulders. She leaned back into him as she stared at the enchanting sight. Wisps of mist wafted up and dissolved. Cordes revealed itself, one slow inch at a time.

"I wish Louise could see this," said Chantal. Her heart ached for the child.

"Someday, she will."

Chantal reached up to squeeze one of his hands in hers. He pressed a quick kiss to her neck.

CHAPTER TWENTY-FIVE

They reached the stream twenty minutes later. Chantal still struggled to shake off the lingerings of melancholy that Louise hadn't been able to share in the glorious sight of Cordes' hill rising above the mist. At least the child might remember something of the views around the stream from her visits there before the accident.

Chantal took in the wide grassy area that sloped gently towards the stream. The water ran between narrow shingle shores except in a few places, where the shingle turned to mud banks, lined by jaunty daffodils. A large, flat-topped stone, speckled with gray-green and yellow lichen, dominated the grass to the left and proved to be the Morels' preferred picnic spot. As Chantal watched Louise, well ahead, dragging a camping chair at a trot that allowed her to keep up with her more heavily-laden father, she had to admit that Louise evidently suffered no self-pity.

Chantal joined them in time to hear the girl ask for a snack.

Berenger paused in unrolling the ground rug beside two already unpacked chairs. "The kitchen can't serve snacks until the fishing department has caught at least ten minnows. Chantal will be our judge to count them, won't you?"

"Of course," Chantal laughed. "Let's finish setting things up and then, Louise, before we go fishing, I have a surprise for you."

"What is it?"

"Not telling. Do you need help with that chair?"

Louise shook her head and went back to tugging the chair free of its nylon bag.

Once order had been established, Chantal drew Louise down onto the rug. She pulled the little box from her coat pocket. "Surprise time. Can you hold out a hand, please?"

Louise grinned and her fingers clutched the box as soon as it touched her palm. Her thumb discovered the lid and her other hand lifted it off. She danced her fingers over the rustling tissue paper that Chantal had packed the bracelet in.

"Not just paper?"

"Of course not. Just go slowly."

Louise's solution was to upend the box between her knees and use both hands to find a way into the wrapping. She emerged triumphant. "It's my bracelet! You remembered!" Sightless green eyes looked up at Chantal, their odd flicking almost hidden in the width of a smile.

Louise rose up on her knees and leaned in to Chantal, wrapping her arms around her neck. Chantal returned the hug warmly.

"I promised you, Louise. I just needed time to choose the right beads."

Louise sat back down and held out the bracelet. "Tell me them."

Rather than take the bracelet, Chantal cupped one hand under Louise's. "Give me a finger, and we'll go down the pattern one bead at a time."

Louise grinned and held out a stiff finger. Chantal guided it to the first bead.

"The bracelet is green and blue and red. Here we go. What shape is this first one?"

Louise brought up her thumb to roll the bead. "Round!" she announced.

"Yes. And it's blue, a deep blue like the summer sky or the Mediterranean Sea." Best not to say the color also reminded her of Louise's father's eyes. She had been so absorbed in Louise and the bracelet that she'd momentarily forgotten Berenger's presence just a couple of feet away.

"What's next?" asked Louise.

"You tell me."

Louise moved her fingers on further. "It's round again. Is it blue?"

"Yes, all the round ones are blue. Keep going. What can you feel?"

"A squashed egg shape."

"It's called an oval. Guess its color."

"Red?"

Chantal smiled. "No. I'll tell you a secret, Louise. There's only one red bead, and it's a very special one. But we haven't got to it yet."

Louise swung her head towards Berenger. Though the girl wasn't looking at her, Chantal could tell Louise's face shone with happiness. "Can you see, Papa? What Chantal made for me?"

"I can." His voice sounded unusually deep.

"I'm going to find the red one in a minute." Louise rolled the oval bead before glancing sideways at Chantal, her expression now one of someone making a difficult but important choice. "I think this one is green."

"Well done! It is. All the ovals are green, a really bright green, like young leaves on a tree in spring. So, go back to the start and see if you can tell me the colors in order."

Louise laughed, gleefully taking on the challenge. "Blue, blue, green, green, blue…blue, green, blue—" She paused as her fingers hit a new and different shape. Rapidly, they explored its surface. "It's a heart! Is it red?" Again she looked across to Chantal to hear the confirmation she couldn't see.

"It is. Right in the center. I chose it for you."

"Why?"

The directness of the child's question drew an instinctive response. "Because I like you. You were the first friendly face I met in Cordes and that makes you my special friend."

Louise smiled. "Is Papa your special friend, too? He helped you that night."

Chantal's access to affectionate words evaporated faster than a water drop on a hotplate. "He's…"

"A lot harder to get to know and like than you, Chérie," said Berenger. "So it's not a fair question."

Chantal half glanced round to give him a small nod of thanks before turning back to Louise. "What is a fair question, though, is how long will it take us to catch ten minnows so we can earn our snack?"

"Ten minutes! My special bracelet will attract them."

"Best leave that safe with me, Louise," warned her father. "You don't want to lose it in the stream."

Warm in knee-high rubber boots, Louise soon waded a couple of steps into the gentle current, her net at the ready, and her jam jar of water waiting on the shingle. Chantal guided her to a promising area beside a stepping stone, and, with a hand on the child's shoulder, looked back for a second at the picnic rock. Berenger had moved to lie full length on the picnic rug. Another act of trust.

Chantal focused on Louise, ready to move if she stumbled. As the little net dipped in and out, the falling water droplets caught the sun and glistened with tiny rainbows. They were gems, fit for any store window.

Jewelry in Cordes held such appeal. Chantal felt certain she could persuade one or two shops to stock her line. She'd offer them on a sale or return basis, meaning there'd be no risk to the store-owner.

Louise had collected eight minnows when a shadow fell across the stream.

"An aperitif, Chantal?" Berenger offered her a plastic wine goblet trimmed with blue. "It's a sparkling white from Gaillac. Think of it as grown-up lemonade."

Chantal refused with a smile. "It's far too early for me. I'd love some juice, though."

Berenger shook his head theatrically and sighed. "Juice it is."

"Me too, Papa! And a *croquant*. We've caught lots of fish."

Berenger inspected the jar. "Eight is nearly ten, I suppose, and you've been working hard. Time for a break."

Fortified by her quick snack, Louise announced she wanted to hunt through the shingle for pebbles that felt like the beads on her new bracelet.

"Don't go in the water," Berenger warned, as he stood to take her back to the shingle. "You can do more fishing later."

He returned and looked down at Chantal who had claimed the rug. "It's getting warm at last," he commented, pushing back his sleeves.

Chantal lifted her face to the sun's heat, eyes shut against the glare, and nodded her agreement.

"Now," he said and sat down so close that their thighs touched.

The contact's zing snapped her eyes open again.

"Explain why you were smiling when I came over with the wine before."

"I was working out how to run a jewelry business here. Stockists, distribution."

His deep-set blue eyes narrowed. "And that makes you smile?"

"It does. Like wine makes you smile. On the inside, at any rate."

"You make me smile." To prove it, he let a slow grin spread over his face. The transformation sapped her breath once more. She dropped her eyes to the rug.

"Go on. Distribution."

"It's very hard to concentrate on business when you smile, you know." She screwed her eyes shut and let the images of Cordes' store windows return. "I've a business proposition for you, actually."

Where did that come from?

Surprise chased his lingering smile away. After a quick glance to check on Louise, his attention returned to Chantal.

"Number 8. You want the downstairs rooms, the backyard, and the basement." The words spilled from a pocket of her subconscious. "I need the upper rooms for storage and manufacture. And some window space downstairs. I propose—" She paused to let the deal take shape in her mind.

"Isn't proposing usually the male prerogative?" As usual, he teased with a straight face.

"This is business," countered Chantal. "I propose that if the house ends up mine, I'll go halves with you. All legal and proper. Will you do the same if it goes your way?"

"You want half for your jewelry business? Does this mean you're planning to stay in Cordes?" His tone blended intensity and skepticism in equal measure.

In that instant she realized that while she'd not planned anything formally yet, she did want stay in the town. She laughed in surprise, and held up her glass with an expectant expression, ready to clink it enthusiastically against his if he agreed.

He ignored the gesture and looked towards the stream again. Louise's dark head bobbed as she scooted sideways a couple of feet to find new pebbles.

Chantal lowered her hand slowly.

His gaze returned to Chantal. "If I'm going to be sharing a house with you, Chantal, even on a strictly business footing, then it's time you told me your story." His gaze held her as powerfully as a sci-fi tractor beam. "I want to know what makes you tick."

Chantal sat up and pushed the hair back off her face.

This was it, then.

She'd never told it all in one go. Like the first time she'd had to talk about Aunt Jeanne's death, she had no pat phrases to draw on and no clear pathway through it.

Now it was her turn to stare at Louise's figure by the stream, but all she saw was a scene from two years before. A room full of people, chatter, and business cards changing hands.

"His name was Steven. We met at a venture capital event. Boutique investors on one side, businesses with modest needs on the other. I had a strong lead with a UK fashion chain, but nowhere near the resources to develop it."

Steven had been an investor. He'd also been big and blond, with a ready grin. For a share of the profits, he'd offered two capital injections. The first would be due after the chain approved the designs, the second, and larger one, after the chain placed the first big order.

Steven turned out to be an active investor. He came along on buying trips, made recommendations on her designs, even fetched coffee and cakes when she worked through the night. His smile kept her cheerful when she wanted to cry with fatigue.

The day the fashion chain approved her designs, they went out to celebrate and ended up spending their first night together. When he gave her a key and asked her to move in with him, she agreed. It was an escape from her mother's house, and she was falling in love with him, after all. She ignored the inner voice that warned her she was taking an easy way out.

The bliss of a new man and real success in her business didn't last long. A conversation she overheard at Steven's raucous thirtieth birthday party revealed he had a habit of picking investment opportunities by the prettiness of the women running the ventures. It sounded like he'd moved most of the other women into his apartment—and moved them out again in time for the next meet.

She wanted to believe she was different, that he'd meant it when he said he loved her. It didn't take much probing to find out she'd heard the truth. On past form, she'd last a couple more months at best.

She moved out before he could make the decision for her. He tried, repeatedly, to plead his case, but she refused to listen. Within days, the big order came in. The operation changed gear and work almost drowned out her bruised heart.

On the due date, Steven's bank wired a tenth of what she'd expected. She rang him. They remained business partners, if no longer lovers, and she had a contract. He promised to sort it out. Certain the money was coming, she continued to write checks and hire workers.

Another small payment came through. This time, Steven's fury at his bank's error was incandescent. He stormed off to sort it out. No payments appeared.

When she contacted his bank, the clerks denied he'd made any contact. Steven's treachery left her high and dry with commitments she couldn't possibly meet. She had no time to find another investor, no spare cash to set a lawyer on Steven for breach of contract.

Berenger squeezed her hand gently. She returned the pressure.

"My father offered help," she said. "But I refused. You know I'm not much good at accepting help. This time I felt mostly responsible for the mess I'd landed in."

And for taking the convenient, easy option.

"The jewelry deal went south," she sighed. "I sold my car and took on three jobs to clear the debts. It took me eight straight months on five hours sleep a night." She gazed at the little stream. This time, the painful scenes of the past cleared and she could see Louise, still busy hunting pebbles.

"And Steven?" Berenger asked quietly. "What of him?"

"Never saw him again. Never went looking."

"That was quite some revenge he extracted, Chantal."

"And they talk about women scorned." She tried to make her voice light.

"You're very determined, aren't you? And strong." He brought her hand to his lips and kissed it. "I had noticed, of course. By the way, the answer is yes."

She shot him a baffled look.

"Yes, I will go halves with you in Number 8 if it's mine. If you're staying, I'll do whatever I can to make it work."

His words sealed a new level of understanding between them. Chantal wanted time to stop. She wanted to stay forever on the rug in the sun, with a bright future beckoning.

Time ticked by, of course. Armand appeared in the early afternoon and set off to play with Louise. The sight of the retired diplomat playing Explorers with his granddaughter charmed Chantal. Armand finally paused for a couple of *croquants* washed down with coffee from their thermos.

Softly, he asked Berenger how Louise had been when they'd arrived. The older man explained to Chantal, "When she goes to places she remembers being with her mother, she can grow sad."

It reminded Chantal of how much Louise—and her father—had lost, and how relatively recently. Too recently for Berenger to commit to a new relationship? She kicked herself. They'd only known each other a few days; she had no right to expect anything.

Berenger scowled at his father. "Louise hasn't reacted that way in months, you know that."

"Granted. But you haven't come here since last summer. I couldn't help wondering."

Soon after, they packed up, keen to escape the cooling day. Berenger asked his father to run Louise back so he could take Chantal on elsewhere while the good weather held.

"Somewhere special," he murmured, so only Chantal

could hear. The warmth in his eyes reassured her that he enjoyed her company and wanted more.

Louise, inevitably, took some persuading to leave, but a promise of a pebble-sorting session later with Chantal eventually persuaded her.

As Armand's car disappeared, Berenger put his arm around Chantal's shoulder. "There's a place I want to show you. A special place." He led the way to his car.

Five miles down the main road he swung the wheel over to the left. They entered a narrow, rutted lane. Where were they headed? Chantal shivered in anticipation.

CHAPTER TWENTY-SIX

The ride down the lane pitched Chantal from side to side. "Where are you taking me?" she laughed. She held on to him, her fingers barely reaching around half his arm.

"Wait and see."

Rows of vines flicked past on the right. At the ends of some rows, spring-flowering roses flashed stark red against the chalky soil. By contrast, clumps of dandelions waved yellow from the ditch that ran between the road and the vines. On the left, cows grazed in lush pasture.

Another hundred yards on, the lane ended in a wide forecourt where grass and gravel mingled.

A long, single-story farm building stood before them, with a vast barn beyond it. The farm's newly re-pointed mortar and freshly-painted blue shutters couldn't hide its age. The roof line of heavy terracotta shingles bowed and waved, and a tie-rod piercing the ancient masonry showed where it had needed reinforcing.

Through a wisteria-lined archway to the right of the building, Chantal could see stone flags.

Berenger killed the engine. "This is it."

She climbed out and Berenger guided her through the arch to the flagged yard. Here the land, striped with vines, fell gently to a glinting river. On the far side, a yellow tractor plowed a bare field, its engine rumbling.

Berenger slid his fingers through hers. "Welcome to La Picarie."

She'd guessed as much.

Berenger nodded at the water rippling below. "That's the stream we picnicked at. We haven't driven far but it's twisted and turned three times the distance to get here. You can see how much wider it is now." He tilted his head back to breathe in La Picarie's air and his shoulders relaxed.

"My special place." His gaze shifted to the tractor tacking to and fro on its far bank. "Kept me sane two years ago. If I'd been in an office in a big city, I'd have gone mad. But being out here helped."

He wanted to talk, and she wanted to learn all she could about him. "How?" she asked.

He sighed. "At home, even in the estate winery, people surrounded me. Suffocated me. Talked at me. About things that had broken and things that couldn't be fixed. Ever." The pressure on her fingers tightened. "I felt they all watched me. Judged me."

Chantal listened in silence.

"Looking back, I can see they were concerned for me," he admitted. "But I have a tendency to assume the worst. All those schoolyard fights. Bite before I'm bitten. Don't wait to listen."

He paused and Chantal risked a gentle nudge. "And La Picarie helped?"

"Out here I could be alone. And I could create. Setting up to make good wine from the best soil in these parts. Out here I wasn't patching up what was broken, but making something new and worthwhile. Come and look." Still holding her hand, he jumped down the three steps that led to the rough soil and drew her to the nearest vines.

"This row is Ondenc. It's still rare around here, replanted from vines brought back from the Barossa

Valley, the ones I told you about in the café." He ran a finger over a shoot about to burst into life. "The vine's still young, you see?"

She nodded.

"Next year will be my first harvest."

They walked on. Berenger held her hand in his, but his free hand surfed gently over the sprouting vines. "A heritage variety grown on my mother's family land. It's the best of the past, but combined to make something new and unique."

Berenger fell silent. At the row's end, they turned back.

Chantal looked ahead to the low stone building. "You must have a lot of happy memories here, too? Sharing it with Louise and Mireille?"

"Mireille rarely came here. Louise likes it, though. She's a real country girl at heart."

"Mireille wasn't?"

"Not really." His clipped tone closed down her enquiry.

Chantal looked around again, from the old building to the ranks of young vines and on to the fast-flowing river below. The late afternoon sun cast it all in a golden glow. "It's marvelous."

"A marvelous amount of work," he grumbled. "Drainage, plantings, pruning. Year after year."

"Perfectly horrible."

"You're right, Chantal. I love it all."

They headed back to the farm past a stack of old barrels. Chantal expected a further lecture on wine-making. Instead, Berenger stopped at the edge of the patio, one step below her, their heads level. His eyes burned gas-flame blue. "What's your verdict? Too boring? Nothing to do if you're not obsessed by wine?"

"Not remotely boring. Give me a blanket down by the river, my macramé board and fifty beads, and I won't move all day."

"It's pretty basic inside, you know."

She slid her arms around his neck, sensing he needed comfort. "Listen to me. Rural settings don't scare me, nor does roughing it once in a while. I'm not a Girl Scout type, but if I've lived in cities, it's been by necessity. I know nothing about wine-making but you could safely leave the coffee to me."

His drew in a breath. "Believe me, Chantal, I'm not thinking of wine now. I'm thinking of you."

Chantal couldn't resist teasing. "And I thought you were fixated on soil and piping and—"

He silenced her with a kiss, as she'd hoped he would. His arms pulled her in close and the weight of his mouth rested cashmere-soft on hers. She caught his scent of nutmeg. At his nape, she twined her fingers around the little curls.

Straining closer, she wriggled her arms under his sweater and shirt. Her fingers stroked the warm skin between his shoulder blades. A mental image of his naked back drew a tiny groan from her.

The sound jolted Berenger like another electric shock. He broke off the kiss and whispered, "Shall we go inside? There's a heater."

"Good," she muttered back. "I want to be warm enough to take my coat off."

His eyes darkened. In one smooth movement, he swept her into his arms. Chantal snuggled into his chest for the short journey to the blue-shuttered door, and enjoyed feeling protected.

He reached for a key. Inside, he pushed back the window shutters. The light angled in on mismatched furniture. A large, old-fashioned sofa and an armchair sat around a rich, red rug. An inevitable chill came off the stone walls, and Berenger at once switched on a gas heater.

He guided her across the rug and then hesitated. "This sofa folds out to a bed. Shall we open it? Or will you make that coffee you talked about, and then I'll drive you home? Either is OK with me."

His restraint won her in ways that pushiness never could have. Their physical chemistry couldn't be denied, but it went deeper. The sense of discovering the essential Berenger, layer by layer, had intoxicated her.

Her fingers longed to touch him again. She smiled her answer.

He moved in close. "I can tell you this, Chantal. I've wanted you from that first night we met in the street. I should only have been worried about Louise, and instead I found myself thinking about you, a total stranger."

She could spend all afternoon listening to him talk about wanting her.

His arms tightened around her. Standing this close to him felt the safest place on earth. "I haven't noticed a woman in two years. Then you came along. I felt guilty, I suppose."

"To Mireille's memory."

"No, Chérie."

He'd never called her Chérie before. It captivated her. She had to drag her attention back to his next words.

"Not Mireille, but Louise. I swore she'd be the one woman in my life after the crash. Yet here you are."

Chantal smiled gently. "You weren't looking for anyone, and I know for sure I wasn't looking for a man. I wonder how we got here."

"Do you?" He kissed her, his lips like warm feathers on hers. She imagined that sensation on other parts of her body and heat flared inside her.

She glanced at the bed.

"Give us a chance, Chantal. Not today, if you don't want to, but soon."

"I do want to," she said. "A lot. Now. Unfold it." She was surprised to hear how unsteady she sounded.

He didn't need telling twice.

He sat down on the newly spread blankets and pulled her onto his lap. Enjoying the calm before the inevitable storm, they kissed.

Without breaking contact with her mouth, Berenger eased her out of her cardigan. His hands traveled up her body, thumbs extended, straining for the first contact with her breasts. He traced their sensitive undersides from side to side. Slowly, he rolled his thumbs over the top and down across her nipples. A shudder ran through her.

She leaned back to pull her blouse over her head. Looking down, she saw a head of dark, wiry hair obscuring the lacy white fabric of her bra. Warm kisses filled the shallow valley between her breasts.

Deft fingers unhooked her bra and let it drop to the bed. Berenger raised his head a little to look at what he'd revealed. "You're perfect," he murmured. "Beautiful." He cupped each breast in turn and kissed its upper curve.

"Am I the only one who's going to get naked?" Her whisper brought Berenger's face up to hers. He kissed the corner of her mouth.

"No, Chérie, I'd be glad to join you." His sweater was off in a second. When he reached for the buttons of his shirt, she put her hand out to stop him. "My job," she whispered. "Why don't you lie down?"

He obliged, and she straddled his belly. He stretched his arms up to stroke hers. She inched a little higher and undid his top two buttons. For long seconds, her fingers explored, luxuriating in the first touch of his chest. Fine, even hair covered his upper torso. Slowly, she undid the buttons down to his waistband. Below his pectorals, the hair funneled into an inverted triangle. It was a signpost, pointing down.

Chantal could follow directions.

She wriggled lower for room to undo his belt and found herself sitting on the hard evidence of his desire.

"Do you mind?" Berenger asked through gritted teeth. "Some bits of me really can't take any more pressure."

Chantal smiled wickedly. "I was working towards releasing it all, actually."

Berenger sat up and held her firmly to him. Instead of

the embrace she expected, he swiveled and reversed their positions. "My turn to stoke the fire."

"You could start by taking your shirt off," murmured Chantal. "I'm sure that would raise my temperature a few degrees." She reached an arm up to slip one shoulder out of the fabric. He shook off the other.

The sight of him above her, half naked in the afternoon light, spoke to a primal instinct. A powerful male, a protector. His shoulders were like steel joists. The muscles in his arms and chest bunched as he kept his weight off her body.

Adrenalin flushed into her blood, wakening the very few parts of her not already on full alert. She pulled his head down to hers, urgently seeking out his lips. He responded, cradling her body against his. She was dimly aware he could have crushed her to him. His gentleness moved her more than his raw strength.

A wholly new sensation interrupted her thoughts. Berenger's mouth had drifted below her neck. By millimeters, he made his way towards her breasts. As she waited, her nipples ached, anticipating the touch of his mouth. When he reached his destination, an invisible conduit sprang up, linking her breasts to her lower abdomen. He teased her nipples, one after the other, and the pressure between her legs grew. He was assailing her tenderly on so many fronts. His hands roamed over her, stroking, cupping. His mouth tickled and nibbled.

Chantal lay in a daze of pleasure. What he was doing was wonderful, but she wanted them to reach journey's end together. She rolled towards him and he gracefully ceded the upper position.

He refused to lie passive, though. Even while she enjoyed evoking his mounting excitement with her hands and lips, he continued exploring her. It became a dance of give and take, gifts generously offered, and eagerly accepted. Somewhere in the ebb and flow of their lovemaking, they shed their final pieces of clothing. The sensation of Berenger's skin against hers seared itself into Chantal's mind. The first top-to-toe contact became a lifetime memory in a second.

Their movements grew more feverish, their bodies communicating a shared and rising passion. Chantal longed for the final intimacy. She sat astride him. The choice of moment belonged to her alone.

She chose.

Berenger responded with a steady, deep thrust, filling her and making them both quiver. They began to move together, their well-matched height an asset.

Berenger's eyes fixed on hers. She had nowhere to run, nowhere to hide. She knew her face told Berenger all he needed to know of her pleasure.

Eventually, Berenger's gaze grew unfocused. She wanted to stay with him, but her mind wouldn't co-operate. The torrent of their passion swept her attention away.

They surged on, clinging together in the tumult. The current overwhelmed them both. Within seconds of each other, they reached the lip of a chasm and plunged over, twisting and turning in the limitless fall.

Chantal gasped and swept sweat-slick hair off her forehead. She collapsed onto Berenger's chest and his arms immediately encircled her. She could hear the pistons of his heart hammering beneath her cheek.

They rested, unmoving, drained by the intensity of their union. Chantal shivered slightly and Berenger rescued a tangled blanket from the floor for her. She snuggled into the crook of his arm, her chin propped on his chest.

"OK?" he asked tenderly, his voice deep.

"Wonderful," she smiled.

"Weren't we?" He traced a strong finger across her eyebrows. "You're becoming very special to me, Chantal Harrison. I hope you never leave."

Every last vestige of her defenses against him crumbled. She had no desire to stop her headlong plunge toward love. "I'm very glad to hear it," she whispered at last. "I don't want to be the only one losing control around here."

They held fast to each other and fell asleep.

The real world intruded an hour later when the metallic tones of Berenger's cell phone woke them. Groaning, he tumbled out of bed and grabbed for his jacket.

She vaguely heard the conversation. A note of alarm in Berenger's voice brought her upright. He snapped the phone off and headed for his clothes. "Delgarde rang from the shop," he said tersely. "He was locking up and thought he heard a crash from inside Number 8. Could be Mulberry."

She swung her legs over the bed, already tensing for action. There'd be more intimate times with Berenger. Meanwhile, they had an intruder to catch.

CHAPTER TWENTY SEVEN

Berenger held the blue-shuttered door open for Chantal and his fingers stretched out to trace along her cornflour-smooth cheek as she hurried by.

He ought to be hurrying, too. With every minute, it grew more likely Mulberry would escape. Yet Berenger stood and stared at the empty arch in the twilight, trying to paint Chantal's image into its frame. He could only capture a fleeting glimpse of auburn hair. Suddenly, he doubted she'd ever been with him.

He snatched at his sweater, hunting for a trace of her scent. The heavy oriental perfume he'd caught on her that first night, she'd told him, had been her aunt's Italian bath oil. At last he caught the scent that was unequivocally Chantal's: apple from her hair, mixing with a light rose scent. It should have reassured him, but the old ghosts rose all about him.

For so long, his life had shuttled between work and Louise. Was he wrong to add a third element? To want a passionate woman who seemed to return his growing feelings?

She'll grow bored. And then she'll want to leave Cordes.

Berenger clenched his jaw. He knew this negative voice

all too well. It would goad him all day if he let it.

"Hurry up!" Chantal's call cut into his reverie. "Mulberry won't wait."

On the way back to Cordes, he kept his foot hard on the gas, yet sneaked glances at Chantal whenever the dark road allowed it. She'd tucked her hair behind her ear. A small, gold-striped blue bead set off the delicate lobe and he longed to trace its outline with his lips.

At Grand' Rue, he pulled the SUV over at the door of his store. Delgarde, in his late forties, but looking younger under his thick, dark brown hair, came out to meet them. Berenger tossed him the keys. "Park it for me, would you? I don't know how long we'll be."

"Wait, *patron*, I've remembered something." He rubbed his hand across his mouth, revealing the woven leather band he liked to wear on his wrist.

Fleetingly, Berenger wondered what Chantal thought of the bracelet.

"A tourist came in earlier, *patron*," said Delgarde. "I said we'd soon be closing, but he wanted to look at what we had. Then the phone went and while I was answering it, I heard the gong for the front door opening."

"You sure he left the shop?"

"No. I'm not. What if he opened the door enough to trigger the gong, then went through the yard to your new place? Could be he caused that crash I heard from over the wall."

"What did he look like?" Chantal asked eagerly.

Delgarde addressed his answer to Berenger as if Chantal didn't exist. It didn't surprise his employer; Delgarde was old school at heart, whatever his trendy accessories. "Short, broad. Couldn't see much of his face, what with his scarf and beret. He sounded like a foreigner, though he didn't look it."

To a local like Delgarde, who, Berenger knew, had barely traveled a hundred miles from Cordes in his life, that could mean anything from a Norman to a Norwegian.

Chantal's eyes lit up at Delgarde's description, though.

"Stay here," Berenger ordered the older man. "Forget the car for now. Don't let anyone in or out of the front door, understand?"

"Got it."

Berenger led the way swiftly through the shop, knowing how readily Chantal would court danger to catch Mulberry.

The little room at the back had been a storage area. Awaiting the alterations, it stood empty except for drapes at the window, and an empty wooden packing case. One day soon, he hoped this room would become part of the extended tasting area. Usually, its south-facing aspect kept it warm, but now it felt cool. The French doors that opened onto the walled yard hung open. Delgarde's doing, or Mulberry's?

Berenger checked behind the drapes and then looked outside. The little yard offered nowhere to hide, but one of the metal chairs had been moved hard up to the wall. The ivy above it bore signs of damage, and a few freshly fallen leaves suggested someone had scrambled over not long before.

Chantal was close behind him. He caught her scent.

"Let's go out and listen," he said softly, putting a restraining arm around her. Given a choice, he'd have her in the main shop with Delgarde standing over her, but he knew he'd as much chance of that as of growing another six inches.

They stepped quietly out into the twilight. Berenger caught no more than a faint hum from Grand' Rue. Nothing happened. He began to relax. The man might have left. Or Delgarde might have been mistaken.

A door rattled on the other side of the wall.

They both froze.

A short jangle and a slight squeak from old hinges came over the wall.

"The kitchen door," breathed Chantal, her eyes wide.

Berenger put himself between Chantal and the wall. The next second, he changed his mind and gestured urgently for her to move back into the shop. She resisted until he made it clear he was coming, too. They hid behind the drapes, and Berenger held open a spy-hole between the fabric and the door frame.

He planned to tackle the man the instant he landed in the yard. He'd need room to do it and hoped to heck Chantal would stay put this time.

Something heavy scraped over the flagstones on Number 8's side of the wall.

"He's moving the rubbish bin," Chantal whispered.

Adrenalin flooded Berenger's body.

Any second…

A figure appeared, high on the other side of the wall.

"Mulberry!" gasped Chantal in his ear.

The man wore his signature scarf, muffling half his face, with the scarf ends tucked into a gray jacket. He swung a short leg over the wall and dropped down.

Berenger sprang.

This time the odds favored him, and he pounced before Mulberry could find his balance. With his fist clenched around the purple scarf, Berenger hauled him to his feet. As the man's arms flailed, Berenger gave the scarf a sharp twist, feeling a stab of primitive satisfaction as the man choked. Mulberry had hurt his woman. Now he would pay.

Mulberry wrenched at the scarf. Berenger seized Mulberry's wrist and twisted it sharply behind his back. Pinned by neck and arm, Mulberry kicked back hard.

"Damn!" The pain in Berenger's shin shredded any self-control he had left. Using the scarf and arm as control points, he propelled his captive to the storeroom.

"You're going to throttle him!" Chantal stood back to let them pass, her eyes wide.

"Chantal, remember who this is. A house-breaker. An attacker!" At each word he shook his prisoner hard. "And, let's not forget, a poisoner."

"No!" Mulberry gurgled in protest.

Berenger slackened the pressure on the scarf an inch. Mulberry dragged in a deep breath in relief.

"You're denying it? We'll soon see about that." Berenger turned to the front of the shop and yelled, "Delgarde!"

Mulberry jumped in his grip at the bellow.

"Bolt the front door, we've caught him. And bring a chair."

"We should call the police," Chantal said.

"Yes! The police, please," agreed Mulberry. It was clear he preferred his chances with the law than in Berenger's furious grip. With the scarf away from his face, he appeared to be in his early fifties, with a weather-beaten complexion and straight, black hair graying at the temples. His stocky frame appeared suited to wrestling, but there was no doubting this was the man who had twice out-sprinted Berenger.

"No police yet," said Berenger. "Let's hear what he's got to say for himself first. Lock those doors, please, Chantal. I don't want to have to chase him over the wall. He's more agile than a mountain goat."

"Berenger, this is a matter for the police. They know we're on his trail. If he ends up hurt…" Her gray eyes widened with concern.

Frustration burned inside him. How could she be so tender-hearted? If he let himself imagine what could have happened if she'd met Mulberry alone in the graveyard as she'd planned…

Still, he couldn't go on throttling the man forever. "OK, OK."

When Delgarde came through, Berenger managed to keep a reasonable tone. "Our intruder, as you see, Delgarde. We're going to have a little conversation with him. Ten minutes from now, I want you to call Inspector Riberon in Albi and let him know the situation. Tell him this man climbed into our yard from Jeanne Lamarque's house. That should get his attention."

Delgarde received the instructions impassively. He set down the chair. "Yes, *patron*. Shall I find some rope?"

Berenger turned to Mulberry. "What do you say?" He couldn't resist giving the man another shake. "Will you sit quietly and wait for the police, or shall we tie you up?"

"I'll sit." Mulberry's voice rasped despite the removal of the scarf's pressure. Berenger deposited Mulberry firmly on the hard, wooden seat and Delgarde, glancing at his watch to begin the ten-minute countdown, returned to his guard duty at the front door.

Mulberry rubbed his throat. He pointedly ignored Berenger and looked across at Chantal who had retreated to perch on the wooden crate. The low seat placed her lower than their prisoner, and Berenger saw her smile tentatively at Mulberry, as if to build a bridge of goodwill.

Perhaps they could play this good cop, bad cop. Berenger was judging the right moment to begin his interrogation when Mulberry started talking.

"I'm very sorry I hurt you on the stairs last week, Mam'selle. I was scared, not thinking." Though he spoke with none of a foreigner's hesitation, Berenger hadn't heard the accent before. The fellow was smart, though, leading off with an apology.

It worked a charm with Chantal. She smiled warmly and leaned forward. "I know. I was scared, too."

"My name is Yvan Vico." He thumped his chest with his fist. "From Corsica."

Chantal flashed Berenger a glance. He knew what it meant. *The photo album.* Calvi, in Corsica.

Chantal introduced herself, and Berenger, and continued, "Yvan, you knew Jeanne Lamarque, my great-aunt, who lived in that house?" She pointed outside, across the yard wall.

Confusion rode across Yvan's features.

"Either you knew her or you didn't," Berenger

snapped. The man was playing games, encouraged by the good cop.

In answer, Yvan turned away from his interrogator to face Chantal. "She was your great-aunt? I'm so sorry. You must be sad at losing her."

The Corsican had simply ducked the question. That signaled guilt as clearly as his skill at breaking in.

Chantal seemed unaware of the man's tactics. "Yes, I am, very sad. Are you?"

He sat silent so long that Berenger thought he would refuse to answer. Finally he said, "Who isn't sad when his mother dies?"

Chantal grasped Yvan's sleeve. "Jeanne was your *mother*?"

"Yes. But I never knew her. My father always told me she was dead. And then my father died a month ago."

"I'm sorry." Chantal's sympathy at Yvan's bereavement touched even Berenger. "And he told you the truth before he died?" she asked softly.

"No, Tanta, our village's wise woman, told me, after we buried my father. She knew my mother slightly, they were a similar age. She told me my mother ran away after I was born, scared, not trusting in my father's love for her. Tanta said she never heard from my mother again after she left Corsica, until she wrote to Tanta six weeks ago. She sent it to an old address, but in Calvi everyone knows everyone."

"Aunt Jeanne wrote to this woman, this Tanta? Why?"

"Tanta said my mother feared she had become ill in her mind. She wanted Tanta to help her make amends before she died — or before she went mad."

At these words, Chantal threw Berenger another look, and he could tell she believed this tale. She couldn't see that Vico wanted to lull them into believing he hadn't done the poisoning.

"You were in Corsica all this time?" Berenger asked.

"Of course," Yvan said curtly. He addressed Chantal, "Tanta showed my father the letter, but he destroyed it.

She said he refused to speak of it, or her. I knew nothing of this. Two weeks later, he died. Then I found this in his things."

He wriggled a hand inside his shirt. Berenger leapt forward and clamped his hand on Yvan's arm.

"You think it's a gun? Maybe a proper Corsican knife?" Scorn carved the lines around Yvan's mouth more deeply. "For you, maybe, but not for my cousin." He bowed his head politely at Chantal and asked her, "You'll allow me?"

She looked at Berenger, impatience on her face.

Berenger ignored it. They would do this his way.

"I pull your arm out of your shirt," he said. "You show me what you've got under there. If it's OK, I'll let go."

Yvan made an exaggerated shrug into an insult. Berenger felt a new surge of anger. Roughly, he hauled the Corsican's hand into sight. From Yvan's stubby fingers dangled a silver locket, still attached to a chain around his neck. Berenger let him go.

Yvan unfastened the chain and handed the locket to Chantal. "I wanted to bury it with her. That's why I went to the graveyard. To put it near her in her tomb. Not to disturb her rest."

Chantal took it gently and opened it. She gasped. "Oh, Berenger, see — it's Aunt Jeanne." She stood to show him the two pictures inside. "She can't have been more than twenty."

That fitted with the dates in Mezaute's notes and with the missing photo album. "1947 or '48," he muttered.

Yvan nodded. "Yes. I'm fifty-one."

Berenger squinted at the locket. "That's you."

Yvan laughed for the first time. "No, that's my father. We're very alike."

"Oh, he liked to terrify women and break into other people's houses too, did he?"

"Berenger!"

"I never terrified her! But I did enter her house. I needed to know about her. It was like—like a constant hunger." He drew a deep breath. "I used the key from under the flowerpot twice, till you changed the lock. By then I had a copy of the back door key and I used this shop to get through. It was easy." Yvan threw the comment at Berenger, his chin jutting in challenge. Berenger's fist itched to punch it.

"Mulb—Yvan," Chantal began gently, "Why didn't you just explain who you were? Why this sneaking and stealing?"

Yvan's eyes flashed. "I never stole!"

"She means the photo album you helped yourself to."

"I brought it back, didn't I? I wanted to make copies to keep. I never stole it."

"All right," said Chantal. "Not stealing. But you were sneaking. Every time we saw you, you ran."

"Damn fast, too," said Berenger in a bitter tone that made Yvan smile.

"For a short man, eh? I was the Corsican sprint champion in '69. And I still like to run." He glanced across. "You weren't that slow. For a man with spider legs."

Blood vessels bulged in Berenger's neck at the Corsican's arrogance.

"Will you two stop it?" Chantal said in exasperation. "Yvan, what stopped you asking me directly about Aunt Jeanne?"

"I couldn't come to you." There was a hint of despair in the way he shook his head. "I was too guilty."

Berenger clenched his fist. Here it came, the admission of how Yvan had in fact tried to scare Jeanne away. His tormented lovechild story was no more than a cover.

"What did you do?" Chantal prompted.

"I caused my mother's death. By accident."

A police siren wailed in counterpoint to his whisper. He jumped, and Berenger sprang forward.

"Not so fast. You killed her when your scare tactics failed, didn't you? What drove you to it? She wouldn't accept you as her own, so you killed her and started hunting for hard proof of your birth? Trying to stake a claim to her property as her son?"

Yvan answered with a howl of anguish. He hid his face in his hands. From behind them, and over the noise of the approaching siren, he gasped out his tale. "I came here to Cordes for the first time only last Friday. With the locket, to show it to her, to talk to her. The church bells were ringing and I waited for them to stop. Then I knocked, but the door was already open. She stood at the head of the stairs. My heart was so full I couldn't say anything. She saw me. Maybe she thought she saw my father. She clutched, here—" he slapped his hand to his chest, "—and then she slipped. I jumped to catch her, but I had too little time. She landed hard with her neck bent. She had no pulse, no breath. An accident."

He rubbed his face as if to scrub away the horror. "And then?" Chantal prompted.

"I knew she was dead. I'm ashamed now that I left her like that. I ran back to my hotel in Toulouse. But I couldn't stay away."

Outside, the siren wound down to silence. Next came slamming doors and shouts. The noise interrupted Berenger's thoughts. They'd missed something. Before he could grasp it, Delgarde brought in two local policemen.

"Riberon sent us, Monsieur. Said we're to take an intruder into custody, and asked for you to come and give statements at Albi by Monday latest, please."

Chantal tried to protest, but Yvan made it easy. "Don't distress yourself, cousin. I'll tell them what I told you. They'll find the proof that it's true."

The police group was leaving when Berenger caught the niggling thought. He grabbed Yvan's shoulders. "Wait! When were you there on Friday? How many times did the church bells chime?"

Startled by the unexpected question, Yvan answered simply, "Twelve. She died a minute after noon."

Berenger clenched his fist again, this time in victory.
At last.

"Thank you, Monsieur Vico." He inclined his head with a level of courtesy he usually reserved for his better customers. "This time, you've done me a great service, and in front of impeccable witnesses. Chantal, come on, we've got something big to celebrate. We're going halves in an old house."

CHAPTER TWENTY-EIGHT

In the doorway of the wine shop, Chantal leaned back against Berenger. The police car maneuvered around Berenger's SUV, still illegally parked, and disappeared over the crest of the hill. Chantal watched it go with a mix of regret and relief. She'd gained a family member, but not in circumstances she'd have chosen.

"Yvan's behind it all. He's denying half of it to bolster his claim that Jeanne's death wasn't murder." Berenger kissed the back of her head to soften the brutal words. "We'll go to Albi and give Riberon our statements soon. This is one case he doesn't need imagination for. There's opportunity, means, and one heck of a motive."

"I don't want a murderer, or a vindictive brute for a relative," she sighed. "I want to believe what he said."

"I know." His voice grew gentle. "But he's had time to concoct that story, Chérie. I think he stirred in just enough truth to make it sound believable."

"I suppose so. But his remorse seemed real. So did his desperate need to find out more about Aunt Jeanne."

"He's desperate all right, but I doubt it's for happy family photos. Illegitimate children can inherit in France now, you know. He may have demanded full recognition.

If she rejected him a second time…"

"And if things turned ugly," Chantal continued his line of reasoning and shivered, "Aunt Jeanne paid the ultimate price."

Berenger's arm came around her in a circle of comfort, shutting out the cool evening and the worst of the pictures in her head.

"I don't want a cent of my purchase money to go to him," he said grimly. "I want you to have it."

"I don't care about the money. I truly don't. And maybe Yvan does deserve something for the years of abandonment. I wonder who brought him up. If his father married someone kind."

"Chantal, you're too soft-hearted." Impatience mixed with amusement in his tone.

He drew her back inside and told Delgarde he could leave. The man donned his beret and muttered a goodbye to his boss while giving Chantal only the briefest of nods. The courtesy bell on the door announced his departure.

Berenger scooped his car keys off the counter. "Now, could we forget Yvan for a while and go and celebrate?"

"Don't you think we should check Number 8 first? What if Yvan left a mess?" Chantal couldn't identify the source of her unease. "I'd like to set my mind at rest, that's all. Wouldn't you, too? As the new owner?" she added knowingly.

He sighed. "Do you want to jump over the wall or shall we walk around?"

They opted to park the car legally before their luck ran out, and then walk on to Number 8. They covered the distance down Les Rampes and onto Rue Obscure arm-in-arm, Chantal enjoying again how well matched they were in height. The nighttime chill through the arch became her friend, offering a good excuse to snuggle a little closer. When they reached Number 8, Berenger used his left hand to unlock Aunt Jeanne's front door—his front door, now—which kept her tight by his side for another few seconds. It also, Chantal noted, allowed him to enter first and protect her from any danger. After the recent drama of capturing Yvan, she cheerfully relinquished any heroic lead role, and followed him in.

Berenger turned back to her, a crooked half-smile on his lips. "Welcome to my house."

She clasped her arms around his neck and gave him a victor's kiss. He returned it with searing intensity.

"So you believe what Yvan said about Aunt Jeanne's time of death?" she whispered.

"I do. That bit rang true. Number 8 is mine." His arms tightened around her as if to suggest not only the house belonged to him.

She smiled up at him. "And how are we going to celebrate your good news?"

"I have one idea in mind," he rumbled against her ear. Already, she could feel the evidence of that particular notion against her belly. "But it'll be sweeter for the wait," he said, "and even sweeter after a little of the best champagne."

"Aunt Jeanne liked good champagne, but there's nothing here I'd trust to drink."

"But there is in the chiller at our place. So let's make sure this house is in order and then get down there to share the good news."

Reluctantly they drew apart, but their fingers interlaced. They climbed upstairs hand-in-hand to start their rounds, in what Berenger referred to as Chantal's share of the house. As they peered around doors and in cupboards, where nothing appeared to have been disturbed, Chantal found herself choosing the room she'd like for her workshop. It had to be the one with the photo albums, the room that enjoyed the best of the wide, unbroken view over the valley to the south.

Back downstairs, she showed Berenger where she'd hidden the key to Aunt Jeanne's office. She led the way into the little room, feeling sure, with the key in its hiding place, that nothing unpleasant awaited on the other side. The document box with Aunt Jeanne's Eye of the Needle research sat safely on the desk where she'd left it.

"Smells like the Historical Society's library in here," said Berenger, wrinkling his nose.

"You don't like it either?" Chantal said, happy to find another thing they shared, however trifling. She gestured at the crammed shelves. "Somewhere here there might be a hint about Yvan and his father. I'm struggling so much with the idea of my kind and generous great-aunt deserting a baby. She was a loving person. To me, to the house, even to all the different causes she supported over the years. It seems so out of character."

"Sounds like she was compensating. Not with you, but with all the attention on this house. And with those good causes—fixing what was broken."

Chantal looked at him in surprise. "Hark at Dr. Freud. But that makes a lot of sense."

"I've spent a lot of time around psychologists, remember, for Louise. Some of it's stuck."

"But how awful, to have one early mistake cast a shadow over your whole life. Poor Aunt Jeanne. She never married, never had any more children." Chantal felt tears welling up and turned away, staring at the shuttered window and fighting down the pity that twined in her chest. "It's too sad," she said crossly, annoyed at how easily her tears seemed to flow.

In answer, a warm hand caressed her neck and a soft kiss landed on the back of her head. "I didn't know your great-aunt well, Chérie, but, from what I heard at the wake, I'd say she enjoyed life and gave pleasure to others. Most lives combine light and shade."

She had to agree, and spun back to him, knowing being in his arms would chase shadows away.

When they broke apart, foreheads still touching, she could feel the smile on her face.

"Good," Berenger said. "You look happier. How about

after the champagne I take you to Le Grand Ecuyer? They've just opened for the season."

She knew it was the best restaurant for miles around, a gastronomic, Michelin-starred jewel, where princes and presidents had dined. She'd walked past its Gothic-arched doors on Grand' Rue a thousand times without ever going in. The notion of entering on Berenger's arm stirred up a mix of excitement and apprehension. "On a Saturday night? Without a booking?"

"You're underestimating the Morel charm."

"I bet you went to kindergarten with the maitre d'."

"His daughter," he chuckled, giving her a tight squeeze. Chantal wriggled in playful response and her thigh knocked the document box. It thudded to the floor and its lid popped open, letting a sheaf of papers slither out like a white snake. The scroll rolled away under the desk.

"Damn."

Berenger caught her shoulder before she could stoop to tidy the mess. "My fault, and there's only room for one of us. I'll do it."

His large hands quickly gathered the sheets back into the box and, with a stretch, he gripped the scroll.

"Careful," murmured Chantal, reaching down to take it from him. "It's the original of the map that shows the Eye of the Needle symbol. Aunt Jeanne found it when the kitchen fireplace got repaired."

Berenger stood up again with a grunt of effort. "Do you want to show it to me?"

She wrinkled her nose at him in disgust. "Go to the basement? Haven't we had enough adventure for the day with Mulberry?"

"I meant the scroll, or a copy of it. But yes, I could stand a little more adventure. Especially if you had to press very close to me in the darkness because you were scared." He flashed her a wolfish grin.

"More likely because the passageways are too narrow," retorted Chantal.

"That sounds good, too. Come, one last adventure before champagne and food." He held out a hand to her.

She clasped it, but shook her head. "No. Enough. We meant for today to be a rest from sleuthing and chasing. I'm not going into the cold and dark so you can check whether I've been imagining things. Not when there's champagne and gourmet food waiting." She reached for the document box. "But I'll take Aunt Jeanne's copy of the map if I can find it quickly. Then you can see the clues I followed."

"Very well," he grumbled, but she could hear the teasing in his voice. "Whatever Mam'selle wishes. But let's hurry, hey? First I have to deal with the restaurant, and, if I succeed, I have the even tougher job of telling Ah Wong we won't be eating her dinner. She hates late changes to her meal plans, and my track record this last week has been terrible."

Chantal spotted Aunt Jeanne's copy of the map among the first few papers in the box, and flourished it above her head. "Got it. Let's go, so you can battle your dragons."

CHAPTER TWENTY-NINE

Ten minutes later, the SUV scrunched to a halt on the chateau's gravel. Another ten minutes after that, in the family room, Berenger poured champagne into six glasses with a steady, practiced hand.

"A local vintage?" asked Chantal.

Berenger shook his head, concentrating on the pale yellow liquid. "By definition, champagne is made only in the Champagne region up north. Though our *perlés* are as fine, in their own way."

"*Mon Dieu*," said his father, catching sight of the label for the first time. "That isn't regular champagne. You've gone for a *grand cru*."

"It isn't every day I gain something so precious." Berenger sought out Chantal's gaze for a long moment, and her heart rate ratcheted up a notch as she watched his eyes turn twilight blue.

"Indeed," Armand agreed, missing their private look. "Number 8, the missing piece in your wine business."

"I certainly hope so." As he finished pouring, Berenger twisted the bottle to prevent even a drop going to waste.

Ah Wong joined them, her repeated head bobs showing how pleased she was to hear the news. Wilbur took a glass and the last, smallest portion went to Louise, now dressed in her pajamas.

She'd turned cranky, tugging at Ah Wong's sleeve, then Chantal's and her grandfather's. She wanted another round of her afternoon game of Explorers. The special treat of wine finally silenced her, and peace descended.

"To my house on Rue Obscure," toasted Berenger, holding up his crystal flute.

"The house on Rue Obscure," they all echoed, and sipped.

Armand forgot his manners enough to smack his lips in appreciation.

"You know this bottle was made by the sixth generation of vintners, all from the same family?" Berenger said, holding his glass to the light. "A wine dynasty. I'd like that. To build a business that could far outlive me."

"You forget, Berenger." Armand squeezed his son's shoulder. "You're already a fourth-generation vintner on your mother's side. *Her* grandfather developed La Picarie. He might not have borne the name Morel, but he's as much in your blood as anyone in the direct paternal line."

"A good thought," nodded Berenger, before taking another swallow of the fine vintage.

Chantal could tell by the relaxed lines around Berenger's eyes how much he was enjoying knowing the house was his. Or would be, as soon as the lawyers received the necessary paperwork from the police.

And if he ever asks you to marry him, you'll know it's not because he's trying for a legal way to get the house.

Louise soon resumed her sleeve-tugging.

"It's too late to explore," Chantal said firmly, backing up Ah Wong who had said the same. "But if you bring the pebbles you collected from the stream, we can sort some of them, like I promised you." Chantal took a quick look at her watch; dinner was booked for eight, and she needed time to freshen up and conjure a new and romantic look from the one smart dress in her small suitcase.

Louise swung her head to and fro in stubborn refusal. "I've been exploring in the basement," she explained at last. "At the far end. Come and tell me what you see."

"The basement? You not go there, Louise," Ah Wong said at once. "I tell you many times. Too many things could hurt you."

"I'm sorry!" said Wilbur who had bumped into Armand and splashed champagne onto a side table.

Ah Wong shook her head but quickly fetched a serviette. "You stay away from cellars, Louise," she urged again, as she deftly mopped up the spill.

"What are you worried about, Ah Wong?" said Wilbur, leaning his thin frame against the mantelpiece. "There's nothing much down there, and I'm a regular visitor, as you know. You hiding a secret down there, maybe?"

"You have secret there, not me," she hissed.

"What does Ah Wong mean?" asked Louise, distracted from her whining. "What's your secret, Monsieur Sanders?"

Wilbur's brown eyes twinkled. "One your pa and grandpa know all about, whatever Miz Wong may say. When I'm hard at work, I sometimes like a bottle of wine. She found me helping myself one night and still sees me as a thief. Don't you, Miz Wong?"

The housekeeper's eyes shrank to reptilian slits. "You always walking around, late."

"Walking helps me think, when I have a problem with my Ph.D."

"I see you last night, too, in the basement!"

"Now, Ah Wong," interjected Armand, in a placating tone. "Wilbur had gone to find a paper he thought he'd thrown in the trash."

"I not see him near trash bags."

"Like I said," shrugged Wilbur. "I walk around. And how about you, hey?" He returned her glare. "If you see me sometimes at night, you must be out walking the corridors too."

"I protect my family! Everyone trusts me. But I not trust you." She clamped her lips into a tense, angry line.

"Now, Ah Wong," repeated Armand, but she marched off, slamming the door into the kitchen behind her.

"Why does she say I shouldn't go down to the basement?" asked Louise, apparently unconcerned by Ah Wong's dramatic departure. "I don't want wine or the trash bags."

"Because she doesn't want you hurt," explained her father. "Old furniture and heavy boxes could fall on you. And now it's time for bed."

Berenger ushered Louise around for good night kisses from Chantal and Armand, ignoring her pleas for a few minutes longer.

When only three of them remained in the living room, Armand apologized to Wilbur for the scene, but his guest laughed it off.

"Ah Wong seems to be growing more protective, not less. You'd think after two years…" Armand shook his head. He invited Chantal to tell them more of the events with Yvan, but she excused herself to get ready for dinner.

Upstairs, she washed and dressed. The flowing lines of the bias-cut georgette offset its stern color. A pearl-gray wrap in fine wool kept her shoulders snug. Against the black and gray, her hair glowed like an autumn sunset. A jet and crystal bead necklace completed the effect.

Berenger's eyes blazed in approval when he met her at the top of the staircase.

She wasn't immune to the sight of him in formal dress, either. If they'd been alone in the house, she'd have been sorely tempted to slide his well-cut suit jacket off his broad shoulders, loosen his dark blue tie and slowly, oh so slowly, unbutton his crisp white shirt.

He could read it in her eyes. The corner of his mouth twitched. "Later," he whispered.

Yes, please, said the little voice.

CHAPTER THIRTY

On the dot of eight, Berenger held open the arched door of Le Grand Ecuyer for Chantal. She stepped inside for the first time.

The restaurant's interior resembled a sitting room for one of the great French kings. The dining chairs were high-backed and covered in richly patterned red brocade. By contrast, lacy white cloths lay over the round tables, setting off the red satin undercloths that reached to the floor. Gold-framed mirrors glinted back light from the chandeliers and electric candelabra. In one corner, a sumptuous flower arrangement half hid a delicate escritoire.

"This is marvelous," Chantal said as they relaxed with a glass of kir before ordering. "Fit for royalty."

"Certainly for nobility. This building started life as a hunting lodge for Raymond of Toulouse, the Count who founded Cordes." He broke off, and focused on someone behind her, his eyes narrowing. "What's the right etiquette for when you see a man you believed was a villain, until you caught the real one?"

She turned to see who he meant. Mezaute, and a plump, gray-haired woman she guessed to be his wife, sat at a far table. She faced Berenger again, wrinkling her nose in thought. "He could still be a villain, you know. He knew about the baby. And his medical notes were obtuse in the extreme."

Berenger quietly moved his chair around to avoid looking across at the pair. "They were to you. You'd suffered like Jeanne. Mezaute did prescribe reasonable remedies, after all. Seems to me he's only guilty of poor doctoring."

Chantal sniffed. She hadn't forgotten the way Mezaute tried to fob her off with the mention of haunting. "Go and speak to him if you want. I'm staying here."

"And I'm staying with you. If he comes over, I'll do the talking." He opened the menu.

Chantal watched with amusement. Berenger chose a set menu from the six on offer in a matter of seconds. With her agreement, he settled on the one that offered a truffle appetizer. He then concentrated with knotted brows for five minutes on the wine list before settling on an old white Burgundy to accompany the risotto. "Have to go outside Gaillac to get a wine that will stand up to truffles," he muttered.

By contrast, his choice of a local Duras to pair with the sage-infused lamb took a fraction of the time. He promised her the Duras would look almost inky-black in their glasses.

"Poor Yvan won't be dining in this sort of luxury," sighed Chantal. "Do you really think he could have been behind the absinthe and the sugar?"

"Yes," said Berenger firmly. "Obviously he's been slinking around Cordes much longer than the few days he admitted to. Pushing for his inheritance."

"I can't see Aunt Jeanne refusing her child, though."

"I can," Berenger countered. "If Yvan inherited, that would cut you out. Illegitimate children have the same legal standing as legitimate ones, once they've demonstrated their relationship. And it seems to me you were the child—or maybe grandchild—Jeanne never had. She knew and loved you. Yvan's a stranger."

"I can't believe Aunt Jeanne would have rejected him twice, though. Imagine how that must have felt. I could almost forgive him."

The Burgundy arrived and diverted Berenger. He plunged into a brief but intense conversation with the black-aproned sommelier as to the logic for his earlier wine-food match choice. After he had tasted the white, he gestured for the waiter to pour. The risotto came shortly after, pungent with fine slices of black truffle.

The wine and food appeared to soothe him. "How about we wait for the police to make more checks on Yvan next week? Let the evidence do the talking," he suggested. "There's the Corsican end, as well as the hotel he stayed at here. Number 8 for prints, too."

"They're certain to find them. He seems to have spent enough time there." Chantal chased a sliver of truffle around the wide dish, determined not to let a scrap escape. "And the lab reports from Toulouse will surely prove the food and drink had been spiked. That should help build the case."

"Especially linked to such a strong motive."

A waitress cleared their plates and their conversation shifted direction.

"Do you hope Louise will follow you into the wine business one day?" Chantal asked. "The fifth generation?"

The creases above Berenger's nose deepened. "On the sales side maybe, working the phones…"

"Why couldn't she be a winemaker?" Chantal leaned in. "Louise has a unique advantage with her blindness. It's already enhancing her sense of smell, from the little I've seen. Presumably her taste buds aren't far behind. With her genes and her uncommon talents, she could be—" Chantal looked around for something to make her point. A tea-light in a shallow crystal cup illuminated their table. She scooped it up and held it out to Berenger on her palm.

"She could be *luminous.*"

"You believe in her?" he murmured, and took the finely-cut candle holder from her. Its shimmering light threw shadows across his hand, highlighting the tendons beneath his wind-tanned skin.

"I do," Chantal affirmed. "Her confidence amazes me. If she can retain even half of it as she grows up, she'll be unstoppable."

He stared at the tea-light between his fingers. "You've no idea what it means to hear that."

"Why?" she murmured.

"Because we all think of her as damaged." He sighed. "You've only known her as blind, and so you accept her as she is. And imagine what she could be." He set the crystal cup back on the tablecloth. "I've spent all this time wanting to fix her."

"Of course you have," said Chantal roundly. "You're her father. Louise's life would be easier if she could see, yes, but who's to say it would be more fulfilled?"

He answered by covering her hand with his. "Do you want children some day?" he asked.

"I do. Three, I think. And each of them the old-fashioned way. With a man I'm married to, who wants them as much as I do."

"Lucky fellow."

The lamb arrived. Their hands slid apart and they leaned back to give the waiting staff room to work. Chantal watched the almost-black Duras as the sommelier poured it, noting how the tea-light, sitting behind her glass, chased deep red highlights from the depths of the wine. If she couldn't truly appreciate the flavor, she could certainly enjoy the color, and imagine capturing it in her jewelry.

The Mezautes left a few minutes later, their raincoats rustling, and merely nodded as they passed by. The sight of them reminded Chantal of Aunt Jeanne's map. When she had regretfully finished the last of the tender lamb, she pulled the paper from her purse.

"Here. A map to adventure," she said, handing it to Berenger.

"No adventure, not after all this food."

The subdued restaurant lighting made him squint to focus. After a few seconds, he looked up, baffled. "It's hard to read the pencil notes, but I'm guessing this oval shape standing on its end could be the Eye of the Needle everyone talks about?"

Chantal nodded, and quickly explained the main points she'd gleaned from Aunt Jeanne's notes. "You can see from this why I went into the basement looking for signs of the Eye. You think I imagined it, but I'm sure I found the entrance."

"If you found it, Chantal," Berenger said, tilting his head to soften his words, "surely your aunt would have found it before you? And if she *had* found it, she'd have rubbed the Historical Society's nose in it, fast." He held up his hands to stop her objection. "And she'd have had every right, Chérie, after their poor treatment of her."

"But what if Aunt Jeanne didn't find it? What if the person who found it *came from the other side*? I've not had time to tell you, but the recess leading to the passage down to the Eye had been hidden behind a false wall, and all the rubble from its demolition lay inside Jeanne's basement." She leaned so far forward the table dug into her full stomach. "I can see it as clearly as I see you now."

"OK." Berenger held out a placatory hand. "Let's say it's real. This person, presumably your dear cousin Yvan, must have smashed through recently, or else Jeanne would have seen the hole and the rubble. And that would fit with our belief that Yvan arrived in the last few weeks or so."

"Maybe the wall came down recently. But Aunt Jeanne didn't often go down to the basement. And the hole in the wall is hidden behind great piles of clutter." Chantal took a sip from her water glass.

"And how did Yvan get to the far side of the wall anyway, to smash through to Jeanne's basement?"

Berenger tapped his index finger on the map, and then pointed at the second Eye symbol, near the base of the triangle. "Could this other Eye mean something? The far end of a passage?"

"There's no line joining the Eyes," objected Chantal. "The upper Eye is on the top dotted line, which Aunt Jeanne thought could be the lost tunnel." She reached across and ran her finger along the map. "You can see how these dots—let's guess they're the tunnel—only run horizontally through the hill, not down."

"But those myths. Don't they say the Eye is the path to true treasure? This other Eye down below has to mean something." He took a mouthful of the Duras and shook his head. "I'm a winemaker, not a treasure hunter. My father and Wilbur would have some ideas."

Chantal frowned.

"What?"

"I suppose it's silly, but I'd rather we figured it out." Her gaze fell to the tea-light, still burning steadily. "I don't want people who were unkind to Aunt Jeanne getting the glory from all her hard work, you know? Even your father."

"No problem. He's old enough to fight his own battles." Berenger's mouth twitched in a tiny smile. "And you know I want to help you fight yours."

Chantal smiled back at him. Perhaps it was becoming easier for her to accept help from this man.

Berenger checked the time. "Would you like more to eat? They're famous for their chocolate soup, and there's a sweet dessert wine I can recommend to go with it."

"Not a thing, thank you. That was wonderful." She stretched her fingers across her stomach. "If I eat any more, I'll look like one of those plump Catholic leaders Wilbur spoke about. I'd never fit through the Eye."

CHAPTER THIRTY-ONE

A few minutes later they left the restaurant and walked out into light drizzle. Saint Michel struck ten as Berenger opened a large golf umbrella over them. In the car, Chantal asked him to stop at Rue Obscure for a piece of her jewelry kit she'd left behind.

"I'm coming in with you," he said as he pulled up a few doors down from Number 8. "To hell with the parking for a few minutes. I don't want to find you shriveled to a crisp from some left-over Indiana Jones booby-trap."

"I'll be fine. I promise I'll even slip on the galoshes for extra protection before I turn any lights on." She unlocked the house and walked through to the dark scullery. Despite her brave words, Chantal listened for Berenger's footsteps to reassure herself he was only a few paces behind.

The iron latch on the basement door felt cool under her fingers. She opened it and held her breath to avoid inhaling the cold and damp. Her hands swept to the left, feeling for the galoshes.

A weak, wordless cry came from the depths.

High-pitched.

Child-like.

She forgot the galoshes, forgot about not breathing.

The cry came again.

She spun round. "Berenger!"

His hand slapped the nearest light switch, uncaring of the danger of any more booby-traps. The scullery appeared, familiar and benign. "What's wrong?"

"A cry. I heard a cry." He pushed past to listen.

They could both hear only silence.

"It was a child's cry," Chantal insisted. The skin at the back of her neck prickled.

"You've heard so much crazy stuff in this house, Chérie."

"Are you saying this is a flashback?" she snapped, her chin thrusting up.

"It's possible." He held up a hand to stop her inevitable objections. "I'll go down and listen from there."

He turned on the basement light.

Chantal peered around his broad form. The view down the stairs looked the same as before, with stacks of boxes nestled against shrouded shapes. Berenger descended onto the basement floor and stood motionless, listening again. After a minute of silence, he shrugged. "Maybe you heard a cat. Stuck somewhere."

That made Chantal feel no better. She could no more ignore an animal in need than a child. "Let's at least search around, Berenger. Maybe the sound will come again and guide us. I'll fetch the flashlight."

She joined him in the basement a minute later, breathing lightly to avoid the odor of damp earth. The temperature hadn't budged since her last visit. The basement would make a fine cellaring place for Berenger's wine inventory.

"Here," she said, pushing the light into his hand. "You take this. At least I've got an idea of where I'm going."

"You can't wander around here," he objected, taking the flashlight. "Your dress."

"It'll wash." All the same, she wrapped her shawl around herself both for a little warmth and protection from cobwebs, and held it together securely in one hand.

Berenger promptly grasped her empty hand with his free one. "If you're staying, I want to know you're safe." He deliberately moved in front of her, putting himself between her and the shrouded shapes. "Be a back seat driver for once, eh? Which way?"

"Might as well start with where I think I saw the rubble. Could be an animal has wandered in through the passage, poor thing." Her empathy for a frightened animal made her keen to move forward, rather than retreat to the kitchen. "This way," she said, gesturing with the hand clasped in his.

The narrow path past the table appeared in the flashlight's golden beam.

"Down here. Single file. Head to the wall by those crates."

They squeezed past the table and shuffled forward to the far wall. Berenger peered around the crates and the pressure of his hand on hers tightened. "*Mon Dieu!*"

He played the flashlight to and fro, and in its darting light, Chantal caught glimpses that proved she'd imagined nothing. Shards of brick, the pile of rubble and the sledgehammer, they all leapt to life in the light. For a moment, the beam illuminated the great gash in the wall and the white of the chalk in the recess beyond, before they fell back into darkness.

Berenger guided the beam along the shaft of the sledgehammer. He swore, dropped her hand, and strode over to the heavy tool.

Chantal crept forward, and gripped the rough edge of the hole in the wall to orient herself in the blackness. "What is it?" she whispered.

"Our sledgehammer. It's been missing a month or more. I needed it at La Picarie, and when I looked for it at home, it had gone. There's a blue paint stain on it I recognize."

Chantal felt a zephyr of air in her hair, coming from the

hole in the wall, and turned towards it. In her mind's eye she saw Aunt Jeanne's map and the lower Eye symbol. "Berenger!"

He grunted in reply, and she heard the sledgehammer handle clunk back on the rubble heap.

"If that hammer came from the chateau, then there must be a way between it and here." She spoke in a hoarse whisper. It felt hard to speak normally. "Maybe those two Eyes on the map *are* connected after all, but the line between them has faded away. Invisible ink or something."

"Could be." He joined her at the jagged opening in the wall. "If I were a Cathar," he mused as he probed the thin, rough brick with his thumb, "I'd want an escape route in case of trouble. Wouldn't you? Maybe that's the true treasure, a secret exit from Cordes."

"It would make sense." She paused as the flaw in her argument became clear. "Except the Cathars were long gone by the time your family built the chateau, so the lower Eye can't be in it."

"There was a cave on our land long before our house, though, remember. *Lagrotte.*" Berenger traced around the gash in the wall with the flashlight. With the recess beyond, it resembled the mouth of a cave. "Maybe the passage came out through there."

"And I'm willing to bet today the opening is somewhere in your basement, long forgotten."

"But someone's remembered," Berenger warned, looking towards the sledgehammer.

If she'd been alone, the words would have made Chantal shiver apprehensively, but with Berenger in tow she felt brave. When he pointed the flashlight into the recess, she nimbly climbed over the lip into the little chamber, stooping under its low ceiling.

Before he could object, she said, "The passage down to the Eye starts right at the back, on this side. I'll go through, and you come behind me with the flashlight."

"No, wait."

"There's not much room for two tall people. I'll be fine. Just follow me." Chantal trailed a hand along the chalk wall, closing her eyes to shut out the leaping beam, hoping to give her night vision a chance to return before she reached the sloping passage to the Eye. It struck her how much her pose resembled Louise's the first night they'd met, out on the twilit street.

Chantal heard Berenger climbing into the recess. She moved further in, secure in his company, eyes still shut. Under her fingers, the chalk wall ended. She brought her shoulder to the passage opening and felt a stronger draft on her cheek. "It's here," she whispered. She turned left into the passageway, sure of her way.

One step in, and she tripped over something. Her hands came down hard. The right one hit the passage's chalk floor. The left landed in something.

Something thin and floppy.

Almost at once, the thing responded, folding itself around her, seeking her wrist. She recoiled, opening her eyes, but seeing only a dark shape, flapping round her hand. Mewing with fear, she flailed her arm, but it stuck fast, snagged on her watch strap and weighing her arm down.

"Chantal!" Berenger's voice from the entrance to the passage was intense but low. The flashlight beam stabbed toward her and blinded her.

Now even more disoriented, she swung her arm wide. This time, the thing flew off, back towards the recess. She heard it smack into a surface and fall to the floor,

A grunt told her it had hit Berenger.

He ignored it, and another grunt told her he had pushed into the passage, half bent to avoid the low ceiling. "Are you hurt?" His hand cupped her face, and kept the beam pointing sideways to avoid blinding her again. She shook her head against it. The warm, dry skin of his palm instantly soothed her.

Very gingerly, she reached down to where the thing had

fallen. It gave way under the slight pressure of her fingers. Berenger tracked the beam down her arm. She held up her trophy to the light.

And yelped.

She dropped the mask. The distorted head flopped onto the chalk floor. Berenger squatted beside it and slipped a hand inside. "Anyone you know?"

He held up a donkey head.

"I saw this," she hissed. "But I thought it was another hallucination. The lousy little rat."

Yvan had left the mask here, handy, in the little passageway. With it, he'd have had free run of the house. She imagined him walking past Aunt Jeanne as she babbled with fear, laughing as she wrestled with demons he'd put into her head. And he'd not stopped when she, Chantal, had moved in.

Icy anger chilled her even more than the bone-aching underground cold. She sniffed the rubber mask, hoping for aftershave, something to link it once and for all to Yvan. All she could catch was the smell of the mask itself.

Berenger crouched beside her and pulled her to him. His warmth and scent soothed her.

"I'm OK," she murmured, reaching for his free hand. "But I'm not letting you go again."

"Good plan," he agreed, before shining the flashlight further down the passage.

He sucked in a breath.

Looking over his shoulder, Chantal could see the stone-rimmed Eye of the Needle.

"I'm sorry I doubted you."

They stood up together and crept down the passage, their movements becoming freer as the ceiling rose higher.

At the Eye, Berenger paused. "It's too narrow," he murmured. "Like an arrow slit. We can't get through." He waggled the beam through the gap. From under his arm, Chantal caught glimpses of more white walls. Chalk? Plaster?

The high-pitched cry came again from their right. They both stiffened. It cut off almost at once.

"Who's there?" roared Berenger. The echoes bounced off the white walls and made her gasp.

Silence answered him.

He flung himself at the slit. His shoulder went in, but his chest stuck fast. He tried to haul himself through but only wedged tighter. "Pull," he wheezed, breathing out to deflate his ribcage.

Chantal clamped her hands around his free wrist and yanked. He staggered back into the passage, and hauled in a deep gulp of air.

"I'm going to call and check Louise is safe in bed. Because you were right. That was no flashback, and it sounded like my daughter."

Hand in hand, they retreated through the recess to the basement, and Berenger bounded up the stairs.

In the bright kitchen, he jabbed a speed dial number on his mobile phone. Chantal watched him wait for someone to pick up. And wait. And wait.

He gave up.

"We'll go back home," he said, pushing his hand through his hair. "Find out what's happening. Call the police. "

"You go. I'll try and get through. I'm sure I could."

"Like hell you will! I may have lost Louise. I'm not risking you as well."

It fell short of hearing 'You can't go because I love you', but it drove some sense into Chantal.

"OK. But let me wait here. I might hear or see something helpful. When you get back, once you know Louise is safe, I'll fill you in."

The edges of his nostrils were white. He held her by the shoulders, tightly, his eyes dark with emotion. "Do you promise me you won't go through that Eye? And that you'll wait in the recess out of sight?"

She hesitated. She hated dark places, but a child in need

was a powerful motivator.

"Because I know what you're like with danger, Chantal. You don't give a thought for your safety. But I do. I can't—" His lips disappeared as he pressed them together. "I can't bear it when you're hurt." Breath gusted from his nose and fanned her forehead. "So promise me. Whatever you hear, stay put. Please."

"I promise."

She meant it. If she could possibly avoid going through the slit, she would.

He kissed her, hard, and vanished into the night.

Chantal picked up the flashlight, pulled a woolen coat of Aunt Jeanne's from a peg above the galoshes, and straightened her back. The basement's musty autumn air embraced her as she descended the wooden stairs one more time. From under a shroud, she fished out a rickety wicker chair, a damaged cousin of the one in the spare bedroom, and part-dragged, part-lifted it through to the recess. Aunt Jeanne's coat around her shoulders kept out some of the creeping chill.

Berenger would be back soon. Twenty minutes. Thirty at the most. All she had to do was listen and wait.

Scuffling and rustling.

She stiffened.

Grunts.

The sounds drew her down to the Eye, her breath coming in short, frightened bursts. She softened the flashlight beam to a soft glow behind a fold of her shawl.

As she reached the Eye, the wordless cry rang out again.

"Now, swim!" rasped an enraged voice.

The thin cry grew loud for a second before it ended in a splash. More panicked splashes echoed down the tunnel.

Chantal catapulted herself at the Eye, wriggling and twisting her way through.

Any memory of her promise was lost in the terrible urgency to save a drowning child.

CHAPTER THIRTY-TWO

Berenger's car surged down Cordes' hill, but its pace felt like a dawdle. He stabbed the speed dial on his mobile phone again, straining to control the SUV with one hand on the wheel, while he listened to the endless dial tone from the handset clamped to his ear.

Where was everybody?

He hated to leave Chantal behind. Her headstrong nature when facing danger frightened him. But if his daughter languished in those ancient Cathar tunnels—and he prayed she did not—he needed someone Louise would trust. She might have to follow Chantal's voice to safety.

Let my daughter be safe at home in bed.

He hauled the wheel over at the sharp right turn below the town wall and stamped on the gas again. The tires squealed, echoing his fears that the two key people in his life were in great peril.

Chantal had grown more precious to him each day over the last week. He couldn't ask for more than Chantal to share his life, and Louise's, in Cordes. The right woman had been the missing item. Now, with Chantal, his life would be complete.

His words to her at La Picarie had only told the first

chapter of what lay in his heart. The truth—he could admit it, as he hurtled alone through the night—was that he was falling in love with her. His urge to protect Chantal would soon equal his instincts to protect Louise.

Through the chateau gateposts, and around the fountain, he slithered to a halt in a spray of gravel. Unusually, no light shone from the hall. He jabbed at a switch and took the stairs four at a time. To hell with whom he woke. If they could sleep through the phone, he'd didn't care if he disturbed them now.

Louise's door stood ajar. He threw it open. Her quilt lay tossed on the floor next to her favorite teddy.

Her bed was empty.

Adrenalin pumped even harder than before. He spun around and turned on the light. She wasn't in the closet, nor under the bed, nor behind the curtains.

Then he noticed her missing dressing gown. The slamming of his heart eased. It meant Louise had to be somewhere around the house. Ill, maybe, a nightmare. Or worse, at the hospital, which would be why no one had answered his call. Ah Wong or his father would be with her.

But your cell phone's been on. Nobody's called.

He strode up the corridor. For once, no light came from under Wilbur's door. Berenger's hand clasped the bedroom's door knob, ready to turn it, when the sound of snoring drifted out. His hand slid off; pointless to wake a man who had slept through the insistent ringing of the phone. He headed to Ah Wong's bedroom instead. Her door stood open, her bed tidily made. He found the same in his father's room.

Downstairs, his pace picking up once more, he could find no one in the kitchen. The living rooms stood empty. He came back to the hall. A white square gleamed on the telephone table. He snatched up the message he'd passed in the dark the first time. His father's elegant script began with the hour he'd penned it: 9:45 p.m.

"The Musketeers!" it read. His father had obviously gone to discuss some exciting theory or even discovery in the History Society's papers. That explained one absence.

But where were Ah Wong and Louise? Remembering the hospital theory, he turned down the short corridor to the garage. Only his father's car was missing.

Coming back, he passed the little room and paused, mid-stride. Could Louise be in there?

He went in. The familiar scents assailed him with memories of the final years of his marriage, and his one enduring secret. Only old ghosts inhabited the space. He banged the door shut on his way out.

Another minute ticked by. Where to next?

Think.

If Louise was with Ah Wong, her other committed protector, she'd be safe. Ah Wong had reacted strongly to Louise's nagging about the basement earlier. Could his daughter have returned to her exploring? Ah Wong might have followed much the same search path he had taken in the last five minutes, and tracked Louise down under the house.

He had to check—and he had to hurry. For every second he spent searching, Chantal sat patiently waiting, alone in the chill of another basement. At least, he hoped to hell she'd kept her promise to stay inside the recess and not push through the Eye.

The Eye. Chantal had found the upper Eye. Could Louise have found the lower one, deep in the chateau's basement? Could she have disturbed whoever had hauled the chateau's sledgehammer up to Jeanne's basement?

A fresh shot of adrenalin sluiced ice-water under his skin.

He ran through the kitchen and down the stone steps. They stored a large flashlight on a hook at the bottom and he snatched it, gratefully. Under the vaulted brick roof, the wine racks stretched out before him, filling the near end of the long, rectangular room. Like Wilbur, Berenger rarely needed to go any further than this. Small anterooms to either side of him held trash and firewood.

"Louise! Ah Wong!"

No answer.

Beyond the wine racks, he knew, lay a jumbled, dusty storage area of bric-a-brac, much like Jeanne's, with two more anterooms off to either side, and one at the furthest end.

He'd not listened closely to Louise's griping about her exploring. Had she mentioned the far end of the basement? It'd be a rat's nest to search.

Berenger took a chance on the furthest anteroom. It had to be a good bet for a link to a long-lost cave and passageway. He jogged towards it as quickly as he could, dodging and weaving dusty obstacles like a quarterback.

When he reached the far end, he thrust past a stack of antique traveling trunks, and in his haste almost stumbled over a small wine cask that lurked unseen in the shadows. He paused to regain his balance and bearings. His light flicked to and fro across the back of the anteroom. It reminded him of the recess at Number 8 except that here the walls were bare brick instead of plaster-rendered.

The air smelled musty with no draft to freshen it.

The flashlight beam reflected off a white scrap caught under a stack of old wine crates. He pulled it out. The empty white plastic bag rustled in his hand. It bore the logo of Albi's big supermarket, one that had only been open for a year.

His pulse quickened again.

He kicked the crates and his shoe thudded hollowly. The crates sounded half empty, just like the stack in Jeanne's basement. He heaved them aside. A strip of old, dark sheet hid the bricks behind. He snatched it down. The tacks that had held it up tinkled on the floor. He pointed the flashlight ahead.

Before him ran a stone-flagged passage, its floor running level, and its ceiling gradually heightening till it reached an eight-foot-high, stone-trimmed ellipse ahead.

He recognized the pattern only too well, but this lower Eye had been attacked on one side, its arch ragged-edged, and the fine stone smashed to debris underfoot.

Had Ah Wong brought Louise through this passage instead of returning her to bed? And if so, why? To escape from someone? Or had Wilbur hit on a glimmer of truth—did Ah Wong have something to hide down here, something she had to protect even more fiercely than Louise? He pushed his hair back. The idea was madness.

He glanced at his watch: over fifteen minutes had ticked by since he'd left Chantal. But this passage would surely bring him to her. And, he fervently hoped, to Louise along the way.

He stepped through the Eye, widened enough to make it easy for a man of his stature. Three steps in and the tunnel roof lowered sharply. He didn't see it coming and scraped his head. With the adrenalin coursing through his blood, the pain barely registered.

He had to move along with his back hunched and neck thrust forward, turtle-like, straining to see ahead. The stone lining soon gave way to marl-gray clay walls, secured with occasional stout wooden posts. He shed his jacket, dropping it on the floor behind him. His tortured posture began to wring sweat from every inch of skin. The stale air barely refreshed his lungs.

The flashlight picked out stone steps in the distance, spiraling tightly upward. *Up to Louise and Chantal?* Number 8 had to be forty or fifty yards above the chateau. The stairs must link this clay passage to the white chalk tunnel he'd glimpsed through the upper Eye.

He lengthened his stride. An unseen line twanged hard across his shins and snapped audibly. He ignored it.

Puffs of dust appeared ahead, blocking out the stairs. He stopped so abruptly that he toppled forward onto his knuckles. The flashlight survived the shock, and its beam shone on, illuminating a white haze, thicker than fog. A heavy shower of silt fell sighing to the floor, coating his sweating back. Desperately, he swung around in the confined space.

A rumble overhead put springs in his legs. He had time for one lunging dive back the way he'd come.

Berenger was flying through the air when the dead weight of Cordes' hill descended on him.

CHAPTER THIRTY-THREE

Chantal straightened up from the effort of squeezing through the narrow gap of the Eye. Immediately, she cracked her head on the low passage roof. Rubbing the agony away with one hand, she pointed the flashlight toward the splashes. Had they grown weaker?

The passage led around a bend to the left. Chips of white stone littered the floor, all from chiseled gouges in the tunnel wall. The tool marks surrounded dressed limestone blocks set into the wall about four feet from the floor and spaced about three feet apart. The row of blocks disappeared into the darkness ahead, resembling a dotted line, like the line on Aunt Jeanne's map.

Someone—Yvan? Yvan's accomplice?—had attacked each limestone block, trying to pry it free of the tunnel wall, as if believing it concealed a secret cache. The chiseling must have taken hours of work, and the noise would surely have reached into Number 8.

A clanging of metal on stone.

She'd heard the chiseling, on the same night she'd seen the donkey-headed man. Crazy sights and weird sounds, and she'd dismissed them both as hallucinations. As she'd been meant to. As Aunt Jeanne had been meant to.

Everything that had happened in Number 8 had been designed to give someone the chance to hunt, undisturbed, for long-lost Cathar treasure in this long-lost tunnel.

She tried to jog, bent over, even though the debris underfoot risked a turned ankle. The glare of the flashlight off the chalk bothered her, and as she hurried along, she swathed it in a corner of her shawl again to reduce the dazzle.

The white floor disappeared in front of her, and a black pit yawned across the full width of the passage.

She gasped and stumbled to a halt at its brink. A fragment of stone rolled forward and over. It plopped faintly. The light reflected on ripples slicing through stale water an arm's length below. Metal staples, surprisingly shiny, made a makeshift ladder downward.

The cistern was no more than three and a half feet across but, without headroom to jump, it stretched like the Atlantic. A long plank laid across the center offered the only way across. She'd have felt braver if it had lain closer to the wall, for support. There was no time to shift it over, though. While she dithered, a child was drowning in another pit.

Two steps. Just two steps, and it's done.

Perspiration had made her feet slick in her low-heeled pumps. She slipped the shoes off for the crossing. The plank flexed horribly, but held.

Panting now, shoes back on, she followed the passage further around the bend. Her flashlight beam grew weaker. Fear of the dark writhed inside her until she realized a competing light source had washed hers out. Ahead, strong, yellow light spilled from the left through a generous gap in the passage wall. It shone brightly enough to show her the lip of another cistern in the passage floor just beyond the gap.

The splashes echoed up from its depths.

A passing glance into the entrance at the left half-blinded her as she hurried past. She could hear shuffling and metallic scraping from the direction of the bright light, but she had no time to investigate. As the dancing spots faded from her eyes, she shone the flashlight into the black shaft.

The water chopped and heaved five feet below her as two small arms struggled. The beam caught a young white face, green eyes staring. Lank, black hair plastered across the forehead. A cruel gag stretched the mouth back in a monstrous parody of laughter. The tightly tied cloth dipped below the water, then rose clear again.

Louise.

The burden of responsibility felt twice as heavy. She felt a momentary spurt of anger against Berenger. This was his child, damn it. Why wasn't he here to do the hard work?

He's doing his best. He'd be here if he possibly could.

Chantal dropped to her knees and whispered the girl's name, torn between calling clearly to allay the child's panic and attracting the attention of the person in the side passage. Louise responded by twisting her head from side to side. There were more shiny staples set into this cistern, too. They descended in a line directly below where Chantal knelt. Louise's hand flailed only a foot away from the lowest.

"Louise! Follow my voice," she hissed. She tried to tell Louise what to do, but the girl was too distraught to obey.

Chantal had no choice. She slipped off her pumps again and ditched her shawl. She set her foot on the rungs. They were set close to the wall and she had to scrunch her toes to fit the metal under the balls of her feet.

The descent was a lot harder than it looked in the movies. The rungs cut into her hands and feet, and fear and adrenalin couldn't mask the pain. Under the bone-achingly cold water, she found one more rung.

Now she could grab one of Louise's hands and curl it over the first dry staple. Louise brought her other hand to clutch Chantal's ankle, all the time making heart-wrenching pleading sounds. Chantal glanced up to the top of the shaft. She knew she couldn't manage the climb one-handed, holding the girl in her other arm.

"Louise, hold on tight. Please. Another minute or two. I can't lift you. I have to find something else." She pried the cold fingers off her leg and pushed them onto the rung.

It broke her heart to do it.

She scrambled back up. Even while she ached to help Louise, Chantal hunted for a way to make a rope. Her shawl made a good sling, but it wasn't long enough. She scoured the floor, finally edging toward the bright gap. There, just inside the passage, lay cut lengths of white cord, camouflaged on the chalk. She snatched them up, wondering if they had recently been around Louise's wrists.

"Louise!" she whispered over the girl's endless whimpers. "I've found rope! Hang on. I have to knot it all."

The longest piece measured two feet. She chose it to bind the shawl's tips together. What knot would use minimal line, yet hold the tapering ends tightly? She drummed her fist on her forehead. She could almost see the page from one of her books of knots. The icicle hitch.

Wrap from right to left, going under. Then what? A bight to the right, push the working end through. Ram the two top twists up against each other. Pull tight. There were five other pieces of cord. Five fisherman's knots gave her a few working feet and offered handholds for the job ahead.

She propped the flashlight on a lump of stone so it shone partway into the pit. Sucking in a deep breath, she tackled the vicious rungs once more. To wrap the sling under Louise's armpits she had to break the girl's life-or-death grip on the rungs. Then she had to lever the clinging hands off her wrist and ankle again. Tears smeared her eyes as she bolted up the staples before Louise could reattach herself.

Any time now, Berenger. Please.

Maybe he heard her silent plea and somehow sent her strength, because the haul proved easier than she'd dared hope. The moment Louise felt the upward pull, she released the rungs and clamped her hands on the shawl. Forty-five pounds of precious child hung on five knots tied in haste and in half-light. Chantal didn't dare contemplate what the breaking strain of fine wool threads might be.

Up. Pull.

Louise appeared over the lip of the shaft. Chantal paused to gather breath. One more heave and they'd hightail it down the passage back to Jeanne's. Somehow they'd cope with the plank crossing. She didn't give a damn who was beyond the gap, nor why. She only hoped that whatever had kept Louise's kidnapper engrossed so far would last till they were well past the gap. All that counted was escaping this infernal tunnel.

Lying half out of the pit, safe at last, Louise came to life. She wriggled sideways onto the safety of the floor. Chantal tugged again to help her clear the last short stretch.

It was sheer bad luck that Louise's scrabbling foot kicked the flashlight over the edge. They heard its farewell splash. Two seconds later, the bulb shorted.

The pit went black.

CHAPTER THIRTY-FOUR

As he fell, Berenger tried to draw his hands back to his face to create an air pocket. The jarring impact as he hit the passage floor shot a cloud of fine clay silt upwards, filling his nose. However hard he strove to control his breathing, it found its way into his mouth, drying and half-choking him. His eyes watered madly.

He felt no pain from the waist down, only a massive, unyielding weight. The silt settled like concrete around him. It reminded him of his sister burying him at the beach when they were young. But this was a very different place and time.

He could still move his ribcage to breath. The silt pressed in on all sides but weighed lighter on his head and shoulders than further down his body. But breathing was no damn good without oxygen. Already, his lungs were straining to suck every scrap from the thin air.

His will to live burned fiercely, but each moment in the boundless dust hurt like hell. He had to act, or suffocate.

He strained his head back, risking a mini-avalanche of clay filling his little air pocket. His head moved an inch. A second push gained another inch. He squirmed his shoulders. The weight shifted and the load on his head lessened.

Hope blazed.

Blinded, working by touch alone, he fought on. His lungs shrieked, but he focused on Chantal and Louise. His head came free. Dust floated thickly in the passage air. He felt its grittiness on his teeth and down his throat. It was the sweetest air he'd ever known.

Coughing and panting by turns, he twisted his shoulders to free more inches. After two minutes, he slumped. He'd forced head, neck and an arm free. The rest wouldn't budge.

He'd failed.

A muscle jumped in his left leg. It reminded him of the sensation of snapping cord on his shins seconds before the roof fall.

Another booby-trap.

He tried not to think about Louise. His gut told him his daughter lay somewhere in these tunnels, that it was her cry he'd heard echoing down the chalk passage far above. That meant she'd somehow avoided the booby-trap. Had she been taken hostage, and marched past this obstacle by someone who knew exactly where it lay? Was Ah Wong with her?

He groaned.

With this lower exit blocked, Chantal could be in grave danger, too. Anyone on the other side of the roof fall now, in all likelihood, had only one way out. That route that would lead right past her, as she waited for him in Jeanne's basement.

The police had Yvan in their custody. For a moment he relaxed, knowing the Corsican could not be wandering the tunnels above, preying on Louise. But if someone had driven Louise and Ah Wong this way, it meant Yvan had an accomplice. Perhaps someone who visited the chateau. Or, more likely, someone who worked on the estate. How hard would it have been to steal and copy Berenger's keys during a work day on the estate? Harder than with Jeanne's keys, but possible.

He slumped, his body worn out from the struggle.

A hand shook Berenger gently. Disoriented, he opened dust-encrusted eyes. More dust fell in, drawing a protesting cry from his throat. He clamped his eyelids shut. In the second his eyes had been open, he'd glimpsed a pair of sharply-pressed trousers.

"Berenger." He'd known the voice all his life, but it bore an uncharacteristic note of urgency. "Was anyone behind you? Is someone buried in there?"

"No," he croaked.

"Ahead of you? You were following someone out?"

"No. No one's gone to fetch help." The effort of speaking made him cough and stirred up more dust. Silence followed. "For God's sake," he managed. "Help me."

"I will. Tell me first. What happened?"

"Louise missing. Booby-trapped before I could reach the stairs."

"So you've not seen anyone in here?"

Berenger shook his head. The questions puzzled him, but if they were the price of help, he'd pay.

A hand patted his arm. "You stay there. I'll fetch help."

"No! Dig me out! Louise is up there, I'm sure." He coughed again. "I have to get to the other entrance."

He heard a rustle as the man stood up. "Not much point," came the cultured voice. "I know the other entrance is too narrow for either of us. But this roof fall is most helpful. Now I know the treasure's exit route. It may have escaped Montségur, but it won't escape me."

Berenger did his best to bellow in protest. It came out as a feeble cry. The footsteps faded.

CHAPTER THIRTY-FIVE

Chantal hugged Louise close with one arm, trying to transfer warmth to the shivering little body. The soaked shawl lay discarded. "Are you hurt?" she whispered in her ear and felt relief at the slight shake of the child's head against her collarbone.

With the other hand she explored the gag's knot. The water had tightened it, but her fingers told her she faced an undemanding granny knot. After a minute of waggling, it came free. A balled-up handkerchief tumbled out of the girl's mouth. It was a wonder she hadn't choked.

"I want to go home," Louise croaked.

"Me, too, sweetie, but we've lost the flashlight. It's too dangerous in the dark." She stroked the wet, dark hair. "The person who hurt you has a light, though. I can see it."

The bright light that poured through the gap in the wall lured her as powerfully as a full moon did a moth. From beyond it came grunts and the sound of metal squeaking on stone. Louise shrank further into Chantal. Whoever was through there, it could not be Yvan. He was locked in a jail cell in Albi.

Chantal picked the child up, whispering to her to keep

quiet. Louise's arms locked around Chantal's neck, as tightly as a limpet to a shoreline rock.

Chantal shifted warily toward the gap. On the other side, it opened into a recess of similar size to the one she'd left not long before. An electric lantern shed light from its perch atop an upturned wooden crate, that looked a twin to the ones stacked in Jeanne's basement. A step to the side brought into view a pair of heavy boots and thin lower legs clad in royal blue overalls. A man knelt close to the recess wall on the right.

"At last, at last," he muttered. "Not out there in the tunnel, but in here. At last." The American accent was unmistakable.

Chantal backed away to whisper in Louise's ear. "*Wilbur Sanders* brought you here?"

She felt the answering nod against her neck. "He caught me in the basement. I couldn't sleep, and I wanted to go exploring again, back to where I'd found a bag of clothes hidden today."

"Ah Wong didn't stop you?"

Again the head shook against Chantal's shoulder. "There's a back way. And when I was half through the basement, he grabbed me and stuffed that thing in my mouth."

Chantal hugged her a little closer, hoping her touch gave some comfort.

"His arm squeezed round me so tightly, I couldn't move. He carried me through a narrow place and bumped my head a lot. We climbed up stairs that wound round and round. Then we stopped."

"And then the water?" Chantal whispered gently.

"I kept trying to get back down the stairs. He tied my ankles. I still tried. He said he'd throw me in a pit."

The brute.

The sudden urge to lash out, to repay pain with pain, almost overwhelmed her. Louise squeaked in protest as Chantal's arms squeezed hard.

The sound shocked Chantal back to their current predicament. Her pulse cantered, but she had to stay calm, to figure out how to protect Louise until Berenger could reach them. "Sorry, *petite*," she breathed.

A thud and an exclamation drew her nearer the gap again. She angled to a new position. At the corner of her field of vision lay Louise's purple dressing gown, but her attention locked onto Wilbur. He'd backed up to the center of the little room and was bent over a small brown box that sat on a square of oilskin beside the lantern. His shoulders heaved with excitement.

He panted instructions to himself as he lifted a wrapped package out of the chest. "Careful. Gently now." His long thin fingers deftly peeled open the folds of cloth. The fragile fabric, undisturbed for centuries, shed broken strands that sparkled in the lantern's light as they spun and fell.

Inside lay two small books in dark bindings, one larger than the other. He laid the smaller one on the oilskin.

"One quick look. Don't damage the spine." He opened the larger volume and gasped.

Chantal caught a glimmer of gold from its page.

Wilbur stretched out a reverent finger to caress the edge of the book. He eased a page over. "The *Consolamentum*!" He drew a long, shuddering breath.

The second book sent him into further raptures. His hand hovered over the oilskin to wrap the volumes back up again, when a bell tinkled. Moments later, a shudder shook the tunnel.

Chantal stumbled sideways, off balance with Louise's weight in her arms.

Wilbur didn't hear her. He grabbed something from a corner out of her sight. A second later, a gun glinted in his hand. "Too late, dear friend. Caught you in my trap." Taking the lantern, he vanished through a dark opening at the back of the recess, presumably heading to the spiral stairs Louise had described.

The thing Chantal wanted most from Wilbur—the lantern—had gone. Louise's dry dressing gown remained, though, and she longed to make the girl more comfortable. She whispered her plan to Louise and left her huddled by the gap in the wall. In the blacked-out recess, inspiration struck. Instead of simply turning back to the passage with the robe, Chantal scrabbled across the floor. Her hand touched the books and then the chest. She added them to her booty and headed for the gap.

It had disappeared.

A course of smooth stone with chalk rising above it met her fingertips. Disoriented, she felt the panic of her first hallucination in Jeanne's bedroom rising. She whispered urgently, "Louise! Talk to me! Say anything. Guide me back. Quick."

"This way. This way. This way," Louise responded.

Scooting sideways towards the chanting voice, Chantal's fingers soon felt the opening back into the passage. There, Chantal quickly bundled Louise out of her wet pajama top and into the dry dressing gown. So much for the easy part. For the next bit, she had to find the edge of the cistern.

Chantal dropped to her knees and crawled awkwardly to where she hoped it was. One hand clutched the wooden chest; the other swept the passage floor for the first sign of the pit's rim. Chunks of stone dug agonizingly into her knees. She preferred the pain to the dread of pitching headfirst into the water if she moved any faster. She picked up her shawl on the way. Louise followed, hanging onto the hem of her dress.

Wilbur had still not returned. Chantal had time to sort out the chest and its contents by touch alone. When she finished, she drew Louise into the crook of her arm. "Now we wait," she whispered.

CHAPTER THIRTY-SIX

Chantal and Louise waited, shivering, in the dark. After ten minutes, a gleam of light in the recess. A cheerful humming accompanied it.

Chantal hoped to heck her idea would work.

The humming disappeared in a roar of anguished rage.

She'd soon find out.

Wilbur's thin body pushed into the passage. He held the lantern thrust out. The instant glare off the white walls dazzled her, but the brightness didn't blind her to the polished metal of the gun. For once she was glad Louise couldn't see.

Chantal settled her palm more firmly on the end of the chest. It overhung the cistern by three inches. A small push would send it on its way.

"You!" Wilbur's surprise was fleeting. He didn't care about her, nor about Louise. He only cared about the treasure. "Where is it?" he snarled. Even as he asked, he saw the chest under her hand.

The lantern swayed and she heard a ratcheting from the gun. Sweat flooded her palm, reducing her grip on the wood.

"That chest's mine!"

"Maybe." She pushed the chest out another inch. The wood squeaked.

"I'll shoot the kid." He pointed the gun.

Chantal instinctively brought her hand up to shield Louise's face.

Wilbur sneered at her paltry effort. "This is a Glock 23. I may not be a good shot, but it's got thirteen .40 rounds in it. One of them'll get her, and maybe your hand right along with it."

The riskiness of her gamble constricted her throat. She cleared it. "Go ahead. I'll push this box in a millisecond later. Louise might survive, but your pretty books won't."

"They're priceless," he snarled.

"Louise is priceless," she hissed back. Her confidence rose a notch. At least Wilbur was talking, not shooting. He hadn't rushed her. Could she keep Wilbur talking till Berenger arrived?

"Where's young Morel? I heard him shouting earlier. It's like half the town's down here tonight—of all nights."

Wilbur's question made her catch her breath; it was as if he'd peered into her mind. After quick reflection, she couldn't see any harm in telling him the truth: the exit through Jeanne's basement currently lay clear.

"I'll give you a spare flashlight." His tone grew coaxing. "Give me the chest. You can walk out just ahead of me. We'll go our separate ways."

The offer tempted Chantal. But without the chest he'd have no reason not to shoot. Or to force them both into the pit. "No, thanks."

For a minute, neither spoke, but they dueled with their eyes. Chantal caved first, dropping her gaze even as her fingers tightened their grip on the little chest. "I'd rather talk it through."

"You think I'm going to talk till the cavalry get here? Because I'm sure Morel hasn't quietly gone home to bed. D'you think I'm stupid?"

"Not at all. It took brains to find this. My great-aunt

tried and failed, but you found it. The first person in hundreds of years."

"You've no idea. If I wrote a book on it, it'd be the bestseller of the century."

Flattery worked? She'd trowel it on. "I believe it. You knew all along the Cathars had hidden something precious here, didn't you? And you were very convincing when you told everyone the treasure myths only referred to something spiritual."

"I didn't lie. Those are spiritual books. Holy of holies."

Chantal manufactured a little sigh. "Can't you tell me more? Are they Bibles?"

To her delight, he leaned back on the wall. The gun still pointed at Louise, but she could see the historian in him itching to hold forth.

"They're sacred books. The little one is the Gospel of St John. Gold leaf. Illuminated on every page. But the other…" He shook his head in wonder. "The ritual of the *Consolamentum*. That was the Cathars' special ceremony, y'know. A kind of laying on of hands. No one's ever seen the liturgy for it before…" His voice trailed away as the scholar gained control over the brigand.

"How did you ever get on the trail of this treasure?" she asked quietly.

"Destiny. In the Rare Books room of the Butler Library." The gun drooped several degrees. "Destiny. I'm one of the few students of the Cathars in Cordes in the whole US of A, and I find an unlabeled map of the town. No one else would have recognized it. But I did. It was meant to be. Meant to be mine." He smiled greedily. "They'll clamor to offer me the best posts after this."

"Yours was the same map Aunt Jeanne found by the well a few years ago?"

He shrugged. "You never showed it to us, did you? But your description at dinner that night sounded mightily similar. You made me step up my…little surprises…around the old house. I had to distract you, encourage you to leave. Preferably go home to London. Same as I did with your dear, dead aunt."

Louise whimpered at the word *dead* and Chantal tried to hold her closer, while hunting urgently for a new angle to keep him talking. "A scholar like you couldn't rig all those booby-traps. The boiler, the kettle."

He laughed bitterly. "I'm a Jack of all trades. I came to studying very late. I was a roadie with a rock band once. Learned about electrics. The merchant navy taught me a lot about plumbing. All the travel taught me to be interested in other countries and times, too. That hooked me into studying. And it's all been leading to this." He fixed a predatory gaze on the chest.

"Aunt Jeanne's map had no X to mark the spot. Did yours? How did you find the chest?"

He jerked his head towards the tunnel behind him, and his gun lowered a few inches. "Kept at it every night of my study leave here. Chiseling at all those limestone blocks. Even drove staples in to explore the cisterns. I was so sure it had to be in the lost tunnel itself. Turns out those Cathars bluffed. They'd buried the chest in a corner of that little room."

Chantal shifted uncomfortably on the cold stone floor, but resolved to ask questions all night if she had to. "And Yvan's your partner, yes? But I can't figure out how you ever met."

"Yvan?" Wilbur's surprise sounded genuine.

"Yvan Vico. The Corsican, who's been hanging around Aunt Jeanne's house this last week. Was he looking for more clues for you?"

"Never heard of him."

Her head felt muzzy. "You must have. I know you have a partner."

"Who says?" His chin and the Glock lifted together.

Chantal's hand instinctively rose to shield Louise's head again, and the flutter of fear cleared her mind. "Who was the gun for, then, when you went to check out that roar earlier? You said 'dear friend' as you left."

His eyes narrowed. "OK. You're sharp." He wiped a hand across his mouth. "That noise was a roof fall. It was easy to rig up in the silty earth down there. A welcome mat for my partner. I do have one, more's the pity. And he knew how close I'd be to the treasure tonight. He doesn't trust me with it. And he shouldn't. No, sir. I've done all the hard work. He's getting none of it."

"Then why team up?"

"He discovered what I was really after. Sneaked into my room last year. Found the map. So much for honor among Musketeers."

Wilbur shifted his shoulders and retrained the gun. Chantal increased the pressure of her fingers on the chest in reply, and tried to snuggle Louise a little closer.

A Musketeer. Not Yvan at all. The partner had to be his previous year's host, Mezaute. Her instincts about him had been right. She was glad Yvan had been telling the truth after all. He'd never tried to hurt Jeanne.

"He gave me an ultimatum that night. If I shared the hunt and the find, he'd give me active help and support. If I refused, he'd remove my access to the archives and smear my name so badly locally that I'd make no progress."

That fitted. As the History Society President, Mezaute would have had the power.

"And Aunt Jeanne? Why did you have to scare her? Why not pretend she'd won a cruise?"

"Cost," he said laconically. "And we knew enough about her. Your aunt had a horror of losing her mind in old age. That was her Achilles' heel."

As her doctor, Mezaute would have known that fear only too well.

"That's why we sourced LSD. Tiny doses at first, getting bigger. I came through the basement whenever I wanted, and mixed it into drinks, condiments, even her weird old tooth powder. You got the full dose. Fun, huh?"

Chantal bit back the furious retort she wanted to throw at him for the hell she and Aunt Jeanne had endured. She had to keep herself under control. "And you succeeded in driving my aunt from her beloved home so you could make all the noise you wanted. But then I arrived."

"I had to start all over. Time was getting short. I knew you were onto the drugs. Martin told me you'd asked about a testing lab. He's been useful, though he doesn't know what for. His stepdad got him out of some scrapes a while ago and Martin's being repaying his debt helping us get hold of narcotics."

"But Martin isn't Mezaute's son," she objected, her mind whirring too slowly to keep up this time.

"Mezaute?" he barked a laugh. "You think he's my partner? That yellow-bellied fool, who sees ghosts behind every set of drapes? No. Among those Musketeers, it's all for one and Grenier for himself. Mezaute and Morel have no idea. They share their old maids' gossip and Grenier picks all the handy stuff out of it."

Grenier. It felt like a slap in the face.

A mighty clang of metal on stone reverberated up the passage. They all gasped at the assault on their ear drums.

"Berenger!" She wanted to leap to her feet, but the chest kept her locked down on the floor.

"Papa!" Louise struggled in Chantal's arm. Another metallic crash shook the air.

"No, Louise! Stay here! There's another pit along the passage."

The Glock rose again and Wilbur took aim. "I liked our talk. You're too smart for that brute of a grape farmer. But the stakes are high tonight." He waggled the gun. "Last chance. Leave the chest."

Chantal shook her head mutely.

"Bad choice, lady."

He fired. The flare made her clutch Louise and they both shuddered at the deafening roar that drowned out the clanging from Berenger's sledgehammer.

Wilbur's warning shot slammed into the chalk wall. Razor-sharp slivers of stone sprayed into Chantal's scalp and left arm. The shock jolted her right hand on the chest.

It nudged further over the pit.

Now only the pressure of her sweat-slick hand stopped it falling. "Drop the gun, Wilbur." The stinging in her arm and scalp clouded her judgment. Had the time come?

"No way."

"Bad choice," she echoed.

She pushed the chest hard. From the corner of her eye she saw it tumble over and over.

Wilbur howled in protest. His skinny legs propelled him in a grasshopper's leap towards the pit. The lantern and gun came for half the journey, forgotten in his frantic stretch for the chest. They slid from his fingers. The gun flew into the passage beyond. The lantern crashed at the edge of the pit.

As it went out, the water splashed twice, first with the chest, then with Wilbur. The gun clattered in the blackness.

The sledgehammer rang out again.

"Let's go." Louise tugged at her.

"There's no light. Your father will be here soon. He's widening the gap so he can get into this tunnel."

Splashes and heaving breaths rose from the cistern as Wilbur repeatedly dived for the chest.

"I don't care. Monsieur Sanders could climb out."

Delayed shock hit Chantal and her limbs shook. Tears began to trickle down her face. "Louise," she whispered brokenly between the hammer blows. "I can't face it. There's another pit in our way. Like this one." She wanted to stay put and wait for Berenger.

"I'll help you," Louise insisted. "Come *on*." The girl yanked her sleeve again. "I'll go ahead. I can smell the water."

"It's not safe," protested Chantal, but she fumbled behind her for the bundle of her shawl.

"*He's* not safe." Louise crept forward in the lead, holding Chantal's hand. If the girl felt the stab of the stone chips in her bare feet, she didn't complain. Her gait felt like a series of dancing steps. Chantal worked out that Louise was stretching a foot forward to feel for solid ground, before bringing the other foot up to meet it.

Noise assailed them from both sides with continued splashes from behind and mighty crashes from in front.

"It's close," shouted Louise. She inched forward.

"There's a plank in the middle, Louise," said Chantal. "We have to move it to the side. The wall will guide us. Help us balance."

They crouched together and found it. Chantal jiggled it sideways. Trapped crumbs of chalk screeched against the wood, adding to the bedlam around them.

Chantal left a gap of a few inches between the passage wall and the plank, so they could creep along sideways, chests to the wall, toes overhanging the plank. She crossed first, moving as lightly as she could, every sense quivering to help her gauge distance and angle. Louise followed, making the crossing in half the time.

Then Louise led again. Chantal could hardly credit the girl's bravery. She tried to copy her. They moved along, faster now, around the bend in the passage.

"That's better," the child shouted over the ringing of the hammer. "Now we've got a bit of light, see. Papa must have got a lamp close to that narrow doorway."

Chantal nodded. There was indeed a soft gleam from up the passage. Then she stopped. "What did you say, Louise? Surely you can't *see*?"

CHAPTER THIRTY-SEVEN

"But I *can* see, Chantal, I can!" Louise's voice echoed loudly in the suddenly quiet passage. The hammer blows had ceased. She spun round to Chantal and peered eagerly up in the faint light. "I can see you." She giggled. "You're prettier than I thought."

Chantal smiled through the mist of her tears. Louise jigged up and down, as if the trauma of the last hour had passed her by. "I have to tell Papa. Will you be OK?" The little face looked worried for a moment. "There's light now. You can just walk to it."

Chantal nodded dumbly. Louise skipped up the passage, her bare feet dodging the debris in her way. "I hope you like every new thing you see from now on," Chantal whispered, a hand pressed to her mouth. If only the little girl suffered no relapse.

"Papa, Papa!" Louise's shouts echoed back.

"Louise?" The passage brightened, lit by a small lantern held in a powerful hand.

"Chantal?" Berenger bellowed.

"I'm fine," she called, wishing her quivering voice didn't give the lie to her words.

"Papa, guess what! You'll never guess, but guess!"

"Wait," came the command. Berenger struggled into the now-wider opening. Before he was half way through, his daughter was pouring out her wonderful news. With a final wrench, Berenger made it into the tunnel.

Chantal's heart lifted at the sight of his broad form.

"This can't be true." Emotion deepened his voice.

"Papa, you're a funny color." She retreated a step. "What happened? Your hair is gray!"

Now she was closer, Chantal could see Louise's words proved her sight was back. Gray mud covered all of Berenger. It looked like he'd got soaking wet and then showered in ash.

He sank to his knees, cupping his daughter's head in his huge hands. A moment later, she disappeared into a hug. Chantal slowed her pace to give them time together. She watched Berenger cover Louise's face with kisses before hugging her again.

Louise broke the embrace. "But that's not all, Papa," she announced. "I brought Chantal, too. See?"

Berenger squinted past the lantern. The remains of tears glistened on his cheeks, tracks running through the caked mud. Chantal's heart cramped, and she found herself jogging to him, unable to stay away any longer.

"Chérie." His voice was husky, but the arm he stretched out to her was steady. His other arm hugged Louise. He made no effort to rise. The shawl dropped at her side as she collapsed into his gray mud-coated lap, both arms going around his neck.

His hard muscles offered a homecoming. It felt wonderful to press against the reassuring slab of his chest, but the power of the feeling went beyond the physical. Her heart had come home, too. The truth jolted her. She'd stopped falling in love with him. There was nowhere further to plummet. She'd hit bedrock.

She was in love with him.

The tunnel was as cramped and gloomy as ever, yet it seemed full of golden light. All because of a man covered in filth. Tears rolled down her cheeks. She couldn't stop them.

He pulled her tightly to him. Her cuts hurt in his grip, but she didn't care. He kissed the tears and then her ear, because it was the part of her closest to him. She replaced it with her mouth.

Louise giggled again.

"Get used to it, *petite*. I plan to do this a lot," said Berenger before returning to Chantal's lips.

Chantal took one arm from his neck and stretched it out to Louise. A three-way hug united them.

"Promise you won't disappear from me again like that," said Berenger hoarsely over their heads. "I thought I'd go mad tonight with not being able to reach you, or help you."

"But we came back, Papa."

"Yes, you did. You, able to see again after two whole years. And you—" His breath fanned Chantal's forehead. "We'd barely started, and I thought I'd lost you."

She dropped a kiss on his chin. "No way," she sniffed. The American phrase made her twist around sharply and stare into the gloom. "Wilbur! He's in the second cistern. He's the one who's caused all this. He and Grenier."

"Grenier's tied up in the basement, with my father standing guard till the police arrive. I called them as we drove back here. My father rescued me." He sighed. "It's a long story."

Louise wriggled. "Let's go up to Grand-Papa. I don't want to stay here."

Berenger loosened his hold on them. "Chérie, why don't you both go up? I'll deal with Wilbur." He sounded as if he relished the prospect.

"No, Papa! Monsieur Sanders has a gun. It fell the other side of the pit. But he might have found it again."

"A *gun?*" With tremendous strength, Berenger stood up, lifting both Chantal and Louise from the floor, and spun around to protect them from any attack from the dark tunnel. A second later, he pushed them both through the Eye. "We'll all go up to the basement. Easier to see, easier to guard the exit." He paused to pick up the lantern.

Louise, reveling in her newly regained sight, skipped ahead up the gloomy passage before her father or Chantal could offer to carry her. "Grand-Papa! Grand-Papa!"

"Louise? Thank God!" A bulky shape blocked out the soft light spilling from the recess.

"Guess what! Papa couldn't guess and you won't be able to either."

"Walk slowly," warned her grandfather. "You might trip over something."

"I won't, Grand-Papa. I know I won't, because I can *see*!" She reached her grandfather and stretched up into his arms.

Heavy boots drummed on the basement's wooden stairs. The sound drowned out Armand's answering cry of amazement.

Berenger squeezed Chantal's shoulder. "The police."

Together they stumbled through the recess and straightened up to see Riberon ducking around the stack of crates. He trained the beam of his huge flashlight on them, making them recoil. The inspector's expression told Chantal how dreadful they must both look.

"Are you never off duty, Riberon?" quipped Berenger.

"You've a knack for calling when I'm passing this town," the inspector replied. "What's down there?" He swung the flashlight into the recess.

"A man swimming in a cistern. Louise said he had a gun at one point. I can show you the way."

Riberon whistled to someone behind him. "The *gendarme* and I will go. You've been through enough, and this young lady could do with some attention. Is that blood, Mademoiselle?"

The question distracted Berenger. Chantal relaxed in the luxury of his fussing while the policemen moved off.

Chantal had Berenger to herself.

"I can't check your wounds if you try to kiss me."

"Kisses are the only medicine I want right now."

They helped themselves to that remedy. Chantal pushed her fingers through Berenger's hair and wondered at the grit that fell in whispers to the basement floor.

"We've all got stories to tell, Chérie," he said to her unspoken question. "I think it's time we went home, washed, and slept. We can talk at breakfast."

"Not till I've seen Wilbur. I've something to show him."

Riberon and the gendarme soon returned in single file through the recess, with a dripping and cursing Wilbur shackled between them. Chantal leaned back against Berenger as the trio climbed over the lip of the wall into the basement.

"Philistine!" Wilbur snarled at her. "Those books were unique!"

Chantal opened her shawl and flipped back the oilskin inside to show him two dark-bound books.

He lunged for them, his desperate energy dragging the policemen with him. Berenger pulled Chantal out of the way with one arm and jabbed forwards with the other. His fist smacked into Wilbur's jaw, and the American sagged in the cuffs.

"Nicely done," observed Riberon. "But now we have to carry him."

"Bump his head as you go," said Chantal with feeling, recalling what he'd done to Louise up the spiral staircase.

Riberon chained Wilbur to the same pipe as Grenier. The lawyer strained at his bonds to keep as far from his groggy accomplice as possible.

Once Riberon had called the station for backup, he turned to Berenger and Chantal. "Come to Albi soon, please," he said. "I'll need statements on this pair and the Corsican from you."

"I don't want to press charges against Yvan, Inspector," said Chantal. "Wilbur was the one who scared

Aunt Jeanne from her beloved home. I know that now."

Berenger made a sound of surprise, but she waved it away. "Like you said, we've all got stories to tell from tonight."

She wanted to share one lot of stories with Yvan, to fill in the last fifty years for him. Stories about Aunt Jeanne, illustrated with all the albums and keepsakes she could find.

Riberon looked around to where Armand stood with Louise in his arms, wrapped in his jacket for extra warmth. Armand had his back turned to Grenier, and Chantal guessed the lawyer's treachery had shaken him deeply.

"I think I will need to hear from both of you, too," said Riberon. "This young lady seems to have had an adventurous evening and will have a perspective to add."

"I can see again, Monsieur!" said Louise, swallowing a huge yawn.

"A miraculous evening," agreed her grandfather. "But, if the Inspector will allow us, we should all get back to baths and beds."

"I need to tell Ah Wong my news," protested Louise.

"We'll have to find her first," Berenger muttered. He stepped over to Wilbur, leaned down and grabbed the collar of his overalls. Before Riberon could intervene, Berenger shook the adventurer, hard.

Wilbur groaned and his ponytail swung to and fro.

"Where's Ah Wong?" Berenger shook him again. "What have you done with her?"

Riberon pulled Berenger away and Wilbur slumped sideways onto Grenier. The lawyer recoiled in distaste.

"If I tell you where your housekeeper is, will you please move me away from this criminal? He's starting to dribble."

Riberon shrugged. "Very well. Talk first, then I'll get my *gendarme* to tie you up in the kitchen."

Grenier nodded. "She's asleep on the floor of your walk-in pantry. I'd say she'd been drugged. In my haste to ascertain what this criminal was up to, I may have closed the pantry door a little more firmly than I intended. The latch might have dropped into place on the outside."

"Will Ah Wong be OK?" wailed Louise. "I have to tell her my news."

"We'll go and find her right now," soothed Armand, turning to the stairs.

"I think we can say you've eaten your last meal at the chateau, Grenier," said Berenger. He put an arm around Chantal. "Come on. One more rescue and then a wash and bed."

CHAPTER THIRTY-EIGHT

Chantal woke late to the happiest morning she could remember having for years. Ah Wong, released unharmed from the pantry the previous evening, had been too groggy to absorb Louise's momentous news, and Chantal could empathize with the disorienting aftermath of being drugged.

The housekeeper's resilience became evident the next morning, however, when she came downstairs before anyone else, and set to work preparing a large batch of crêpes and chocolate sauce. The tantalizing aroma drew them all from their beds.

Her resilience broke down when Louise, her face shining with excitement, demonstrated her newly regained sense of sight by pouring a chocolate sauce smiley face on her first crêpe. Ah Wong could only gulp phrases in her native Shanghainese as she tried to take in the miracle. Then, still struggling to believe, she insisted Louise take her on a tour of the house and describe what she could see.

They all joined in. Like a young Pied Piper, Louise led the adults from room to room, and up the stairs, on a journey of discovery. She found things she'd long known and loved, but had never seen, like her favorite lace-trimmed, heart-shaped cushion and a yellow plastic shape-sorting toy. Each one she described for them, her eyes bright with excitement. The adults' eyes were more often misty, and Chantal heard Armand blow his nose as they finally made their way downstairs.

No one minded that their crêpes had cooled. They sat around the table to exchange their stories. Chantal listened, horrified, to Berenger describing the roof fall, and his eventual rescue by Armand after Grenier had callously left him half-entombed.

"Grenier called a sudden meeting of the Musketeers," Armand explained. "About 9:30 or so. He said he'd found out something about the Eye of the Needle. Of course, we raced over to the Society library. He never showed up and when we rang his home, his wife said he'd been out for hours. I came home to find the drive half blocked with Berenger's SUV and Grenier's Jaguar pulled up behind it.

"I couldn't find anyone in the house, except for Wilbur snoring away in his bed and—"

"Wait." Berenger held up a hand. "I heard snoring too, when I came in, desperately hunting for Louise. But we know Wilbur was up in the lost tunnel, not asleep in bed."

"I go look," announced Ah Wong firmly.

"I'll come with you," said Berenger. "He might have booby-trapped something."

When they returned, Berenger carried a tape recorder. He placed it on the table and pressed the 'play' button. At once, snores filled the air. "A three-hour tape. I can only hope recording it gave him a very sore throat."

"Sit down," urged Chantal. "I want to hear the rest of Armand's story."

Armand explained that he'd glimpsed Grenier coming out of the basement and leaving by a back door. "It was very odd, but I can't say I suspected anything. I went down to the basement more on a whim than anything. Then I saw the flashlight had gone from its hook, and Grenier's shoes had left dusty footprints. Once I'd found a light, I followed the trail, right into the passage. And I found Berenger buried from the chest down." He looked across at his son, his pupils darkening. "I hauled him out," he finished abruptly.

"And we drove to Number 8 and caught up with Grenier in the basement, where he seemed to be waiting for someone to emerge from the Eye," continued Berenger. "I suspect I hadn't shut the front door properly when I left you. We politely pointed out to him that he shouldn't have left me to choke in that dusty hellhole." He rubbed his knuckles thoughtfully.

Chantal reached over and covered his bruised knuckles gently with her hand. "Between punches and tricking Wilbur over the treasure," she murmured, "I think we scored a few points for the good guys last night, don't you?"

The crooked half smile he gave her in reply made her wish for a moment they were alone, but then she looked around the table and saw a group of people she felt very proud to be associated with. To one of them in particular she owed a great deal for his actions the night before, and she realized she knew exactly how to repay him.

"Armand, now that you've seen the stone arch of the Eye in Jeanne's basement, I expect you'll want to look at the map that caused all this," offered Chantal "I have Jeanne's copy in my bag from last night." In a few moments, she'd laid it before him.

Armand scrabbled in his breast-pocket for his glasses.

Berenger shook his head. "He won't move for hours now."

Chantal ignored his teasing and leaned over Armand's shoulder, pointing out the various features she'd deciphered with the help of Aunt Jeanne's notes. "Berenger noticed how the passageways could have offered an escape route as well as a hiding place for treasure."

"After the fall of Montségur they'd never want to be trapped again," Armand agreed.

"We worked out that the Eyes were a way of marking the tunnel as Cathar territory. As ascetics they could all fit through the Eye, but the leading men of the organized church, the men who'd called that awful persecution down on them, they weren't. They were well-fed."

Armand slapped the table. "And a camel can't pass through the eye of a needle, eh?"

"Exactly."

He leaned closer and sighed. "Ah, this is marvelous. And you have the treasure too?"

Chantal felt a momentary spurt of panic. Where *had* she left the two little books? Then she saw them in her mind's eye and relaxed. "In my shawl, in the hall. Would you—"

"Of course he would," said Berenger. "It'd be better than all his birthdays come at once. Not to mention seeing the treasure before Mezaute does."

"Can I see the treasure?" asked Louise, looking up from the last swirl of chocolate sauce on her plate.

"Any minute now," said Chantal, heading to the hall. As she returned, carefully carrying the books, she saw Berenger put his hand on Louise's head.

"Things are going to be different now you can see again," he said. "For a start, you can't pretend you don't know how much sauce you've poured."

"Well, now I can see everything you're doing," retorted Louise. "Like kissing…"

There was more laughter, but Chantal couldn't stop her blush. Remarkably, Armand dragged his attention away from the Cathar books she carried and shook his head in mock dismay. "You think your father should keep that sort of thing private?"

"I think people can kiss in public if they're married," replied Louise, apparently considering the matter for the first time. "But Papa and Chantal aren't married yet."

Her final word hung in the air.

"Well, give me time, *petite*. If things would calm down for a day or two I might get a chance to ask. And now," Berenger continued smoothly before anyone, including Chantal, could say anything, "I think it's time you caught up on more sleep. You've been yawning non-stop." Berenger shepherded Louise upstairs, with the promise that the treasure would be waiting when she came down.

"Those precious books, Chantal," said Armand, his eyes tracking their path towards him. "Perhaps the desk in my office would be a safer place to put them down than a messy breakfast table? May I?" He held out his hands like a communicant at the altar.

She laid the oilcloth and its contents on his palms.

"I'll be most careful with them," he promised. "And we must discuss who to inform of this discovery. Toulouse University perhaps."

Chantal nodded absently as he quickly left the room, her mind still spinning with Berenger's recent words. *Marriage*? Talk about a whirlwind romance. She wanted to join Ah Wong in stacking the dirty plates, keen to keep herself busy with simple tasks while she tried to process what he'd said.

Her hand twitched forward as the housekeeper stretched for the sauce jug, but she pulled it back. "Sorry," she muttered, ducking her head.

"You want to help?"

Chantal looked up in surprise.

The Chinese woman smiled. "Can. Yes." She pointed at the jug. "Please."

Now Chantal had two extraordinary remarks to process. By the time she and Ah Wong had stacked the dishwasher and wiped down the table in companionable silence, she'd concluded that rescuing Louise from the cistern had earned her so much gratitude that it trumped protecting the family fiction about Berenger's mother never doing chores.

The third surprise came when Armand appeared at her

elbow and guided her to the seats opposite the fireplace.

"Surely you've not finished with those Cathar books already? I thought we might not see you for days!" she joked.

He invited her to sit, his face solemn. "I've been staring at the books, but my thoughts all stray back to Louise. I need to know, Chantal. What happened in those passages to make my granddaughter see?"

She'd been wondering the same herself. If they knew why, they might be able to figure out how permanent it would be. "The bottom line, Armand, is that she was blind when I reached her in the cistern and sighted when we returned to Jeanne's basement."

Armand tapped his chin. "I wonder. Louise feels she rescued you, doesn't she?"

"She should," said Chantal. "Without her, I couldn't have made it back along the passage."

"Without her, you wouldn't have had to," he pointed out. "You did it all to save her. I'm very grateful for that."

Chantal brushed his thanks aside. "We don't need a scoreboard of who helped whom the most."

He gave a little shrug. "The thing is that Louise feels she rescued you. She lost her sight when the opposite happened. When she couldn't stop Mireille dying."

"You're saying that by helping another woman, it's made up for what she couldn't do in the car crash?"

"You're not just another woman, are you, Chantal? She's only known you a few days, but no other young woman has spent as much time with her here as you have. You're the closest thing to a mother figure she's had since the accident."

Yet again, Chantal couldn't stop the flush in her cheeks. "I'm not trying to take her mother's place, Armand. I've no right."

"From what I've seen, Louise wants to give you that right." He added quietly, "I don't know if you want to take it, of course. That's between you and my son."

Berenger entered the room. His glance flicked between them. "Private conversation? Shall I come back later?"

"No, no. You two stay in here. I'll go back to those priceless books." Armand patted his son's shoulder as he left.

Berenger looked inquiringly at her.

"We were talking about Louise's sight. Hoping it's back for good."

Berenger sank down beside her on the sofa and took her hand, his thumb tracing circles on her skin. His eyes were hidden deep under gathered brows. Something was coming.

"I owe you so much," he said in a low voice. "You saved my daughter's life, who knows how many times. The cistern. The gun. You handled it all."

"You were unavoidably detained," she reminded him. "I know you were trying like crazy to reach us."

His thumb stopped its tracing. "I can't think how to repay you. But if you stay here in Cordes…" He lifted her hand to his lips. "And I hope with all my heart you do, maybe I'll figure out how." He took a deep breath. "You've not been here long, Chérie, but already you fit in. To my life, to Louise, to this place. I'm finding it hard to imagine life without you."

She should have been happy at the words. Instead, cold washed under her skin. She could see the future as Berenger saw it, and it felt all wrong.

He leaned down to kiss her. She barely responded.

"What's wrong?"

She twiddled his shirt buttons. It would be easier to open his shirt and lose herself in her need for him. Far easier than confronting him with her fears. Because if he couldn't allay them, she'd be in a place far worse than perilous dark tunnels.

"Chérie, what's wrong?" he repeated.

Chantal found herself by the long windows, gazing out at a clump of tulips in a pot on the back terrace. The bright yellows and reds bobbed in a light breeze.

"What's wrong, Berenger, is that you want me to be the patch to fix your life." Her voice wobbled and she had to stop. "I'm the consolation prize. Good enough, but not great. What does that make me? A convenience." Her fears etched acid into the word.

She'd promised herself after Steven she'd never settle for a relationship that contained expediency on either side. A few years along, and Berenger would come to resent her. She never wanted to hear him say the hurtful things her mother had to her father, or see his eyes fill with boredom. Most of all, she didn't want Louise to grow up surrounded by meanness. She knew only too well how corrosive that could be.

He came over to her and folded her in his arms. For long moments he did nothing but kiss her hair. "A convenience, eh?" he managed, a little raggedly. "There's nothing convenient about *this* at eleven in the morning." He pressed his hips into her. "And it happens whenever I kiss you."

"Then don't kiss me." Her abrupt tone silenced them both.

Berenger tried to tilt her chin up to see into her eyes, but she pushed his hand away. It was one thing to recognize the state of her emotions in the tunnel, in the aftermath of danger. It was another to tell him to his face in this comfortable lounge and risk agonizing disappointment.

Better than making everyone pay a much higher price years down the track.

She gulped a deep breath. "I love you, Berenger. I know it's very early days, but I don't think you feel the same way." She stared up at him as she said it, daring him to interrupt. "I know you want me. I know you care about me. Two out of three's not bad. But it's not enough. I need to be more than a good fit. Just because I'm prepared to move here—"

"Chantal." He put his palms to her cheeks to stop her words. There was no blue left in his eyes, nothing but dark pools of passion. "Is it possible, after all we've been through, that I've not told you, clearly, how I feel?"

She shook her head.

There was a rueful twist to his smile as he said, "Like I never denied I'd hurt your aunt. I thought I'd been telling you this in all sorts of ways. God knows I've been feeling plenty about you."

She hung on every word, waiting, hoping.

He traced her lips with a finger. "I want you to listen very carefully. I'm falling in love with *you*, Chantal." In between each word, he dropped tiny kisses around her mouth. "Every day. More and more. A month ago, I had Louise and my work here in Cordes. Now I have you, and I've come alive. You've even made me smile again."

She wanted to believe him. Not just that he loved her, but that he loved her the way she needed. For her own sake. Not for where she wanted to live or out of gratitude for saving Louise.

He stood back and gazed at her, sensing her hesitation. "What?"

"Everyone says you're still in love with Mireille. It's only been two years."

"I loved Mireille. Of course I did. And she'll always be part of my life because of Louise. But I've moved on. I couldn't prove it till I met someone special. You."

"Am I like her?"

"No."

"What was she like? To you. Apart from beautiful."

There was a long pause. "She was a butterfly. A party girl. Loved crowds." He stared over her head at the window. "She seemed fragile. Made me want to shield her. But I also remember a lot of tears and sulks."

"What about?"

He sighed and Chantal could see his eyes lose focus as his mind replayed old scenes. "Her dull life here in Cordes, mostly. After Louise was born, Mireille took her to visit her parents in Paris a lot. That last day, she'd set off on a trip there." He stopped. His gaze fastened back on her face. "It's *you* I love. If I don't tell you every day, Chérie, kick me. Please."

He drew her mouth to his. Desperation thrummed in his kiss, as if he was trying to pour into it every ounce of reassurance he could find.

"Will you stay here for a couple of minutes?" he murmured when they finally moved apart. "I need to fetch something."

She nodded, her lips tingling from the pressure of his embrace. As the door closed, a grin slowly spread from the corners of her mouth, widening and stretching till it commandeered every muscle on her face. He *loved* her. He loved *her*.

But would he love you if you weren't such a great fit to his life? She sighed. Some demons were hard to shake off.

The minutes stretched, and with them her nerves. When would he come back? Beyond the door, the short corridor to the garage and the kitchen were empty.

Only two other doors opened off this part of the passageway. One, she felt sure, led to where Armand displayed his Chinese celadons, the place Ah Wong had once called "Master's private room", and the other Chantal had not yet entered. It stood ajar and she peeped inside to find a walk-in pantry with rows of preserves. Empty. That left the private room. Could Berenger be in there for some reason?

She knocked loudly. When no one answered, she stepped inside. Brocade curtains blocked out most light. She fumbled for the switch.

Soft rays lit up more than she could bear to see.

She had entered a shrine, but not one dedicated to the study of thirteenth-century Chinese pottery.

This shrine honored a beautiful, dead woman called Mireille.

CHAPTER THIRTY-NINE

Chantal could see no photos, but the room shrieked the identity of the woman whose memory it served.

A dressing table served as Mireille's altar.

Two distinctive perfume bottles stood like votive candles at each end. On little mats, silver-backed brushes nestled to the right and a range of cosmetics to the left. In the center, in pride of place, sat an open jewelry box. Someone had painstakingly spiraled golden and beaded necklaces. In cushioned slits, rings spelled out an 'M'.

Bile rose in Chantal's throat.

Sultry, amber-infused perfume filled the air. She traced the source to a flimsy screen of scarves and shawls that hung from a wire. Their shades were mostly greens and aquamarines, perfect for a woman with black hair and huge green eyes.

Berenger hadn't moved on emotionally from Mireille. He'd lied.

Why?

She knew why. Because, after two years, he wanted someone to share his bed and be a mother figure to his daughter. Five minutes ago, Chantal had made it plain she needed to hear she meant more than that—and he'd readily obliged.

He'd sounded sincere. This room told her otherwise. Berenger had said what she wanted to hear.

She pressed her hands to her temples. The last twenty-four hours had been an insane roller coaster and now she was plummeting downwards. She'd stay long enough to confront Berenger. She'd drag him into this hidden room and listen to his sad excuses.

And then she'd run. Leave before her misery overwhelmed her. The last person she wanted comfort from was Berenger.

She strode into the corridor and saw him at the foot of the stairs.

"Chérie, I wondered where you'd gone. Sorry I took so—"

"Come here," she ordered. She turned around without waiting for his agreement.

"Can it wait? There's something important…"

Chantal kept walking toward the door she had left open.

"What's up?" A moment later, he gave a muffled curse.

At the threshold she spun round and leaned on the door jamb, affecting a look of polite enquiry.

He held his hands up to her, a champagne bottle awkwardly grasped between thumb and palm and a little box clasped in his remaining fingers. "It's not what it seems."

"Of course not."

"I've been thinking about you, not her. I forgot to mention it."

"*You forgot?* I asked you what Mireille was like, and it never crossed your mind to say, 'Well, darling, she's got a room down the hall. Come and meet her'?"

"Listen to me!"

"No, you listen. You tell me you love me and then I find this." Her voice cracked on the last word, but the surge of fury, born of disappointment, carried her on.

"Why lie to me? Just tell me it's too soon, that you still love your dead wife."

"I didn't lie! I do love you, Chantal. This room isn't for me, it's for Louise."

"*Louise?* Look at it!" She grabbed his arm and pulled him into the room. "This is a grown man's temple to a dead lover. All sensuous scents and sensations." She snagged a scarf off the wire and threw it at him.

"Chantal!" he thundered. He tossed the bottle onto the bed, and reached for her.

She recoiled and darted back into the corridor. "Don't you dare touch me, Berenger Morel." The tears were perilously close. She flew down the short passage to the door leading to the garage and wrenched it open.

"Where are you going?"

She sensed his long stride narrowing the distance between them.

"Away!"

Armand's golden Jaguar loomed, and Chantal's wild momentum nearly carried her into it. She stumbled around the rear of the vehicle and past Berenger's dark green SUV. They'd all driven back from Number 8 in it the night before. The elation of that trip felt an eon ago.

Chantal had meant to head for her hired car, but as she passed Ah Wong's small, white Peugeot she spotted its keys dangling from the ignition.

Thank God the garage roller door was up. Berenger shouted more excuses about Louise, but Chantal's focus had shrunk to the task of escaping before she lost control.

She yanked the Peugeot door open and threw herself into the driver's seat. Her thumb flipped the door lock mechanism. It responded with a chunky click.

Just in time.

Berenger reached the car, pulling on the door handle. He slapped the window and bellowed through it, "Chantal, you're not listening! Why are there are no photos in there? Because the room was for Louise when she couldn't see."

She turned the key and rammed the shift into Drive.

"Chantal, please stop!" Another blow from his palm rattled her window.

She gunned the engine. The Peugeot's tires squealed on the concrete floor and the little car shot across the gravel and down to the gateposts. A minute later she turned onto the main road heading south. It didn't matter where.

The weak sunlight glistened on the drizzle-slick tarmac. Its glare rubbed like sandpaper on her tired eyes, yet the heavy oncoming traffic demanded she concentrate. She needed to turn off, to find a quiet layby and let the river of tears begin.

Her hands shook slightly on the wheel. The seat, set up for Ah Wong, made her knees bang the lower edge of the dashboard.

A car behind her honked loudly. She knew she was right on the speed limit. A glance in the rear view mirror showed a dark green SUV close behind. It resembled Berenger's. She was the one obsessed now; it couldn't be him, he couldn't have latched onto her trail so fast.

Again, the horn blared, its harsh tone scraping on her taut nerves. "What, for heaven's sake?"

She could see an arm protruding from the following vehicle. It waved up and down in the international symbol for 'slow down'. Was it Berenger? On a straight stretch, she took her foot off the gas. Now, if ever, the SUV would overtake and she'd see the driver.

She never got the chance to find out.

An oncoming van swerved slightly towards the midline to avoid some hidden obstacle. Chantal reacted slowly. When she did finally swing the wheel to the right, she went too far, too fast.

The Peugeot skated on the wet road. A front wheel snagged the verge. The vehicle slewed round.

Chantal saw a green ditch rise up before her. Without her safety belt on, she slammed into the steering wheel.

It was the turn of the Peugeot's horn to blast, on and

on. Grass pushed in at her window, tickling her cheek. A familiar voice shouted her name. Before she could work out whose it was, everything slid into peaceful blackness.

*   *   *

Much later, it seemed, her senses began to return. Smells came first, bringing antiseptic laced with the fragrance of spring freesias. Next she became aware of rubber-soled footsteps squeaking on a shiny surface and something metallic rattling nearby. She tried opening her eyes but the sunlight stabbed them and set her head pounding. When she tried to lift a hand to probe for injuries, her arm felt too heavy to move.

She slept fitfully.

When she next woke, the light in the room had almost gone. She guessed at early evening but had no idea what day.

A cool hand picked up her wrist. Chantal cautiously rolled her head to the side and saw a nurse's pale blue uniform.

"Ah, you're awake. That's good. I'll get the doctor now you've come around properly."

"How—how long…?" The sentence, so clear and simple in her mind, croaked to a rusty halt halfway through.

"How long have you been here? Two and a half days, drifting in and out of consciousness. You came in Sunday lunchtime with serious concussion, extensive bruising and a cracked rib." The nurse gently set Chantal's arm down and walked to the chart at the end of the bed.

"Is anyone…"

"Your father's here," the nurse answered as she jotted down notes. "He arrived yesterday morning."

"My father?" she slurred.

"He won't be far away." The nurse hung the clipboard back on its hook. "Your other regular visitor's rather nice, too," she added with a smile. "He's brought flowers twice, and I think his little girl left that homemade card." She pointed to the bedside table before leaving.

Chantal craned to the left with effort. Her ribcage had morphed into a wrap-around bruise. On a folded piece of foolscap paper, she glimpsed a crayon drawing of a green body with enormous fingers. The person lay on a bed under a wobbly, long-rayed sun. "Louise," she whispered. The memories rushed back.

Mireille's room, the spinning car.

Berenger shouting.

Her heart turned over at the mere thought of him. She ached in bone and body, but another, deeper, pain lay beneath the purely physical hurts, somewhere in the region of her heart. Berenger didn't love her the way she loved him. A powerful longing swept through her, and she groaned.

A figure stepped into the room and crossed swiftly to the bed. She looked up to see the familiar figure of her father, Terry. Tall and lean, so like herself, but his head topped with the blond hair, now graying, that he'd given her twin sister, Lotty. This man, she knew with absolute certainty, loved her for herself. That reassurance gave her the strength to squeeze out a small smile for him. "Dad," she rasped.

"Darling? Are you in pain?" Her father's trademark cheery grin dissolved in his concern. He crouched beside the bed, bringing the familiar wide planes of his tanned face close to hers.

Carefully, slowly, she shook her head. She doubted the hospital stocked medication to ease the kind of hurt that tore away at her.

Her father softly stroked a finger down her cheek. "I'm so glad to see you awake at last, darling. Your mother will be too."

"Is she here?"

Her father shook his head briefly. "She'll be pacing a

path into the carpet by the phone waiting for an update on you. I know I would be."

Chantal didn't doubt her mother would be worried, but the minute better news arrived, she expected the tune would revert to more familiar Helene-centric themes.

"How did you…"

Once more, her father proved adept at interpreting her half-questions.

"That Berenger chap tracked me down and called me about your accident. I flew down late Sunday night. We've been sharing shifts here since."

Her eyes flew to her father's.

"He's been looking miserable and stressed since your accident. Well, I don't know what he's like in happier times, but his father Armand commented."

Chantal's heart lifted a little.

"Berenger says he followed you along the highway. Tried to make you slow down. You'd had a row and driven off upset? I think he's feeling very guilty that he failed."

So it had been Berenger behind her in the green SUV. She wanted more than guilt from him, though. Much more.

"The harrowing thing is that you crashed on the same stretch of road where his wife died. I think it's been *déjà vu* for him, poor man."

Her heart shriveled. Whatever showed on her face was enough to send her father hurrying for the doctor. Chantal lay as rigid as ice. If nothing else, her ribs hurt less when she stopped moving. The doctor came and went. The extra medication in her IV drip eased her body if not her mind. She dozed off.

A shadow fell across her. She opened her eyes to see a sheaf of red roses held by a strong, tanned hand. The flowers moved and revealed a pair of piercing blue eyes.

She immediately looked away. The rapid action sent a shooting pain through her head.

"At least now you can't run away," said Berenger

grimly. "I can't make you look at me, but I can make you listen."

"You're supposed to ask me how I am." Chantal found her throat more relaxed than before and kept going. "Not lecture me."

"There's no point me being nice," he said shortly. "You don't believe what I say." She heard a crackle as the paper around the flowers settled on the bedside table. "But for the record, I was hugely relieved that your injuries weren't serious. When I saw the car skid down into the ditch—"

"You thought about Mireille," she finished for him.

"I thought about losing you, actually." His lips thinned to a pencil line. "As we waited for the ambulance, you were so pale. I was afraid I'd worsened your injuries by pulling you out." He exhaled in a rush. "But if I'd left you and the car had caught fire…"

His words conjured up a hideous vision of her rag-doll body slumped in a burning car with her hair a torch of flames. She shivered.

"The ambulance team had to pry you away from me. If you've got extra bruises on your shoulders, blame me."

"Thank you," she said in a small voice.

"For the bruises?"

"For rescuing me. For protecting me."

He shrugged.

Silence followed, but it seemed to Chantal they'd established a small truce. Gingerly, she rolled to face him. He pulled up a hard plastic chair and sat down, bringing their faces level. Blue and gray watched each other warily.

She noted his weariness, his eye sockets more deeply shadowed than ever before.

"You wanted me to listen."

"I do." He folded his arms. Before the crash he'd have reached for her. Chantal ignored the yearning inside her.

"That room you found was part of Louise's therapy. For months after the accident, she not only blanked out her sight, she blanked out memories of her mother. The doctors believed Louise needed to get those memories back as part of the journey to seeing again. We designed it to appeal to the senses she had left. Scents. The trinkets and fabrics she'd loved playing with before. It gradually worked. We didn't take the room's contents away, though, because Louise liked to go there sometimes."

It sounded so plausible. A doubt nagged at her, though, and she dragged it to the front of her mind. "If it's for Louise, why did Ah Wong call it 'Master's private room'?" Chantal closed her eyes, picturing the chateau's corridors. "I got confused with the doors. I thought she'd meant your father's celadon room."

Berenger rocked back on the chair, further increasing the distance between them. His gaze remained locked on hers, however.

"Until yesterday, Ah Wong didn't know Louise's blindness was hysterical. Remember? The experts said Louise shouldn't know it herself, so we told no one. We never spoke about it, but I knew Ah Wong thought the room was because I was hung up on Mireille. I might add she's very upset with me for not telling her the truth."

An unrelated thought struck Chantal. "Tell Ah Wong I'll pay to have her car fixed. Please."

"You can tell her tonight. She wants to come and visit."

"Berenger." A spurt of fear injected urgency into her tone and her hand stretched to him instinctively. His eyes flicked down to it, but he made no move. "Berenger, is Louise OK? Has my accident on that stretch of road affected her sight?"

The answering shake of his head filled her with relief. "I thought it might," he admitted, "but so far so good."

Silence fell.

"Well?" He raised an eyebrow. She could hear the question as if he had spoken it.

"I guess I believe you. It's hard, tripping over these secrets in your life, Berenger, and having to absorb them. Is this the last?"

He strode to the window and stared out. "Would you say you were good at keeping secrets?"

"I kept the one about Louise's blindness."

"But this one," he drummed his nails on the windowsill, "concerns Mireille."

"How does that make it different?"

"The dead can't defend themselves."

"Does she need to?"

He shrugged slowly, and ran his fingers through his hair in the gesture she had come to know so well. After a pause, he pulled a folded envelope from his back pocket and tapped it against the pane. "I don't know what to do, Chantal," he confessed. "Instinct told me to bring this today, but now I don't know. It's something between Mireille and me. I never thought I'd show anyone. Lord knows why I didn't burn it."

"So why tell me?"

"Because it's my last chance to persuade you Mireille's no threat." He turned to face her at last. "I want you in my life, Chantal. I've told you: you're the one I love." His raw need stretched his face, narrowing his eyes and thinning his lips once more. He crossed the floor and dropped the letter onto the blankets. "Can you read without getting a headache?" he murmured.

She nodded. She'd go through a migraine to read the contents of that envelope. Berenger worked the crank to tilt her bed up.

Chantal slowly pulled out the letter and unfolded its stiff, blue paper. She took a deep breath.

Dear Berenger,

I have to end this. To end us. I am so unhappy living in Cordes. You know this, you've known it for years, and yet you won't compromise to help me be happy.

I'm taking Louise. Please don't fight me for her. Leave me that much at least.

Mireille

"I found it the afternoon she left. The afternoon she died." Berenger sat back down in the plastic chair. "As you can see, things had been bad between us for a long time. She didn't just sulk about the country life; she hated it. But I loved my work on the estate. It was all I ever wanted to do and in the place I wanted to be. I wasn't prepared to leave. Things eased when Louise was born, but then it started again."

A new emotion crept into Chantal's heart. Compassion. For Mireille, whose husband wouldn't compromise.

"My father retired from the diplomatic service and my parents came back to the chateau. We knew they'd be distressed about our problem, so we hid it. It became a habit." He grimaced. "A stressful habit."

The chair squeaked as he shifted his weight. "I should have encouraged Mireille to go away more. Instead, I accused her of neglecting her family and insisted she stay." He drew a hand over his face. "And I told her that if she ever left me, I'd file for custody of Louise."

"That's why she took Louise when she finally went." What mother wouldn't? "But I don't understand, Berenger. Why did you keep up the pretense after she died?"

"Because it would have discredited her. I owed her that much. That's why I never told anyone the truth until two minutes ago." The blue of his eyes drilled into her. "If I wasn't prepared to spend my life with you, Chantal, it would still be a secret."

She could see that he expected an answer. The last time he'd offered her this act of faith it had taken their relationship to a new level. He had to be expecting the same. A reward for his risk. A resolution to the barriers between them.

Instead, she felt strangely disconnected. It sounded like someone else who quietly asked him, "What if I wanted to leave Cordes in a year or two, Berenger? You'd demand I stay, or else?"

"Do you think I learned nothing from the situation with Mireille? I'd encourage you to go off on trips."

She heard him, but his words didn't help. "You see, I remember what happened after I told you I could see my future in Cordes. You took me to La Picarie. We made love." She paused to rest her aching ribs for a moment and plucked at a non-existent thread on the beige blanket. "If I'd said I had to get back to London, I don't think that would have happened." She lifted her eyes, tears smudging her view of intense blue.

The blue half-disappeared behind narrowed lids. "I should only love someone who detests where I live and what I do? That's madness."

"I think your love shouldn't be conditional on Cordes." She was nearly choking. "Berenger, this is nothing to do with poor Mireille. This is about us." A long, shuddering breath did nothing to ease the pain in her throat, and cruelly hurt her ribs. "I think you love me mostly because I complement your existing life. But I need you to love me for me. And right now, I don't believe you do."

He didn't deny it. The silence stretched between them. She couldn't meet his gaze but raised her eyes far enough to see his bunched jaw muscles.

"What will you do?" he asked at last between clenched teeth.

"Go back to England with my father. I think perhaps you'd better not visit again," she added in a whisper.

She slowly rolled away from him, drawing the blanket up to hide her face while she sobbed, oblivious now to the pain in her ribs. When her tears finally eased, Berenger had gone.

CHAPTER FORTY

Chantal aimed a foot at her new front door, trying to close it, but the heavy cardboard box in her arms made her stagger, and she missed. It didn't matter. Her car held several more boxes. She'd be back outside in thirty seconds. Tomorrow she'd bring Harry over to this small, ground-floor rented apartment. Her cat's undemanding company would make her new address feel like home faster than pictures on the wall and books on the shelves.

The chestnut tree outside the kitchen window wore the brown-tinged green of late summer. Four months had crept by since she'd left...France. She always avoided his name. It was a puny defense against the deep ache that had taken root in her, but it gave her a veneer of control.

The pain had changed her, though. Old shackles had dissolved in its acid. She'd hunted Steven down, easily bluffing her way past his well-manicured receptionist. His stricken look as she'd walked into his gleaming office in the City of London had almost been worth the long weeks of three-job grind he'd caused her months earlier.

Her regret for her lost business had now been swamped by a much greater loss, and it threw Steven's deceit into perspective. His actions, she'd come to see, had been petty revenge that said far more about him than it did about her. In forgiving herself for trusting him, she'd found she'd forgiven him, too. She'd told him so and walked out, leaving him behind forever.

She'd made the long overdue break from her mother's at last. Her mother had kicked up surprisingly little fuss at the prospect of losing her live-in nurse and companion. Chantal wondered if it had something to do with a new client her mother had acquired for her translation business. Hubert, an aristocratic Frenchman in his sixties, had taken to calling round more often than necessary. The Harrison women, it seemed, had developed a passion for Frenchmen.

Chantal sighed as she squeezed the box onto the coffee table, already cluttered with odds and ends. She stretched her shoulders. It had been a physically demanding weekend. The day before, her father had helped her move in her modest stock of furniture. To his delight, she had even allowed him to buy a few pieces for her.

Learning to accept help more readily had been another change for the better. Help didn't have to signify weakness. Since the night she'd followed a blind child in a black tunnel, she'd learned help could simply mean someone else had better skills and resources to confront a problem. And that night had had such a joyous outcome. Chantal couldn't wish she'd refused the help.

The box she'd just brought in contained some of her most cherished keepsakes from Aunt Jeanne's office. Lelou had organized the storage of Number 8's contents to allow the new owner to progress his alterations in time for the summer season. Chantal paid to have the documents from Jeanne's office and all papers collected from around the house shipped to London.

For long evenings, she'd combed through them, setting aside items she wanted to copy to share with Yvan—and hunting for an explanation of how and why she had abandoned her baby. Eventually becoming interested in

Chantal's search for the truth, Helene had taken charge of all documents in Italian, including the stack of letters Chantal had seen in one of the green document boxes in the office. Heart-breakingly, each had been addressed, but never posted, to the son she'd left behind.

Those letters told and retold an old, familiar story. Aunt Jeanne had fallen in love across Corsica's national divide, she a Juliet descended from French Corsicans, and he, Petru, the Italian Corsican Romeo. Jeanne's pregnancy lost her the support of the cousins she was staying with, and Petru's family refused to countenance marriage. Petru lacked Jeanne's adventurous spirit, insisting they stay in his native Corsica, close to his family and fishing boat—the other *Jeanne* in his life—rather than fleeing to the mainland together.

Petru had been out fishing when a powerful storm had swept through. That night, scared and alone, Jeanne had gone into labor in a tumbledown shack in the woods near Petru's village, and Yvan had been born amid the thunder and lightning, premature and unresponsive. When Petru's nonna woke Jeanne from exhausted sleep in the morning, the new mother saw another old woman from the village holding Yvan. The woman declared the baby a vegetable, as good as dead, perhaps soon to die, and join his father in Heaven. Petru's fishing boat had been found wrecked in a neighboring cove at dawn. Then the nonna had howled that Jeanne must be cursed, for all the terrible misfortune she'd brought on the family, and that she must leave at once.

Bewildered and bereft, Jeanne had obediently fled instead of demanding to hold and keep her son, and to stay to bury his father's body. Chantal wondered if that one submissive act did not explain all Jeanne's fighting thereafter.

"It explains why she left her entire estate to you instead of sharing it with the wider family," sniffed Helene, revisiting a well-worn theme. "You were her surrogate child. Look at all your cards and letters that she kept, too."

Some of those old pieces of correspondence lay in the box Chantal had brought in. She ran her finger thoughtfully over the cardboard flaps. By storing her letters, Aunt Jeanne had preserved part of Chantal's history, records of events and people half-forgotten. Her parents held nothing comparable.

And if Aunt Jeanne had been the custodian of Chantal's past, she had also provided the springboard for her future. Lelou had wired through her legacy. Chantal, refusing to think about whose bank account the money had once sat in, had transferred almost all of it to a high-interest account while she laid plans to resurrect her jewelry business. Thanks to Aunt Jeanne, she had no need of venture capital, and could go it alone. Her father had suggested a couple of low-risk ways she might enter the market and she had research running on one of them.

Despite her need for capital, she had offered some of her inheritance to Yvan. She made the gesture at the same time that she sent him the packet containing the story of his past. He wrote back thanking her for the documents, which he said brought him both great pleasure and deep pain when he reflected on the lies, omissions and lost years. He also gently refused her generous offer of a share of the inheritance. He had his father's estate, and his dairy business had enjoyed a run of good years.

From the edge of the coffee table she picked up another small sign of progress: a bracelet in pink and white cord. She'd finally solved how to knot love hearts to stand proud of the base braid. On this piece, she'd not allowed enough length for the series of complex knots, and it would only fit a child. She laid it down regretfully. She missed Louise and she'd managed not to think about…France…for several hours.

The front door squeaked and broke in on her melancholy thoughts. The wind?

Heavy footsteps came over the threshold. Her heart

rate kicked up. "Who's there?"

The feet didn't slow and their owner didn't answer. This was supposed to be a good neighborhood, but in London it always paid to be vigilant—and she'd left the door open. The nearest weapon was a wine bottle she used as a candlestick, its neck a kaleidoscope of wax rivulets. She grabbed it and backed up to the counter. The last time she'd defended herself with a bottle…

A giant of a man ducked into the room, his broad frame filling the doorway. Piercing blue eyes flicked between the bottle and her face. "I know I have a bad habit of barging into your houses, Chantal. But the door was open, and I didn't want to talk to you on the doorstep."

The air drained from her lungs. She wanted to give vent to the whirlwind of anger that roared in with the shock of seeing Berenger again, but no sound came out. Her eyes bulged in their sockets.

He stood just inside the lounge door as if unwilling to invade her space any further. He was more deeply tanned now, yet a pallor lay beneath the bronze.

"I have something to say to you, Chantal, if you'll let me. It won't take long."

She managed a strangled sound. She had no idea what she'd said, but he took it as agreement and walked in.

"I'll try and say this clearly. I know I tend to duck saying the really important things straight out." He drew a breath. "My love for you. It doesn't depend on where you want to live, or how willing you are to put up with the winery life." His bright blue gaze bored into her and made her pulse race even faster.

He broke off and pushed his fingers though his hair. "I don't expect you to believe me. Frankly, I didn't know the answer myself for a while. That's why I couldn't deny it when you accused me at the hospital. My love for Cordes and my lifestyle there were all mixed in with my love for you."

He was right. She didn't believe him. He couldn't walk in after one hundred and eighteen days and think that saying the words she longed to hear would make it all better.

"I thought about you every day while I worked on the alterations at Number 8. You were like a mantra in my mind. You still are." The blue was giving way to black under the force of emotions he held fiercely in check. "Maybe that's why we got the job done so fast. I should have been pleased, shouldn't I? But the person I most wanted to share it with wasn't there. That's when I realized the truth."

He took a short step forward, his palms turned toward her. "Chantal, paradise would be you, me and Louise in Cordes. I can't deny it. But I've figured out that next on my list is you, me and Louise. Anywhere."

She found her voice with difficulty. "It's easy to say these things, Berenger. What if I called your bluff?"

"You'd be too late, Chérie." He drew an envelope from his shirt pocket. A tremor shook his fingers as he pulled out a piece of paper and handed it to her.

It bore the letterhead of an international school ten miles away. Louise had the offer of a place for the start of the new school year in September, in a few days' time.

"Half the lessons are in French," he explained. "I thought it would be less of a culture shock for her. Now that she can see, she handles new places no problem."

Chantal needed the support of the kitchen counter at her back. "But her friends. Armand."

"My father's quite capable of travel. He's been around the world a hundred times. But there's more in here."

The other two pieces of paper detailed the agreements for British wine distributors to stock Berenger's *Blanc de Cordes* wine. "I should have done it years ago, but I refused to do anything that took me away from Cordes. Long term, I aim to build my own distributorships around Europe, promoting a range of wines from the Gaillac area.

For now, I've left Delgarde holding the fort. I've not decided how to staff the estate long term."

He crossed the distance between them. She caught a hint of nutmeg and glimpsed dark hairs in the 'V' of his collar. They prompted a fierce longing in her for him to hold her against the solid muscle of his chest. He made no move to touch her, though. She realized the first move had to be hers. She'd been the one to walk away. Now, she had to decide if she would walk back.

"You've done so much, Berenger," she whispered. "It's a shame it's all for nothing."

He flinched and drew a sharp breath in through his nose. The pallor under his tan intensified.

She reached to smooth the tension out of his tightly clenched jaw and then to cup his face. "Darling, I don't want to live in London. Or England. If you're prepared to change your life to follow me here, then I know I want to live with you and Louise in Cordes. I've never stopped loving you. And now at last I know, for sure, that you love me."

He gave a wordless cry and crushed her to him. She heard his rasping breaths and luxuriated in the familiar feel and fragrance of him.

"Thank you," she murmured against his shirt.

"For what?"

"For being willing to do so much to show me you love me. Any other man would have given up."

"Not this one." He kissed her forehead.

"Is our deal still on?"

He moved back to focus on her face, his eyebrow lifting in query.

"To share Number 8. You know I have the money to buy half of it back. I need a place to base my jewelry business in Cordes. And," she raised her chin, anticipating resistance, "I need my own space to get to know you better from."

"I have a better idea, and I have that scoundrel Grenier

to thank for it." His voice was as deep as distant thunder, but his eyes danced. "You can live upstairs in Number 8 for a year, rent-free, and then, if I haven't scared you off, we'll do what Grenier advised. We'll fully commingle our assets."

She brought her face close to his again, smiling.

"Anything else?" he rumbled.

She nodded. "If we do decide in a year's time that we want to commingle our assets," she grinned at the ridiculous phrase, "then I want to do it in Place de la Bride. Bridal Place."

"Bridle Place, as you well know." A hint of laughter joined the happiness in his eyes. "And a bridle could be what I need to keep you by my side."

She shook her head. "No more running, Berenger. Now I know you truly love me, I'm staying put."

Their lips melded in a searing passion that pledged them both to a shared future.

"We couldn't get married in September next year, even if we decided we wanted to," Chantal said a few minutes later, her breath ragged. "You'll be in the middle of harvest."

"Perfect," he said with satisfaction. "It'll be damnably inconvenient."

Chantal disappeared once more into the protective circle of his arms. This was her home. Anywhere with this man would be home.

EPILOGUE

The café on Place de la Bride, no longer part-owned by Grenier, buzzed with female activity. Louise walked to and fro in front of a mirror, admiring her full-length pink bridesmaid's dress and her posy of tiny white and pink roses. They matched the knotted love heart bracelet she'd insisted on wearing. At her heels, as always, followed Harry the cat, who had transferred his feline affections to her on his arrival in France. He also wore a crocheted and beaded collar in honor of the day, in flattering tones of green and silver, chosen to complement his ginger fur.

Ah Wong, standing on a stool, tweaked the flowers in Chantal's headdress. A steady hiss suggested the housekeeper hadn't yet achieved perfection. Lotty, her simpler bridesmaid's flowers already pinned in place with Tricia's help, walked nervously to and fro. She'd arrived from Australia only thirty-six hours before and had slept most of the time since. Chantal's niggling worry that she might not get enough time to catch up properly with her twin was the only blot on her happiness.

Outside in the September morning, friends and family milled around. Half of Cordes had gathered beyond the roped-off area to see the town's most eligible widower married off.

Chantal peered through the window, searching for a dark head that ought to stand proud of the crowd. She had urgent news for him. He had to be the first to know.

She spotted him at last, leaning on the wall at the edge of the square, next to her father. No doubt they were refining plans for the first stage of work at La Picarie. They'd decided to convert the barn into a family home, bit by bit. Terry's building skill had already contributed several good ideas to the project.

Her mother came over, tapping her watch. "You've done a lovely job, Ah Wong. She looks perfect. But I think we'd better get going. Ten minutes till kick-off." The last three days with her mother in Cordes had been the most relaxed they'd spent together in years. Hubert, now deep in conversation with Armand, had become a fixture in her mother's life and his admiring attention had given her mother something she'd been lacking for years.

Chantal took Louise's hand and a deep breath. Then, with Lotty alongside, the three of them walked out into the square. All eyes turned, but hers remained fixed on the broad-shouldered man waiting by the priest.

"You look fabulous," he murmured as he took her hand and gripped it tightly. "You should wear white more often."

She couldn't keep her news to herself a moment longer. "Don't tell the priest," she replied in English, "but white is stretching the truth. Under the circumstances."

His eyes narrowed. "What are you saying?"

"That baby makes four. In a bit over seven months."

The priest shifted his weight and cleared his throat. Berenger paid no attention. His face lit up with the biggest smile Chantal had ever seen him wear. It sapped the strength from behind her knees, but she needn't have worried. He clutched her to him and flipped back her veil to kiss her fervently.

There were cheers from the crowd and a gurgle of

surprise from the priest.

"Papa!" said a cross voice from behind them. "You're supposed to do that *afterwards.*"

Berenger drew away slowly. Chantal could see his profound love for her darkening his eyes. She hoped he could see its reflection in her own.

"I can't wait to call you my wife, Chantal. I want to spend the rest of my life with you." His eyes crinkled and he dropped a quick kiss on her hand. "And we'd better hurry up and make this little person of ours official."

They turned to the priest. Below them, the last of the morning mist dissolved, and a light breeze from the south carried the promise of a warm day.

THE END

WHAT'S NEXT?

If you enjoyed reading *The House on Rue Obscure*, please help others find the book by leaving a review on Amazon. It would make all the difference and be very much appreciated.

You can find out more about Sarah W. Sparx and her books at her author website, www.sarahwsparx.com. This is where you can sign up to her newsletter to receive notification of the release of the next two books in the *Echoes of the Cathars* series: Lotty's story, set in 2004 and Louise's, set in 2016.

25289787R00204

Printed in Great Britain
by Amazon